MURDER
AT THE SAVOY

Also by
MAJ SJÖWALL and PER WAHLÖÖ

MURDER
AT THE
SAVOY

MAJ SJÖWALL and
PER WAHLÖÖ

Translated from the Swedish by Amy and Ken Knoespel

PANTHEON BOOKS, *A Division of Random House, New York*

ISBN: 0-394-47081-8

Library of Congress Catalog Card Number: 77-162551

Manufactured in the United States of America
by The Colonial Press Inc., Clinton, Massachusetts

9 8 7 6 5 4 3 2

First American Edition

MURDER
AT THE SAVOY

1.

The day was hot and stifling, without a breath of air. There had been a haze quivering in the atmosphere, but now the sky was high and clear, its colors shifting from rose to dusky blue. The sun's red disk would soon disappear beyond the island of Ven. The evening breeze, which was already rippling the smooth mirror of the Sound, brought weak puffs of agreeable freshness to the streets of Malmö. With the gentle wind came fumes of the rotting garbage and seaweed that had been washed up on Ribersborg Beach and in through the mouth of the harbor into the canals.

The city doesn't resemble the rest of Sweden to a very great degree, largely because of its location. Malmö is closer to Rome than to the midnight sun, and the lights of the Danish coast twinkle along the horizon. And even if many winters are slushy and windblown, summers are just as often long and warm, filled with the song of the nightingale and scents from the lush vegetation of the expansive parks.

Which is exactly the way it was that fair summer evening early in July 1969. It was also quiet, calm and quite deserted. The tourists weren't noticeable to any extent—they hardly ever are. As for the roaming, unwashed hash-smokers, only the first bands had arrived, and not so many more would show up either, since most of them never get past Copenhagen.

It was rather quiet even in the big hotel across from the railroad station near the harbor. A few foreign businessmen were deliberating over their reservations at the reception desk. The checkroom attendant was reading one of the classics undisturbed in the depths of the cloakroom. The dimly lit bar contained only a couple of regular customers speaking in low voices and a bartender in a snow-white jacket.

In the large eighteenth-century dining room to the right of the lobby there wasn't much going on either, even if it was somewhat livelier. A few tables were occupied, mostly by people who were sitting alone. The pianist was taking a break. In front of the swinging doors leading to the kitchen stood a waiter, hands behind his back, looking contemplatively out of the big open windows, probably lost in thoughts of the sand beaches not too far away.

A dinner party of seven, a well dressed and solemn gathering of varying sexes and ages, was sitting in the back of the dining room. Their table was cluttered with glasses and fancy dishes, surrounded by champagne coolers. The restaurant personnel had discreetly withdrawn, for the host had just risen to speak.

He was a tall man in late middle age, with a dark-blue shantung suit, iron gray hair and a deep suntan. He spoke calmly and skillfully, modulating his voice in subtly humorous phrases. The other six at the table sat watching him quietly; only one of them was smoking.

Through the open windows came the sounds of passing cars, trains switching tracks at the station across the canal, a switch-yard that is the largest in northern Europe, the abrupt hoarse tooting of a boat from Copenhagen, and somewhere on the bank of the canal a girl giggling.

This was the scene that soft warm Wednesday in July, at approximately eight-thirty in the evening. It's essential to use the expression "approximately," for no one ever managed to pin down the exact time when it happened. On the other hand, what did happen is quite easy to describe.

A man came in through the main entrance, cast a glance at the reception desk with the foreign businessmen and the uniformed attendant, passed the checkroom and the long narrow lobby outside of the bar, and walked into the dining room calmly and resolutely, with steps that weren't notably rapid. There was nothing remarkable about this man so far. No one looked at him; he did not bother to look around either.

4

He passed the Hammond organ, the grand piano and the buffet with its array of glistening delicacies and continued past the two large pillars supporting the ceiling. With the same resolve he walked directly toward the party in the corner, where the host stood talking with his back turned to him. When the man was about five steps away, he thrust his right hand inside his suit coat. One of the women at the table looked at him, and the speaker half turned his head to see what was distracting her. He gave the approaching man a quick, indifferent glance, and started to turn back toward his guests, without a second's interruption in the comments he was making. At the same instant the newcomer pulled out a steel-blue object with a fluted butt and a long barrel, aimed carefully and shot the speaker in the head. The report was not shattering. It sounded more like the peaceful pop of a rifle in a shooting gallery at a fair.

The bullet struck the speaker just behind the left ear, and he fell forward onto the table, his left cheek in the crenelated mashed potatoes around an exquisite fish casserole *à la Frans Suell.*

Sticking the weapon into his pocket, the gunman turned sharply to the right, walked the few steps to the nearest open window, placed his left foot on the sill, swung himself over the low window, stepped into the flower box outside, hopped down onto the sidewalk and disappeared.

At the table three windows away a diner in his fifties became rigid and stared with amazement, a glass of whisky halfway to his mouth. In front of him was a book that he had been pretending to read.

The man with the suntan and the dark-blue shantung suit was not dead.

Stirring, he said, "Ow! It hurts."

Dead people don't usually complain. Besides, it didn't even look as if he were bleeding.

2.

Per Månsson was sitting in his bachelor den on Regementsgatan, talking to his wife on the telephone. He was a Detective Inspector with the Malmö police force, and although he was
married, he lived as a bachelor five days out of the week. For
more than ten years he'd spent every free weekend with his wife—
an arrangement which had so far satisfied both of them.

He cradled the receiver with his left shoulder while he mixed a
Gripenberger with his right hand. It was his favorite drink, consisting simply of a jigger of gin, crushed ice and grape soda in a
big tumbler.

His wife, who'd been to the movies, was telling him the plot of
Gone With the Wind.

It took some time, but Månsson listened patiently, because as
soon as she had finished the story he planned to ward off their
usual weekend get-together with the excuse that he had to work.
Which was a lie.

It was twenty minutes after nine in the evening.

Månsson was sweating in spite of his light clothing—a fishnet
undershirt and checkered shorts. He had closed the balcony door
at the beginning of the conversation so that he wouldn't be disturbed by the rumble of the traffic from the street. Although the
sun had long ago sunk behind the roofs of the buildings across the
street, it was very warm in the room.

He stirred his drink with a fork, which he was embarrassed to
admit had been either stolen or taken by accident from a restaurant called "Översten." Månsson wondered if a person could take
a fork by accident and said, "Yes, I see. It was Leslie Howard
then who . . . No, huh? Clark Gable? Uh-hmm . . ."

6

Five minutes later she'd got to the end. He delivered his white lie and hung up.

The telephone rang. Månsson didn't answer immediately. He was off work and wanted to keep it that way. He slowly drained his Gripenberger. Watching the evening sky darken, he lifted the receiver and answered, "Månsson."

"This is Nilsson. That was a helluva long conversation. I've been trying to get you for half an hour."

Nilsson was an Assistant Detective, on duty that night at the central police station on Davidshall Square. Månsson sighed.

"Well?" he said. "What's up?"

"A man has been shot in the dining room at the Savoy. I'm afraid I'm going to have to ask you to get over there."

The glass was empty but still cold. Månsson picked it up and rolled it against his forehead with the palm of his hand.

"Is he dead?" he asked.

"Don't know," said Nilsson.

"Can't you send Skacke?"

"He's off. Impossible to get hold of. I'll keep looking for him. Backlund is there now, but you probably ought to . . ."

Månsson gave a start and put down the glass.

"Backlund? Okay, I'll leave right away," he said.

He promptly called a taxi, then put the receiver on the table. While dressing, he listened to the rasping voice from the receiver mechanically repeating the words "Taxi Central, one moment please" until his call was finally put through to the operator.

Outside the Savoy Hotel several police cars were carelessly parked, and two patrolmen were blocking the entrance from a growing crowd of curious evening strollers jammed together at the bottom of the stairs.

Månsson took in the scene as he paid for the cab, put the receipt in his pocket, observed that one of the patrolmen was being rather brusque and reflected that it wouldn't be long before Malmö's police force had as bad a reputation as their colleagues in Stockholm.

He said nothing, however, only nodded as he walked past the

7

uniformed patrolmen into the lobby. It was noisy there now. The hotel's entire staff had gathered and were chatting with each other and with some customers streaming out of the grill. Several policemen completed the picture. They seemed at a loss, unfamiliar with the surroundings. Evidently no one had told them how to act or what to expect.

Månsson was a big man in his fifties. He was dressed casually in dacron pants and sandals, with his shirt out. He took a toothpick from his breast pocket, pulled off the paper wrapper and stuck it in his mouth. As he chewed, he methodically took stock of the situation. The toothpick was American, menthol-flavored; he'd picked it up on the train ferry *Malmöhus,* which provides such things for its passengers.

Standing by the door leading to the large dining room was a patrolman named Elofsson, whom Månsson thought was a little smarter than the others.

He walked over to him and said, "What's the story?"

"Looks like someone's been shot."

"Have you had any instructions?"

"Not a word."

"What's Backlund doing?"

"Questioning witnesses."

"Where's the man who was shot?"

"At the hospital, I guess."

Elofsson turned slightly red. Then he said, "The ambulance got here before the police, obviously."

Månsson sighed and went into the dining room.

Backlund was standing by the table with the gleaming silver tureens questioning a waiter. He was an elderly man with glasses and ordinary features. Somehow he'd managed to become a First Assistant Detective. He was holding his notebook open in his hand, busily taking notes. Månsson stopped within hearing distance, but said nothing.

"And at what time did this happen?"

"Uh, about eight-thirty."

"*About?*"

8

"Well, I don't know for sure."

"In other words, you don't know what time it was."

"No, I don't."

"Rather odd," said Backlund.

"What?"

"I said, it seems rather odd. You have a wrist watch, don't you?"

"Of course."

"And there is a clock on the wall over there, if I'm not mistaken."

"Yes, but . . ."

"But what?"

"Both of them are wrong. Anyway, I didn't think of looking at the clock."

Backlund appeared overwhelmed by the response. He put down the pad and pencil and began to clean his glasses. He took a deep breath, grabbed the notebook and started writing again.

"Even though you had two clocks at your disposal, you still didn't know what time it was."

"Well, kind of."

"We've got no use for 'kind of' answers."

"But the clocks aren't synchronized. Mine's fast, and the clock over there's slow."

Backlund consulted his Ultratron. "Odd," he said, writing something down.

Månsson wondered what.

"So, you were standing here when the criminal walked by?"

"Yes."

"Can you give me as full a description as possible?"

"I didn't really get a good look at him."

"You didn't see the gunman?" said Backlund, startled.

"Well, yes, when he climbed out the window."

"What did he look like?"

"I don't know. It was pretty far away, and that table was hidden by the pillar."

"You mean you don't know what he looked like?"

"Not really."

"How was he dressed then?"

"In a brown sport coat, I think."

"Think."

"Yeah. I only saw him for a second."

"What else did he have on? Try pants, for example."

"Sure, he had pants on."

"Are you certain?"

"Well, it sure would have seemed a little . . . like you said, odd, otherwise. If he hadn't had any pants on, I mean."

Backlund wrote furiously. Månsson started chewing on the other end of the toothpick and quietly said, "Say, Backlund?"

The other man turned around and glared.

"I'm in the middle of questioning an important witness . . ."

He broke off and said sullenly, "Oh, so it's you."

"What's going on?"

"A man was shot in here," said Backlund in great earnest. "And you know who?"

"No."

"Viktor Palmgren. The corporation president." Backlund laid heavy stress on the label.

"Oh, him," said Månsson. And thought, this'll be a helluva time. Aloud he said, "It happened over an hour ago and the gunman climbed out the window and got away."

"It may look that way."

Backlund never took anything for granted.

"Why are there six police cars outside?"

"I had them close off the area."

"The whole block?"

"The scene of the crime," said Backlund.

"Get rid of everybody in uniform," Månsson said wearily. "It can't be very pleasant for the hotel to have police swarming around in the foyer and out on the street. Besides, they must be needed more some place else. Then try to get up a description. There has to be a better witness than this guy."

"Naturally, we'll question everybody," said Backlund.

"All in due time," said Månsson. "But don't detain anyone who doesn't have something crucial to say. Just take names and addresses."

Backlund looked at him suspiciously and said, "What are you planning to do?"

"Make some telephone calls," said Månsson.

"Who to?"

"The newspapers, to find out what's happened."

"Was that supposed to be a joke?" said Backlund coldly.

"Right," said Månsson absentmindedly and looked around.

Journalists and photographers were roaming around in the dining room. Some of them must have been there long before the police, and one or more had been on the spot in the grill or the bar when the famous shot was fired. Probably. If Månsson's suspicions proved correct.

"But the manual requires . . . ," Backlund began.

Just then Benny Skacke hurried into the dining room. He was thirty years old, and already an Assistant Detective. Previously he had been with the National Homicide Squad in Stockholm, but had asked to be transferred after taking a rather foolish risk that had almost cost the life of one of his superiors. He was dedicated, conscientious, somewhat naive. Månsson liked him.

"Skacke can help you," he said.

"A Stockholmer," said Backlund skeptically.

"Right," said Månsson. "And don't forget that description. That's all that matters now."

He threw his shredded toothpick into an ashtray, went out into the lobby and headed for the telephone across from the reception desk.

Månsson made five calls in rapid succession. Then he shook his head and went into the bar.

"Well, look who's here!" said the bartender.

"How's it going?" Månsson said and sat down.

"What can we give you today? The usual?"

"No. Just a grape soda. I've got to think."

Sometimes everything gets messed up, Månsson thought. This

case had really got off to a bad start. In the first place, Viktor Palmgren was important and well known. True, it was hard to tell exactly why, but one thing was certain—he had plenty of money, at least a million. The fact that he had been shot down in one of the most famous restaurants in Europe didn't help matters. This case would attract a lot of attention and could have far-reaching consequences. Immediately after the shooting, the hotel personnel had carried the wounded man out to a TV lounge and fixed a makeshift stretcher. They'd alerted the police and an ambulance at the same time. The ambulance had come very quickly, picked up the wounded man and taken him to General Hospital. For a while there had been no sign of the police. In spite of the fact that a patrol car had been parked at the railroad station—in other words, less than 200 yards from the scene of the crime. How had that happened? He had received the explanation now, but it wasn't especially flattering to the police. The call had been misinterpreted at first, the case judged to be less urgent than others. The two patrolmen at the train station had therefore spent their time picking up a completely harmless drunk. Only after the police had been alerted a second time had cars and uniformed men been dispatched to the hotel, with Backlund fearlessly in the lead. What had then been undertaken in the way of investigation seemed totally slipshod. Månsson himself had sat rehashing *Gone With the Wind* with his wife for more than forty minutes. Besides that, he'd had two drinks and been forced to wait for a taxi. When the first policeman arrived, half an hour had passed since the shot was fired. As to Viktor Palmgren's condition, the situation was equally unclear. He had been examined at the emergency ward in Malmö, then referred to a neurosurgeon in Lund, about fifteen miles away. At this very second the ambulance was still on its way. One of the most important witnesses, Palmgren's wife, was also in the ambulance. She'd probably sat across from him at the table and had been the person most likely to get a close look at the gunman.

An hour had already gone by. An hour wasted, and every second of it was precious.

Månsson shook his head again and glanced at the clock above the bar. Nine-thirty.

Backlund marched into the bar, followed closely by Skacke.

"And you just sit here?" Backlund said, quite surprised.

He strained his eyes to stare at Månsson.

"How's the description coming?" said Månsson. "We've got to get a move on."

Backlund fumbled with his notebook, put it on the bar, took off his glasses and began cleaning them.

"Listen," Skacke said quickly, "this is the best we can come up with right now. Medium tall, thin face, thin dark brown hair, combed back. Brown sport coat, pastel shirt, dark gray pants, black or brown shoes. Age about forty."

"Fine," said Månsson. "Send it out. Right away. Block all main roads, check out trains, planes and boats."

"Right," said Skacke.

"I want him to stay in town," said Månsson.

Skacke left.

Backlund put on his glasses, stared at Månsson and repeated his pertinent question, "And you just sit here?"

Then he looked at the glass, saying with even greater astonishment, "Drinking?"

Månsson didn't reply.

Backlund turned his attention to the clock over the bar, compared it with his watch and said, "That clock's wrong."

"Of course," the bartender said. "It's fast. A little service for guests who're in a hurry to catch a train or boat."

"Hmm," Backlund said. "We'll never get this figured out. How can we determine the correct time when we can't rely on the clock?"

"It won't be too easy," Månsson said absentmindedly.

Skacke came back.

"Well, that's done," he said.

"Probably too late," Månsson said.

"What in the world are you talking about?" Backlund said, seizing his notepad. "About this waiter . . ."

Dismissing him with a gesture, Månsson said, "Wait. We'll take that later. Benny, go call the police in Lund and ask them to send a man to the neurosurgeon at the hospital. The man they send should have a tape recorder with him so he can take down anything Palmgren says. If and when he regains consciousness. He'll have to question Mrs. Palmgren, too."

Skacke departed again.

"About this special waiter. I'd say he wouldn't have noticed a thing if Dracula himself had fluttered through the dining room," the bartender said.

Irritated, Backlund kept quiet. Månsson waited to say anything else until Skacke came back. Since Backlund was officially Skacke's superior, he carefully addressed his question to both of them.

"Who do you two think is the best witness?"

"A guy named Edvardsson," said Skacke. "He was sitting only three tables away. But . . ."

"But what?"

"He isn't sober."

"Liquor's a curse," Backlund said.

"Okay, we wait with him until tomorrow," said Månsson. "Who can drop me off at headquarters?"

"I can," said Skacke.

"I'll stay here," Backlund said stubbornly. "This is officially my case."

"Sure," said Månsson. "We'll be seeing you."

In the car he mumbled, "Trains and boats . . ."

"Do you think he's gotten out of here?" asked Skacke hesitantly.

"He could have left. Any way you look at it, we've got a whole lot of people to call. And we can't worry about waking anybody up."

Skacke looked sideways at Månsson, who was taking out another toothpick. The car swung into the courtyard of the main police station.

"Planes," Månsson said to himself. "It could be a rough night."

The station seemed large, grim and very empty at this time of day. It was an impressive building. Their steps echoed desolately on the broad stone staircase.

By nature, Månsson was as slow-moving as he was tall. He detested rough nights, and besides, most of his career was behind him.

The opposite was true of Skacke. He was twenty years younger, thought about his career a lot and was eager and ambitious. But his previous experience as a policeman had made him careful, anxious to do what was expected.

So, in fact, they complemented each other quite well.

Inside his room Månsson immediately opened the window, which faced the station's asphalt courtyard. Then he sank down in his desk chair and sat silently for several minutes, reflectively spinning the platen on his old Underwood.

Finally he said, "Get all the radio messages and calls sent up here. Take them on your telephone."

Skacke had a room on the other side of the corridor, across from Månsson.

"You can leave the doors open," Månsson said.

And after several seconds he added with mild irony, "That way we'll have a real tracking center."

Skacke went into his room and began using the telephone. After a little while Månsson followed him. He stood with a toothpick in the corner of his mouth, one shoulder propped against the doorpost.

"Have you given this any thought, Benny?" he said.

"Not very much," said Skacke carefully. "It seems incredible, somehow."

"Incredible is the word for it," Månsson said.

"What I don't get is the motive."

"I don't think we should give a damn about the motive until we get the details straight."

The telephone rang. Skacke made a note.

"The person who shot Palmgren had only one chance in a thousand of making it out of the hotel dining room afterward. Up to the second the shot was fired, he acted like a fanatic."

"Something like an assassination?"

"Right. And afterward? What happens? Miraculously enough he escapes, and then he doesn't act like a fanatic any more, but panics."

"Is that why you think he's trying to leave town?"

"Partly. He walks in and shoots and doesn't care what happens afterward. But then, like most criminals, he panics. He simply gets frightened and only wants to get away from there, as far and as fast as possible."

That's one theory, Skacke thought. Seems rather loosely founded, though.

But he said nothing.

"Of course it's only a theory," Månsson said. "A good detective can't rely just on theories. But for the time being I don't see any other line we can work on."

The telephone rang.

Work, Månsson thought. What a helluva way to work.

And he was supposed to have a day off!

It was a rough night in the sense that nothing really happened. Some people who more or less fitted the description were stopped on the highways leading out of the city and at the train station. None of them seemed to have anything to do with the case, but their names were taken.

At twenty to one the last train left the station.

At quarter to two the police in Lund sent the message that Palmgren was alive.

At three o'clock another message came from the same source. Mrs. Palmgren was in shock, and it was difficult to question her thoroughly. However, she had seen the gunman clearly and was sure she didn't recognize him.

"Seems on the job, that guy in Lund," said Månsson with a yawn.

Just after four the Lund police got in touch again. The team of doctors treating Palmgren had decided for the present not to operate. The bullet had penetrated behind his left ear; it was impossible to tell what damage had been caused. The condition of the patient was reported to be as good as could be expected.

Månsson's condition wasn't good. Tired, his throat very dry, he went out to the washroom time after time to fill up on water.

"Is it possible for someone to live with a bullet in his head?" asked Skacke.

"Yes," said Månsson, "it's been done before. Sometimes it's enclosed by the tissue, and the person recovers. If the doctors had tried to remove it, however, he probably would've died."

Backlund had evidently stuck to the Savoy for a long time, for at four-thirty he called to say that he had blockaded and sealed off an area in anticipation of the technical squad's investigation of the scene of the crime, which might take place in several hours, at the soonest.

"He wants to know if he's needed here," said Skacke, holding his hand over the receiver.

"The only place he could possibly be needed is at home in bed with his wife," said Månsson.

Skacke conveyed the message but modified the wording somewhat. Soon after this Skacke said, "I think we can rule out Bulltofta. The last plane left at five after eleven. Nobody on board answered the description. The next one takes off at six-thirty. It's been booked up since the day before yesterday, and there's nobody on the waiting list."

Månsson mulled over that for a while. "Hmm," he said finally. "Guess I'll call up somebody who sure isn't going to like being dragged out of bed."

"Who? The police chief?"

"No, he probably hasn't slept any more than we have. By the way, where were you hiding out last night?"

"At the movies," said Skacke. "You can't sit home and study every night."

"I've never sat home and studied," said Månsson. "One of those hydrofoils left Malmö for Copenhagen at nine o'clock. Try to find out which one it was."

That was an unexpectedly difficult task, and half an hour went by before Skacke could report, "It's called *Springeren,* and right now it's in Copenhagen. It's unbelievable how sore some people get when you call and get them out of bed."

"You can comfort yourself with the fact that I've got a much worse job now," said Månsson.

He went into his room, picked up the telephone, dialed Denmark, 00945, and then the home number of Police Captain Mogensen, Danish Bureau of Investigation. He counted seventeen buzzes before a thick voice said, "Mogensen."

"This is Per Månsson in Malmö."

"What the hell do you want?" said Mogensen. "Do you know what time it is?"

"Yes," said Månsson, "but this could be very important."

"It'd better be goddamned important," the Dane said threateningly.

"We had an attempted murder here in Malmö last night," said Månsson. "There's a chance that the gunman flew to Copenhagen. We have a description."

Then he related the whole story, and Mogensen said bitterly, "For chrissake, do you think I can work miracles?"

"Why not?" said Månsson. "Let us know if you find out anything."

"Go to hell," said Mogensen in a surprisingly clear voice and slammed down the receiver.

Månsson shook himself, yawning.

Nothing happened.

Backlund called later to say that they'd begun investigating the scene of the crime. It was then eight o'clock.

"Hell, he's really on the ball," Månsson said.

"Where do we go from here?" asked Skacke.

"Nowhere. Wait."

At twenty to nine Månsson's private line rang. He lifted the receiver, listened for a minute or two, broke off the conversation without saying so much as thanks or good-bye and yelled to Skacke, "Call Stockholm. Right away."

"What should I say?"

Månsson looked at the clock.

"That was Mogensen. He said a Swede who gave his name as Bengt Stensson bought a ticket from Kastrup to Stockholm last night and then waited stand-by for several hours. He finally got on an SAS flight that took off at eight twenty-five. The plane should have landed at Arlanda ten minutes ago at most. The guy might fit the description. I want the bus from the airport into the city stopped at the air terminal, and this man taken into custody."

Skacke rushed to the telephone.

"Okay," he said breathlessly half a minute later. "Stockholm will take care of it."

"Who did you talk to?"

"Gunvald Larsson."

"Oh, him."

They waited.

After half an hour Skacke's telephone rang. He yanked the receiver to his ear, listened and was left sitting with it in his hand. "They blew it," he said.

"Oh," Månsson said laconically.

But they'd had twenty minutes, he thought.

3.

A similar expression was used in the main police station on Kungsholmsgatan in Stockholm.

"Well, they blew it," said Einar Rönn, sticking his sweaty red face through a crack in the door to Gunvald Larsson's room.

"Which one?" Gunvald Larsson asked absentmindedly.

He was thinking about something completely different, specifically three unusually brutal robberies in the subway the night before. Two rapes. Sixteen fights. This was Stockholm, quite a different place. Even though there were no murders last night, not even a homicide. Thank god. How many burglaries or thefts had been committed, he didn't know. Or how many addicts, sexual offenders, bootleggers and alcoholics the police had taken into custody. Or how many policemen had worked over presumably innocent people in patrol cars and local stations. Probably too many to count. He minded his own business.

Gunvald Larsson was a First Assistant Detective on the Assault and Battery Squad. Six foot three, strong as an ox, blond, blue-eyed, he was very snobbish for a policeman. This morning, for example, he was dressed in a pale gray, lightweight suit with matching tie, shoes and socks. He was an odd character; not many people liked him.

"You know, that bus to Haga air terminal," Rönn said.

"Well, what about it? They blew it?"

"The patrolmen who were supposed to check the passengers didn't get there soon enough. When they arrived the passengers had all got out and disappeared, and the bus had driven off."

Finally switching his thoughts to the subject at hand, Gunvald Larsson glared at Rönn with his blue eyes and said, "What? But that's impossible."

"Unfortunately not," said Rönn. "They just didn't get there on time."

"Have you gone crazy?"

"I'm not the one who was in charge of this," Rönn said. "I wasn't the one."

He was calm and good-natured, originally from Arjeplog in the north of Sweden. Although he had lived in Stockholm for a long time, he still used some dialect.

Gunvald Larsson had received Skacke's call quite by chance and considered checking this bus as a simple routine measure. He scowled angrily and said, "But goddammit, I called Solna promptly. The man on duty there said they had a patrol car on Karolinskavägen. It takes three minutes at most to drive to the air terminal from there. They had at least twenty minutes. What happened?"

"The guys in the car seem to have been detained on the way."

"Detained?"

"Yes, they had to issue a warning. And when they got there the bus had already left."

"A warning?"

Putting on his glasses, Rönn looked at the piece of paper he was holding in his hand. "Right. The bus's name is Beata. Usually it comes from Bromma."

"Beata? What kind of asshole has started giving names to busses?"

"Well, it's not my fault," Rönn said sedately.

"Do the geniuses in the patrol car have names, too?"

"Very likely. But I don't know what they are."

"Find out. For chrissake, if busses have names, patrolmen must have them too. Although really they should only have numbers."

"Or symbols."

"Symbols?"

"You know, like kids at nursery school. Like boats, cars, birds, mushrooms, bugs or dogs."

"I've never been in a nursery school," Gunvald Larsson said scornfully. "Now find out. That guy Månsson in Malmö is going to die laughing if there's no reasonable explanation."

Rönn left.

"Bugs or dogs," Gunvald Larsson said to himself. And added, "Everybody's crazy."

Then he went back to the robberies in the subway, picking his teeth with the letter-opener.

After ten minutes Rönn came back, glasses on his red nose, paper in hand. "I've got it now," he said. "Car three from the Solna police station. Patrolmen Karl Kristiansson and Kurt Kvant."

Gunvald Larsson jerked forward suddenly, nearly committing suicide with the letter-opener. "Christ, I should have known. I'm hounded by those two idiots. They're from Skåne, too. Get them over here on the double. We've got to straighten this thing out."

Kristiansson and Kvant had a lot of explaining to do. Their story was complicated and not at all easy. Besides, they were scared to death of Gunvald Larsson and managed to postpone their visit to the police station on Kungsholmsgatan for nearly two hours. That was a mistake, for in the meantime Gunvald Larsson made successful inquiries on his own.

Finally they were standing there anyway, uniformed, proper, caps in hand. They were six foot one, blond and broad-shouldered, and looked woodenly at Gunvald Larsson with dull blue eyes. They were wondering to themselves why Gunvald Larsson would be the one to break the unwritten but golden rule that police aren't supposed to criticize the actions of other policemen or to testify against each other.

"Good morning," said Gunvald Larsson in a friendly manner. "Nice that you could make it."

"Good morning," said Kristiansson hesitantly.

"Hi," said Kvant insolently.

Gunvald Larsson stared at him, sighed and said, "You were the ones who were supposed to check the passengers on that bus in Haga, weren't you?"

"Yes," said Kristiansson.

He reflected. Then he added, "But we got there late."

"We couldn't make it on time," Kvant improved.

"I've gathered that," said Gunvald Larsson. "I've also gathered that you were parked on Karolinskavägen when you got the call. Driving to the air terminal from there takes about two minutes, three at most. What make of car do you have?"

"A Plymouth," Kristiansson said, squirming.

"A perch does a mile and a half an hour," said Gunvald Larsson. "It's the slowest fish there is. But still it could've easily covered that stretch in a shorter time than you did."

He paused. Then roared, "Why the hell couldn't you get there on time?"

"We had to caution somebody on the way," said Kvant stiffly.

"A perch probably could have come up with a better explanation," Gunvald Larsson said with resignation. "Well, what was this caution about?"

"We . . . were called names," Kristiansson said feebly.

"Abuse of an officer of the law," said Kvant emphatically.

"And how did that happen?"

"A man riding by on a bicycle shouted insults at us."

Kvant was still acting the part while Kristiansson was standing saying nothing, but looking more and more uneasy.

"And that prevented you from carrying out the orders you'd just received?"

Kvant had the answer ready. "In an official statement, the National Chief of Police himself said that a complaint should definitely be brought against anyone who abuses an officer, especially an officer in uniform. A policeman can't be made a laughing stock."

"Is that so?" said Gunvald Larsson.

The two patrolmen glared at him unsympathetically.

He shrugged and went on: "Now I grant you that the potentate you mention is famous for his official statements, but I doubt that even he could have said anything so utterly stupid, for chrissake. Well, how did those insults go?"

" 'Pig!' " Kvant said.

"And you think you didn't deserve that?"

"Absolutely not," Kvant said.

Gunvald Larsson looked searchingly at Kristiansson, who shifted his weight and mumbled, "Yes, I suppose so."

"Yeah," Kvant said. "And even if Siv would say . . ."

"What is Siv?" said Gunvald Larsson. "Is that a bus, too?"

"My wife," said Kvant.

Gunvald Larsson disentangled his fingers and put his enormous hairy hands on the desk top, palms down. "Here's how it happened," he said. "You were parked on Karolinskavägen. You had just gotten the alert. Then a man rode by on his bicycle and shouted 'Pig!' at you. You were obliged to caution him. And that's why you didn't make it to the air terminal on time."

"That's right," said Kvant.

"Yeeaah," said Kristiansson.

Gunvald Larsson watched them for a long time. Finally he said in a low voice, "Is that true?"

No one answered. Kvant began to look apprehensive. Kristiansson nervously fingered his pistol holster with one hand, wiping the sweat off his forehead with his cap.

Gunvald Larsson remained quiet for a long time, letting the silence deepen. Suddenly he raised his arms and slammed his palms down on the table, with a smack that made the whole room shake.

"It's a lie," he shouted. "Every single word is a lie; and you know it, too. You'd stopped at a drive-in. One of you was standing outside the car eating a hot dog. As you said, a man rode by on a bicycle and someone shouted something at you. But it wasn't the man who shouted, it was his son who was sitting in the kiddie carrier on the back of the bike. And he didn't yell 'Pig!' but 'Daddy, this little pig . . .' He is only three years old. He plays with his toes, for chrissake."

Gunvald Larsson broke off abruptly.

By now Kristiansson and Kvant were as red as beets. At long last Kristiansson mumbled indistinctly, "How on earth did you know?"

Gunvald Larsson looked piercingly from one to the other. "All right, who was eating the hot dog?" he asked.

"Not me," said Kristiansson.

"You sonovabitch," Kvant whispered out of the corner of his mouth.

"Well, let me answer the question for you," Gunvald Larsson said tiredly. "The man on the bicycle simply wouldn't let two idots in uniform bawl him out for more than fifteen minutes for something a three-year-old happened to say. So he called here to complain and had every right to do so. Especially since there were witnesses."

Kristiansson nodded glumly.

Kvant tried to make a final defense: "It's easy to hear the wrong thing when you've got your mouth full of . . ."

Gunvald Larsson cut him off by raising his right hand.

He pulled over his notepad, took a pencil out of his inside pocket and printed in large letters, "GO TO HELL!" He tore off the page and shoved it across the desk. Kristiansson took the sheet, glanced at it, turned a deeper shade of red and gave it to Kvant.

"I can't bear to say it one more time," Gunvald Larsson said.

Kristiansson and Kvant took the message and left.

4.

Martin Beck didn't know anything about all that.

He was in his office at the South police station on Västberga Allé, working on quite different problems. He had pushed back his chair and was sitting with his legs outstretched and his feet on the lower desk drawer, which he'd drawn halfway out. He bit down on the filter tip of a newly-lit Florida, thrust his hands deep into his pants pockets and squinted out the window. He was thinking.

Since he was a Chief Inspector in the National Homicide Squad, it might be supposed that he was meditating on the ax murder on the South Side, which was still unsolved after a week. Or on the unidentified female corpse that had been fished up from Riddarfjärden the day before. But that wasn't the case.

He was brooding over what he should buy for his dinner party that night.

At the end of May, Martin Beck had found a two-room apartment on Köpmangatan and moved away from home. He and Inga had been married for eighteen years, but the marriage had been on the rocks for some time, and in January, when his daughter Ingrid had moved in with a friend, lock, stock and barrel, he'd talked to his wife about separating. At first she'd protested, but when the lease was ready, and she was faced with the facts, she accepted. Rolf, their fourteen-year-old; was her favorite, and Martin Beck suspected that she was actually pleased to be alone with the boy.

The apartment was cozy and large enough, and when he'd finally arranged the few things he'd taken with him from his and Inga's home out in the dismal suburb of Bagarmossen and bought what he still needed, he'd had an attack of recklessness and invited his three best friends for dinner. Considering that, at best, his knowledge of cooking consisted of boiling eggs and brewing tea, that was reckless to say the least; he realized that now. He tried to recollect what Inga used to serve when they had company, but managed only to evoke diffuse images of hearty dishes whose preparation and ingredients were totally foreign to him.

Martin Beck lit another cigarette and thought with confusion of Sole Walewska and filet of veal *à la Oscar*. Not to mention *cœur de filet provençale*. Furthermore, there was one more detail that he hadn't taken into consideration when he extended his unpremeditated invitation. He had never seen three people with appetites so voracious as those of the forthcoming guests.

Lennart Kollberg, who was the person he worked with most closely, was both a gourmet and a gourmand; he'd had the chance to observe this the times he'd ventured down to the lunchroom. In addition, Kollberg's size indicated a strong interest in the delicacies of the table—not even an ugly knife wound in the stomach about a year earlier had been able to remedy that peculiarity. Gun Kollberg didn't have her husband's figure, but did have quite a good appetite. Åsa Torell, now a colleague of his, too, since she had been placed on the Vice Squad after graduating from the Police Academy, was a real Gargantua.

He remembered very distinctly how small, thin and spindly she'd looked a year and a half earlier, when her husband, Martin Beck's youngest Assistant Detective, had been shot to death on a bus by a mass murderer. She'd got over the worst now, regained her appetite and even become a little rounder. Presumably she had an astounding metabolic rate.

Martin Beck considered asking Åsa to come earlier so she could help, but dismissed the thought.

A meaty fist rapped on the door, which was promptly opened, and Kollberg came into the room.

"What are you sitting here thinking about?" he said, throwing himself into the extra chair, which creaked precariously under his weight.

Nobody would suspect that Kollberg knew more about burglars' tricks and the science of self-defense than perhaps anyone else on the force.

Martin Beck took his feet down from the drawer and pushed the chair nearer the desk. He put out his cigarette carefully before answering.

"About that ax murder in Hjorthagen," he lied. "Nothing new's turned up?"

"Have you seen the autopsy report? It says that the guy died after the first blow. He had an unusually thin skull."

"Yes, I've seen it," Martin Beck said.

"We'll have to see when we can talk to his wife," Kollberg said. "She's still in deep shock, according to what they said at the hospital this morning. Maybe she bludgeoned him to death herself, who knows?"

He stood up and walked over to open the window.

"Close it," said Martin Beck.

Kollberg closed the window.

"How can you stand it?" he complained. "It's like an oven in here."

"I'd rather be baked than poisoned," Martin Beck said philosophically.

The South police station was located very near to Essinge Parkway, and when the traffic was heavy, like now, at the beginning of vacation time, it was obvious how thick the air was with exhaust fumes.

"You'll only have yourself to blame," Kollberg said and lumbered over to the door. "Try to survive until tonight, anyway. Did you say seven?"

"Yes, seven," Martin Beck said.

"I'm hungry already," said Kollberg provocatively.

"Glad you can come," Martin Beck said, but the door had already slammed shut behind Kollberg.

A moment later the telephone began ringing and people arrived with papers to sign, reports to read and questions to answer, and he had to push aside all thoughts of the evening's menu.

At quarter to four he left the police station and took the subway to Hötorgshallen. There he walked around shopping for such a long while that finally he had to take a taxi home to Gamla Stan to have time to fix everything.

At five to seven he'd finished setting the table and surveyed his work.

There was matjes herring on a bed of dill, sour cream and chives. A dish of carp roe with a wreath of diced onion, dill and lemon slices. Thin slices of smoked salmon spread out on fragile lettuce leaves. Sliced hard-boiled eggs. Smoked herring. Smoked flounder. Hungarian salami, Polish sausage, Finnish sausage and liver sausage from Skåne. A large bowl of lettuce with lots of fresh shrimp. He was especially proud of that, since he had made it himself and to his surprise it even tasted good. Six different cheeses on a cutting board. Radishes and olives. Pumpernickel, Hungarian country bread, and French bread, hot and crusty. Country butter in a tub. Fresh potatoes were simmering on the stove, sending out small puffs of dill fragrance. In the refrigerator were four bottles of Piesporter Falkenberg, cans of Carlsberg Hof and a bottle of Løjtens schnapps in the freezer compartment.

Martin Beck felt very satisfied with the results of his efforts. Now only the guests were missing.

Åsa Torell arrived first. Martin Beck mixed two Campari sodas for them and she made a tour of inspection, drink in hand.

The apartment consisted of a bedroom, living room, kitchen, bathroom and hall. The rooms were small, but easy to take care of and comfortable, too.

"I don't really have to ask if you like it here," Åsa Torell said.

"Like most native Stockholmers, I've always dreamed of having an apartment in Gamla Stan," Martin Beck said. "It's great to get along on my own, too."

Åsa nodded. She was leaning against the window frame, her ankles crossed, holding the glass with both hands. Small and delicate, she had big brown eyes, short dark hair and tanned skin, and she looked healthy, calm and relaxed. It made Martin Beck happy to see her so, for it had taken her a long time to get over Åke Stenström's death.

"How about you?" he asked. "You moved not very long ago, too."

"Come see me sometime and I'll show you around," said Åsa.

After Stenström's death, Åsa had lived with Gun and Lennart Kollberg for a while, and since she didn't want to return to the apartment where she'd lived with him, she'd exchanged it for a one-room apartment on Kungsholmsstrand. She had also quit her job at a travel agency and started studying at the Police Academy.

Dinner was a great success. Despite the fact that Martin Beck didn't eat much himself (he did so seldom, if ever), the food was disposed of rapidly. He wondered anxiously if he'd underestimated their appetites, but when the guests stood up from the table, they seemed full and content, and Kollberg discreetly unbuttoned the waistband of his pants. Åsa and Gun preferred schnapps and beer to wine, and when the dinner was over, the Løjtens bottle was empty.

Martin Beck served cognac with coffee, raised his glass and said, "Now let's all get a real good hangover tomorrow, when we have time off on the same day for once."

"I don't have time off," Gun said. "Bodil comes and jumps on my stomach at five and wants breakfast."

Bodil was the Kollbergs' almost two-year-old daughter.

"Don't think about it," Kollberg said. "I'll take care of her tomorrow, hungover or not. And don't talk about work. If I'd been able to get a decent job, I'd have quit after that incident a year ago."

"Don't think about it now," Martin Beck said.

"It's damned hard not to," Kollberg said. "The whole police force here is going to fall apart sooner or later. Just look at those poor clods from the country, who meander around in their uniforms and don't know what to do with themselves. And what an administration!"

"Oh, well," Martin Beck said to divert him and grasped his cognac.

Even he was very worried, most of all by the way in which the force had been politicized and centralized after the recent reorganization. That the quality of the personnel on patrol was getting lower all the time hardly improved things. But this was hardly the proper occasion to discuss the matter.

"Oh, well," he repeated wistfully and lifted his glass.

After coffee Åsa and Gun wanted to wash the dishes. When Martin Beck protested, they explained that they loved to wash dishes anywhere but at home. He let them have their way and carried in whisky and water.

The telephone rang.

Kollberg looked at the clock.

"A quarter after ten," he said. "I'll be damned if it isn't Malm telling us that we have to work tomorrow anyway. I'm not here."

Malm was Chief Superintendent of Police and had succeeded Hammar, their previous chief, who had recently retired. Malm had come from nowhere, that is to say from the National Police Board, and his qualifications appeared to be exclusively political. Anyway, it seemed a bit mysterious.

Martin Beck picked up the receiver.

Then he grimaced eloquently.

Instead of Malm, it was the National Chief of Police, who said gratingly, "Something's happened. I have to ask you to go to Malmö first thing tomorrow morning."

Then he added, somewhat belatedly, "Please excuse me if I'm disturbing you."

Martin Beck didn't respond to that, but said, "To Malmö? What's happened?"

Kollberg, who'd just mixed a highball for himself, raised his eyes and shook his head. Martin Beck gave him a look of defeat and pointed to his glass.

"Have you heard of Viktor Palmgren?" said the Chief of Police.

"The executive? The V.I.P.?"

"Yes."

"Of course I've heard of him, but I don't know much about him other than that he has a million different companies and he's loaded. Oh, yeah, he also has a beautiful young wife who was a model or something. What's wrong with him?"

"He's dead. He died tonight at the neurosurgical clinic in Lund after he was shot in the head by an unknown assailant in the dining room of the Savoy in Malmö. It happened last night. Don't you have newspapers out in Västberga?"

Martin Beck again refrained from replying. Instead he said, "Can't they take care of it themselves down in Malmö?"

He took the glass of whisky Kollberg offered him and took a drink.

"Isn't Per Månsson on duty?" he continued. "He surely ought to be capable of . . ."

The Chief of Police cut him off impatiently.

"Of course Månsson is on duty, but I want you to go down and help him. Or rather to take charge of the case. And I want you to leave as soon as you can."

Thanks a lot, thought Martin Beck. A plane did leave Bromma at a quarter to one in the morning, but he didn't plan to be on it.

"I want you to leave early tomorrow," the Chief of Police said.

Obviously he didn't know the schedule.

"This is an extremely complicated, sensitive matter. And we have to solve it without delay."

It was quiet for a moment. Martin Beck sipped his drink and waited. Finally the other man continued, "It's the wish of someone higher up that you take charge of this."

Martin Beck frowned and met Kollberg's questioning look.

"Was Palmgren that important?" he said.

"Obviously. There were strong vested interests in certain areas of his operations."

Can't you skip the clichés and come out with it? Martin Beck thought. Which interests and which certain areas of which operations?

Evidently it was important to be cryptic.

"Unfortunately I don't have a clear idea of what kind of operations he was engaged in," he said.

"You'll be informed about all that eventually," the Chief of Police said. "The most important thing is that you get to Malmö as quickly as possible. I've talked to Malm, and he's willing to release you. We have to do our utmost to apprehend this man. And be careful when you talk to the press. As you can well understand, there's going to be a good deal written about this. Well, when can you leave?"

"There's a plane at nine-fifty in the morning, I think," Martin Beck said hesitantly.

"Fine. Take it," said the Chief of Police and hung up.

5.

Viktor Palmgren died at seven-thirty-three on Thursday evening. As recently as half an hour before the official declaration of death, the doctors involved in his case said that his constitution was strong and the much-discussed general condition not so serious.

On the whole, the only thing wrong with him was that he had a bullet in his head.

Present at the instant of death were his wife, two brain surgeons, two nurses and a first assistant detective from the police in Lund.

There had been general agreement that an operation would have been much too risky, which seemed fairly sensible, even to a layman. For the fact remained that Palmgren had been conscious from time to time and on one occasion in such good shape that they could communicate with him.

The detective, who felt more dead than alive by this time, had asked him a couple of questions: "Did you get a good look at the man who shot you?" And, "Did you recognize him?"

The answers had been unambiguous, positive to the first question and negative to the second. Palmgren had seen the would-be killer, but for the first and last time in his life.

That didn't exactly make it any more comprehensible. In

Malmö Månsson's face was creased with heavy lines of misgiving, and he yearned for his bed, or at least for a clean shirt.

It was an unbearably hot day, and the main police station was by no means air-conditioned.

The only small lead he'd had to go on had been bungled.

Those Stockholmers, Månsson thought.

But he didn't say it, out of consideration for Skacke, who was sensitive.

Furthermore, how much had that lead been worth?

He didn't know.

Maybe nothing.

But still. The Danish police had questioned the staff of the hydrofoil *Springeren,* and one of the hostesses on board during the nine o'clock trip from Malmö to Copenhagen had noticed a man, primarily because he had insisted on standing on the afterdeck during the first part of the thirty-five-minute journey. His appearance, meaning mostly his clothing, corresponded somewhat to the scanty description.

Something actually seemed to fit together.

The fact is, you don't stand up on the deck of these hydrofoils, which in most respects resemble airplanes more than boats. It's even doubtful whether you would be permitted to stand out in the fresh air during the passage. Eventually the man had wandered down and sat in one of the armchairs. He hadn't purchased tax-free chocolate, liquor or cigarettes on board and thus hadn't left any written notes behind him. To buy anything, you have to fill out a printed order form.

Why had this person tried to remain on deck for as long as possible?

Perhaps to throw something into the water.

In that case, what?

The weapon.

If, in fact, the same person was involved. If, in which case, he wanted to get rid of the weapon.

If, in fact, the man in question hadn't been afraid of becoming seasick and had therefore preferred the fresh air.

"If, if, if," Månsson mumbled to himself and broke his last toothpick between his teeth.

It was an abominable day. In the first place, the heat, which was next to unbearable when you were forced to sit inside. Moreover, inside the windows, you were completely unprotected from the blazing afternoon sun. In the second place, this passive waiting. Waiting for information, waiting for witnesses who had to exist but didn't get in touch.

The examination of the scene of the crime was going badly. Hundreds of fingerprints had been found, but there was no reason to assume that any of them belonged to the man who had shot Viktor Palmgren. They'd placed their greatest hopes on the window, but the few prints on the glass were much too blurred to be identified.

Backlund was most irritated by not being able to find the empty shell.

He called several times about that.

"I don't understand where it could have gone," he said with annoyance.

Månsson thought that the answer to that question was so simple that even Backlund should be able to think it out for himself. Therefore he said with mild irony, "Let me know if you have a theory."

They couldn't find any footprints, either. Quite naturally, since so many people had tramped around in the dining room, and also because it's next to impossible to find any usable impressions on wall-to-wall carpeting. Outside the window the man had stepped into a window box before hopping down onto the sidewalk. To the great detriment of the flowers, but offering scarcely any information to the criminal technicians.

"This dinner," Skacke said.

"Yes, what about it?"

"It seems to have been some sort of business meeting rather than a private gathering."

"Maybe so," Månsson said. "Do you have the list of the people who were seated at the table?"

"Sure."

They studied it together.

> Viktor Palmgren, executive, Malmö, 56
> Charlotte Palmgren, housewife, Malmö, 32
> Hampus Broberg, district manager, Stockholm, 43
> Helena Hansson, executive secretary, Stockholm, 26
> Ole Hoff-Jensen, district manager, Copenhagen, 48
> Birthe Hoff-Jensen, housewife, Copenhagen, 43
> Mats Linder, vice-president, Malmö, 30

"All of them must work for Palmgren's companies," said Månsson.

"It looks like it," said Skacke. "They'll have to be questioned thoroughly once more, of course."

Månsson sighed and thought about the geographical distribution. The Jensen couple had already returned to Denmark the previous evening. Hampus Broberg and Helena Hansson had taken the morning flight to Stockholm, and Charlotte Palmgren was at her husband's bedside at the clinic in Lund. Only Mats Linder was still in Malmö. And they couldn't even be really sure of that. As Palmgren's second in command, he traveled a lot.

Thus the day's misfortunes seemed to culminate in the message of death, which reached them at a quarter to eight and which at once transformed the case into murder.

But it was to get worse.

It was ten-thirty and they sat drinking coffee, hollow-eyed and weary. The telephone rang and Månsson answered.

"Yes, this is Detective Inspector Månsson."

And immediately afterwards:

"I see."

He repeated the phrase three times before he said good-bye and hung up.

He looked at Skacke and said, "This isn't our case any more. They're sending a man down from the National Homicide Squad."

"Not Kollberg," Skacke said anxiously.

"No, it'll be the one and only Beck. He's coming tomorrow morning."

"What'll we do now?"

"Go home to bed," said Månsson and stood up.

6.

When the plane from Stockholm landed at Bulltofta, Martin Beck didn't feel very well.

He'd always had a distinct aversion to flying, and inasmuch as this Friday morning he was also suffering from the effects of the party the night before, the trip had been particularly unpleasant.

The hot, heavy air struck him when he came out of the relatively cool cabin, and he began to sweat even before he'd finished walking down the steps. The asphalt felt soft under his shoe soles as he walked toward the domestic arrivals building.

The air in the taxi was sweltering despite the open window, and the imitation leather covering on the back seat felt red-hot through the thin cloth of his shirt.

He knew that Månsson was waiting for him at the police station, but he decided to go to the hotel first to shower and change. This time he had reserved a room not at the St. Jörgen's, as he usually did, but at the Savoy.

The doorman greeted him so exuberantly that for an instant Martin Beck suspected that he was being confused with a long-lost guest of great importance.

The room was airy and cool, facing north. From the window he could see the canal and the railway station and beyond the harbor and Kockum's wharf, a white hydrofoil, which was just disappearing into the pale blue haze on its way over the Sound to Copenhagen.

Martin Beck undressed and walked around the room naked while he unpacked his suitcase. Then he went into the bathroom and took a long, cold shower.

He put on clean underclothes and a fresh shirt, and when he had finished dressing he noticed that the time on the clock at the train station was twelve exactly. He took a cab to the main police station and walked directly up to Månsson's room.

Månsson had the windows wide open onto the courtyard, which lay in shadow at this time of day. He was in shirt sleeves, drinking beer while he leafed through a bundle of papers.

After they had greeted each other, and Martin Beck had taken off his suitcoat, settled down in the extra armchair and lit a Florida, Månsson handed him the bundle of papers.

"For a start you can take a look at this report. As you'll see, the whole thing was handled horribly from the very beginning."

Martin Beck read through the papers carefully and now and then put questions to Månsson, who filled in with details that weren't in the report. Månsson also recounted Rönn's slightly modified version of Kristiansson's and Kvant's behavior on Karolinskavägen. Gunvald Larsson had refused to have anything more to do with the case.

When Martin Beck had finished reading, he laid the transcripts on the table in front of him and said, "It's obvious that we'll have to first concentrate on questioning the witnesses properly. This really hasn't been very productive. What do they mean, anyway, by this curious phrase?"

He hunted out a piece of paper and read, " 'The deviation from the correct time of various clocks existent on the scene of the crime at the moment of the commission of the crime . . .' Does that mean anything?"

Månsson shrugged.

"That's Backlund," he said. "You've met Backlund?"

"Oh, him. I see," said Martin Beck.

He had met Backlund. Once. Several years ago. That was enough.

A car drove into the courtyard and stopped below the window. Then noises were heard, car doors being slammed shut, people running and loud voices shouting something in German.

Månsson got up slowly and looked out.

"They must have made a clean sweep on Gustav Adolf

Square," he said, "or down by the wharves. We've stepped up surveillance there, but it's mostly teenagers who have a little hash for their own use who get picked up. We seldom get at the big shipments and the really dangerous dealers."

"Same thing with us."

Månsson shut the window and sat down.

"How's Skacke doing?" Martin Beck asked.

"Fine," Månsson said. "He's an ambitious boy. Sits at home and studies every night. He does a good job, too, very careful and doesn't do anything rash. He really learned a lesson that time. He was very relieved, by the way, when he heard that you were coming, and not Kollberg."

Less than a year before, Benny Skacke had been more or less the direct cause of Kollberg's being stabbed in the stomach by a man that both of them were going to arrest at Arlanda airport.

"Good reinforcement for the soccer team too, I hear," Månsson said.

"Is that so?" said Martin Beck disinterestedly. "What's he doing right now?"

"He's trying to get hold of that man who was sitting alone several tables away from Palmgren's party. His name is Edvardsson, and he's a proofreader for *Arbetet*. He was too drunk to be questioned last Wednesday, and yesterday we couldn't get hold of him. He was probably at home with a hangover and refused to answer the door."

"If he was drunk when Palmgren was shot, maybe he's not worth much as a witness," Martin Beck said. "And when can we question Palmgren's wife?"

Månsson took a swallow of beer and wiped his mouth on the back of his hand.

"This afternoon, I hope. Or tomorrow. Do you want to deal with her?"

"Maybe it'd be better if you did it yourself. You must know more about Palmgren than I do."

"I doubt it," Månsson said. "But okay, you're the one to decide. You can talk to Edvardsson, if Skacke gets hold of him. I have a feeling that he's the most important witness so far, despite everything. Say, would you like a beer? It's warm, I'm afraid."

Martin Beck shook his head. He was extremely thirsty, but warm beer didn't appeal to him.

"Why don't we go up to the canteen and have some mineral water instead?" he said.

They each drank a bottle of mineral water standing at the bar and then returned to Månsson's room. Benny Skacke was sitting in the extra chair reading something from his note pad. He stood up quickly when they came in, and he and Martin Beck shook hands.

"Well, did you get hold of Edvardsson?" Månsson asked.

"Yes, eventually. He's at the newspaper right now, but should be home about three o'clock," Skacke said.

He looked at his notes.

"Kamrergatan 2."

"Call and say that I'll come at three," Martin Beck said.

The building on Kamrergatan seemed to be the first finished in a series of new structures; on the other side of the street were low, old houses that had been evacuated and would soon fall prey to bulldozers to make room for newer and larger apartment buildings.

Edvardsson lived on the top floor and opened the door soon after Martin Beck had rung the bell. About fifty years old, he had an intelligent face with a prominent nose and deep furrows around his mouth. He squinted at Martin Beck before he threw open the door and said, "Superintendent Beck? Come in."

Martin Beck preceded him into the room, which was frugally furnished. The walls were covered with book shelves, and on the desk by the window was a typewriter with a half-typed sheet of paper in the platen.

Edvardsson removed a stack of newspapers from the room's only armchair and said, "Please sit down and I'll get something to drink. I have cold beer in the icebox."

"Beer sounds good," Martin Beck said.

39

The man went out into the kitchenette and returned with glasses and two bottles of beer.

"Beck's Beer," he said. "Appropriate, eh?"

When he had poured the beer into the glasses he sat down on the sofa with one arm over the back.

Martin Beck took a big swallow of beer, which was cold and good in the oppressive heat. Then he said, "Well, you know what my visit is about."

Edvardsson nodded and lit a cigarette.

"Yes, about Palmgren. I can't exactly say I regret his passing."

"Did you know him?" Martin Beck asked.

"Personally? No, not at all. But you couldn't help but run into him in every possible connection. The impression I had was of a domineering, arrogant man—well, I've never gotten along with that type of person."

"What does that mean? 'That type'?"

"People for whom money means everything and who don't hesitate to use any means to get it."

"I'd like to hear more about Palmgren later, if you'd like to clarify what you think of him, but first I want to know something else. Did you see the gunman?"

Edvardsson ran a hand through his hair, which was a bit grizzled and lay in a wave over his forehead.

"I'm afraid I can't be of too much help. I was sitting reading and didn't really react until the fellow was already halfway out the window. At first I only noticed Palmgren, and then I saw the gunman—but kind of out of the corner of my eye. He took off very quickly, and when I got around to looking out of the window, he'd disappeared.

Martin Beck took out a crumpled pack of Floridas from his pocket and lit one.

"Have you any idea what he looked like?" he asked.

"I seem to remember that he was dressed in rather dark clothes, probably in a suit or a sport coat and pants that didn't match, and that he wasn't a young man. But it's only an impression I have—he could have been thirty, forty, or fifty, but hardly older or younger than that."

"Was Palmgren's party already seated when you got to the restaurant?"

"No," said Edvardsson. "I'd already eaten and had a whisky when they came. I live alone here, and sometimes it's nice to sit in a restaurant and read a book, and then I end up sitting there for quite a long time."

He paused and added, "Even though it gets damned expensive, of course."

"Did you recognize anyone besides Palmgren in this gathering?"

"His wife and that young man who's said to be—have been—Palmgren's right-hand man. I didn't recognize the others, but it looked as if they were employees, too. A couple of them spoke Danish."

Edvardsson took a handkerchief out of his pants pocket and wiped the perspiration off his forehead. He was dressed in a white shirt and tie, pale dacron trousers and black shoes. His shirt was soaked with sweat. Martin Beck felt his own shirt begin to grow damp and stick to his body.

"Did you happen to hear what the conversation was about?" he asked.

"To tell you the truth, I did. I'm fairly curious and think it's fun to study people, so, in fact, I was eavesdropping a little. Palmgren and the Dane talked shop—I didn't catch what it was all about, but they mentioned Rhodesia several times. He had a lot of irons in the fire, Palmgren—I even heard him say that himself on at least one occasion—and there were a number of shady deals underway, I've heard tell. The ladies talked about the kind of things that that kind of ladies usually talk about—clothes, trips, mutual acquaintances, parties . . . Mrs. Palmgren and the younger of the other two talked about someone who'd had her sagging breasts operated on so that they looked like tennis balls right under her chin. Charlotte Palmgren talked about a party at "21" in New York, where Frank Sinatra had been, and someone called Mackan had bought champagne for all of them the whole night. And a million other things like that. A fantastic bra for 75 kronor at Twilfit. That it's too warm to wear a wig in the summer, so you have to put your hair up every day."

Martin Beck reflected that Edvardsson couldn't have read much of his book that night.

"And the other men? Did they talk shop, too?"

"Not very much. It seems they'd had a meeting before dinner. The fourth man—not the Dane and not the young one, that is— said something about it. No, their conversation wasn't on a very high level either. For example, they talked a long time about Palmgren's tie, which unfortunately I couldn't see since he sat with his back to me. It must have been something special, for they all admired it, and Palmgren said that he'd bought it for 95 francs on the Champs-Elysées in Paris. And the fourth man told them that he had a problem that kept him awake at night. His daughter had actually moved in with a Negro. Palmgren suggested he send her to Switzerland, where there are hardly any blacks."

Edvardsson got up, carried the empty bottles out into the kitchenette and returned with two more bottles of beer. They were misty and looked extremely tempting.

"Yes," Edvardsson said, "that's most of what I remember from the table conversation. Not especially helpful, is it?"

"No," Martin Beck said truthfully. "What do you really know about Palmgren?"

"Not much. He lives in one of the largest of those old upper-class mansions out toward Limhamn. He made a pile of money and also spent plenty, among other things on his wife and that old house."

Edvardsson was silent a moment. Then he asked a question in return: "What do *you* know about Palmgren?"

"Not too much more than that."

"God save us if the police know as little as I do about characters like Viktor Palmgren," said Edvardsson and drank deeply from his glass of beer.

"Right when Palmgren was shot, he was giving a talk, wasn't he?"

"Yes, I remember, he stood up and started rambling on—the usual sort of nonsense. Welcomed them and thanked them for good work and lectured the ladies and had his fun. He seemed skilled at it; he sounded overwhelmingly jovial. The whole staff withdrew so they wouldn't disturb them, and even the music stopped. The waiters had vanished into thin air, and I had to sit there sucking on ice cubes. Don't you really know what Palmgren was doing, or is it a police secret?"

Martin Beck eyed the glass of beer. Took it. Took a sip cautiously.

"I don't know very much, in fact," he said. "But there are others who probably know. A lot of foreign business and a real estate agency in Stockholm."

"I see," Edvardsson said and then seemed lost in thought.

After a moment he said, "The little I saw of that murderer, I already told them about the day before yesterday. Two fellows from the police were on me. One fellow who kept asking what time it was, and also a younger one who seemed a little sharper."

"You weren't quite sober at the time, were you?" Martin Beck said.

"No. Lord knows, I wasn't. And then yesterday I tied on another one, so I'm still hungover. It must be this damned heat."

Splendid, thought Martin Beck. Hungover detective questions hungover witness. Very constructive.

"Maybe you know how it feels," Edvardsson said.

"Yes, I do," said Martin Beck. Then he took the glass of beer and emptied it in one gulp. He stood up and said, "Thank you. Maybe you'll be hearing from us again."

He stopped and asked another question:

"By the way, did you happen to see the weapon the murderer used?"

Edvardsson hesitated.

"Come to think of it now, it seems to me I caught a glimpse of it, at the moment he stuck it in his pocket. I don't know much about guns, of course, but it was a long, fairly narrow thing. With a kind of roller, or whatever you call it."

"Revolving chamber," said Martin Beck. "Good-bye and thanks for the beer."

"Come again sometime," Edvardsson said. "Now I'm going to

have a pick-me-up, so I can put things into a little better shape here."

Månsson was still sitting in about the same position behind his desk.

"What shall I say?" he said when Martin Beck slipped in through the door. "How did it go? Well, how did it go?"

"That's a good question. Rather badly, I think. How's it going here?"

"Not at all."

"How about the widow?"

"I'll get her tomorrow. Better be careful. She *is* in mourning."

7.

Per Månsson was born and grew up in the working-class section around Möllevång Square in Malmö. He'd been a police officer for more than twenty-five years. Having lived with Malmö his whole life, he knew his city better than most—and liked it, too.

However, there was one part of the city he'd never really got to know, and this section had always made him feel uneasy. That was Västra Förstaden, with areas like Fridhem, Västervång and Bellevue, where many rich families had always lived. He could remember the famine years of the twenties and thirties, when many times as a little kid he had trudged in his clogs through the blocks of mansions on the way to Limhamn, where somehow it might be possible to find herring for dinner. He recalled the expensive cars and the uniformed chauffeurs, maids in black dresses with aprons and starched white caps, and upper-class children in tulle dresses and sailor suits. He'd felt so utterly outside of all that; the whole environment had appeared incomprehensible, like a fairy tale to him. Somehow it still felt the same way by and large, despite the fact that the chauffeurs and most of the servant girls were gone and that by now upper-class children didn't differ very much on the surface from any other children.

After all, herring and potatoes was not a bad diet. Although fatherless and poor, he'd grown up to be a big strong man, taken the "hard road" and eventually done quite well. At least he thought so himself.

Viktor Palmgren had lived in this same area; and consequently his widow probably still lived there.

So far he'd only seen pictures of the people around the fated dinner table and didn't know very much about them. About Charlotte Palmgren, however, he knew that she was considered an exceptional beauty and had once been crowned Miss Something—was it only of Sweden or of the whole universe? Then she'd made herself famous as a model and after that become Mrs. Palmgren, twenty-seven years old and at the height of her career. Now she was thirty-two and outwardly fairly unchanged, as only women can be who haven't had children, and who can afford to spend a lot of time and an unlimited amount of money on their appearance. Viktor Palmgren had been twenty-four years older than she, a fact which might give an indication of the mutual motives for the marriage. He'd probably wanted something good-looking to display to his business acquaintances and she, enough money so that she never again would need to do anything that might possibly be characterized as work. And that is the way it seemed to have worked out.

However, Charlotte Palmgren was a widow, and Månsson couldn't avoid a certain measure of conventionality. Therefore, much to his dislike, he put on his dark suit, white shirt and tie before he went down and got into the car to drive the relatively short stretch from Regementsgatan to Bellevue.

The Palmgren residence seemed to correspond to all of Månsson's childhood memories, which had perhaps become covered with a patina of slight exaggeration over the years. One could catch only a glimpse of the house from the street, a bit of the roof and a weather vane, for the hedges were not only well-clipped and richly verdant, but also very high and thick. If he wasn't mistaken, there was likely to be a wrought-iron fence behind it. The lot seemed immense, and the lawn rather resembled formal gardens. The gate to the drive was just as impenetrable as the hedge; it was of copper, green with age, high, broad, and embellished with spiraling pinnacles. On one half of the door was a row of oversized brass letters, which formed the name that was not totally unknown by now—Palmgren. On the other half was a mail slot, the button for an electric doorbell and directly over it a square opening through which potential visitors could be scrutinized before being granted admission. Clearly it wasn't a matter of just walking in any old way. As he cautiously pressed down the handle, Månsson almost expected an alarm to start ringing somewhere inside. The door was locked, of course, and the opening hermetically sealed. Nothing could be seen through the mail slot— obviously it opened into a closed metal box.

Månsson raised his hand to the doorbell, but changed his mind, let his arm sink back and looked around.

Besides his own old Wartburg, two cars were parked by the curb—a red Jaguar and a yellow MG. Did it seem plausible that Charlotte Palmgren would have two sports cars parked on the street? He stood still listening and thought for an instant that he discerned voices from within the park. Then the sounds died away, perhaps stifled by the heat and the stagnant, quivering air.

What a summer, he thought. One that comes only about once every ten years. And here you stand like a blockhead in a tie, shirt and suit instead of lying on the beach in Falsterbo or sitting at home in shorts with a cold drink in your hand!

Then he thought about something else. The mansion was old, probably from the turn of the century or so, certainly rebuilt and modernized for a million or two. These houses usually had a gate in the rear, where the gardener, cooks, maids, messengers and nursemaids could slink in without the master and mistress being irritated by the sight of them.

Månsson walked along the hedge and turned down the next

side street. The lot seemed to extend over the whole block, for the hedge was even, unbroken and still just as impenetrable. He took a right again, went around to the rear, and found what he was looking for. A pair of double wrought-iron gates. From here the house wasn't visible, since it was enclosed by tall trees and dense foliage. However, he could see a big garage, rather newly built, and an older, smaller building—a tool shed, undoubtedly. There was no name plate on the rear entrance.

He placed his hands on both sides of the gate and pressed. The sides swung in and open. This meant he didn't have to find out if the gate was locked or not. In the shade of the trees he felt how warm it really was; drops of perspiration ran down inside his collar and ran down his back in a tickling rivulet between his shoulder blades. He pushed the gates shut.

On the gravel driveway to the garage, car tracks were visible; the paths that wound into the garden were covered with slate slabs.

Månsson walked across the grass under the trees in the direction of the house. This took him between rows of blooming laburnum and jasmine and, as calculated, brought him to the back of the house, which was quiet and deserted, with closed windows, kitchen and cellar stairs, and various mysterious adjoining buildings. He looked up at the house but couldn't see much of it, since he was far too close. He followed the path to the right, climbed over a flower bed, peeked around the corner and stood stock-still among the showy peonies.

The scenery was breathtaking in several respects. The lawn was very large and green, as well kept as an English golf course. In the middle was a kidney-shaped swimming pool lined with light blue tile, with clear green, shimmering water. At its farthest end there were a sauna, parallel bars and Roman rings. An exercise bicycle beside the sauna. Presumably this was where Viktor Palmgren had built up his excellent physical condition that everyone talked about. In something resembling a Bruno Mathsson chair at the edge of the pool, Charlotte Palmgren was sitting, or rather, lying, naked, her eyes closed. She had a very deep suntan, evenly apportioned over her whole body, and blond hair. If anyone had ever fostered the suspicion that she wasn't a genuine blonde, it was refuted by the fact that the sparse triangular patch of hair between her legs was so light that it appeared almost white against her suntanned skin. Her face had thin, apathetic features, a clean profile and a straight mouth. She was very thin, with almost unnaturally slender hips, a small waist and girlish breasts. Her nipples were small and pale brown and the area around them lighter than the other skin. There was nothing about her that appealed to Månsson. She could just as well have been a mannequin in a store window.

Just look at that, a naked widow!

Why not, anyway? Widows have to be naked, too, sometimes.

Månsson stood among the peonies feeling like a Peeping Tom, which of course he was.

What induced him to remain there, however, wasn't what he saw but what he heard. Somewhere in the immediate vicinity but out of sight came clinking noises from someone who was moving and doing something.

Then Månsson heard steps, and a man came forward out of the shade cast by the house. He was suntanned, too, although not nearly so deeply as Charlotte Palmgren. He was dressed in flowered Bermuda shorts and carried two tall glasses containing a pale red liquid. Straws and ice cubes. Not a bad idea at all.

Månsson recognized the man immediately from the photographs. It was Mats Linder, closest associate and protégé of Viktor Palmgren, deceased for less than forty-eight hours.

He walked across the grass toward the swimming pool. The woman in the reclining chair raised her left leg and scratched her ankle. Still without opening her eyes, she stretched out her right arm and took one of the glasses from the man's hand.

Månsson retreated behind the corner of the house. Listened. Linder said something first, "Is it too sour?"

"No, it's okay," the woman said.

He heard her put the glass down on the tiles.

"Aren't we terrible?" Charlotte Palmgren said apathetically. "Anyway, it's damned nice."

"You can say that again."

Her voice still had the same indifferent tone.

It was quiet for a while. Then the widow said in a suggestive and affected tone, "Mats, why can't you take those stupid pants off?"

If Linder replied at all, Månsson would never find out, for he promptly left his place among the peonies.

He walked briskly and silently the same way he'd come, closed the gate behind him and continued along the hedge, went around both street corners and stopped in front of the green copper door. Without a second's hesitation he pressed the doorbell.

Chimes sounded in the distance. It didn't take more than a minute before light steps were heard approaching. The peephole was opened, and a light blue-green eye stared at him. He also saw a lock of blond hair and exaggeratedly long, technically perfect eyelashes.

Månsson had taken out his identity card and held it up in front of the opening.

"I'm sorry to bother you," he said. "My name is Månsson. Detective Inspector."

"Oh," she said childishly. "Of course. The police. Could you please wait a few minutes?"

"Of course. Am I intruding?"

"What? No, not at all. Just a couple of minutes for me to . . ."

Apparently she couldn't invent an appropriate conclusion, for the aperture banged shut and the light steps withdrew much faster than they had come.

He looked at his watch.

It took her only three and a half minutes to return and open the door. Wearing silver sandals and a severe gray dress of a light material.

She could hardly have had the time to put on anything underneath it, thought Månsson, but it wasn't necessary anyway. She had nothing special to show off or to hide.

"Please come in," Charlotte Palmgren said. "I'm so sorry you had to wait."

She locked the door and walked ahead of him to the house. Out on the street a car started. Evidently there were others besides the widow who were quick on their feet.

For the first time Månsson had the opportunity to see the mansion in its entirety and he stared at it with amazement. It wasn't a house, actually, but a kind of diminutive castle with pinnacles and towers and strange projections. Everything indicated that the original builder had suffered from a severe case of megalomania and that the architect had copied the design from a picture postcard. Recent modernizations with added porches and glass verandas hadn't improved the over-all impression. It looked atrocious, and one didn't know whether to laugh or cry or maybe send for a demolition team to blow up the whole business. The building seemed extremely substantial; dynamite was probably the only thing that could budge it. Along the drive stood a row of hideous sculptures of the type found in Germany in the Kaiser's day.

"Yes, it's a beautiful house," Charlotte Palmgren said. "But it wasn't cheap to modernize. Now everything's in tiptop shape."

Månsson managed to tear his eyes away from the house and proceeded to look at the surroundings. The lawn, as he'd already had the chance to remark, was fastidiously well kept.

The woman followed his eyes and said, "The gardener comes three days a week."

"I see," Månsson said.

"Do you want to go in or sit outside?"

"Makes no difference," Månsson said.

Every trace of Mats Linder was gone, even the glasses, but on a cart on the porch in front of the large veranda stood a seltzer bottle, a bucket of ice and some bottles.

"My father-in-law bought this house," she said, "but he died many years ago, long before Viktor and I met."

"Where did you meet?" Månsson asked irrationally.

"In Nice, six years ago," she said. "I was in a fashion show there."

She hesitated a second, then said, "Maybe we should go inside."

"Fine," Månsson replied.

"I can't offer you anything special. A drink or two, of course."

"Thank you but no."

"You understand, I'm all alone here. I've sent the servants away."

Månsson didn't say anything, and after a moment she said, "After what's happened, I thought it would be better to be alone. All alone."

"I understand. My sympathies."

She inclined her head slightly but wasn't capable of expressing anything but disgust and total apathy.

Probably she wasn't talented enough to be able to look sorrowful, Månsson thought.

"Mm-m," she said, "Let's go in then."

He followed her up a flight of stone steps beside the veranda, crossed a large gloomy hall and entered a colossal drawing room stuffed with furniture. The mixture of styles was grotesque—ultramodern mixed with old wing chairs and semi-antique tables. She directed him to a group of four sofa units, a couch and a gigantic table with a thick plate-glass top. It looked new and expensive.

"Please sit down," she said conventionally.

Månsson sat down. The chair was the largest he'd ever seen; he sank down so deep that it felt as though he would never get back on his feet again.

"Are you sure you wouldn't like anything to drink?"

"Nothing, thanks," Månsson said. "I won't disturb you for long. But unfortunately I have to ask you several questions. As you understand, we're anxious to get hold of the person who killed Mr. Palmgren as quickly as possible."

"Yes, you *are* a policeman. Well, what should I say? It's been terribly sad, this whole thing. Tragic."

"You saw the gunman, isn't that right?"

"Yes, but it all happened so terribly fast. I sort of didn't react until afterward. Then the horrible thought struck me that he could have shot me too. All of us."

"Had you ever seen this man before?"

"No, absolutely not. I can't remember names or things like

that, but I have a good memory for faces. The police in Lund asked me the same question."

"I know, but you were upset then, naturally."

"Certainly, it was horrible," she said with little conviction.

"You must have given this a lot of thought during the past few days."

"Yes, of course."

"And you did see the man clearly. You were looking in his direction. What did he actually look like?"

"Well, what can I say? He looked terribly ordinary."

"What kind of impression did he make? Was he nervous? Or desperate?"

"You know, he looked completely ordinary. Quite common."

"Common?"

"Yes, no one we'd ever associate with, I mean."

"What were your feelings when you saw him?"

"Nothing, until he pulled out the pistol. Then I was afraid."

"You saw the weapon?"

"Of course. It was some kind of pistol."

"You couldn't say what kind?"

"I don't know a thing about guns. But it was some kind of pistol. Pretty long. Like the kind they use in Westerns."

"But what could you say about the man's facial expression?"

"Nothing. He looked ordinary, as I said. I got a better look at his clothes, but I've already talked about that."

Månsson gave up on the description. Either she wouldn't or couldn't tell any more than she already had. He looked around the curious room. The woman followed his glance and said, "This sofa grouping is quite dashing, don't you think?"

Månsson nodded and considered how much it could have cost.

"I bought it myself," she said with a certain pride. "At Finncenter."

"Do you live here all the time?" Månsson asked.

"Where else would we live when we're in Malmö?" she asked sheepishly.

"But when you're not in Malmö?"

"We have a house in Estoril. We live there during the winter. Viktor often did business in Portugal. And then the company apartment in Stockholm, of course. It's on Gärdet."

She reflected and added, "But we only live there when we're in Stockholm."

"I understand. Did you usually accompany your husband on his business trips?"

"Yes, when there were social affairs, I always went along. But not to the meetings."

"I understand," Månsson repeated.

What did he understand? That for the most part she'd served as a living mannequin, something young to hang expensive creations on, things that would have been of no use to ordinary people. That for persons like Viktor Palmgren, a wife who attracted universal admiration was included in the stage properties.

"Did you love your husband?" he asked suddenly.

She didn't look surprised, but searched for an answer.

"Love sounds so silly," she said finally.

Månsson took out one of his toothpicks and began to chew on it contemplatively.

She looked at him with amazement. For the first time she displayed something resembling real interest.

"Why do you do that?" she asked.

"A bad habit I picked up when I stopped smoking."

"Oh," she said. "I see. Otherwise, there are cigarettes and cigars in the case over there."

Månsson looked at her a second. Then he tried a new tack.

"The dinner last Wednesday was almost a business gathering, wasn't it?"

"Right. They'd had a meeting in the afternoon. But I wasn't there. I was at home changing then. I was at the luncheon earlier in the day."

"Do you know what this meeting was about?"

"Business, as usual. What, I don't really know. Viktor had so many irons in the fire. He used to say that himself, too. 'I have a lot of irons in the fire.' "

"You knew all the people there, didn't you?"

"I've seen them now and then. No, as a matter of fact, not the secretary who'd come with Hampus Broberg. I'd never seen her before."

"Are you good friends with any of the others?"

"Not really."

"Not with Mr. Linder, for example? He does live here in Malmö."

"We've seen each other now and then. At company parties and things like that."

"You don't see each other privately?"

"No, only through my husband."

She was answering in a monotone and seemed completely impassive.

"Your husband was giving a speech when he was shot. What was he talking about?"

"I wasn't listening very carefully. He welcomed everyone and thanked people for their cooperation—things like that. They were all employees. Besides, we were going to leave for a while."

"Leave?"

"Yes, we were going to go sailing on the West Coast for several weeks. We have a cottage in Bohuslän—I forgot to tell you that, of course. And then we were going to leave for Portugal."

"And that meant that your husband wasn't going to see his staff for a while?"

"Right."

"And you weren't, either?"

"What? No, I was going to accompany Viktor. We were going to play golf in Portugal. Later. In the Algarve."

Månsson had lost the main battle. Her indolence made it impossible to determine when she was lying or telling the truth, and her feelings, if she had any, were well concealed. He formed a last question which he thought was idiotic and which in any case was meaningless. But it sort of belonged to the routine.

"Can you think of anyone or of any group who wanted to get rid of your husband?"

54

"No, I couldn't possibly."

Månsson raised himself up out of the Finnish super-armchair and said, "Thank you. I won't take up any more of your time."

"You're welcome."

She followed him to the door. He was careful not to turn his head and look at the house of mourning.

They shook hands. He thought that she held his hand strangely, but only when he was sitting in the car did he realize that she had expected him to kiss it.

She had thin hands with long, narrow fingers.

The red Jaguar was gone.

It was insufferably warm.

"Oh, hell," Månsson said to himself and turned on the ignition.

8.

After a night of heavy and dreamless sleep, Martin Beck awoke late on Saturday morning, at five after nine. The evening before he'd eaten a hearty *skånsk* dinner with Månsson at the hotel, and he still felt slightly groggy, an aftereffect of what the kitchen had to offer in Scandinavia's best-known restaurant.

After opening his eyes with a sense of general well-being, he lounged for several minutes, pondering the fact that his appetite had improved, and his sensitive stomach had begun to behave quite decently since he had been separated from his wife. So, his suffering, which had gone on for so many years, had been psychosomatic, which was exactly what he had suspected all along.

The evening had been very enjoyable and rather long. Early on, Månsson had suggested that they shouldn't mull over the Palmgren case, since up to now there was so little that was concrete to say about it. This was obviously a good idea, for they were both in great need of a meal in peace and quiet, to be rounded off with a solid night's sleep. Simply to feel free for several hours and to gather their forces for continuing the investigation. The material was meager, and they both had a feeling that the case was complicated and could be painfully difficult to solve.

Martin Beck threw off the sheet and got up. He pulled up the shade and looked with pleasure out the open window. It was already hot, and the sun was beaming. Beyond Ferdinand Broberg's magnificent 1906 Post Office he saw the sparkling white hull of a boat on the Sound, blue and appealing despite the water pollution. The train ferry *Malmöhus* was making a wide swing, turning around outside of the harbor mouth in order to head the prow in the right direction. A fine boat, built at Kockum's in 1945 and constructed according to time-honored principles.

When boats still looked like boats, Martin Beck thought.

Then he took off his pajamas and went into the bathroom.

He was standing under the shower when the telephone rang.

It rang many times before he'd managed to turn off the cold water, wrap a bath towel around himself, shuffle over to the night stand and pick up the receiver.

"Yes, this is Beck."

"Malm here. How's it going?"

How's it going? The eternal question. Martin Beck frowned and said, "Hard to say at this point. The investigation has just begun."

"I tried to contact you at the police station but only found Skacke," the Chief Superintendent complained.

"I see."

"Were you sleeping?"

"No," said Martin Beck truthfully, "I wasn't asleep."

"You have to catch the murderer. On the double."

"Okay."

"A lot of pressure's been put on me. Both the Chief and the Attorney General have been on me. And now the Foreign Office is involved, too."

Malm's voice was shrill and nervous, but that was only normal.

"So it's got to be done quickly. As I said before, on the double."

"How are we supposed to do that?" said Martin Beck.

The Chief Superintendent neglected to answer his question, but that was to be expected, since he knew next to nothing about practical police work. He wasn't a very good administrator, either.

Instead he said, "This call is going through the hotel switchboard, isn't it?"

"I suppose so."

"Then you'll have to ring me from another telephone. Dial my home number. As soon as possible."

"I don't think there's any risk. You can keep talking," Martin Beck said. "In this country only the police have time to tap people's telephones."

"No, no, it's no good. What I have to say is extremely confidential and important. And this case takes precedence over anything else."

"Why?"

"That's just what I'm going to tell you. But you have to call back on a direct line. Go to the police station or somewhere. And fast. I'm in a tight spot. God knows, I wish I could get rid of the responsibility for this."

"Bull," Martin Beck said to himself.

"I can't hear. What did you say?"

"Nothing. I'll call back right away."

He hung up, dried himself and put on his clothes at a leisurely pace.

After a suitable length of time, he picked up the receiver, requested an outside line and dialed the number of Malm's home in Stockholm.

The Superintendent must have been hovering over the telephone, for he answered before the first signal had faded away.

"Yes, this is Superintendent Malm."

"Beck here."

"At last. Now listen carefully. I'm going to give you some information regarding Palmgren and his activities."

"Not a moment too soon."

"It's not my fault. I was given these details only yesterday."

He fell silent. All that could be heard was a nervous rustle.

"Well?" Martin Beck said finally.

"This is no ordinary murder," Malm said.

"There aren't any ordinary murders."

The reply seemed to confound the man. After a moment's reflection, he said, "Well, you are right, in a way. I haven't had the same practical experience as you have . . ."

No, you really haven't, Martin Beck thought.

". . . since mostly I've been involved with larger administrative problems."

"Now, what was Palmgren involved in?" said Martin Beck impatiently.

"He was in business. Big business. As you know, there are certain countries with which we have very sensitive relations."

"Such as?"

"Rhodesia, South Africa, Biafra, Nigeria, Angola and Mozambique, to name a few. It's difficult for our government to maintain normal contacts with these nations."

"Angola and Mozambique aren't nations," said Martin Beck.

"Now, don't get hung up on details. Anyway, Palmgren did business with these countries, among others. A large part of his operations were located in Portugal. Even though his official headquarters were in Malmö, he's thought to have made a great many of his most profitable transactions in Lisbon."

"What did Palmgren deal in?"

"Weapons, among other things."

"Other things?"

"Well, he handled practically everything. For example, he had a real estate company. Owns a lot of buildings here in Stockholm. The firm in Malmö is considered to be not much more than a façade, even if it's a very impressive one."

"Then he made piles of money?"

"Yes, to say the least. They've no idea how much."

"What does Internal Revenue have to say about that?"

"A great deal. But they don't know anything definite. Several of Palmgren's companies are registered in Liechtenstein, and they believe that most of his income went into accounts in Swiss banks. Even though his operations here were handled impeccably, they're well aware that records of the bulk of his money were inaccessible to the Internal Revenue people."

"Where does this information come from?"

"Partly from the Ministry for Foreign Affairs, and from the Revenue people. Now maybe you understand why they're so worried about this case higher up."

"No, why?"

"You really don't understand the implications?"

"Let's say that I don't quite grasp what you're getting at."

"Now listen to me," Malm said, exasperated. "In this country there's a small, but very militant, political group that violently opposes Sweden's getting involved with the countries I just mentioned. And also a much larger group of people who believe the official assurances that there aren't any Swedish interests in Rhodesia or Mozambique, for example. Palmgren's activities have been kept pretty much under cover, and still are, but from certain sources we happen to know that extremist groups here were well acquainted with them, and that he was on their black list. To use a trite expression."

"It's better to use a trite expression than one that doesn't make any sense," Martin Beck said encouragingly. "How do we happen to know all this? About the black list?"

"The Security Division of the National Police Board has done some research into the matter. Certain influential people insist that the Security Division should take over the investigation."

"Wait a second," Martin Beck said.

He put down the receiver and began hunting for cigarettes. Finally he found a crumpled pack in his right pants pocket. During this time he was thinking feverishly. The National Police Board's Security Division, known derisively as Sepo, was a special institution, despised by many but primarily renowned for its unsurpassed incompetence. On the rare occasions it had managed to break a case, or even seize a spy, without exception the culprit had been delivered by the public, trussed like a turkey on a platter and garnished with full evidence. Even the military counterespionage was more effective. Anyway, it was seldom talked about.

Martin Beck lit a cigarette and returned to the telephone.

"What in the world are you doing?" Malm asked suspiciously.

"Smoking," Martin Beck said.

The Chief Superintendent said nothing. It sounded as though he had hiccupped or possibly gasped with surprise.

"What was that about Sepo?" Martin Beck asked.

"The Security Division? It's been suggested that they should take over the investigation. And they seem to be interested in the case."

"May I ask a question? Why would Security be interested?"

"Have you thought about the murderer's *modus operandi?*" Malm said ominously.

"Modus operandi." I wonder where he read that, Martin Beck thought. Aloud he said, "Yes, I've thought about it."

"As far as I can see, it presents many similarities to a classic political killing. A fanatic who thinks about one thing only, which is to carry out the task in hand, and who doesn't worry about whether he gets caught or not."

"Yes, there's something to that," Martin Beck admitted.

"Many people think that there's a great deal to it. Among them the Security Division."

Malm paused, probably for the sake of effect. Then he said, "Now, as you know, I hold no brief for the personnel of the Security Division and have no inside knowledge of their affairs. But I've been tipped off that they're sending down one of their specialists. But then they've probably already done it. There are also secret agents stationed in Malmö."

Martin Beck put out the half-smoked cigarette from pure disgust.

"Officially, the responsibility for the investigation lies with us," said Malm. "But presumably we can count on the Security Division's making a parallel investigation, so to speak."

"I see."

"Yes, and that, of course, means avoiding conflicts."

"Certainly."

"But above all it means getting your hands on the murderer as soon as possible."

Before the secret police do, Martin Beck thought. In that case, there's no big rush for once.

"As soon as possible," Malm said with determination.

And he continued: "It'll be a feather in your cap, at the very least."

"I don't have a cap."

"This is nothing to joke about."

"I can always buy one though."

"This is nothing to joke about," Malm repeated disparagingly. "Besides, this is urgent."

Martin Beck gazed defeatedly at the sun-drenched panorama outside of the window. Hammar had been troublesome in his fashion, especially during his last few years, but at least he had been a policeman.

"What's your view on how the investigation should be set up?" Martin Beck asked blandly.

Malm did some heavy thinking. Finally he came up with the following solution: "That is a detail which I'm turning over to you and your assistants with complete confidence. You do have a great deal of experience."

It was beautifully said. The Chief Superintendent also sounded quite happy when he continued, "And now we'll give it all we've got, right?"

"Right," Martin Beck said automatically.

He was thinking about something else. Then he said, "Then Palmgren's firm here in Malmö is more or less of a front?"

"I wouldn't go so far as to say that. On the contrary, it's probably an excellent operation."

"What kind of business is it?"

"Import and export."

"Of what?"

"Herring."

"Herring?"

"Yes," said Malm with surprise. "Didn't you know that? They buy up herring from Norway and Iceland and then export it. Where, I don't know. The whole thing is managed legitimately, as far as I can see."

"What about the company in Stockholm?"

"It's mainly a realty company, but . . ."

"But what?"

"Experts claim that Palmgren made his real fortune somewhere else, with means that we have no way of checking on or becoming involved with."

"Okay, I understand."

"Furthermore, I'd like to impress a couple of things on you."

"What things?"

"In the first place, that Palmgren was a powerful man in this country, with many influential friends, quite apart from his African and other foreign deals."

"Yeah, I get it."

"Therefore we must proceed with caution."

"I see. And secondly?"

"That you take into consideration the possibility that this could be a political killing."

"Yes," Martin Beck said and for once grew serious, "I'll take that into consideration."

With that the conversation was terminated.

Martin Beck called the police station. Månsson hadn't been heard from yet, Skacke was busy, and Backlund had gone out.

That was a good idea. Go out.

The weather was tempting, and besides, it was Saturday.

The foyer was rather crowded when he went down several minutes later. People were checking in and out in several different languages, but in the crowd in front of the reception desk was someone who couldn't help but attract attention.

He was a rather young, corpulent man, dressed in a hounds tooth checked suit of modern, youthful cut, a striped shirt, yellow shoes and socks of the same fierce color. His hair was wavy and shiny; he also had a little upturned mustache, no doubt waxed and prepared with a mustache form. The man was leaning nonchalantly on the reception desk. He had a flower in his buttonhole and was carrying a copy of *Esquire* rolled up under his arm.

He looked like a model out of a discothèque advertisement.

Martin Beck knew him. His name was Paulsson, and he was a First Assistant Detective from Stockholm.

When Martin Beck walked over to leave his room key, Paulsson gazed at him with a look that was so exquisitely empty and indolent that three other people felt it necessary to turn around and stare.

The secret police were on the scene.

Martin Beck suddenly felt an almost uncontrollable desire to laugh. Without looking at his secret colleague, he turned around abruptly and went out into the sun.

In the middle of Mälar Bridge, he turned around and studied the special style of the hotel building. It wasn't bad. The impressive façade had been preserved, and the tall *art nouveau* tower was a striking element of the cityscape. He even knew who had designed the building once upon a time—Frans Ekelund.

Paulsson was standing on the hotel steps spying. Because of his appearance, which looked almost like a disguise, there was hardly a public enemy who would not recognize him. Besides, he had an amazing gift for being seen on TV in connection with demonstrations and other public brawls.

Martin Beck smiled to himself and wandered out toward the harbor.

9.

The room that Benny Skacke rented was on Kärleksgatan, only a block from the police station. It was large and cozy, the furniture comfortable and practical, even if somewhat worn. He'd obtained the room from a police sergeant who'd been transferred to Landskrona. The landlady, a friendly, motherly old woman, was a police widow; all she required of boarders was that they be police officers.

His room was next to the hall, within convenient reach of the bathroom and kitchen, and he had unlimited access to both.

Benny Skacke was a man of habit, or rather, was in the process of making himself one. It wasn't really part of his nature to make a routine out of his existence, but he thought it would be easier for him to accomplish the tasks he'd set out for himself in order to reach his goal if he followed a definite schedule. His goal was to become Chief of Police.

Every morning he got up at six-thirty, did exercises and worked out with bar bells, took an ice-cold shower and rubbed himself dry before getting dressed. He ate a nourishing breakfast, usually consisting of sour milk and cereal, a soft-boiled egg, wholewheat bread and a glass of fruit juice. Since his working hours could be highly irregular, he had to fit his athletic training into the leisure offered during the course of the day. He swam at least three times a week, took long bicycle rides and sometimes put on his sweat suit to go jogging on Limhamn's field. He diligently took part in the Malmö policemen's soccer practice, in addition to having a position on the team and playing in all the matches on Mariedal's field. At night he studied law; he'd already completed two terms toward his law degree and hoped to be ready for the third in the fall.

At eleven o'clock every morning and at nine every evening he called his fiancée, Monica. They had become engaged in Stockholm the week before he started working in Malmö. A recent graduate, she had applied for a job as a physiotherapist in Malmö, but hadn't managed to find anything closer than Helsingborg. That was an improvement, at any rate, since they could now meet on the rare occasions when their free days happened to coincide.

This warm and sunny Saturday morning, however, he deviated from the schedule to the extent that he got up an hour later and skipped breakfast. Instead he filled a thermos with cold chocolate milk and put it in a canvas bag along with bathing trunks and a bath towel. On his way to the police station, he went into a bakery on Davidshall Square and bought two cinnamon rolls and a vanilla heart. He walked past the large copper doors of the main entrance of the police station, turned on Verkstadsgatan and went into the courtyard, where his bicycle was standing. It was black, a Danish make. On the oblique frame he'd hand-painted the word POLICE in white letters. He hoped that would scare off possible bicycle thieves.

With the bag on the carrier rack, he pedaled off through the luxuriant foliage of Castle Park and on to the bathhouse on Ribersborg. In spite of the early hour, it was already blazing hot. He took a swim, sunbathed for about an hour, and then settled down on the beach grass and ate the lunch he'd brought along.

When Skacke entered his office at nine-thirty, his desk was decorated with a message from Backlund:

Månsson at the widow's, Beck at the Savoy until further notice. Answer the telephone if it rings. Back at noon.

Backlund

Skacke sat down at the desk and listened for the telephone, which didn't make a sound, while he mused over the murder of Viktor Palmgren. What could the motive have been? Since Palmgren had been rich, money should be a convenient explanation. Or power. But then who would benefit from his death? Charlotte

Palmgren was the closest and—as far as he knew—the only heir to the money; Mats Linder should be next in line for his job. Considering Mrs. Palmgren's much-talked-of beauty and relative youth, the motive could also have been jealousy. It wasn't inconceivable that she'd had a lover who'd grown tired of playing second fiddle. But in that case it was a strange way to do away with the husband. Whatever the motive was, the method seemed poorly planned. The assailant had actually escaped, but his chances of getting away must have appeared extremely small if he'd plotted the whole thing beforehand. Moreover, the victim had died after a lapse of twenty-four hours; he might have survived, if the murderer's luck had been really bad—or good. The man must have known that Palmgren would be in the dining room of the Savoy at that exact moment, unless, of course, he were a complete lunatic who'd simply barged in and shot the first guest he caught sight of.

The telephone rang. It was Chief Superintendent Malm in Stockholm, looking for Martin Beck. Skacke informed him that he was probably still at his hotel, and Malm hung up without thanking him or saying good-bye.

Benny Skacke had forgotten his train of thought and became lost in daydreams. He imagined that he came up with the solution, tracked down and caught the murderer singlehanded. He would be promoted, and after that the only direction he could go would be up. He was close to becoming Chief of Police when a new ring of the telephone interrupted his visions of the future.

It was a woman's voice. At first he didn't understand what she was saying; her *skånsk* accent was hard for a Stockholmer to comprehend. Before his transfer to Malmö, Skacke had never been in Skåne. It didn't surprise him that he found certain *skånsk* dialects difficult to understand. However, it didn't cease to amaze him that he couldn't always make himself understood. He who spoke perfectly correct Swedish.

"Uh, it's about the murder that was in the newspaper," he heard the woman say.

"Yes," he said and waited.

"This is the police I'm talking to, isn't it?" she asked suspiciously.

"Yes, this is Assistant Detective Skacke," he said.

"Assistant? Isn't your boss there?"

"No, he's away for the moment. But you can talk to me just as well. I'm working on this case, too. What did you have on your mind?"

He thought his tone inspired confidence, but the woman didn't seem at all convinced of his authority.

"Maybe it'd be better if I came over," she said solemnly. "I don't live so far away."

"Yes, please come up," said Skacke. "Just ask for Assistant De—"

"Maybe the boss will be back by then," she added and hung up.

Twelve minutes passed. Then there was a knock on the door. If the woman had sounded skeptical on the telephone, she seemed even more so when she caught sight of Skacke.

"I'd really imagined someone older," she said, as though she were choosing an article in a store.

"Very sorry," said Skacke stiffly. "But it so happens that I'm on duty at the moment. Please sit down."

He moved the armchair a little closer to the end of the desk, and the woman sat down carefully on the very edge of the chair. She was small and pudgy, dressed in a pale green summer coat and a white straw hat.

Skacke returned to his place behind the desk and said, "Well, Mrs., uh . . ."

"Greta."

Is there such a name? Skacke thought. Apparently so.

"Well, Mrs. Gröngren. What is it you have to say about what happened last Wednesday?"

"The murder," she said. "Uh, you see, it's just that I saw the murderer. Well, I didn't know then that it was him, not until this morning when I read the newspaper. Then I understood."

Skacke leaned forward, his hands clasped on the blotter.

"Tell me about it," he said.

"Uh, I'd been over to Copenhagen shopping for groceries, you see, and then I met a ladyfriend, and we had coffee at Brønum; so I came home rather late. When I got to the corner at Mälar Bridge across from the Savoy the DON'T WALK sign was on, so I had to stand there and wait. Suddenly I saw a man jump out of one of the windows of the dining room at the Savoy—I've been there several times to eat dinner with my nephew, so I know it was the dining room. Well, my first thought was: What a rat! He's making off without paying the bill. But I couldn't do anything since the light was red, and there was no one around."

"Did you see where he went after that?" Skacke asked.

"Yes, I did. He went over to the bicycle rack to the left of the hotel, got on a bicycle and pedaled away toward Drottning Square. Then the light turned green, but I lost sight of him. I thought that the manager of the restaurant could surely afford to lose that money, so I didn't worry about it and went home."

She paused briefly.

"Well, when I'd crossed the street, people came out of the hotel entrance and stared, but by then he was already gone."

"Can you describe the man?" Skacke said with ill-concealed fervor and pulled over his note pad.

"Uh, he was about thirty, maybe forty. More like forty. He was quite bald—no, not bald, but almost. He had dark hair. And he had a brown suit on, a yellowish shirt and a tie—I don't know what color. Shoes black or brown, I think—must've been brown, since his suit was brown."

"What did he look like? His face, build, anything unusual about him?"

She seemed to reflect.

"He was thin," she said. "Thin body, thin face. Nothing special. Pretty tall, I thought. Shorter than you, but pretty tall. I don't know what else I can tell you."

Skacke sat quietly and looked at her for a while. Then he said, "When you lost sight of him where was he?"

"At the traffic light, I think. At the crossing on Bruksgatan.

The light must have been red there. Then the WALK sign came on, and when I walked across the street he was gone."

"Hmmm," said Skacke. "Did you see what the bicycle looked like?"

"The bicycle? Like any other bicycle, I suppose."

"Did you see what color it was?"

"No," Mrs. Gröngren said and shook her head. "Cars were going past the whole time. They got in the way."

"I see," said Skacke. "There's nothing else you can remember about this man?"

"No. Not that I can think of now. Will I get a reward for this?"

"I don't believe so," said Skacke. "The public has a moral obligation to help the police. Could I have your address and telephone number so that we can get in touch if necessary?"

The woman gave her address and telephone number. Then she stood up.

"Well, good-bye now," she said. "Do you think I'll get in the newspaper?"

"It's quite possible," Skacke said to encourage her.

He got up and followed her to the door.

"Good-bye and thanks an awful lot for the help. And for the trouble."

After he had shut the door and sat down at the desk, the door was opened again, and the woman stuck in her head.

"You know, that's right!" she said. "Before he got on the bicycle, he took something out of the inside of his jacket and put it in a box, a cardboard container, on the carrier rack. I'd completely forgotten about that."

"Oh," Skacke said, "you didn't happen to see what it was? The thing under his sport coat?"

"No, he was sort of turned away from me. The box was about this big. Almost as big as the carrier and about four inches thick. I saw it later as he was riding away."

Skacke thanked her once again, and Mrs. Gröngren left, this time apparently for good.

Then he dialed the number of the hydrofoil terminal.

When it was new, he'd written on the cover of his notebook:

Assistant Detective B. Skacke

While waiting for an answer, he wrote in front of that: *First.*

10.

Just after one on Saturday afternoon, Martin Beck and Per Månsson ran into each other in the doorway to the police station canteen.

Martin Beck had strolled around in the Industrihamn docks, which were quiet and deserted on Saturdays like this during summer vacation. He'd walked all the way out to the oil wharves, where loading had been momentarily interrupted, to view the strange science-fiction landscape. Milky water stagnated in ponds surrounded by rectilinear bars of sand, on which trucks and excavators had made deep tracks. He had marveled at how much the harbor area had grown since he'd seen it for the first time about fifteen years before. He'd suddenly felt hungry—a new and pleasant phenomenon the day after a hearty meal. It doesn't take long to get used to having an appetite again, he thought contentedly. Returning to the center of the city as quickly as possible in the blazing sun, he wondered what could be on the lunch menu at the police station.

Although Månsson wasn't especially hungry, he was extremely thirsty. He had refused the drink Charlotte Palmgren offered him. But now, sitting in his stifling car, he saw the light red drinks in Mats Linder's hands, clinking with ice. They danced before his eyes. For a second he considered driving home and mixing a Gripenberger, but decided it was too early in the day and compromised. A glass of cold soda water at the canteen would have to do.

Martin Beck's hunger diminished somewhat when he entered the canteen, and since he didn't feel so sure of his stomach, he ordered a ham omelet, a tomato and a bottle of mineral water. Månsson duplicated the order.

When they were settled down with their trays, they caught sight of Benny Skacke, who was desperately looking over in their direction. Backlund was sitting across from him, with his back turned to Beck. Backlund had pushed his plate aside and was pointing his first finger threateningly at Skacke. They couldn't hear what he was saying, but to judge from the look on Skacke's face, he was giving him some kind of lecture.

Martin Beck ate his omelet quickly and then walked over to Backlund. Putting his hand on his shoulder, he said kindly, "Forgive me for borrowing Skacke awhile. There are a couple of things I have to go over with him."

Backlund seemed irritated by the interruption but could hardly protest. That cocky Stockholmer *had* been sent down by the National Police Board to head the investigation. As if they couldn't manage it themselves.

Visibly relieved, Skacke stood up and went with Martin Beck. Månsson finished his meal, and they left the canteen. Backlund gazed after them with a grieved look on his face.

They went to Månsson's room, which was moderately cool and ventilated. Månsson sat down in the swivel chair, took a toothpick from the penholder and, after peeling off the paper, stuck it in the corner of his mouth. Martin Beck lit a cigarette and Skacke went directly across the corridor to get his note pad. Then he sat down in the chair next to Martin Beck and placed the pad in his lap.

Martin Beck caught sight of the writing on the pad's cover and smiled. When Skacke saw his glance he blushed and closed the pad quickly. Then he began to give an account of what the new witness had had to say.

"Are you positive her name's Gröngren?" Månsson said skeptically.

When Skacke was through, Martin Beck said, "You'd better check that out with the crew on the hydrofoil. If it was the same man they saw standing on the afterdeck, they should've seen the box. If he still had it with him."

"I've already called," Skacke said. "The boat stewardess who saw him isn't working today. But she's making the crossing tomorrow morning, so I'll go down and talk to her then."

"Good," said Martin Beck.

"You understand Danish then," Månsson said in a doubtful tone.

"Is it really that hard?" Skacke said, wide-eyed.

Then it was time for Martin Beck to tell them about Malm's phone call and the arrival of their colleague.

"Hmm, Paulsson's his name," said Månsson. "I wonder if I haven't seen him on TV. He sounds a lot like a security guy we have here, too. He's a secret agent called Persson. Always wears the same kind of suit. Dresses strangely. I thought you already knew about the herring export business, but I've never had an inkling about the weapons deals."

"That's not so strange, really," Martin Beck said. "It wasn't exactly intended that too many people should know about it."

Månsson broke the toothpick in half and put it in the ashtray.

"Well, something like that did enter my mind when the naked widow told me that Palmgren did a lot of business in Portugal."

"The *naked* widow?" Martin Beck and Skacke chorused.

Taking a new toothpick out of the penholder, Månsson said, "I was going to say the merry widow. But she wasn't—either happy or sad. She seemed indifferent to everything."

"But naked," said Martin Beck.

Månsson recounted the morning's visit to the Palmgren mansion.

"She was good-looking, huh?" Skacke said.

"No, I didn't think so," Månsson said curtly.

Then he turned to Martin Beck and said, "Do you have anything against my questioning Linder?"

"No," Martin Beck said, "but I'd really like to meet him, too. Besides, it might take the two of us to handle him."

Månsson nodded. After a while he said, "Do you believe that stuff about a political motive?"

"Sure, why not? But I'd like to know a little more about Palmgren's activities abroad. How we would work that, I don't know. Mats Linder probably isn't familiar with that part of the operations—presumably his job only includes the herring company. What was the Dane's job, by the way?"

"I don't know yet," Månsson said. "We'll have to find that out. If nothing else works, Mogensen will surely know."

They sat quietly for a while. Then Skacke said, "If the gunman is the same guy who flew to Stockholm from Kastrup, we know he's Swedish. And if the murder had political motives, then he had to be against Palmgren's dealings with Rhodesia and Angola and Mozambique and wherever else it was. And if he was against them, then he has to be some left-wing fanatic."

"Now you're talking like Persson," said Månsson. "He sees extremists under every bush. But there's something to what you say, of course."

"To tell the truth, that same line of thought had occurred to me even before I talked to Malm. It looks amazingly like a political killing. Something very peculiar about the murderer's *modus operandi*—"

Martin Beck broke off sharply. He'd used exactly the same terminology as Malm, and that annoyed him.

"Maybe, maybe not," said Månsson. "The radical groups down here are mainly centered in Lund. I know a little about them, and they're damn peaceful for the most part. Of course Sepo doesn't think so."

"There's nothing that says he comes from around here," Skacke said.

Månsson shook his head.

"Knowledge of the local area," he said. "And if that bit about the bicycle happens to be correct."

"Just think, maybe we could get hold of it," Skacke said optimistically.

Månsson looked at him a long time. Then he shook his head

again and said good-naturedly, "My dear Skacke, tracking a bicycle . . ."

Backlund knocked and stepped in without waiting for an answer; he was polishing his glasses diligently.

"Deliberations, I see," he said with irritation. "Maybe you gentlemen have also concluded where the shell went. We've hunted everywhere. Even in the food. I even made a thorough search of the mashed potatoes. There simply isn't any shell . . ."

"Sure there is," Månsson said wearily.

"But he used a revolver," Martin Beck and Benny Skacke said in the same breath.

Backlund looked as though he'd been struck by lightning.

On Sunday morning when Benny Skacke got off his bicycle at the hydrofoil's pier, *Springeren* was just entering the inner harbor. It had settled down on its keel and was gliding slowly forward to the quay.

The weather was still fantastic; not many people had chosen to cross the Sound in something that closely resembled an airplane cabin. A dozen passengers came climbing out of the boat's interior, hurried over the gangplank and through the station building to fight over the only taxi on the spot.

Skacke waited at the gangplank. After five minutes a blond girl in a hostess uniform came up on the deck. He walked up to her, introduced himself and showed her his identification.

"But I've already told the police about that man," she said. "The police in Copenhagen."

To Skacke's happy surprise, she actually spoke Swedish, but naturally with a noticeable Danish accent.

"Yes, I know," he said, "but there was something they didn't ask you about. Did you happen to notice if that man standing on the deck last Wednesday evening was carrying anything?"

The boat stewardess bit her lower lip and knit her brow.

At last she said hesitatingly, "Ye-es, now that you mention it—I recall that . . . No, wait, didn't he have a box in his hand, a black cardboard box, about this big?"

She approximated the dimensions with her hands.

"Did you see if he still had the box when he came down and took a seat? Or when he went ashore?"

She pondered a moment. Then she shook her head firmly.

"No, I don't remember that. I really don't know. I only saw that he had it under his arm when he was standing up here."

"Thanks anyway," said Skacke. "That's a valuable piece of information. You haven't remembered anything else about that man since you spoke with the police in Copenhagen?"

Again she shook her head.

"No, nothing else," she said.

"Nothing else?"

She smiled at him professionally and said, "No, nothing. Now if you'll excuse me I have to get things ready for the next trip."

Skacke rode his bicycle back to Davidshall Square and went up to his room in the police station. He was actually off work, but it was close to eleven o'clock—time to call Monica.

He preferred to call from his office rather than from home. For one thing, he didn't dare talk so long at home, considering the cost; for another, his landlady was rather curious when he talked on the telephone. And he wanted to be undisturbed when he was talking to Monica.

She was off work, too, alone at home in the apartment she sublet along with a friend from work. The conversation lasted almost an hour, but what did that matter? The police department could pay. Or, better still, the taxpayer.

When Skacke hung up he had on his mind something different from the murder of Viktor Palmgren.

11.

Martin Beck and Månsson met again at the police station at eight o'clock on Monday morning. Neither of them was in the best of humors; Månsson seemed indolent, slow-moving and unenterprising, and Martin Beck grim and pensive.

Without a word, they looked through their papers, but there wasn't anything encouraging. Nothing had happened on Sunday except that the town had become even warmer and emptier. When they informed the afternoon newspapers that "the state of the investigation was unchanged," there was indeed every justification for this empty and worn-out phrase. The only positive thing had been Skacke's vague information from the hydrofoil.

July is a highly unsuitable month for police investigations. If the weather is also beautiful, it's unsuitable for almost anything except for being on vacation. The Kingdom of Sweden virtually closes down; nothing functions, and it's impossible to get hold of people, simply because most of them have gone abroad or to their summer places. That includes almost every category from native professional criminals to government bodies. The relatively few policemen on duty are occupied mostly with checking up on the motley stream of foreigners or trying to keep traffic under control out on the highways.

Martin Beck would have given a lot to be able to talk to his old colleague Fredrik Melander, now Detective Inspector with the Assault and Battery Squad in Stockholm, forty-nine years of age and more than ever equipped with the police force's surest memory for names, dates, circumstances and all the other facts he'd managed to pick up during thirty years on the job. A man who never forgot anything and one of the few who might have something constructive to offer concerning this strange business with Palmgren. But Melander was definitely out of reach. He was on vacation and, as usual when off work, he had isolated himself completely in his summer cottage out on Värmdö. There was no telephone there, and none of his colleagues knew exactly where the place was. His hobby was chopping wood, but he'd chosen to devote this month of vacation to building a new, two-seater outhouse—something that only he and his tall, amazingly ugly wife were aware of, however.

Moreover, Martin Beck and Månsson should both have gone on vacation this week; the knowledge that it was sure to be put off until sometime in the nebulous future was reflected in their gloomy expressions.

On this Monday, however, there was questioning to be attended to, if at all possible. Martin Beck called Stockholm and managed after many if's and but's to persuade Kollberg to take care of Hampus Broberg and Helena Hansson, the executive secretary.

"What'll I ask them about?" Kollberg said mournfully.

"I don't really know."

"Who's the head of the investigation?"

"I am."

"And you don't know? How in the hell am I going to find out anything?"

"I'd like to get a picture of the general situation."

"The general situation? It's bad. I'm dying of heat exhaustion."

"What we need is the motive. Or, rather, we have too many to choose from. Maybe the atmosphere in the Palmgren concern can lead us to the right one."

"I see," Kollberg said skeptically. "This Hansson person, is she good-looking?"

"They say so."

"Well, there's always something to look forward to. Bye now."

Martin Beck had been close to saying, "Let me hear from you," but checked himself at the last second.

"Bye," he said and hung up.

He looked at Månsson and said, "Kollberg'll take care of the Stockholm end."

Månsson nodded and said, "Okay, he's a good man."

Kollberg was more than that, but Månsson didn't know him as well as Martin Beck did.

As a matter of fact, Kollberg was the only person Martin Beck trusted completely. He had sound judgment and was fully capable of managing on his own. Besides this he was imaginative, systematic and implacably logical. They had worked together for many years, and each understood what the other was thinking without having to exchange too many words.

Månsson and Martin Beck sat quietly and listlessly leafing through their papers.

A little after nine they got up and went down to Månsson's car, which was parked in the courtyard.

The Monday morning streets were a bit livelier, but it still didn't take Månsson more than ten minutes to drive to the tall building near the harbor where Viktor Palmgren had his main office in Sweden. By this time Mats Linder ought to be presiding in there.

Månsson parked in a highly illegal manner and put down the visor, which had a rectangular cardboard sign with the word PO-LICE neatly printed on the front.

They took the elevator up to the seventh story and stepped out into a large antechamber with a bright red wall-to-wall carpet and satiny wallpapered walls. There was a low table in the middle of the floor surrounded by comfortable armchairs. On the table top was a stack of magazines—they were mostly foreign, but even *Svensk Tidskrift* and *Veckans Affärer* were there. There were also two large crystal ashtrays, a teak case with cigars and ciga-rettes, an ebony lighter and a heavy Orrefors glass vase with red roses. Behind a long table on the left side of the room sat a blond receptionist of about twenty examining her glossy nails. In front of her was an intercom, two ordinary telephones, a steno pad in a metal stand and a gilded fountain pen on the blotter.

She had a model's figure and was dressed in a black and white dress with a very short skirt. Her stockings·had an ingenious black lacework pattern, and her feet were enclosed in elegant black shoes with silver buckles. Her lipstick was almost white, and her eyelids were covered with powder-blue eyeshadow. She had long silver earrings, even, chalk-white teeth and beneath dark false eyelashes, unintelligent, clear-blue eyes. She was quite flawless, Martin Beck supposed, if you like women that way.

The girl watched them with a touch of scorn and disapproval. Then she pecked at a page of the appointment book in front of her with the long pointed nail of her first finger and said in the broadest conceivable *skånsk* accent, "You must be from the po-lice."

She glanced at her diminutive watch and continued, "You are almost ten minutes too early. Mr. Linder is on the telephone.

He's talking to Johannesburg. Please sit down for the time being. I'll notify you as soon as the conversation is completed. You're Månsson and Back, aren't you?"

"Beck."

"I see," she said indifferently.

She took the gold pen and made a nonchalant little mark in the appointment book. Then she inspected them once again, barely concealing her dislike, and made a vague gesture toward the table with the roses, crystal ashtrays and smoking articles.

"Go ahead and smoke," she said.

The way a dentist says, "Rinse."

Martin Beck felt uneasy in the setting. He glanced at Månsson, who was dressed in a wrinkled shirt with the tail out, unpressed gray pants and sandals. He probably wasn't much more elegant himself, even though he'd put his pants under the mattress the night before. Nevertheless, Månsson seemed totally unaffected. He flung himself down in one of the armchairs, took a toothpick out of his breast pocket and leafed through a number of *Veckans Affärer* for about thirty seconds before shrugging his shoulders and throwing the magazine down on the table. Martin Beck also sat down and carefully studied the selection of expensive smoking articles in the open teak case. Then he took out one of his own Floridas, pinched the filter together and struck a match.

He looked around. The girl had returned to admiring her nails. It was absolutely quiet in the room. Something irritated him very much. After a while he realized what it was—the doors were invisible. They were there, but so well melted into the surrounding wallpaper pattern that a person actually had to make an effort to discover them.

The minutes passed. Månsson absent-mindedly chewed on his toothpick. Martin Beck put out his cigarette and lit another, then stood up and walked over to where a large aquarium with shimmering green water was built into the wall. He stood studying the gaudy fish until a low buzz from the intercom interrupted this activity.

"Mr. Linder will see you now," the receptionist said.

A second later, one of the well-camouflaged doors was opened, and a dark-haired woman of about thirty-five gestured for them to come in. Her movements were rapid and precise, her look steady. A typical executive secretary, Martin Beck thought. Probably she was the one who did the work, if any real work got done within these walls. Månsson stood up and went first, with a heavy, leisurely gait, through a small room with a desk, electric typewriter, filing cabinets and many folders, arranged on shelves against the wall.

Without a word, the dark-haired secretary opened one more door and held it open for them. After they stepped in, Martin Beck had an even stronger impression that they were big, clumsy, uncouth and out of place.

During the time it took Månsson to walk straight up to the desk, behind which Mats Linder was just getting up with a grieved but kind, polite smile, Martin Beck was studying three different things in turn—the view, the furnishings and the individual they'd come to meet.

He had the ability to take stock of situations quickly and felt that it was his greatest asset in his chosen profession. While Månsson took the toothpick out of his mouth, put it in the brass ashtray and shook hands, Martin Beck had the time to grasp the essentials.

The view from the large picture windows was spectacular. Below lay the dock, or rather, the docks, bustling with activity— swarms of cargo and passenger boats, tugboats, cranes, trucks, trains and rows of containers. Beyond the harbor were the Sound and Denmark. The scene was crystal clear. He could see at least twenty boats at one time, among them several passenger boats on their way to or from Copenhagen. The panorama far surpassed the view from his own hotel window, which wasn't so bad, either. All he needed was a good pair of binoculars.

A pair of Carl Zeiss marine binoculars, made in Jena, had been included among the furnishings. They were on the right side of the large steel desk. The desk was so situated that Linder sat with his back to a windowless wall covered by a huge photographic enlargement of a fishing trawler in heavy sea, its freeboard splashed with foam, a huge cascade of water welling up from the prow. Along the starboard gunwale stood a row of men in sou'westers and oilskins, hoisting up the trawl. The contrast was striking—between struggling to catch a meager living from the sea and sitting in peace and quiet in a luxurious office where fortunes were made from these men's toil. The contrast was striking, but probably unintentional. There have to be limits to cynicism. On the wall across from the window hung three lithographs by Matisse, Chagall and Salvador Dali. In the room there were also two leather chairs for visitors and a conference table with six straight-backed rosewood chairs.

According to the detectives' information, Mats Linder was thirty years old. His appearance suited his age and position perfectly. Tall, slender and well built. Brown eyes, neatly parted hair, a thin face with a firm profile and a determined chin. Very soberly dressed.

Martin Beck looked at Månsson and felt sweatier and more wrinkled than ever.

He introduced himself and shook hands with Linder.

They sat down in the leather armchairs.

The man behind the desk leaned on his elbows and sat with his finger tips pressed together.

"Well," he said, "has the murderer been apprehended?"

Månsson and Martin Beck shook their heads simultaneously.

"Then how can I be of help to you gentlemen?"

"Did Mr. Palmgren have any enemies?" Martin Beck asked.

It was a ridiculously simple question, but a beginning had to be made somewhere. Linder, however, seemed to take the question with exaggerated gravity and to consider his answer carefully. At last he said, "When a person is involved in business of the scope that Viktor Palmgren was, he can hardly escape making enemies."

"Can you think of anyone in particular?"

"Far too many," Linder said with a wan smile. "Gentlemen, the world of business is tough today. With the credit market in its present state, there's no room for philanthropy or sentimentality.

Many times it's a matter of kill or be killed. From an economic viewpoint, that is. But . . ."

"Yes?"

"But in the business world we use other methods than shooting each other. Therefore I believe that we can quite simply dismiss the theory that a slighted competitor walked into the dining room of a first-class restaurant with a pistol in his hand, in order, so to speak, to balance his books privately."

Månsson made a movement, as though something had occurred to him, but he didn't say anything. Martin Beck was forced to continue directing the conversation.

"Do you have any idea who it was who shot your boss?"

"I didn't really see him, partly because I was sitting beside Vicke—his intimate friends used to call him that—and consequently I had my back turned to the murderer, and because I didn't realize what was happening at first. I heard the shot—it wasn't loud and didn't seem very frightening—then Vicke fell forward over the table and I immediately stood up and leaned over him. It took several seconds before I realized that he was severely injured. When I turned around the gunman was gone, and the staff came rushing from all directions to help. But I told the police all this that same night."

"I know," said Martin Beck. "Maybe I didn't make myself quite clear. "What I meant was, have you any idea of what kind of person might be involved?"

"A lunatic," said Mats Linder without the slightest hesitation. "Only a person who is mentally ill could act that way."

"Then Mr. Palmgren would be a victim chosen at random?"

The man reflected. Then he smiled his faint smile again and said, "That's for the police to try to figure out."

"From what I gather, Mr. Palmgren did considerable business abroad?"

"Yes, that's correct. His commercial interests were numerous and varied. What we deal with here is the original business—the import and export of fish for the canning industry. This firm was founded by old Palmgren, Vicke's father. I'm too young to have known him. As for other foreign transactions, I really know very little."

He paused and added, "But it seems highly probable that I'll have to become closer acquainted with them now."

"Who is taking over the main responsibility for . . . the concern?"

"Charlotte, I suppose. She should be the sole heir. There aren't any children or any other relatives in the picture. But the corporation lawyers will have to clarify that. The firm's main lawyer had to break off his vacation very hastily. He came home on Friday night and since then has been at work going through the documents with his assistants. For the time being we are working here as usual."

Working? Martin Beck thought.

"Are you planning on being Mr. Palmgren's successor?" Månsson suddenly put in.

"No," Linder said. "I wouldn't say that, actually. Besides, I have neither the experience nor the talent required for managing a business emp—"

He broke off and Månsson didn't pursue the topic. Martin Beck didn't say anything, either. It was Linder himself who continued, "For the present I'm completely satisfied with my position here. And I can assure you that even this part of the business takes some running."

"Is herring a good business?" Martin Beck said.

The other man smiled indulgently.

"Well, we deal in more than herring. In any case, I can assure you that the company's financial status is very sound."

Martin Beck felt it necessary to try a new line of attack.

"I presume that you knew all the people at the banquet fairly well."

He reflected awhile and said, "Yes. Except Mr. Broberg's secretary."

Wasn't there some animosity in his features? Martin Beck felt that there was something afoot and forged ahead.

"Isn't Mr. Broberg considerably older than you, both in terms of age and years with the Palmgren concern?"

"Yes, he's about forty-five."

"Forty-three," said Martin Beck. "And how long has he worked for Palmgren?"

"Since the middle of the fifties. About fifteen years."

It was apparent that Mats Linder disliked the subject.

"Still, you do have a more privileged position, don't you?"

"That depends on what you mean by privileged. Hampus Broberg is located in Stockholm, as vice-president of the real estate company there. He also has charge of the stock activities."

Linder's face expressed strong disapproval. Now we've got to stay with it, Martin Beck thought. Sooner or later we might get the guy to make a slip of the tongue.

"But it seems quite obvious that Mr. Palmgren had more confidence in you than in Broberg. And yet Broberg has worked for him for fifteen years and you for only . . . yes, how long has it been?"

"Almost five years," Mats Linder said.

"Didn't Mr. Palmgren trust Broberg?"

"Too much."

Linder said and tightened his lips as if he wanted to annul the answer and erase it from the report of the proceedings.

"Do you consider Broberg unreliable?" Martin Beck asked immediately.

"I don't want to answer that question."

"Have disagreements come up between you and him?"

Linder sat quietly awhile. It seemed as though he were trying to assess the situation.

"Yes," he said at long last.

"What were these disagreements about?"

"That's a strictly private business matter."

"Don't you consider him loyal to the firm?"

Linder said nothing. It didn't matter now, since he'd already answered the question in principle.

"Well, we'll have to talk to Mr. Broberg about that," Martin Beck said in a casual tone.

The man behind the desk took a long, thin cigarillo out of his inner pocket, peeled off the cellophane wrapper and lit it carefully.

"But I don't understand what this has to do with my boss's murder," he said.

"Maybe nothing at all," Martin Beck said. "We'll just have to see."

"Is there anything else you gentlemen would like to know?" Linder asked, puffing on the cigar.

"You had a meeting on Wednesday afternoon, didn't you?"

'Yes, that's correct."

"Where?"

"Here."

"In this room?"

"No, in the conference room."

"What was the meeting actually about?"

"Internal affairs. I'm not able to give a more detailed account of what was said, and wouldn't if I could. Let's just say that Mr. Palmgren was going to withdraw from the business for a while and wanted a report on the situation here in Scandinavia."

"Did he make any criticisms during this review? Was there anything that Mr. Palmgren wasn't pleased with?"

The answer came after a short hesitation.

"No."

"Perhaps you thought that some criticism would've been in order?"

Linder didn't answer.

"You might have objections to our talking with Hampus Broberg?"

"On the contrary," Linder murmured.

"Excuse me, I didn't catch what you said?"

"It was nothing."

Silence. Martin Beck didn't think he could pursue this track much further. There had to be something rotten here, but nothing that indicated that it had anything to do with the murder.

Månsson seemed totally impassive, and Linder waited to see what would happen.

"In any case, it seems quite clear that Mr. Palmgren had more confidence in you than in Broberg," Martin Beck said, as if stating an obvious fact.

"That's possible," Linder said drily. "But anyhow, it doesn't have anything to do with his death."

"We'll just have to see," Martin Beck said.

The other man's eyes flashed. He had a hard time hiding the fact that he was furious.

"Well, we've already taken up a great deal of your precious time," Martin Beck said.

"Yes, you have, to tell the truth. The sooner this conversation is concluded, the better. For you and for me. I don't see any purpose in going over this again."

"Then we'll leave it at that," Martin Beck said, making an attempt to stand up.

"Thank you," Linder said.

His tone was sarcastic and extremely guarded.

At this point Månsson sat up and said slowly, "If you don't mind, I'd like to ask you a few questions."

"Such as?"

"What kind of relationship do you have with Charlotte Palmgren?"

"I know her."

"How well do you know her?"

"That ought to be my private affair."

"That, of course, is correct. But I'd still like you to answer the question."

"What question?"

"Are you having an affair with Mrs. Palmgren?"

Linder looked at him, coldly and deprecatingly.

After a minute of silence, he crushed his cigarillo in the ashtray and said, "Yes."

"A love affair?"

"A sexual relationship. I sleep with her sometimes, to put it simply, in language that even policemen can understand."

"How long has this relationship gone on?"

"For two years."

"Did Viktor Palmgren know about it?"

"No."

"And if he'd known about it, how would he have reacted?"

"I don't know."

"He might have objected?"

"I'm not so sure. Charlotte and I are broad-minded people. We don't care about convention. Viktor Palmgren was like that, too. Besides, their marriage was more of a practical arrangement than an emotional commitment."

"When did you see her last?"

"Charlotte? Two hours ago."

Månsson dug around in his breast pocket for another toothpick. He examined it and said, "How is she in bed?"

Mats Linder stared at him speechless. Finally he said, "Are you out of your mind?"

They stood up and said good-bye, without receiving an answer. The efficient, dark-haired secretary showed them out to the waiting room, where the blonde at the reception desk was carrying on a private conversation, cooing into one of her telephones.

When they were sitting in the car Månsson said, "Smart kid."

"Yes."

"Smart enough to tell the truth when he knows that a lie could be exposed. You can bet Palmgren had a lot of use for him."

"Mats Linder's obviously had a good teacher," Martin Beck said.

"Is he smart enough not to have people shot? That's the question," Månsson said.

Martin Beck shrugged.

12.

Lennart Kollberg didn't know which way to turn.

The job he'd been assigned to seemed both repugnant and pointless. It never occurred to him, however, that it would turn out to be complicated.

He would call on a couple of people, talk to them, and that's all there would be to it.

A little before ten o'clock he left the South police station in Västberga, where all was quiet and peaceful, largely because of the shortage of personnel. There was no shortage of work, however, for all varieties of crime flourished better than ever in the fertile topsoil provided by the welfare state.

The reasons for this were cloaked in mystery—at least for those who had the responsibility of governing and for the experts who had the delicate task of trying to make the society function smoothly.

Behind its spectacular topographical façade and under its polished, semi-fashionable surface, Stockholm had become an asphalt jungle, where drug addiction and sexual perversion ran more rampant than ever. Unscrupulous profiteers could make enormous profits quite legally on pornography of the smuttiest kind. Professional criminals became not only more numerous but also better organized. An impoverished proletariat was also being created, especially among the elderly. Inflation had given rise to one of the highest costs of living in the world, and the latest surveys showed that many pensioners had to live on dog and cat food in order to make ends meet.

The fact that juvenile delinquency and alcoholism (which had always been a problem) continued to increase surprised no one but those with responsible positions in the Civil Service and at the Cabinet level.

Stockholm.

Not much was left of the city where Kollberg was born and grew up. With the sanction of the city planners, the steam shovels of real estate speculators and the bulldozers of the traffic "experts" had devastated most of the respectable old settlement. By now the few sanctuaries of culture that remained were pitiful in appearance. The city's character, atmosphere and style of life had disappeared, or rather, changed, and it wasn't easy to do anything about it.

Meanwhile more squeaks were appearing in the police machinery, which was overworked, partly because of the shortage of men. But there were other, more important reasons.

It was less important to recruit more policemen than to get better ones—no one seemed to have thought of that.

Thought Lennart Kollberg.

It took a while to get out to the housing project managed by Hampus Broberg. It was located far to the south, in an area that had been countryside in Kollberg's youth, a place where he used to go on school excursions when he was a child. It resembled far too many of the rent traps built during recent years—an isolated group of high-rise apartments, slapped together quickly and carelessly, whose sole purpose was to make as large a profit as possible for the owner while at the same time guaranteeing unpleasantness and discomfort for the unfortunate people who had to live there. Since the housing shortage had been kept alive artificially for many years, even these apartments were in great demand, and the rents were close to astronomical.

Presumably the realty office occupied the best rooms—those built with the greatest care. However, even in these, moisture had seeped through, and the doorposts had warped so much that they'd already come loose from the masonry.

The greatest drawback from Kollberg's point of view, however, was that Hampus Broberg wasn't to be found there.

In addition to Broberg's private office, which was spacious and rather stylishly furnished, there was a conference room and two small rooms, which were inhabited by a caretaker and two female employees—the first a woman of fifty and the second a girl who had barely turned nineteen.

The older woman looked like a real monster. Kollberg guessed that her main duty was to threaten eviction and to refuse repairs. The girl was clumsy and ugly, had acne and looked bullied. The caretaker seemed resigned. He must have had the thankless job of seeing to it that the drains and toilets worked just well enough to get by.

Kollberg proceeded on the assumption that he should talk to the monster.

No, Mr. Broberg wasn't here. He hadn't shown up since Friday afternoon. Then he'd been in his office for about ten minutes and then left again, carrying a briefcase.

No, Mr. Broberg hadn't said anything about when he was coming back.

No, neither of the ladies' names was Helena Hansson, nor had they ever heard of anyone by that name.

However, Mr. Broberg did have another office, in the city. On Kungsgatan, to be exact. Both he and Miss Hansson would certainly be there.

No, Mr. Palmgren didn't concern himself with the upkeep of the properties. Since the area had been built up four years ago, he'd only been there on two occasions, both times in the company of Mr. Broberg.

What did they do at the office? Collect rents and keep the tenants in order, of course.

"And that's not the easiest thing in the world," said the monster caustically.

"Okay, I get the picture," Kollberg said. And left.

He got into his car and drove north toward Stockholm.

On the way he passed temptingly close to his own home in the borough of Skärmarbrink. His family was there—his daughter Bodil, who would soon be two years old, and above all Gun, who seemed to grow prettier and more irresistible every day. Kollberg was a sensualist, and had been careful to choose a wife who would comply with his exacting demands.

He steeled himself, however, sighed deeply, wiped the sweat off his forehead with his shirt sleeve and drove on toward the center of Stockholm. He parked on Kungsgatan and stepped out. Then he went into the entrance to check that he'd gone to the right address.

According to the directory, the house contained mostly film companies and law offices, but it also had what he was looking for.

On the fourth floor, there was listed not only HAMPUS BROBERG INC., but also VIKTOR PALMGREN LOAN & FINANCE.

Kollberg rode up on a creaking, aged elevator and found that both company plaques decorated the same snuff-colored door. He grasped the doorknob and found the door locked. There was a doorbell, but he ignored it and, true to habit, hammered on the door with his fist.

A woman opened, looked at him with big brown eyes and said, "What in the world is the matter?"

"I'm looking for Mr. Broberg."

"He isn't here."

"Is your name Helena Hansson?"

"No, it isn't. Who are you?"

Kollberg pulled himself together and took his identification card out of his back pocket.

"Excuse me," he said. "It must be the fault of this heat."

"I see," she said. "The police."

"Right. The name's Kollberg. May I come in for a minute?"

"Of course," the woman said and stepped aside.

The room he entered looked like a run-of-the-mill office with tables, folders, typewriter, filing cabinets and all the usual accessories. Through a half-open door he could see into another room, which was apparently Hampus Broberg's private office. Smaller than the secretary's, but more comfortable, it seemed almost entirely taken up by a desk and a large safe.

While Kollberg was looking around, the woman had turned the

lock on the door. Then she stared at him inquiringly and said, "Why did you ask me if my name was Hansson?"

She was about thirty-five years old, slender and dark, with thick eyebrows and short hair.

"I thought you were Mr. Broberg's secretary," Kollberg said absentmindedly.

"Actually I am Mr. Broberg's secretary."

"Well, in that case . . ."

"My name isn't Hansson," she continued, "and it never has been."

Looking at her obliquely, he saw that she wore two broad gold bands on the ring finger of her left hand.

"What is your name, then?"

"Sara Moberg."

"You weren't in Malmö last Wednesday when Mr. Palmgren was shot?"

"Certainly not."

"We were told that Mr. Broberg was in Malmö at the time and that his secretary was with him."

"In that case it wasn't me. I never go along on his trips."

"And the secretary's name was Hansson," Kollberg said stubbornly, taking a dog-eared piece of paper out of his pants pocket.

He glared at it and said, "Miss Helena Hansson. That's what it says here."

"I don't know anyone by that name. Besides, I'm married and have two children. As I said before, I never go along on trips."

"Then who could this Miss Hansson have been?"

"No idea."

"Maybe an employee in some other branch of the company?"

"I've never heard of her, at any rate."

The woman looked at him sharply and said, "Until now."

Then she added vaguely, "Of course, there are traveling secretaries, as they're called."

Kollberg dropped the subject.

"When did you last see Mr. Broberg?"

"This morning. He came in a little after ten and stayed in his office for about twenty minutes. Then he left. For the bank, I think."

"Where do you think he is now?"

Glancing at the clock, she said, "Probably at home."

Kollberg consulted his piece of paper.

"He lives out on Lidingö, doesn't he?"

"Yes, on Tjädervägen."

"Is he married?"

"Yes. They have a daughter who's seventeen. But she and his wife aren't home. They're in Switzerland on vacation."

"Do you know that for a fact?"

"Yes. I ordered their plane tickets myself. Last Friday. It must have come up quickly, for they left the same day."

"Has Mr. Broberg been working as usual after what happened in Malmö last Wednesday?"

"Well, no," she said. "No, you could hardly say that. It was very tense around here on Thursday. You see, we didn't know anything definite then. On Friday we found out that Mr. Palmgren had died. Mr. Broberg was in on Friday for maybe an hour altogether. And today, as I said, he was here for about twenty minutes."

"Did he say when he planned to get back?"

The woman shook her head.

"Is he usually in the office longer than that?"

"Oh yes, he's here most of the time. Sits in his office."

Kollberg walked over to the inner door and let his eyes wander over Hampus Broberg's room. He took note of three black telephones on the desk and an elegant suitcase standing next to the safe. The suitcase wasn't big, but it was made of pigskin and had two straps buckled over the top. It looked brand-new.

"Do you know if Mr. Broberg was here on Saturday or Sunday?" he asked.

"Well, somebody was here. We aren't open on Saturday, so I was off work as usual over the weekend. But when I came in this morning I noticed right away that someone had moved things around."

"Can this someone have been anyone else but Broberg?"

"Hardly. We're the only two who have keys to this place."

"Do you think he'll come back today?"

"Don't know. Maybe he went to the bank and then home. That seems quite likely."

"Lidingö," murmured Kollberg. "Tjädervägen."

He was getting even farther away from home.

"Good-bye," he said abruptly and left.

It was sweltering hot in the car by now, and he perspired profusely on the way to Lidingö.

As he crossed the bridge over Värtan and saw the big ships in Frihamnen and the hundreds of pleasure boats full of half-naked vacationers with tans, he reflected that it was idiotic to rush around like this. Of course he should have stayed in his office, used the telephone and asked these people to come to Västberga. But then none of them would have come, and he would've been burned up about that. Besides, Martin Beck had said that it was urgent.

The houses built along Tjädervägen on Lidingö didn't belong to the super-deluxe class, but they were still light-years away from the decrepit housing project he'd visited earlier. Nobody who lived here was so unfortunate as to have to be milked by characters like Palmgren and Broberg. Large, expensive bungalows with meticulous lawns lined both sides of the street.

Hampus Broberg's house seemed closed and completely dead. Car tracks led up to the garage doors, but when Kollberg peeked in one of the small side windows, he found the garage empty. Everything indicated that, until quite recently, two cars had been parked there. No one responded to his ringing and pounding, and the blinds behind the large windows were drawn, so that it was impossible to catch a glimpse of what the house looked like inside.

Kollberg panted as he walked over to the house next door. It was larger and more fashionable than Broberg's; the name on the door was that of a noble family. At least it sounded noble.

He rang the bell and the door was opened by a tall blond woman. She looked cool, and her manner was aristocratic.

When he had identified himself, she peered at him disdainfully and made no move to ask him to come in.

When he stated his business she said coldly, "We are not in the habit of spying on our neighbors. I don't know Mr. Broberg and am unable to help you."

"That's too bad."

"Perhaps for you, but not for me."

"Then please excuse me," Kollberg said.

She looked at him appraisingly and asked a very startling question, "Tell me, who sent you here anyway?"

Both her voice and her clear blue eyes expressed suspicion. She might have been between thirty-five and forty. Extremely well preserved. She reminded him vaguely of someone, but he couldn't recall who.

"Well, good-bye," he said dejectedly and shrugged his shoulders.

"Good-bye," she said emphatically.

Kollberg got into his car and consulted his slip of paper.

Helena Hansson had given an address on Västeråsgatan in Vasastaden and a telephone number. He drove to the police station on Lejonvägen on Lidingö, where several plainclothesmen were brooding over the week's pools coupon while they drank soft drinks out of paper cups.

"Do you know what Go Ahead Deventer could be?" one of them said.

"No idea," Kollberg said.

"What about Young Boys?"

"What were those names again?"

"Go Ahead Deventer and Young Boys. They're soccer teams. Playing in the pools cup matches. But we don't know where they're from. You know, the pools cup."

Kollberg shrugged his fat shoulders. Soccer was one of the things that weren't of the least interest to him.

"Go Ahead Deventer must be from Deventer," he said. "That's a city in Holland."

"Damn. The National Homicide Squad *would* know about things like that. Do you think they're any good?"

"As a matter of fact, I only came here to borrow the telephone," Kollberg said wearily.

"Go ahead. Use any one you want."

Kollberg dialed Helena Hansson's number and got the out-of-order signal. Then he called the telephone company and was consoled with the information that the telephone in question was no longer in use.

"Do you know anything about a Mr. Hampus Broberg?" he asked the two betting policemen.

"Sure, he lives on Tjädervägen. And to live like him, you've got to have plenty of money."

"We only have the better sort of people out here," said one of the policemen.

"Have you ever had reason to have anything to do with him?"

"Nope," the other policeman said and poured out more Loranga orange. "We maintain law and order here."

"This isn't Stockholm," said the first one virulently.

"And if we have any crimes, they're high-class stuff. People don't go around bashing each other's heads in with axes. There aren't any old bums or doped-up kids under every bush. I think we'll put our money on Go Ahead Deventer, anyway."

They had completely lost interest in Kollberg.

"Bye," he said gloomily and left them.

During the long drive to Vasastaden in Stockholm, he considered the fact that even Lidingö had a generous portion of crime behind its polished façade. The only difference was that people were richer and could hide their dirty linen more easily.

There was no elevator in the apartment building on Västeråsgatan, and he had to trudge up five flights of stairs in five different stairwells. The house was dilapidated—neglected by the landlord as usual—and big fat rats ran among the garbage cans on the asphalt courtyard.

He rang doorbells here and there. Several times doors were opened, and various people stared at him in alarm.

People here were afraid of the police—perhaps with good reason.

He didn't find Helena Hansson.

No one could say if a person by that name lived or had lived there. Giving information to the police obviously wasn't a popular pastime, and besides, people in apartment buildings like this one generally knew very little about each other.

Kollberg stood out on the street and wiped his face with a handkerchief that was already soaked with hours of perspiration.

He reflected for several minutes.

Then he gave up and drove home.

An hour later his wife said, "Lennart, why do you look so miserable?"

He had showered, eaten, made love to her and then showered again, and was now sitting wrapped in a bath towel, downing a can of cold beer.

"Because I feel miserable," he said. "That damn job . . ."

"You should quit."

"It's not that easy."

Kollberg was a policeman, and he still couldn't help trying to be as good a policeman as possible. Somehow that drive had been built into his psyche; it was like a burden that, for some reason, he had to carry.

The order he'd received from Martin Beck was simple, a routine matter, and now, because of it, he was at his wit's end. He scowled and said, "Gun, what's a traveling secretary?"

"Usually some kind of call girl, who goes around with her nightgown, toothbrush and birth control pills in a briefcase."

"Then she's nothing but a whore."

"Right. Available for people like businessmen who are too lazy to pick up some girl in the place they're staying."

On reflection, he realized that he needed help. He couldn't get it out in Västberga, where they were hard-pressed for people during vacation.

A moment later he sighed, went over to the telephone and called the Stockholm police on Kungsholmsgatan.

The person who answered was the last person he wanted to talk to.

Gunvald Larsson.

"How's it going?" he said sullenly. "What do you think? I'm up to my neck in stabbings, fights, robberies and insane foreigners who are sky-high on LSD. And almost nobody here. Melander is on Värmdö, and Rönn went to Arjeplog last Friday night. Strömgren is on Majorca. And people seem to get more aggressive in this heat. Lose their judgment entirely. What the hell do you want?"

Kollberg detested Gunvald Larsson, who was, in his opinion, only a big, dumb thug with snobbish ways. As far as his judgment went, what was there to say? Gunvald Larsson had lost his in the cradle.

Thought Kollberg. But he said aloud, "Well, it's about the Palmgren affair."

"I don't want to have a thing to do with it," Gunvald Larsson said immediately. He'd already had enough trouble with it.

Kollberg recounted the tale of his sorrows anyway.

Gunvald Larsson interspersed it with bad-tempered grunts. Once he interrupted and said, "Sitting there jabbering about it won't get you anywhere. It's not my job."

But something must have attracted his attention, for when Kollberg finished, he said, "Did you say Tjädervägen on Lidingö? What was the number?"

Kollberg repeated the number.

"Hmm," Gunvald Larsson said. "Maybe I can do something for you."

"That's decent of you," Kollberg forced himself to say.

"To tell the truth, I'm not doing it for your sake," Gunvald Larsson said, as though he really meant it.

He did, too.

Kollberg wondered why he'd become interested. Generosity wasn't one of Gunvald Larsson's characteristics.

"About this Hansson whore," Gunvald Larsson said dismally. "You'd better talk to the Vice Squad."

"Yes, I'd thought of that."

"Well, of course. It all fits together—she had to show identification down there in Malmö at the first questioning. But she could have made up any damn address she pleased. So probably her name really is Helena Hansson."

Even Kollberg had thought of that, but refrained from making further comment.

He hung up and immediately dialed again.

This time he asked to be connected with Åsa Torell of the Vice Squad.

13.

As soon as the conversation was over, Gunvald Larsson went down, got into his car and drove straight to Lidingö.

His face was taut, set in a strangely grim smile.

He looked at his big hairy hands resting on the steering wheel and chuckled to himself with satisfaction.

Out on Tjädervägen he gave only a passing glance to Broberg's house, which looked just as deserted as before. Then he went over to the house next door and rang the bell. The door was opened by the same cool, blond woman who had dismissed Kollberg so ignominiously a couple of hours earlier.

When she caught sight of the gigantic man on the step her attitude changed.

"Gunvald," she said with consternation. "How in the . . . how can you have the gall to show your face here?"

"Oh," he said banteringly, "true love never dies."

"I haven't seen you for more than ten years, and that I'm grateful for."

"What a nice thing to say!"

"Your picture was in the newspapers last winter. I burned them all up in the fireplace."

"You really are sweet."

She knit her blond eyebrows suspiciously and said, "Did you send that fat guy out here earlier today?"

"As a matter of fact, no. But I'm here for the same reason."

"You must be crazy."

"You think so?"

"After all, I can only tell you the same thing I told him. I don't spy on my neighbors."

"You don't? Well, are you going to let me in? Or should I kick your whole goddamned rosewood door in, alabaster paneling and all?"

"You should just die of shame. But you're probably too thick for that."

"This is getting better all the time."

"Well, I'd rather you came in than stand on the steps and disgrace me."

She opened the door. Gunvald Larsson stepped in.

"Where is that henpecked husband of yours?" he asked.

"Hugold is at the Chief of Staff's office. He has a great deal of responsibility and is very busy now. The General is on vacation."

"Kiss my ass," said Gunvald Larsson. "And he hasn't even managed to knock you up in thirteen years, or however long it's been?"

"Eleven," she said. "And watch yourself. I'm not alone, either."

"Is that so? Do you have a lover, too? Little cadets, maybe?"

"You can spare me the vulgar remarks. An old friend dropped by for tea. Sonja. Maybe you remember her."

"No, I don't, thank goodness."

"She hasn't had an easy time of it," the woman said, touching her blond hair lightly. "But she has a respectable profession anyway. She's a dentist."

Gunvald Larsson didn't say anything. He followed her into a very large, elegant living room. On a low table was a silver tea service, and a tall, slim woman with brown hair sat on the couch nibbling on an English biscuit.

"This is my eldest brother," said the blonde. "Unfortunately.

Gunvald's his name. He's a . . . policeman. Before he was just a thug. The last time I saw him was more than ten years ago and before that the times were few and far between."

"C'mon now, you behave now," Gunvald Larsson said.

"You would say that. Where were you, for instance, the last six years Father was alive?"

"At sea. I was working. And that's more than can be said of any other member of the family."

"You made us take all the responsibility," she said bitterly.

"And who laid their mitts on all the money? And everything else?"

"You'd already squandered your part of the inheritance before you received your dishonorable discharge from the Navy," she said icily.

Gunvald Larsson looked around.

"Oh, fuck," he said.

"What do you mean by that?"

"Exactly what I said. Oh, fuck. Like, where did you get that two-foot silver rooster?"

"Portugal. We bought it in Lisbon during a world cruise."

"How much did it cost?"

"Several thousand kronor," she said indifferently. "I don't remember exactly. What are you called now? Patrolman?"

"First Assistant Detective."

"Father would turn over in his grave. You mean to say you haven't even managed to become a superintendent or whatever it's called? How much do you make?"

"That's none of your business."

"What are you doing here? Maybe you want to borrow money? I wouldn't be surprised."

She looked at her girlfriend, who had been following the discussion in silence, and added matter-of-factly, "He's renowned for his insolence."

"Right," Gunvald Larsson said and sat down. "Now bring another cup."

She left the room. Gunvald Larsson looked at the childhood

friend with a gleam of interest. She didn't return the look, and neither of them said anything.

His sister came back with a tea glass in a silver holder, placed on a small engraved silver tray.

"What are you doing here?" she said.

"You know that already. You're going to tell me every single thing you know about this Broberg and his boss. His name was Palmgren and he died last Wednesday."

"Died?"

"Yes. Don't you read the newspapers?"

"Maybe I do. But that's none of your business."

"He was murdered, moreover. Shot."

"Murdered? Shot? What kind of horrible doings *are* you involved in?"

Gunvald Larsson impassively poured tea into his glass.

"Look, I've already told you. I don't spy on the neighbors. And I said so to that other clown you sent along to me this morning."

Gunvald Larsson took a swallow of tea. Then he put the glass down with a bang.

"Quit making a spectacle of yourself, Kid Sister. You're as curious as a cat and have been ever since you started walking. I know you know a helluva lot about Broberg. About Palmgren, too, for that matter. I'm convinced that you and that lousy husband of yours know both of them. I have a fairly good idea of how things work in those distinguished circles of yours."

"Being vulgar isn't going to get you anywhere. I'm not going to say anything anyway. Least of all to you."

"Sure you are. Otherwise . . ."

She looked at him derisively and said, "Otherwise, what?"

"Otherwise I'll get a local patrolman in uniform to go around with me to every house in a mile's radius. I'll introduce myself and say that my sister is such a goddamn idiot that I have to ask other people for help."

She stared at him speechless. At last she said tonelessly, "Do you mean you'd have the nerve to . . ."

"You're damn right, that's what I mean. So you'd better cough something up right now."

Her friend was now following the dialogue with discreet but obvious interest.

After a long, strained silence, his sister said resignedly, "Yes, I suppose you really are capable of doing something like that."

And immediately afterward, "What do you want to know?"

"Do you know Broberg?"

"Yes."

"And Palmgren?"

"Casually. We've been at a party or two together. But . . ."

"But what?"

"It's nothing."

"Well, what has Broberg been up to these last few days?"

"It's none of my business."

"Quite right. But I've got a damn good idea that you've been peeking every time anyone has made a move in that house. Well?"

"His family went away last Friday."

"I know that already. What else?"

"He sold his wife's car that same day. A white Ferrari."

"How do you know that?"

"A buyer was here. They stood outside of the house bargaining."

"Well, how about that! What else?"

"I don't think Mr. Broberg's slept at home the last few nights."

"How do you know that? Have you been in his house to check?"

With a despairing look, she said, "You're worse than ever."

"Now answer, goddammit."

"It's hard to keep from noticing what goes on in the house next door."

"Yeah, especially if you're nosy. So he hasn't been there?"

"In fact, he's been there several times. From what I've seen, he's moved some things out."

"Has anybody besides that car dealer been there?"

"We-e-ell . . ."

"Who and when?"

"On Friday he came with a blond girl. They stayed for a couple of hours. Then they carried some things out to the car. Suitcases and some other things."

"I see. Keep going."

"There were some people there yesterday. A very distinguished couple and a guy who looked like an attorney. They walked around looking at everything, and the guy who I think was an attorney took notes the whole time."

"What do you think it was all about?"

"I think he was trying to sell the house. I think he was successful, too."

"Did you hear what they said?"

"I couldn't help hearing bits and pieces."

"Of course," Gunvald Larsson said drily. "It sounds like he sold the house?"

"Yes."

"With the furniture and the rest of the crap?"

"What a filthy mouth you have!"

"You don't have to worry about that. Just answer. Why do you think he really managed to sell the house?"

"Because I heard snatches of the conversation. For example, they said that quick deals are always the best and that the transaction favored both parties, under the circumstances."

"Tell me more."

"They parted like old friends. Shook hands and slapped each other on the back. Broberg handed over some things. Keys, among other things, I think."

"What happened then?"

"They drove away. In a black Bentley."

"What about Broberg?"

"He stayed behind for a couple of hours."

"And did what?"

"Burned something in the fireplaces. Both chimneys smoked for a long time. I thought . . ."

She broke off.

"What did you think?"

"That it was peculiar, considering the weather. There's a heat wave."

"And then?"

"He went around drawing all the blinds. Then he drove away. I haven't seen him since."

"Kid Sister," said Gunvald Larsson kindly.

"Yes, what is it?"

"You would've made a good cop."

She made an indescribable grimace and said, "Are you going to go on torturing me?"

"Sure. How well do you know Broberg?"

"We've seen each other now and then. That's hard to avoid when you're neighbors."

"What about Palmgren?"

"Casually, as I said. We were at several parties together at Broberg's home. Once we had a party in the garden here, and he came. You know, in situations like that one always invites the neighbors, on principle. Palmgren just happened to be at Broberg's then, so he came over, too."

"Was he alone?"

"No. His wife was with him. Young and terribly charming."

"I see."

She didn't say anything.

"Well," Gunvald Larsson said, "what's your opinion of these people?"

"They're very well-to-do," she said neutrally.

"You are, too. You and your phony baron."

"Yes," she said, "that's correct."

"Birds of a feather flock together," Gunvald Larsson said philosophically.

She looked at him for a long time and then said sharply, "I want you to understand something, Gunvald."

"What?"

"That these people, Broberg and Palmgren, weren't like us. I mean, they do have a lot of money, especially Palmgren. Did, rather. But they lack style and finesse. They're ruthless businessmen who step on everyone and everything in their way. I've heard that Broberg is some kind of profiteer and that Palmgren did very questionable business abroad. For people like that, their money does give them admission to all the most select circles, but they still lack something. They'll never be completely accepted."

"Um-hmm, well, there's something to that, let me tell you. Then, in other words, you don't accept Broberg?"

"No, I do, but solely because of his money. It was the same thing with Palmgren. His fortune gave him influence pretty much everywhere. You must realize that this society has grown dependent on people like Palmgren and Broberg. In many cases, they have more leverage in the way the country's run than either the Government or Parliament and such. So even people like us have to accept them."

Gunvald Larsson looked at her with disgust.

"Well, if you say so," he said. "But I think that in the not-too-distant future, things are going to happen that will make you and that whole damn upper-class riffraff of yours extremely surprised."

"What would that be?"

"Are you so damn stupid that you don't notice what's happening around us? In the whole world?"

"Don't shout at me," she said coldly. "We aren't children any more. And now, I think it's time for you to get lost."

"I already was. You forget I've been a sailor."

"Hugold is coming any minute. And I don't want you here then."

"He has short working hours, I gather."

"Yes, he does. People with highly qualified jobs often do. Goodbye, Gunvald."

He stood up.

"Well, you've been helpful, at any rate," he said.

"I wouldn't have said a word if you hadn't blackmailed me."

"Yeah, I realize."

"As far as I'm concerned, it could easily be another ten years before I see you again."

"For me too. Bye-bye."

She didn't answer.

Her girlfriend stood up and said, "I'd better be off now, too."

Gunvald Larsson looked at her. She was tall and slim—tall enough to come up to his shoulder at least. Gracefully and elegantly dressed. Just enough make-up. Just right, generally speaking. He hadn't seen a car outside and said, "Can I give you a lift into town?"

"Yes, please."

They left.

Gunvald Larsson glanced over at the house that evidently wasn't Broberg's any longer and shrugged.

When they were sitting in the car he checked to see if she was wearing a wedding ring. She wasn't.

"Excuse me, I didn't catch your name," he said.

"Lindberg. Sonja Lindberg. I remember you from when I was little."

"Oh, really?"

"You were much taller than I was, of course. Then as now."

He found her attractive. Maybe he should ask her out. Well, it could wait. No hurry. He could call her up one of these days.

"Where should I drop you off?" he asked.

"On Stureplan, please. My practice is on Birger Jarlsgatan. I live there too."

Good, he thought. That makes asking unnecessary.

Neither of them said anything before he'd stopped on Stureplan.

"Good-bye and thank you," she said and extended her hand.

He took it. It was slender, dry and cool.

"Bye, Sonja," he said.

He closed the door and drove on.

In his office on Kungsholmsgatan there were about fifteen messages, including one from Kollberg, who was in Västberga and wanted him to call back.

Gunvald Larsson got the most urgent work out of the way before he dialed the number of the South police station.

"Hello," said Kollberg.

Gunvald Larsson related what he'd heard but avoided naming the source.

"Good job, Larsson," said Kollberg. "Then it looks like he's planning to skip the country."

"He's probably left already."

"I don't think so," said Kollberg. "That suitcase I told you about before is still there in his room on Kungsgatan. I just called his secretary, and she said that Broberg had called her half an hour ago and said he wouldn't make it back to the office before five."

"He must be living at some hotel," said Gunvald Larsson pensively.

"Probably. I'll try to check it out. But it isn't conceivable that he's registered in his correct name."

"Hardly," said Gunvald Larsson. "By the way, did you get hold of that broad?"

"Not yet. I'm sitting here now waiting for the Vice Squad to call back."

Silence.

After a while he complained, "I'm really pushed for time. If I can't make it back to Kungsgatan before five, could you see to it that you or somebody else keeps an eye on his damn usury office?"

Gunvald Larsson's natural impulse was to say no. He took the letter-opener out of the penholder and picked between his big front teeth in a preoccupied manner.

"Yes," he said at last. "I'll arrange it."

"Thanks."

Thank my dear sister, Gunvald Larsson thought. Then he said, "One more thing."

"What?"

"Broberg was eating at the same table when Palmgren was shot."

"So what?"

"How in hell can he have anything to do with the murder?"

"Don't ask me," Kollberg said. "Everything seems very hush-hush. Maybe Martin knows."

"Beck," said Gunvald Larsson with distaste.

That was the end of the conversation.

14.

Lennart Kollberg had to wait slightly more than an hour for the information from the Vice Squad. Meanwhile he sat, heavy, inert and sweaty, at his desk out in Västberga. What had looked like a simple matter to dispose of that morning—talking to two witnesses—had somehow developed into hot pursuit.

Hampus Broberg and the mystifying Helena Hansson suddenly emerged as two people wanted by the police, while Kollberg sat clinging to the threads of the dragnet like some kind of spider. The remarkable thing was that he still didn't know why he was out to get these two people. No charge had been filed against either of them; they had already been questioned by the police in Malmö, and common sense seemed to indicate that neither could reasonably have had anything to do with the murder of Viktor Palmgren.

However, he couldn't shake off the feeling that it was important to get hold of them as quickly as possible.

Why?

It's only the policeman's occupational disease creeping up on you, he thought gloomily. A total wreck after twenty-three years of service. Can't think like a normal human being any more.

Twenty-three years of daily contact with police officers had made him incapable of maintaining sensible relations with the rest of the world. In fact, he never felt truly free, not even with his own family. There was always something gnawing at his mind. He'd waited a long time to build this family, because police work wasn't a normal job, but something you committed yourself to. And it was obvious you could never get away from it. A profession involving daily confrontations with people in abnormal situations could only lead in the end to becoming abnormal yourself.

Unlike the overwhelming majority of his colleagues, Kollberg was capable of penetrating and analyzing his own situation clearly. Which he did, surprisingly and unfortunately, with unclouded vision. His problem lay in being both a sensualist and a man of duty, in a profession where sentimentality and personal involvement were luxuries which in nine cases out of ten you couldn't allow yourself.

Why do policemen associate almost exclusively with other policemen? he wondered.

Naturally because it was easier that way. Easier to keep the necessary distance. But also easier to overlook the morbid camaraderie in the force, which had flourished, unchecked, for many years. Essentially that meant that policemen isolated themselves from the society they were supposed to protect and, above all, be integrated with.

For example, policemen didn't criticize other policemen, with rare exceptions.

A rather recent sociological study had shown that vacationing policemen, who were more or less forced to mix with other people, were very often ashamed to admit that they were officers of the law. This was a result of the definition of their role and of the many myths that surrounded their profession.

Constantly encountering fear, distrust or open contempt could make anyone paranoid.

Kollberg shuddered.

He didn't want to be a fear-monger and he didn't want to be distrusted or despised. He didn't want to be paranoid.

However, he did want to get hold of two people whose names were Hampus Broberg and Helena Hansson. And he still didn't know why.

He went out to the lavatory for a drink of water. Although the faucet had been running for several minutes, the water was still lukewarm and flat.

He groaned and sank down at his desk again. Distractedly he drew a small five-pointed star on the blotter. One more. And another after that.

When he had drawn seventy-five five-pointed stars, the telephone rang.

"Yes, Kollberg."

"Hi, this is Åsa."

"Have you found out anything?"

"Yeah, I think so."

"What?"

"We've located this Hansson person."

Åsa Torell paused. Then she said, "At least I'm pretty sure it's the right person."

"So?"

"She's on our books."

"As a hooker?"

"Yes, but upper class. She comes closest to what we'd call a call girl."

"Where does she live?"

"On Banérgatan. This other address is wrong. As far as we know, she's never lived on Västeråsgatan. However, the telephone number didn't just come out of the clear blue. It looks like she had that contact number earlier."

"What about the name? Is Helena Hansson her real name?"

"We're fairly sure of that. She had to show identification down in Malmö last Wednesday, so I don't think she could've cheated on that point."

"Does she have a record?"

"Oh, yes. She's been a prostitute since she was a teenager. Our division's had a great deal to do with her, although not so often during recent years."

Åsa Torell was quiet a moment. He could imagine vividly how she looked at that very instant. She was probably hunched over a desk, just like him, biting her thumbnail contemplatively.

"She appears to have begun like most of the others, usually without being paid. Then she began walking the street, and apparently she's had enough class to work herself up into a more profitable bracket. Belonging to a call-girl ring is considered almost respectable by those kind of people."

"Yeah, I can imagine."

"As a matter of fact, call girls are the pick of the crop among prostitutes. They don't take just any job—only the ones that are guaranteed to be lucrative. Just calling herself a traveling secretary, or even an executive secretary, as she seems to have done in Malmö, shows that she has style and can move in quite high society. There's a big difference between selling the goods on Regeringsgatan and being able to sit at home in an apartment in Östermalm waiting for telephone calls. She probably has a group of regulars and at most takes one assignment or whatever you'd call it a week. Or something like that."

"Does your division have any direct interest in her? At the moment?"

"Yes. That's what I wanted to convey to you. If she's involved in some other kind of crime and is afraid of getting caught, we may have a chance of uncovering a whole call-girl ring."

"We could always try to scare her. Send someone over there to pick her up."

Kollberg thought again. He continued, "Of course, I'd be quite willing to meet her myself, at her home. There's something strange about this whole affair. What it is, I don't know yet."

"What do you mean?"

"I have the feeling that she's more involved in this affair with Broberg and Palmgren than we suspect. Do you know her?"

"I only know what she looks like—from pictures we have here," Åsa Torell said. "Judging from them, she looks very proper and businesslike. But of course that's one of the keys to success in that particular line of business."

"Certainly, they have to be able to keep up a good front. It's important for them not to make any false moves at social events."

"Right. From what I've heard, some of these girls can even take shorthand. At least they can do enough to fool most people."

"Do you have her phone number?"

"No."

"Too bad."

"Maybe, maybe not," said Åsa Torell. "The girls in this business change numbers pretty often. They have unlisted phones as a matter of course, and even then their subscriptions are usually registered under different names. And . . ."

"And . . ."

"And that shows that they're real pros. Big time."

She was quiet awhile. Then she asked, "Why is it so darned urgent for you to get hold of her?"

"To be honest with you, I don't really know."

"You don't know?"

"No. Martin wants her questioned, mostly as a routine measure, about what she saw or didn't see that night in Malmö."

"Well, that's not a bad place to start," said Åsa Torell. "Then maybe the first will lead to the second."

"Just what I was hoping," said Kollberg. "According to Larsson, she was at Hampus Broberg's home on Lidingö last Saturday, and I'm as good as convinced that Broberg is working on something really shady."

"I have a hard time imagining she'd be directly involved in Palmgren's murder. But then most of what I know comes from the newspapers these last few days."

"No. I can't see a direct connection with this shooting, either. However, there are a number of ramifications to this case, and I have a feeling they have to be followed up, even if they don't fall directly in my division."

"What do you think Broberg is up to?"

"Some kind of large-scale financial swindle. He appears to be converting all his assets here into cash incredibly fast. I suspect he's preparing to leave the country today."

"Why don't you call in the fraud boys?"

"Because there's not much time. Before those guys have the time to get onto this, Broberg'll probably be far out of reach. Maybe the Hansson girl, too. But Palmgren's murder does give us a lever. Both of them were witnesses, which means I can move in on them."

"I admit I'm only a novice," said Åsa Torell. "And hardly a murder investigator, besides. But does Martin feel that one of the people who were at the dinner would have gone all out to get Palmgren out of the way, for his own benefit?"

"Yes, that seems to be one of the theories."

"Then this person would've hired a murderer?"

"Yes. Something like that."

"It seems farfetched, if you ask me."

"I think so, too. But it's happened before."

"I know. What other possibilities are they considering?"

"For one thing, a purely political killing. Even Sepo's got into the act. From what I've heard, a man of theirs has been sent down to Malmö."

"That must be terribly pleasant for Martin and the rest of them."

"Yeah, it really is. Of course, Sepo is doing its own investigation as usual. It'll be ready in a year or two, and then they'll go into action."

"And Martin who just loves politics," said Åsa Torell.

What she meant was that Martin Beck detested everything even remotely related to politics and that he promptly retreated into a shell every time there was any mention of demonstrations, assassinations or political involvement.

"Hmm," said Kollberg. "Anyway, now it appears that Palmgren earned most of his millions from something that was the exact opposite of foreign aid. Like making indecent profits on international armaments sales. So neither Martin nor any of the others rules out the possibility that he was actually got out of the way for political reasons. As a kind of warning to others in the same line of business."

"Poor Martin," said Åsa Torell.

There was a certain warmth in her voice now.

Kollberg smiled to himself. He'd become well acquainted with Åsa Torell after Åke Stenström's death, and he thought a lot of her, both for her quick intelligence and for her qualities as a woman.

"Oh, well," he said. "I suggest that you and I go over to see this lovely lady as soon as possible and see if we can weasel something interesting out of her. I'll take the car and pick you up on the way. We'll have to chance it that she's home."

"Okay," Åsa Torell said. "But . . ."

"But what?"

"Well, I'm warning you, she's going to be a pretty hard nut to crack, and we'd be smart to take it easy—at least in the beginning. I know I'm only a beginner, and maybe it sounds crazy to be giving you advice, but I've had some experience with this clientele. Somebody like Helena Hansson knows all about how to act with the police. From long, hard practice, you understand. I don't think the strong-arm treatment would be worth much."

"You're probably right."

"By the way, who's keeping an eye on Broberg?"

"If we're lucky, we may find him in the lady's arms," Kollberg said. "Otherwise, Gunvald Larsson has offered his services, strangely enough."

"Then there'll be strong-arm tactics anyway," Åsa Torell said caustically.

"I suppose so. Let's say I'll come by to pick you up in about twenty minutes."

"Sure, that's fine. See you soon."

"Bye."

Kollberg sat for a while with his hand on the receiver. Then he called Gunvald Larsson.

"Yeah," the latter said antagonistically. "What in hell is it now?"

"We've located the girl."

"Okay," Gunvald Larsson said indifferently.

"I'm going to see her now with Åsa Torell."

"Okay."

"You sound even crosser than usual."

"For good reason," Gunvald Larsson said. "Twenty minutes ago a Turk got his guts ripped open with a stiletto on Hötorget. The devil only knows if he'll pull through. When I saw him it seemed like he had a hard time keeping his insides together."

"Did you catch the person who did it?"

"No. But we know who it was."

"Another Turk?"

"No, not at all. A first-rate, pure-bred Stockholm kid. Seventeen years old and stoned out of his mind. We're hunting for him now."

"Why did he do it?"

"Why? That's a helluva question. He probably got the idea that he could solve the foreigner problem a'l by himself. It gets worse and worse for every passing day."

"That's true," said Kollberg. "Gunvald, I don't think I'll have enough time to make it to Broberg's office."

"Don't worry about it," Gunvald Larsson said. "It'll all work out. I'm beginning to get interested in this guy myself."

They hung up simultaneously, without another word.

Kollberg was left wondering what had made Gunvald Larsson so unusually helpful.

He called the finance company on Kungsgatan.

"No, I haven't heard from Mr. Broberg," said Sara Moberg.

"The suitcase is still in his room?"

"Yes. I told you that the first time you called."

"Excuse me, I just wanted to check."

He also called the realty office that he'd visited in the morning.

They hadn't seen Hampus Broberg there either, or even heard from him, for that matter.

He went out to wash his hands, put a note on his desk and proceeded down to the car.

Åsa Torell was waiting for him on the steps outside of the main police station on Kungsholmsgatan.

Kollberg pulled up by the sidewalk and watched approvingly as she walked down the wide steps and crossed the walk.

In his eyes she was an exceptionally attractive woman, with her short dark hair and big brown eyes. She was small, but had a very promising figure, with fine broad hips. Both slender and firm.

Her manner was highly sensual, but as far as he knew, she'd given up sex after Stenström's death.

He wondered how long that could last.

If I hadn't already had the good sense to find a first-rate wife . . .

Thought Lennart Kollberg.

Then he stretched out his arm and opened the right front door.

"Climb in, Åsa," he said.

She sat down beside him, put her shoulder bag on her lap and advised him, "Now we'll take it easy, like we said."

Kollberg nodded and started the car.

Five minutes later they stopped in front of an old apartment building on Banérgatan.

They got out on either side of the car.

"You should be careful when you walk right into the street like that," said Åsa Torell.

Kollberg nodded again.

"You're so right," he said.

He yearned for a clean shirt.

15.

The apartment was on the third floor, and the name Helena Hansson was actually on the door plate.

Kollberg raised his right fist to pound on the door, but Åsa Torell restrained him by putting her hand on his arm and rang the doorbell instead.

Nothing happened, and after half a minute she rang again.

This time the door was opened, and a young blond woman peered at them with questioning blue eyes.

She was wearing plush slippers and a white bathrobe. It looked as if she'd just taken a shower or washed her hair, for she had a bath towel wound around her head like a turban.

"Police," Kollberg said, hauling out his identification card.

Åsa Torell did the same, but didn't say anything.

"You are Helena Hansson, right?"

"Yes, of course."

"We're here about what happened in Malmö last week. We'd like to talk to you a moment."

"I already told the police down there what little I know. The same evening."

"That conversation clearly wasn't very exhaustive," Kollberg said. "You were naturally rather upset at the time, and testimony given under such conditions tends to be rather sketchy. So we always question witnesses again, when they've had several days to think things over. May we please come in for a moment?"

The woman hesitated. It was obvious she was about to say no.

"It won't take too much of your time," Kollberg said. "This is a purely routine procedure for us."

"Yes," said Helena Hansson. "I don't have much time, but . . ."

She stopped, and they let her think through the conclusion of her sentence in peace.

"Can you please wait out here for a second, while I put something on?"

Kollberg nodded.

"I've just washed my hair," she added. "It'll only take a minute or two."

Cutting off further discussion, she closed the door in their faces.

Kollberg put a warning finger to his lips.

Åsa Torell promptly knelt down and opened the lid of the mail slot, soundlessly and cautiously.

There were sounds from inside the apartment.

First the clicks from a telephone dial.

Helena Hansson was trying to call someone. She obviously got an answer, asked for someone in a low voice and was connected. Then nothing, but Åsa Torell had unusually good hearing and thought she heard the phone ringing for a long time on the other end. At last the woman inside said, "Oh, he's not. Thank you."

The receiver was replaced.

"She tried to call someone she didn't get hold of," Åsa Torell whispered. "Through a switchboard, I think."

Kollberg formed a name on his lips.

"Broberg."

"She didn't say Broberg. I would've caught that."

Kollberg made a warning face again and pointed dumbly to the mail slot.

Åsa Torell put her right ear against the opening. It was her best one.

Various sounds came from inside, and she knit her thick black eyebrows.

After a couple of minutes she straightened up and whispered, "She was doing something in a hurry, obviously. Packing a suitcase, I think, because I thought I heard her lock it. Then she carried or dragged something across the floor and opened and closed a door. Now she's getting dressed."

Kollberg nodded thoughtfully.

A little later Helena Hansson opened the door again. She had a dress on, and her hairdo was suspiciously neat. Both Kollberg and Åsa Torell noticed immediately that she'd put on a wig over her damp hair.

They were innocently standing as far away in the stair well as possible. Åsa Torell had lit a cigarette and was smoking nonchalantly.

"Please come in," Helena Hansson said.

Her voice was pleasant and surprisingly cultivated.

They went in and looked around.

The apartment included a hall, one room and kitchen. It was fairly spacious and attractive, but impersonally furnished. Most of the furnishings seemed new; many of them indicated that the person who lived there at least wasn't short of money. Everything was neat and tidy.

The bed was big and wide. Kollberg looked at the thick bedspread and could clearly see a rectangular impression, as though something like a suitcase had lain there recently.

There were a sofa and comfortable armchairs in the room. Helena Hansson made a vague gesture toward them and said, "Sit down, please."

They sat down. The woman was still standing.

"Would you like something to drink?"

"No, thank you," Kollberg said.

Åsa Torell shook her head.

Helena Hansson sat down, took a cigarette from a pewter mug on the table and lit it. Then she said calmly, "Well, what can I do to help you?"

"You already know why we're here," said Kollberg.

"Yes. That horrible night in Malmö. But there isn't much more I can tell you than that—that it was horrible."

"Where were you seated at the table?"

"At the corner on one side. My dinner partner was a Danish businessman. His name was Jensen, I believe."

"Yes. Mr. Hoff-Jensen," said Kollberg.

"Oh, yes, that was his name."

"What about Mr. Palmgren?"

"He was sitting on the other side. Diagonally across from me. Directly opposite me was the Dane's wife."

"That means you were sitting facing the man who shot Mr. Palmgren?"

"Yes, that's right. But everything happened so fast. I barely had the time to grasp what was going on. Besides, I doubt if anyone understood anything until afterward."

"But you saw the murderer?"

"Yes. But I didn't think of him as a murderer."

"What did he look like?"

"I've already said what I know. Do you want me to repeat it?"

"Yes, please."

"I only have a very general impression of his appearance. As I said, everything happened so fast, and I wasn't concentrating very much on the people around me. I was mostly lost in my own thoughts."

She spoke calmly and seemed thoroughly sincere.

"Why weren't you concentrating, as you worded it?"

"Mr. Palmgren was making a speech. What he was saying didn't apply to me, and I was listening with half an ear anyway. I didn't understand most of what he was talking about; I was smoking and thinking about other things."

"Let's get back to the gunman. Did you recognize him?"

"No, not at all. He was a complete stranger to me."

"Would you be able to pick him out if you saw him again?"

"Maybe. But I couldn't be sure."

"What was your impression of him?"

"That he was a man of thirty-five, or maybe forty. He had a thin face and dark hair—not much of it."

"How tall was he?"

"About average height, I suppose."

"How was he dressed?"

"Fairly neatly. I think his jacket was brown. At any rate, he had a pale-colored shirt and a tie on."

"Can you say anything else about him?"

"Not much. He looked pretty ordinary."

"How would you place him socially?"

"Socially?"

"Well, for example, did he look like someone with a good job, plenty of money?"

"No, I don't think so. More like a clerk or a worker of some kind. I got the impression he was quite poor."

She shrugged and added, "But you shouldn't take what I say too seriously. The fact is I only caught a glimpse of him. Since then I've tried to sort out my impressions, but I'm not positive. Part of what I think I saw could be pure . . . maybe not fantasy, but . . ."

She searched for the right words.

"Construction after the fact," Kollberg suggested.

"Exactly. Construction after the fact. You catch a glimpse of someone or something, and then afterward, when you try to recall the details, it comes out wrong."

"Did you see the weapon he used?"

"In a flash, so to speak. It was some kind of pistol, rather long."

"Do you know much about guns?"

She shook her head.

"No, nothing at all."

Kollberg tried a new approach.

"Had you met Mr. Palmgren before?"

"No."

"And the rest of the party? Were you acquainted with them?"

"Only Mr. Broberg. I'd never met the other people before."

"But you'd known Broberg for some time?"

"He had hired me on several occasions."

"In what capacity were you in Malmö?"

She looked at him with surprise.

"As a secretary, of course. Mr. Broberg does have his own regular secretary, but she never accompanies him on trips."

She spoke openly and confidently. It all appeared very well rehearsed.

"Did you take any shorthand notes or minutes during this trip?"

"Certainly. There was a meeting earlier in the day. I took notes on what was discussed then."

"What was discussed?"

"Various kinds of business matters. To tell the truth, I didn't understand very much of it. I just wrote it down."

"Do you still have the shorthand notes?"

"No. I transcribed all of them when I returned home on Thursday and left the minutes with Mr. Broberg. I threw the shorthand away.

"I see," Kollberg said. "How much did you get for this work?"

"A fee of two hundred kronor—plus traveling and living expenses, of course."

"Oh. Was it a difficult job?"

She shrugged again.

"Not particularly."

Kollberg exchanged a glance with Åsa Torell, who as yet hadn't opened her mouth.

"That should be all for me," Kollberg said.

Helena Hansson lowered her eyes.

"Just one more thing. When the police in Malmö questioned you immediately after the murder, you gave an address on Västeråsgatan here in the city."

"Did I?"

"That was wrong, wasn't it?"

"I really hadn't given it a thought. Don't even remember it. But I was in a daze at the time. In fact, I used to live on Västeråsgatan. I must've simply made a mistake in the general commotion."

"Hmm," said Kollberg. "Yeah, that can happen to anyone."

He stood up and said, "Thank you for the help. I'm through now. Good-bye."

He walked toward the door and left the apartment.

Helena Hansson looked enquiringly at Åsa Torell, who was still sitting in her chair, silent and immobile.

"Was there anything else?" Helena Hansson said uncertainly.

Åsa Torell gazed at her for a long time. They were sitting across from each other. Both women were about the same age, but the similarities ended there.

Åsa Torell let the silence deepen and take effect, then she crushed her cigarette in the ashtray and said slowly, "You're no more a secretary than I'm the Queen of Sheba."

"How dare you say a thing like that?" Helena Hansson said with agitation.

"My colleague, who just left, works for the Homicide Squad."

Helena Hansson looked at her in bewilderment.

"However, I don't," said Åsa Torell. "I'm with the Vice Squad here in town."

"Oh," the other woman said.

Her shoulders collapsed.

"We have a whole dossier on you," said Åsa Torell in an unsparing monotone. "It covers ten years. You've already been picked up fifteen times. That's quite a few."

"All right, but you can't send me up for this, you old slut," Helena Hansson said defiantly.

"Careless of you not to have a typewriter at home. Or even a steno pad. Unless it's in the briefcase over there."

"Don't start poking around in my things without a warrant, you bitch. I know my rights."

"I'm not planning to touch anything here without a warrant," Åsa Torell said.

"What in hell are you doing here then? I can't ever be pulled in for this."

Åsa Torell didn't say anything.

"Besides, dammit, I have the right to go where I want with who I want."

"And go to bed with who you want? Yes, that's perfectly correct. But you don't have the right to be paid for it. How big was that 'fee,' anyway?"

"Do you think I'm so damned stupid I'd answer that question?"

"It isn't necessary. I know the going rate. You got a thousand kronor tax-free and all expenses paid."

"You know a helluva lot," Helena Hansson said impertinently.

"We know most everything about these things."

"Only don't get the idea you can send me up, you goddamned, fucking . . ."

"I probably can. Don't worry. It'll all work out."

Suddenly Helena Hansson sprang up and flung herself across the table, her fingers tensed like claws.

Agile as a cat, Åsa Torell got to her feet and parried the attack with a simple blow that threw the other woman backwards, down into the chair.

A vase of carnations had toppled onto the floor; neither of them bothered to pick it up.

"No scratching," said Åsa Torell. "Just take it easy."

The woman stared at her. It actually looked as though she had tears in her watery blue eyes. The wig had slipped to one side.

"So you're a fighter, too, you fucking whore?" she whined.

She sat still for a while with a desperate look on her face. Then she worked herself up to a new counteroffensive and said hysterically, "Go away, dammit. Leave me alone. Come back when you really have something."

Åsa Torell dug around in her shoulder bag and took out a pencil and note pad.

"What I'm really interested in is something else," she said. "You've never worked free-lance and surely aren't now, either. Who's running the show?"

"Are you so goddamned stupid you think I'll tell you?"

Åsa Torell walked over to the telephone, which was on the dressing table. It was a pale gray Dialogue model. She bent over and jotted down the number, which the telephone company had issued as a sort of small service. Then she picked up the receiver and dialed the number. She got a busy signal.

"Wasn't too clever of you to leave the slip on with the correct number," she said. "You'll get sent up for this telephone, no matter whose name the line's registered under."

The woman slumped even lower in her chair and looked bitter but resigned.

After a moment she looked at the clock and complained, "Can't you get the hell out of here now? You've already shown how smart the cops can be."

"Not yet," said Åsa Torell calmly. "Just hang on."

Helena Hansson now seemed totally confused. She clearly hadn't counted on anything like this. It lay beyond the scope of her instructions and didn't fit with the directions she'd followed earlier. Moreover, the fact that this policewoman had complete knowledge of her past was sufficient to make her drop all pretense.

Still she seemed curiously nervous and kept looking at the clock.

She realized that the other woman was waiting for something, but couldn't figure out what it was.

"Are you going to stand there staring at me for much longer?" she said resentfully.

"No. This won't take long."

Said Åsa Torell and looked at the woman in the chair. She didn't feel anything at all for her. Not even dislike and definitely not compassion.

The telephone rang.

Helena Hansson made no attempt to get up to answer, and Åsa Torell didn't move from the spot.

Six rings echoed in the room.

Then everything returned to the status quo.

Åsa Torell was standing beside the dressing table, her arms hanging loosely and her feet slightly apart.

Helena Hansson was huddled up in the armchair, staring ahead with expressionless eyes.

Once she mumbled, "Well, you can give me a break, can't you?"

And immediately after, "How in the hell can a chick be a cop . . . ?"

Åsa Torell could have asked a question in return but refrained.

The deadlock was broken ten minutes later by heavy pounding on the outer door.

Åsa Torell answered, and Kollberg came in with a piece of paper in his hand. He was flushed and sweaty. It was evident that he'd been hurrying.

He stopped in the middle of the floor, breathed in the sinister atmosphere, glanced at the overturned vase of flowers and said, "Have you ladies been scuffling?"

Helena Hansson looked up at him. There was neither hope nor surprise now; all her professional polish had vanished.

"What the hell do you want now?" she said.

Kollberg held out the piece of paper and said, "This is a warrant to search this apartment. Complete with stamp and signature. I requested it myself, and the prosecuting attorney has given his approval."

"Go to hell," Helena Hansson said thickly.

"No thanks," Kollberg said amiably. "We're going to look around a little."

Åsa Torell nodded toward the closet door.

"I think it's in there," she said.

She took Helena Hansson's purse from the dressing table and opened it.

The woman in the chair didn't react.

Kollberg opened the closet door and pulled out a suitcase.

"Not so big, but incredibly heavy," he mumb' :d.

He put it on the bed and unbuckled the stra׀ ɔ.

"Found anything interesting?" he asked Åsa Torell.

"A round-trip ticket to Zurich and a hotel voucher. She's booked on a flight at a quarter to ten tomorrow morning from Arlanda. Return flight from Zurich at seven-forty the day after tomorrow. The hotel room is reserved for one night."

Kollberg pushed aside a top layer of clothing and various other rubbish and began to rummage around in the bundles of paper lining the bottom of the suitcase.

"Stocks," he said. "A helluva lot of them!"

"They aren't mine," Helena Hansson said tonelessly.

"I didn't think so," Kollberg said.

He walked over and opened the black briefcase.

It contained exactly what his wife had said.

A nightgown, several pairs of panties, cosmetics, a toothbrush and bottles of pills.

It was almost laughable.

He looked at the clock. It was already five-thirty, and he hoped that Gunvald Larsson had kept his promise and was on his toes.

"That's all for now," he said. "You can come with us now."

"Why?" Helena Hansson said.

"Off the cuff I can inform you that you're suspected of intent to engage in illegal traffic in currency," Kollberg said. "You can count on being taken into custody, but that's not my business."

Kollberg looked around, shrugged his shoulders and said, "Åsa, will you see that she gets what they usually take along at a time like this."

Åsa Torell nodded.

"Pigs," said Miss Hansson.

16.

Everything happened on that Monday.

Gunvald Larsson stood by the window in his office, looking out over his city. On the surface it didn't look so bad, but he was too aware of the hotbed of crime that smoldered all around him. True, he came into contact only with assault and battery cases, but they were more than enough. Moreover, they were usually the most unpleasant to deal with. Six new robberies, each one more brutal than the other, and no clues for the time being. Four cases of wife-beating, all rather severe. And one case of the reverse: A woman had attacked her husband with an iron. Larsson had had to go there himself, to an address on Bastugatan on the South Side. The shabby apartment looked like a slaughterhouse. Everything was covered with blood, and he even got bloodstains on his new pants.

In Gamla Stan an unwed mother had thrown her one-year-old child out of a window on the third floor. The child was seriously injured, though the doctors said it would survive. The mother was seventeen years old and hysterical. Her only reason had been that the baby was screaming and wouldn't listen to her.

At least twenty fairly bloody fights in the city center alone. He didn't even want to think what the reports from the modern slum areas in the suburbs would look like.

The telephone rang.

He let it ring for a while before answering.

"Larsson."

Grunting fiercely.

The Turk who'd had his stomach ripped open had died at South Hospital.

"Uh-hmm," he said indifferently.

He wondered if the man's death had really been necessary. The hospitals were filled to overflowing; whole sections were closed because of vacations and a general personnel shortage. There was also a shortage of blood donors.

The assailant had already been caught. A patrol car had picked him up in a junkie hangout in a condemned house in Birkastaden. He was completely dazed and couldn't answer at all when he was addressed. He'd had the bloody stiletto on him, in any case. Gunvald Larsson had looked at him for half a minute and sent for the police doctor.

Apart from the robberies, which seemed well planned, these were all what are called unpremeditated crimes, almost comparable to accidents. Unhappy people, nervous wrecks, were driven into desperate situations against their wills. In almost all the cases, alcohol or drugs were of decisive importance. It may have been partly due to the heat, but more basic was the system itself, the relentless logic of the big city, which wore down the weak-willed and the maladjusted and drove them to senseless actions.

And the lonely. He wondered how many suicides had been committed during the last twenty-four hours and felt almost relieved that it would still be a while before he found out. Those reports were still out in the various police stations where the material was processed and the reports compiled.

It was now twenty minutes to five, time for him to be relieved.

He should've been able to drive home to his bachelor den in Bollmora, shower, put on slippers and a clean bathrobe, drink a cold bottle of ginger ale (Gunvald Larsson came near to being a teetotaler), take the telephone off the hook and spend the evening with a piece of escapist literature.

But now he'd assumed responsibility for something that had nothing to do with him at all. This thing with Broberg, an undertaking he alternately regretted and looked forward to with a certain vindictive delight. If Broberg was a criminal—and Gunvald Larsson was convinced he was—then he was exactly the type of criminal Gunvald Larsson took pure pleasure in sending to jail. A slumlord. A loan shark. Unfortunately, they were usually untouchable, although everyone knew they existed and lived in the best of health, within the formal limits of the inflexible law.

He'd decided not to do this alone. On the one hand, because he'd operated on his own and in his own way many times during his years on the force and had been criticized many times for it. For that matter, so often that his prospects of ever being promoted, as things stood now, seemed negligible. On the other, because he didn't want to take any risks and because this ought to look neat.

For once he was following the rule book, and precisely for that reason he should, of course, be prepared for everything to go haywire.

But where would he find a partner?

There was no one available in his own section, and Kollberg had said that the situation was identical out in Västberga.

In desperation he called the fourth precinct and managed after many if's and but's to get a positive answer.

"If it's all *that* important," the Superintendent said, "maybe I can let you have a man."

"That's generous of you."

"Do you think it's easy, keeping *you* supplied with people too? When it should be the other way around?"

"No, no," Gunvald Larsson said. "I know."

A large part of the uniform force stood glowering outside of various embassies and tourist agencies. Doing no good at all, furthermore, since they couldn't accomplish anything constructive if sabotage or demonstrations were in the offing. Now the National Chief of Police had even forbidden the men to play with their batons, which had been the only bit of entertainment this senseless, deadly dull work had to offer.

"Well," Gunvald Larsson said, "who is this guy?"

"His name's Zachrisson. Comes originally from Maria. Usually works as a plainclothesman."

Gunvald Larsson furrowed his blond eyebrows sternly.

"I know him," he said, without a trace of enthusiasm.

"I see. Well, that ought to be an advan—"

"Just make damned sure he doesn't have a uniform on," said Gunvald Larsson. "And that he's outside the building at five minutes to five."

He thought for a moment and added, "And when I say outside, I don't mean for him to stand right outside the door with his arms crossed like some old bouncer."

"I understand."

"Fine," said Gunvald Larsson and hung up.

He arrived at the building on Kungsgatan at exactly five to five and immediately discovered Zachrisson standing with a sheepish look on his face, staring at a store window with a display of women's underwear.

Gunvald Larsson inspected him grimly. His plainclothes attire was limited to a sport coat. Otherwise he was dressed in regulation pants and shirt with the matching police tie. Any idiot could see he was an officer of the law at a hundred yards. Moreover, he was standing with his feet apart, hands behind his back, rocking back and forth on the balls of his feet. The only thing needed to complete the picture was a paper bag containing his cap and baton.

When he caught sight of Gunvald Larsson he straightened up, and it almost looked as though he was going to stand at attention. Zachrisson had unpleasant memories of their previous work together.

"Just take it nice and easy," said Gunvald Larsson. "What's that in your right coat pocket?"

"My pistol."

"Couldn't you have had the sense to wear a shoulder holster?"

"I couldn't find one," Zachrisson said lamely.

"Christ, then put the hardware inside your waistband."

The man promptly stuck his hand into his pocket.

"Not here, for chrissake," Gunvald Larsson said. "Go and do it in the doorway. Discreetly."

Zachrisson obeyed.

When he returned his appearance was somewhat improved. But not much.

"Now listen here," Gunvald Larsson said. "We can expect a

guy to show up here and walk into the building sometime after five. He looks something like this."

He showed him a picture, which was dwarfed by his enormous right hand. It was poor, but the only one he'd been able to get hold of.

Zachrisson nodded.

"He's going to walk into the building and, if I'm not mistaken, he'll be coming out again in a matter of minutes. He'll probably then be carrying a black pigskin suitcase with two straps around it."

"Is he a robber?"

"Yeah, something like that. I want you to stay outside of the building near the door."

Zachrisson nodded once more.

"I'm going up the stairs. I may grab him there, but I may prefer not to. It's very likely that he'll come in a car and park right in front of the door. He'll be in a hurry, and he may leave the engine running while he's inside. The car ought to be a black Mercedes, but that's not definite. If by any chance he comes out on the sidewalk with the suitcase in his hand without me, then you must stop him, at any cost, from driving away until I can make it out here."

The policeman put on a determined look.

"And for chrissake, try to look like an ordinary human being. Not like you were on guard outside of the U.S. Trade Center."

Zachrisson blushed slightly and looked puzzled.

"Okay," he mumbled.

And shortly after, "Is he dangerous?"

"Could be," Gunvald Larsson said nonchalantly.

His own opinion was that Broberg was about as dangerous as a flea.

"Now try to remember everything," he said.

Zachrisson recovered his dignity with some difficulty and nodded.

Gunvald Larsson walked in the door. The hall was large and deserted, and it looked as if most of the offices had already closed.

He walked up the stairs. Just as he passed the door with the two plaques, HAMPUS BROBERG INC. and VIKTOR PALMGREN LOAN & FI-

NANCE, a dark-haired woman of about thirty-five locked it from the outside. Obviously the secretary.

A glance at his Ultratron showed that it was exactly five o'clock. Punctuality is a virtue.

The woman pressed the button for the elevator without glancing at him. He walked halfway up the next flight of stairs, stood absolutely still and waited.

The wait was fairly long and extremely uneventful. During the next fifty minutes, the elevator was used three times, and on two occasions individuals of no interest to him walked down the stairs —apparently people who had worked overtime for one reason or another. When this happened Gunvald Larsson walked up and met them on the floor above. Then he returned to his post. At three minutes to six he heard the elevator come creaking up and heavy steps approaching. This time they were coming from down below. The elevator stopped, and a man stepped out. He had a bunch of keys in his hand, and, for all Gunvald Larsson knew, it could very well be Hampus Broberg. If so, dressed in a hat and overcoat despite the heat. He unlocked the office, went in and closed the door.

At that moment the person who was tromping up the staircase walked past the door to Broberg's office and came on up. He was heavy-set and wearing work clothes and a flannel shirt. When he caught sight of Gunvald Larsson he stopped short and said loudly, "What are you doing, hanging around here, huh?"

"It's none of your business," Gunvald Larsson whispered.

The man smelled of beer or akvavit, or both.

"It is too my goddamn business," the man said obstinately. "I'm the janitor here."

He set himself in the middle of the staircase, with one hand on the wall and the other on the handrail, as if to block the way.

"I'm a policeman," Gunvald Larsson whispered.

At that very second the office door was opened, and Broberg, or whoever it was, came out with the famous suitcase in his hand.

"Policeman!" said the janitor in a rough, booming voice. "You'd better prove that one before I . . ."

The man carrying the suitcase didn't hesitate a fraction of a second, decided against the sluggish elevator and scooted down the stairs at top speed.

Gunvald Larsson was in an awkward situation. There was no time for bickering. If he hit the guy in the work clothes he'd probably fall down the stairs and break his neck. After a short hesitation he decided to brush him aside with his right hand. This should have been quite easy, but the janitor resisted and grabbed hold of Gunvald Larsson's jacket. When he tried to break loose he heard the material give way and rip. Furious about this new damage to his wardrobe, he turned halfway around and struck the man on the wrist. The janitor let go with a groan, but Broberg now had a considerable head start.

Gunvald Larsson plunged down the stairs. Behind him he heard savage curses and uncertain, shuffling steps.

The state of affairs in the hall on the ground floor was perfectly ludicrous.

Zachrisson had come inside the street door, of course, and was standing with his legs apart. He'd opened his jacket and was fumbling for his pistol.

"Stop! Police!" he howled.

Broberg had stopped abruptly without letting go of the suitcase, which he was carrying in his right hand. He stuck his left hand into the pocket of his overcoat and pulled out a gun, aimed at the ceiling and fired. Gunvald Larsson didn't hear a ricochet and was almost certain that it was a starting gun, a stage revolver or some kind of toy.

Zachrisson flung himself down on the marble floor and shot, but missed. Gunvald Larsson flattened himself against the wall. Broberg ran toward the back of the large hall, away from the policeman by the outer door. There was probably a back door. Zachrisson shot again and missed. The man carrying the suitcase was only ten feet from Gunvald Larsson and was still moving toward the inside of the building.

Zachrisson fired three shots. All of them hit wide.

What in hell do they learn at the Police Academy? Gunvald Larsson wondered.

Bullets ricocheted back and forth between the stone walls.

One of them entered the heel of Gunvald Larsson's right shoe, putting paid to a peerless example of Italian craftsmanship.

"Cease fire!" he roared.

Zachrisson fired again, but there was just a click. He'd probably forgotten to fill the magazine.

Gunvald Larsson took three strides forward and, without a second's hesitation, struck Hampus Broberg on the jaw, as hard as he could. He heard a crunch under his fist, and the man slumped down in a sitting position.

The custodian came down the stairs, swearing and panting heavily.

"What the hell . . . ?" he gasped.

Gun smoke lay like a light blue fog over the hall. The smell of cordite was penetrating.

Zachrisson stood up, looking perplexed.

"What were you aiming for?" Gunvald Larsson said angrily.

"The legs . . ."

"Mine?"

Gunvald Larsson picked up the weapon that had fallen out of Broberg's hand. As he'd suspected, it was a starting gun.

Outside on the street a vociferous crowd was gathering.

"Are you nuts?" the custodian said. "That's Mr. Broberg."

"Shut up," said Gunvald Larsson and dragged the man on the floor to his feet.

"Take the suitcase," he said to Zachrisson. "If you can manage it."

He led the captive out through the door, gripping his right arm tightly. Broberg held his chin in his left hand. Blood trickled out between his fingers.

Without looking around, Gunvald Larsson forced his way through the jabbering crowd and walked over to his car. Zachrisson plodded after him with the suitcase.

Gunvald Larsson shoved the prisoner into the back seat and got in himself.

"Think you can get us to Headquarters?" he asked Zachrisson.

The latter nodded dejectedly and squeezed in behind the steering wheel.

"What's going on?" asked a dignified citizen in a gray suit and beret.

"We're making a film," Gunvald Larsson said and slammed the door.

"Get this goddamn thing moving," he said to Zachrisson, who was fumbling with the ignition.

Finally he got the car started.

On the way to Kungsholmen Zachrisson asked a question that had obviously been on his mind.

"Aren't you armed?"

"Idiot," said Gunvald Larsson wearily.

As usual he was carrying his police pistol on a waistband clip. Hampus Broberg said nothing.

17.

Hampus Broberg said nothing, because he was both unwilling and unable. Two of his teeth had been knocked out, and his jawbone was fractured.

At nine-thirty that night Gunvald Larsson and Kollberg were still leaning over him, shouting senseless questions.

"Who shot Viktor Palmgren?"

"Why did you try to escape?"

"You hired a killer, didn't you?"

"It's no good denying!"

"You'd better come clean."

"Well, who's the gunman?"

"Why don't you answer?"

"The game's up, anyway, so start talking."

Now and then Broberg shook his head, and when Palmgren's

murder was mentioned he contorted his already contorted features into an expression that was probably intended to be a sardonic smile.

Kollberg could imagine what this grimace meant, but not much more.

During the introductory formalities and later, in passing, they'd asked him if he wanted to call his lawyer, but the prisoner still shook his head.

"You wanted Palmgren out of the way so you could sneak off with the money, didn't you?"

"Where is the gunman?"

"Who else was in on the plot?"

"Spill it!"

"You're being held in custody."

"You're in a bad fix."

"Why are you trying to protect other people?"

"Nobody's bothering to protect you."

"Well, come out with it."

"If you tell us who committed the murder it may count in your favor later on."

"You'd be wise to cooperate with us."

Now and then Kollberg tried a gentler approach.

"When were you born? And where?"

Gunvald Larsson ran true to form, the whole time trying to adhere to the doctrine that you have to begin from the beginning.

"Okay, let's take it from the beginning again. When did you decide that Viktor Palmgren had to be got out of the way?"

Grimace. Shake of the head.

Kollberg thought he could read the word "idiots" on the man's lips.

For an instant it struck him that that was quite an adequate description.

"If you won't talk, write on the pad there."

"Here's a pencil."

"We're only interested in the murder. Others will have to take care of the other stuff."

"Do you realize you're suspected of conspiracy?"

"As accessory to first-degree murder?"

"Are you going to confess or not?"

"It'd be best for everyone if you did it now. Right away."

"Let's take it from the beginning. When did you decide that Palmgren had to be killed?"

"Out with it!"

"You know we have enough evidence to have you booked. You're already in custody."

That was true. No doubt about it. In the suitcase were stocks and other securities worth something like half a million kronor, according to a quick calculation. They were homicide detectives, not financial experts, but they knew a little about illegal traffic in currency and securities.

They'd found a one-way ticket to Geneva via Copenhagen and Frankfurt in a folder in the inside pocket of Broberg's suit coat. The ticket was in the name of a Mr. Roger Frank.

In the other inside pocket there was a forged passport, bearing Broberg's picture, but also with the name Roger Frank, engineer.

"Well, how about it?"

"The best thing you can do is clear your conscience."

At last Broberg took the ballpoint pen and wrote some words on the steno pad.

They leaned over the table and read:

Get me a doctor.

Kollberg drew Gunvald Larsson aside and said in a low voice, "Maybe that's what we should do. We can't keep on like this for hours."

Gunvald Larsson frowned and said, "Guess you're right. Is there anything to show he set up that damned murder? Seems to me that's highly unlikely."

"Right," Kollberg said reflectively. "Right."

They were both tired and felt like going home.

But they rounded things off by repeating several questions:

"Who shot Palmgren?"

"We know you didn't shoot him, but we also know you know who did it. What's his name?"

"And where is he?"

"When were you born," said Gunvald Larsson, who was not really concentrating. "And where?"

Then they gave up, sent for the police doctor on call and turned Broberg over to the guards in the detention ward.

They got into their cars and went home, Kollberg to his wife, who was already asleep, Gunvald Larsson to grieve over his ruined clothes.

Before Kollberg fell into bed he tried to call Martin Beck but couldn't reach him.

Gunvald Larsson didn't consider calling Beck or anyone else. He took a long shower and thought about the bloodstains on his pants, his ripped jacket and ruined shoes. Before going to sleep he read two pages of a book by Stein Riverton.

Kollberg had witnessed a more instructive interrogation earlier in the evening.

As soon as he and Åsa Torell had brought Helena Hansson into a bare, inhospitable room at the Vice Squad headquarters, the girl broke down completely and reeled off a confession that had run as freely as her tears. They had to turn on a tape recorder to catch everything she had to say.

Yes, she was a call girl.

Yes, Hampus Broberg was a regular customer of hers.

He'd given her the suitcase, the plane ticket and the hotel voucher. She was going to fly to Zurich and leave the suitcase in the hotel's safe deposit box. He was going to come from Geneva the next day and pick it up.

She was going to get ten thousand kronor for her trouble, if everything went well. She didn't know what was in the suitcase.

Hampus Broberg had said they couldn't risk taking the same plane.

When the police arrived she'd tried to contact Broberg at the Carlton Hotel, where he was staying under the name of Frank, but couldn't reach him.

The fee for the job in Malmö had been fifteen hundred kronor, not a thousand.

She also blurted out the various contact numbers of the call girl ring she belonged to.

She said she was completely innocent, really, and didn't know what it was all about.

She was a prostitute, but then she wasn't the only one, and she'd never done anything else.

She knew absolutely nothing about the murder.

At any rate, no more than she'd already told them.

Kollberg was inclined to believe her on that point, as well as on the others.

18.

In Malmö Paulsson was on the lookout.

The first days—Saturday and Sunday—he'd concentrated on the hotel personnel; he wanted, so to speak, to close in on his prey. He knew from experience that it was easier to carry out an assignment if you knew who it was you were looking for.

He took his meals in the hotel dining room and between times remained in the lobby. He soon found out that hiding behind a newspaper in the restaurant with his ears pricked up gave meager results. Most of the guests spoke foreign languages that were incomprehensible to him, and if the staff discussed Wednesday's event among themselves, they didn't do it in the proximity of his table.

Paulsson decided to play the curious guest who'd read about the drama in the newspaper. He called over the waiter, an apathetic young man with sideburns and a dazzling white jacket several sizes too large.

Paulsson tried to start up a conversation about the shooting, but the waiter wasn't interested and answered in monosyllables.

Every now and then his eyes wandered toward the open window.

Had he seen the murderer?

Ye-e-es.

Wasn't he one of those long-haired types?

No-o-o.

Did he really not have long hair, or was he sloppily dressed at least?

Maybe his hair was a little long. Didn't see too well. He had a jacket on, anyway.

The waiter pretended he had something to do in the kitchen and left.

Paulsson reflected.

If someone usually had long hair and a beard and wore jeans and baggy jackets, it was, of course, the easiest thing in the world to disguise himself. All he had to do was cut his hair, shave and put on a suit, and then no one would recognize him. The problem with such a disguise was that it would take quite a while for that person to regain his former appearance. Therefore he ought to be easy to find.

Paulsson felt happy about this conclusion.

However, many of these left-wingers looked like ordinary people. He'd noticed that many times when he'd been on duty during demonstrations in Stockholm. It had often annoyed him. People who wore work clothes and had big red Mao buttons on their shirts were easy to identify, even when they weren't in groups. But the job was complicated by people who were treacherous enough to go around in business suits, smooth-shaven and clean-cut, with their leaflets and subversive literature in neat briefcases. This meant that he didn't have to go to unhygienic extremes in his own disguise, but it was annoying all the same.

The headwaiter came over to his table.

"Was the meal good?" he asked.

He was short, had close-cropped hair and a humorous twinkle in his eye. He must surely be more alert and talkative than the waiter.

"It was very good, thank you," Paulsson said.

Then he switched to *the* topic.

"I was just thinking about what happened last Wednesday. Were you here at the time?"

"Yes, I was working that night. Horrible. And they haven't caught the murderer, either."

"Did you see him?"

"Uhn—you see, it all happened so fast. When he first came in I wasn't in the dining room. I didn't come in until after he'd fired. So you could say I just caught a glimpse of him."

Paulsson had a brilliant idea.

"He didn't happen to be colored?"

"Excuse me?"

"I mean a Negro, to be blunt. He wasn't a Negro?"

"No, why would he be a Negro?" said the headwaiter with genuine surprise.

"There are rather light-colored Negroes, as you may know. Who don't even look like Negroes, really, if you don't look too closely."

"No, I've never heard of that. Other people saw him much better than I did, so you'd think some of them would've noticed if he was a Negro. And said it. No, he couldn't have been."

"Well, okay," Paulsson said. "It was just an idea that struck me . . ."

Paulsson spent Saturday night in the bar, where he consumed a great number of various nonalcoholic drinks.

When he ordered his sixth, a Pussyfoot, even the bartender, who wasn't easily surprised, looked somewhat astonished.

On Sunday night the bar was closed, and Paulsson stayed in the lobby. He prowled around the reception desk, but the clerk seemed very busy, talked on the telephone, studied the ledger, helped guests and now and then hurried off on an urgent errand with elbows raised and long coat tails flapping after him. Finally Paulsson was able to exchange a few words with him, but didn't receive support for any of his theories. The clerk was particularly emphatic about the fact that the man was not a Negro.

Paulsson finished off the day with a pusztaschnitzel in the grill.

There the clientele was significantly more numerous and youthful than in the dining room, and he overheard several interesting conversations from the tables nearby. At the table next to Paulsson's, two men and a girl were talking about things that, to his great displeasure, he couldn't fathom, but at one point they even mentioned the murder of Viktor Palmgren.

The younger man, with long red hair and a bushy beard, expressed his contempt for the deceased and his admiration for the assailant. Paulsson studied his appearance carefully and made a mental note of it.

The next day was Monday, and Paulsson decided to extend the search to Lund. There were students in Lund, and where there were students there had to be radical elements. Up in his room he had long lists of names of people in Lund who could be suspected of holding deviant opinions.

So in the afternoon he took the train to the university town, which he had never visited before, and set off through the town to search out the students.

It was hotter than ever, and Paulsson perspired in his checkered suit.

He found his way to the university, which was dead and abandoned in the blazing sun. No revolutionary activities seemed to be going on. Paulsson recalled the picture he'd seen of Mao swimming in the Yangtze Kiang. Maybe the Lund Maoists were in the Höje River, following the Chairman's example.

Paulsson took off his jacket and went to have a look at the cathedral. He was surprised that the notorious Giant Finn statue was so small and bought a picture postcard of him to send to his wife.

On his way from the cathedral he caught sight of a notice announcing a dance that the Student Union was going to have that night. Paulsson decided to go to it, but since it was still early in the evening, he had to find some way to pass the time.

He wandered around the town, which was deserted for the summer, strolled under the tall trees in the city park, sauntered along the gravel paths of the Botanical Gardens for a long time and suddenly felt very hungry. He ate a simple dinner at Storkällaren and then sat over a cup of coffee, watching what little activity there was on the square outside.

He didn't have the vaguest idea of how to organize the search for Viktor Palmgren's killer. Assassinations hardly ever occurred in Sweden—he couldn't remember any political murder occurring in modern times. He wished that the information he had to go on wasn't so vague and that he knew a little better where to start looking.

When it was dark, and the street lamps had been turned on, he paid the check and went to find the discothèque.

That venture was also unproductive. About twenty teenagers were drinking beer and dancing to deafening rock music. Paulsson talked to several of them, but it turned out that they weren't even students. He drank a small mug of beer and then took the train back to Malmö.

He ran into Martin Beck in the hotel elevator. Even though they were alone in the elevator, the latter stared fixedly at a point above Paulsson's head, whistling silently to himself. When the elevator stopped he winked at Paulsson, put a finger to his lips and walked out into the corridor.

19.

On Monday afternoon Månsson called his Danish colleague.

"What do you think you're doing?" Mogensen said. "Calling during working hours. Do you think I sit here sleeping at the Bureau of Investigation, too?"

"Beg your pardon," Månsson said.

"Oh, I understand, it's so urgent you can't hold off until tonight. Well, let's hear it, I'm just sitting here twiddling my thumbs."

"Ole Hoff-Jensen," said Månsson. "He's a director of some company that's a part of an international concern owned by Viktor Palmgren. You know, the guy who was shot dead here last week. I'd like to know what kind of company and where its office is. As soon as possible."

"Okay, I get it," Mogensen said. "I'll call back."

Half an hour passed.

"That wasn't so hard," said Mogensen. "Are you listening?"

"Sure. Go ahead," Månsson said and grasped his pencil.

"Mr. Ole Hoff-Jensen is forty-eight years old, married, and has two daughters. His wife's name is Birthe; she's forty-three. They live on Richelieus Allé in Hellerup. The firm is an air freight company called Aero-fragt, which has its main office on Kultorvet in Copenhagen and space out at Kastrup airport. The company has five planes of the DC-6 type. Anything else you want to know?"

"No thanks. That's enough for the moment. How are you, by the way?"

"Horrible. And hot. I think this heat drives people insane. The city's packed with nut cases. Swedes galore. Farewell."

The instant Månsson hung up it occurred to him that he'd forgotten to ask for the telephone number of the airline.

He asked the switchboard to get it, which took a while. When he finally reached Aero-fragt he was informed that Hoff-Jensen couldn't be reached until the following day, and that he could meet with him after eleven o'clock.

It's just as well, Månsson thought. I couldn't have taken another director today.

He spent the remainder of Monday afternoon working on some routine business, which did, after all, have to be taken care of.

On Tuesday morning he picked up Martin Beck outside of the hotel. He'd planned for them to take the hydrofoil to Copenhagen, but Martin Beck explained that he wanted to ride on a real boat, and that they might as well combine work with pleasure and eat lunch during the crossing. He'd found out that the train ferry Malmöhus was due to leave in twenty minutes.

There weren't many passengers on board. Only two tables in the dining room were occupied. They made a round of the smorgasbord to sample the herring, had wienerschnitzel and then went forward to the lounge to drink coffee.

The Sound was as smooth as glass, but the view wasn't entirely clear. The silhouette of Ven shimmered in the haze, but it wasn't possible to distinguish either Backafallen or the small white church. Martin Beck studied the lively traffic with interest and was delighted when he caught sight of a steam-driven freighter with a graceful hull and a beautiful, straight chimney.

Over coffee Martin Beck outlined what Kollberg and Gunvald Larsson had found out from Broberg and Helena Hansson. It was bad enough, but didn't really seem to contribute to the murder investigation.

They took a train from the boat to Central Station and then went on foot across Rådhus Place and through the narrow streets to Kultorvet. Aero-fragt's office was on the top floor of an old building, and since there wasn't an elevator, they had to climb up the steep, cramped flights of stairs.

Although the building was old, the interior decoration of the office was ultramodern. They entered a long, narrow corridor with many doors covered with padded green imitation leather. The wall space between the doors was filled with large photostat copies of old types of airplanes, and under each picture there was a small leather armchair and a brass ashtray on a pedestal. The corridor led into a large room with two lofty windows onto the square.

The receptionist, who was sitting with her back to the window at a white steel-frame desk, was neither young nor very pretty. She had a pleasant voice, however; Månsson recognized it from his telephone call the previous day. She also had gorgeous, strawberry blond hair.

She was talking on the telephone and gestured politely to them to wait in chairs on one side of the room. Månsson dropped into one of the armchairs and took out a toothpick. He'd replenished his supply from the condiments rack in the train ferry's dining room. Martin Beck remained standing and looked at the old tile stove in one corner of the room.

The telephone conversation was being carried on in Spanish, a language in which neither Martin Beck nor Månsson was proficient, and they soon grew tired of listening.

At last the strawberry blonde finished talking and stood up with a smile.

"You gentlemen are from the Swedish police, I gather," she said. "Just a moment, and I'll notify Mr. Hoff-Jensen."

She disappeared through a pair of double doors covered in the same imitation leather, although here they were coffee brown, with large, shiny brass studs. The doors closed noiselessly behind her, and even though Martin Beck strained his ears, he couldn't distinguish voices from within. Barely a minute passed before the doors were opened again, and Hoff-Jensen came toward them with outstretched hand.

He was athletic and suntanned. His broad smile revealed a row of dazzling white, flawless teeth under a well-tended mustache. He was dressed in a style of studied unconventionality, in an olive green shirt of thin raw silk, a darker jacket of soft Irish tweed, chestnut brown trousers and beige moccasins. The thick curly hair that showed at the neck of his shirt was silvery against his bronzed skin. He had a broad chest and a large head with powerful facial features. His closely-cropped hair was platinum blond, as was his mustache. His hips seemed unnaturally narrow in relation to the heavy upper half of his body.

After he'd shaken hands with Martin Beck and Månsson, he held the door open for them. Before closing it, he said to the secretary, "I don't want to be disturbed for anything."

Hoff-Jensen waited until the policemen had each taken a seat, then he settled down behind the desk. He leaned against the back of his chair and picked up the cigar that was smoldering on an ashtray within easy reach.

"Well, gentlemen, you're here about poor Viktor, I assume. You haven't found the guilty man?"

"No, not yet," Martin Beck said.

"I really don't have much more to say than what I said when we were questioned that terrible night in Malmö. Everything happened in a matter of seconds."

"But you had the time to see the gunman, didn't you?" Månsson said. "You were sitting facing in that direction."

"Certainly," Hoff-Jensen said and puffed on his cigar.

He reflected a moment before continuing.

"But before the shot was fired I hadn't noticed the man, and afterward it took me a minute to grasp what had happened. I saw Viktor fall onto the table, but didn't understand right away that he'd been shot, even though I did hear the shot. Then I saw the man with the revolver—I think it was a revolver—rush to the window and disappear. I was taken by surprise and didn't have time to take note of what he looked like. So, gentlemen, you see that I can't be of much help to you."

He lifted his arms and let them fall on the padded arms of the chair in a gesture of apology.

"But you did see him," Martin Beck said. "You must have some impression."

"If I had to describe the man I'd say that he looked middle-aged, a little shabby, perhaps. I don't think I ever saw his face; by the time I looked up he already had his back to me. He must have been in good shape to have got through that window so fast."

He leaned forward and put the cigar out in the ashtray.

"What about your wife?" Månsson asked. "Did she see anything in particular?"

"Not a thing," Hoff-Jensen answered. "My wife is a very sensitive, impressionable woman. It was a terrible shock for her, and it took her several days to get over it. Besides, she was sitting beside Viktor and so had her back to the criminal. You won't insist on questioning her?"

"No. It may not be necessary," Martin Beck said.

"That's kind of you," Hoff-Jensen said and smiled. "Well, in that case . . ."

The man gripped the arm rests as if to stand up, but Månsson hastened to say, "We have a couple more questions, if you don't mind, Mr. Hoff-Jensen."

"Ye-es?"

"How long have you been head of this company?"

"Since it was formed eleven years ago. As a young man I was a pilot, then I studied advertising in the United States and was publicity director for an airline before Viktor made me head of Aero-fragt here in Copenhagen."

"What about now? Are you carrying on as usual, despite his death?"

Hoff-Jensen extended his arms and displayed his beautiful set of false teeth.

"The show must go on," he said.

It was quiet in the room. Martin Beck looked sideways at Månsson, who'd sunk deeper into the chair and was staring disgustedly at the golf bag full of clubs propped up against the tile stove.

"Who will be head of the concern now?" said Martin Beck.

"Well, that's a good question," said Hoff-Jensen. "Young Linder is still too green, probably. And Broberg, uh, like me, I imagine, has his hands full."

"How did you get along with Mr. Palmgren?"

"Very well, I'd say. He had complete confidence in me and in the way I ran the company."

"Exactly what does Aero-fragt do?" Martin Beck asked and realized immediately what the answer would be.

"It flies freight, as the name implies," Hoff-Jensen said.

He held out a cigar case to Månsson and Martin Beck, and when both shook their heads he took a cigar himself and lit it. Martin Beck lit a Florida, exhaled the smoke and said, "Yes, I understand that, but what kind of freight? You have five planes, isn't that right?"

Hoff-Jensen nodded and studied the coal on his cigar. Then he said, "The freight consists mainly of the company's own products, primarily canned fish. One of the planes is also equipped with freezer storage. At times we run charter flights. Some firms in Copenhagen call on us for various carrying jobs—and other interested parties, for that matter."

"What countries do you fly to?" Martin Beck asked.

"Mostly European, if you don't include the Eastern European countries. Africa sometimes."

"Africa?"

"Mostly charter. That's seasonal," Hoff-Jensen said and looked pointedly at his watch.

Månsson sat up straight, took the toothpick out of his mouth and pointed it at Hoff-Jensen.

"How well do you know Hampus Broberg?"

The Dane shrugged.

"Not very well. We see each other sometimes at board meetings, like last Wednesday. We talk on the telephone now and then. That's all."

"Do you know where he is now?" asked Månsson.

"In Stockholm, I suppose. His home is there. And his office." Hoff-Jensen seemed surprised by the question.

"What kind of a relationship did Palmgren and Broberg have?" Martin Beck asked.

"Good, as far as I knew. They may not have been exactly close friends, the way Viktor and I were. We played golf together a lot and saw each other outside business hours. I'd say that Viktor and Hampus Broberg were more like boss and employee."

Something in his tone betrayed a feeling of contempt for Hampus Broberg.

"Had you ever met Mr. Broberg's secretary before?" Månsson asked.

"The blond girl? No, that was the first time. A sweet kid."

"How many employees do you have?" Martin Beck asked.

Hoff-Jensen stopped to think.

"Twenty-two at present," he said. "It varies a little, depending on . . ."

He broke off and shrugged.

"Well, on the season, the nature of the business and so on," he said nebulously.

"Where are your planes now?" Martin Beck asked.

"Two are at Kastrup. One is in Rome and one on Sao Tomé for engine repairs. The fifth is in Portugal."

Martin Beck stood up abruptly and said, "Thank you. Can you

let us know if you think of something else? Will you be staying here in Copenhagen in the near future?"

"Yes, I will," Hoff-Jensen said.

He put down the cigar but remained sitting quietly in the chair.

In the doorway Månsson turned around and said, "You don't by any chance know who could've wanted Viktor Palmgren dead?"

Hoff-Jensen picked up his cigar, gazed steadily at Månsson and said, "No, I don't know. Obviously the person who shot him. Good-bye, gentlemen."

They walked down Købmagergade to Amager Square. Månsson glanced toward Læderstræde. He knew a girl who lived there. She was a sculptor from Skåne, who preferred to live in Copenhagen. He'd met her in connection with an investigation a year earlier. Her name was Nadja, and he liked her very much. They met now and then, usually at her place, slept with each other and had a good time together. Neither of them wanted to make a commitment, and they were careful not to encroach too much on each other's lives. During the past year, their relationship had been practically flawless. Månsson's only problem was that he no longer enjoyed his weekend get-togethers with his wife in the same way; he would rather have been with Nadja.

Strøget teemed with people, most of whom seemed to be tourists. Martin Beck, who detested crowds, dragged Månsson through the throng outside of the entrance to Magasin du Nord and in on Lille Kongensgade. They each drank a bottle of Tuborg at cellar temperature in Skindbuksen, which was also crowded, although the people were more congenial than on the street.

Månsson persuaded Martin Beck to take the hydrofoil home. The boat's name was *Svalan,* and Martin Beck felt sick during the crossing. Forty minutes after they left Danish soil they walked in the door to Månsson's office.

On the desk was a message from the Technical Squad:

Ballistic study finished.
Wall

20.

Martin Beck and Månsson looked at the bullet that had killed Viktor Palmgren. It was lying in front of them on a sheet of white paper, and their shared opinion was that it looked small and innocent.

It had been somewhat knocked out of shape by the impact, but not very much, and even then it hadn't taken the experts many seconds to establish the caliber of the weapon. As a matter of fact, you didn't even have to be an expert to know that.

"A .22," Månsson said thoughtfully. "That seems strange."

Martin Beck nodded.

"Who the hell tries to kill somebody with a .22?" Månsson said.

He inspected the small nickel-cased projectile and shook his heavy head.

Then he answered his own question: "Nobody. Especially if it's not premeditated."

Martin Beck cleared his throat. As usual, he was coming down with a cold, although it was the middle of the hottest summer he'd seen in many years.

How would it be in the fall? When moisture and raw fogs closed in on the country, saturated with every species of virus from the whole wide world.

"In America it's almost considered proof that the gunman is a real craftsman," he said. "A kind of snobbishness. It shows the murderer is a real pro and doesn't bother to use more than what's absolutely necessary."

"Malmö isn't Chicago," Månsson said laconically.

"Sirhan Sirhan killed Robert Kennedy with an Iver Johnson .22," said Skacke, who was hanging around in the background.

"That's right," Martin Beck said, "but he was desperate and emptied the whole magazine. Fired like crazy all over the place."

"He was an amateur, anyway," Skacke said.

"Yes. And the shot that killed Kennedy was a chance hit. The rest of the bullets hit other people in the crowd."

"This guy took careful aim and fired a single shot," Månsson said. "From what we know, he cocked the gun with his thumb before pulling the trigger."

"And he was right-handed," said Martin Beck. "But then almost everyone is."

"Hmm," said Månsson. "There's something screwy about this."

"Yeah, there really is," Martin Beck said. "Are you thinking about anything in particular?"

Månsson grumbled under his breath for a minute. Then he said, "What I'm thinking about is that the fellow acted so professional. Especially with the gun. And he knew exactly who he was going to shoot."

"Yes . . ."

"And yet he only fired one shot. If he'd been unlucky the bullet could've struck the skull and ricocheted. As it turned out, it struck obliquely, and that was enough to take away some of the momentum."

Martin Beck had wondered about that, too, but couldn't arrive at any logical conclusion from the reasoning.

In silence they began to study the report of the technicians who'd examined the bullet.

Ballistic science had made great progress since 1927, when it made its international breakthrough during the lengthy, famous trial of Sacco and Vanzetti in Dedham, Massachusetts, but the principles were still the same. Then Calvin Goddard had brought out the helixometer, the micrometer microscope and the comparative microscope, and since then great numbers of criminal cases throughout the world had been decided on the basis of ballistic evidence.

If the bullet, the shell and the weapon were available it was the simplest thing in the world for any specialized criminologist to establish whether a particular projectile had been fired from a particular gun or not. If two of the components were available—usually the bullet and the cartridge—it was fairly easy to deduce the type of weapon.

Different makes of gun leave different characteristics on the shell as well as on the bullet in the second that the firing pin hits the detonator cap and the bullet goes its way out through the bore. After Harry Söderman, who'd been an apprentice of Locard in Lyons, constructed the first Swedish comparison microscope in the early thirties, they had slowly but surely built up an exhaustive collection of tables, from which one could read off the effect of different types of gun on the cartridge used.

But, in this case, the science, despite its generally acknowledged precision, let them down because they only had the bullet to go on and because, moreover, it was misshapen.

Nonetheless, the ballistics man had compiled a list of possible weapons.

Martin Beck and Månsson could contribute several that weren't possible. Only a little common sense was required for that.

First and foremost, all automatics were eliminated—they reject the shell when the barrel recoils, and no shell had been found in this instance. It's true that shells can end up in the most unlikely places—in a dish of mashed potatoes, for example, as Backlund had suspected, in clothes or just about anywhere. There had been examples of spent cartridges finding their way into pockets and pants cuffs and not being discovered until much later.

But the testimony seemed to be conclusive. Even if no one involved seemed to be a weapons expert, everything pointed to one thing—that the murderer had used a revolver. Which, as everyone knows, doesn't reject shells; they stay in the cartridge cylinder, waiting patiently until someone takes them out.

The statement from the ballistics expert was very long, and even when Martin Beck and Månsson had spent an hour of their precious time cutting it down, it was still pretty lengthy.

"My, my," Månsson said, scratching his head. "This document

doesn't give us much to go on, unless we can locate either the gun or something else that points in some definite direction."

"Like what?" Martin Beck asked.

"Don't know," said Månsson.

Martin Beck wiped the perspiration off his forehead with a folded handkerchief. Then he unfolded it and blew his nose.

He looked at the list of revolvers and babbled dismally, "Colt Cobra, Smith & Wesson 34, Firearms International, Harrington & Richardson 900, Harrington & Richardson 622, Harrington & Richardson 926, Harrington & Richardson Side-Kick, Harrington & Richardson Forty-Niner, Harrington & Richardson Sportsman . . ."

"Sportsman," Månsson said to himself.

"I'd like to have a word with these Harrington and Richardson guys," Martin Beck said. "Why can't they be satisfied with one model?"

"Or none at all," Månsson said.

Martin Beck turned the page and continued to mumble.

"Iver Johnson Sidewinder, Iver Johnson Cadet, Iver Johnson Viking, Iver Johnson Viking Snub . . . We should be able to cross that one out. Everybody says the barrel was long."

Månsson walked over to the window and looked thoughtfully out over the station courtyard. He wasn't listening any more. He heard Martin Beck's voice only as background noise.

"Herter's .22, Llama, Astra Cadix, Arminius, Rossi, Hawes Texas Marshal, Hawes Montana Marshal, Pic Big Seven—God, is there no end to this."

Månsson didn't answer. He was thinking of something else.

"I wonder how many revolvers there are in this city alone," Martin Beck said.

The question could hardly be answered. They must have been legion—inherited, stolen and smuggled. Hidden away in closets and drawers and old trunks. Illegal, of course, but people didn't worry about that.

And then, naturally, there were people who actually had licenses, but not many.

The only ones who definitely didn't have revolvers, or at least didn't wear them, were policemen. The Swedish police were equipped with 7.65 mm Walther pistols, stupidly enough. Although it's easier to change the magazine on automatics, they have the unpleasant habit of getting caught in clothing and other things, just when it's important to draw fast. "To snag," as it is called in the jargon.

They were interrupted in their reflections when Skacke knocked on the door and came in.

"Somebody has to talk to Kollberg," he said. "He doesn't know what he's going to do with these people in Stockholm."

21.

What to do with Hampus Broberg and Helena Hansson was a problem, to put it mildly.

In addition, Martin Beck and Kollberg had to resolve the matter on the telephone, which took quite a while.

"Where are they now?" Martin Beck said.

"On Kungsholmsgatan."

"In custody?"

"Yes."

"Can we get them booked?"

"The prosecuting attorney thinks so."

"Thinks?"

Kollberg sighed deeply.

"What are you trying to say?" Martin Beck asked.

"They're being held for planning to violate the currency laws. But for the moment there isn't any formal charge against them."

Kollberg paused significantly. Then he said, "This is what I'm trying to say. The only conclusive evidence against Broberg is that he had a forged passport in his pocket and fired a blank from a starting gun when Larsson and that trigger-happy patrolman were about to pick him up."

"Yes?"

"And the broad's confessed that she peddles her ass. She also had a suitcase full of securities. She says Broberg gave her the suitcase and the securities and the ticket and the whole works and offered her ten grand to smuggle everything into Switzerland."

"Which is probably true."

"Sure. The problem is that they never had time to get under way. If Larsson and I'd had our heads on straight, we would've let them keep going for a while. We could've tipped off customs and the passport check-point so they would've got caught out at Arlanda."

"Then you mean there won't be enough evidence?"

"Right. The prosecuting attorney claims there's a possibility the judge will refuse the arrest warrant and will think it's enough to issue an injunction against their leaving his jurisdiction."

"And let them go?"

"Exactly. Unless you . . ."

"What?"

"Unless you can convince the prosecuting attorney down there in Malmö that they're being held because they have vital information about Palmgren's murder. If you can do that we can book them and send them down to you. That's what the lawyers suggest."

"What do you think?"

"Not too much. It seems really obvious that Broberg was planning to make off with an ungodly amount of money. But if we take that approach, the matter has to be handed over to the Fraud boys."

"But does Broberg have anything to do with the murder?"

"Let's just say that since last Friday his conduct has been dictated by the fact that Palmgren died on Thursday night. It looks clear as day, doesn't it?"

"Yes. Seems like the only logical explanation."

"However, Broberg has the world's best alibi for the murder itself. Just like Helena Hansson and the other people sitting at the table."

"What does Broberg say?"

"He's reported to have said 'Ow!' when the doctor bandaged his jaw. Otherwise he hasn't said a word—literally."

"Wait a second," Martin Beck said.

He wiped off the sweaty telephone receiver with his handkerchief.

"What are you doing?" Kollberg asked suspiciously.

"Sweating."

"Then you should see me. To get back to this goddamn Broberg, he's not very cooperative. For all I know, this money and all these stocks could actually be his."

"Hmm," Martin Beck said. "If that were true, where would he have got them?"

"Don't ask me. The only thing I know about money is that I don't have any."

Kollberg seemed to be thinking over this sorrowful remark. Then he said, "Anyway, I have to have something to tell the prosecuting attorney."

"How is it with the girl?"

"A lot easier, as far as I can see. She's talking her head off. The Vice Squad is reeling in the whole call-girl outfit, which is apparently spread out over the whole country. I just talked to Sylvia Granberg, and she claims they can hold Helena Hansson without any trouble, at least as long as their investigation lasts."

Sylvia Granberg was a sub-inspector with the Vice Squad and, among other things, Åsa Torell's boss."

And besides they have some interests to tend to in Malmö," Kollberg went on. "So if you want to meet Helena Hansson you shouldn't run into any trouble."

Martin Beck said nothing.

"Well?" Kollberg said finally. "What should I do?"

"It would undoubtedly be interesting if certain confrontations took place," Martin Beck mumbled.

"I can't hear what you're saying," complained Kollberg.

"I've got to do some thinking about this. I'll call you in about half an hour."

"Absolutely no later. Any time now everybod 's going to jump on me and start yelling. Malm, the Chief of Police and the whole bunch."

"Half an hour. I promise."

"Good. Bye now."

"Bye," Martin Beck said and hung up.

He sat for a long time with his elbows on the desk, his head buried in his hands.

After a while the picture grew clearer.

Hampus Broberg had converted all his assets into cash in Sweden and tried to escape from the country. He'd first got his family to safety. Everything suggested that his situation had become untenable the moment Palmgren died.

Why?

In all likelihood, because he'd embezzled large sums of money during the course of many years from the Palmgren enterprises he controlled, primarily the real estate agency, the stock transactions and the finance company.

Viktor Palmgren had trusted Broberg, who could consequently feel relatively secure as long as the head of the company was alive.

But with Palmgren gone, he didn't dare remain longer than was absolutely necessary. Thus he'd felt in danger, if not of his life, at least of financial ruin and perhaps a long prison term.

In danger from whom?

Hardly the authorities, for it didn't seem likely that the police or Internal Revenue could ever straighten out Palmgren's tangled affairs. Even if it were possible, it would in any case take a very long time, probably years.

The one who had best access was Mats Linder naturally.

Or possibly Hoff-Jensen.

But Linder's aversion to Broberg was so strong that he'd been unable to conceal it during the police enquiry.

Hadn't he strongly hinted that Broberg was a swindler? That Palmgren had trusted his man in Stockholm too much?

In any case, Linder had the best chances in an eventual struggle for power over the Palmgren millions.

If Broberg had embezzled large amounts, Linder was in the position of being able to demand an immediate audit of the various companies' accounts and bring a charge against him.

However, Linder had as yet taken no action, even though he must know or at least suspect that he didn't have much time.

The police had stopped Broberg instead, but it had happened almost by accident.

Which could indicate that Linder was in a precarious position himself and didn't dare take the risk of possible recriminations.

Anyhow, Broberg didn't seem to have had anything to gain from Palmgren's death, and above all he hadn't expected it.

Everything he had done since Friday had been relative to Palmgren's sudden death, as Kollberg had quite correctly pointed out, but everything indicated that he had acted quickly, almost in panic, and so must have been virtually unprepared.

Then didn't this clear Broberg of any suspicion concerning the murder proper?

Martin Beck felt convinced of one thing—if there really had been a conspiracy behind the act of violence, that conspiracy was economic, not political.

Then who had something to gain from doing away with Palmgren?

There could be only one answer.

Mats Linder.

The man who'd already managed to win Palmgren's wife and who held the best cards in the financial power game.

Charlotte Palmgren was much too content with her existence to get involved in plots at such a high level. Besides, she was simply too stupid.

Hoff-Jensen certainly didn't have sufficient control of the Palmgren business empire.

But would Linder really take such an obvious risk?

Why not?

When you play for high stakes you have to take big risks.

It would be interesting to confront Hampus Broberg with Mats Linder and hear what the two gentlemen had to say to each other.

What about the girl?

Had Helena Hansson only been a paid pawn? Clearly a functional one, useful as secretary, smuggling courier and bedmate.

Her own statements indicated that, and there wasn't actually any reason to doubt them.

But lengthy experience showed that a great deal was revealed in bed. And Broberg was one of her regular clients.

Martin Beck's thoughts matured into a decision.

He got up and left the room. Took the elevator down to the ground floor, where the public prosecution authorities had their offices.

Ten minutes later he was sitting behind the desk in his borrowed room again, dialing the number to Västberga.

"Fabulous!" Kollberg said. "You're right on the dot."

"Yeah."

"And?"

"Have them booked."

"Both of them?"

"Yes. We need them as witnesses down here. They're essential to the investigation of the murder."

"Really?"

Kollberg sounded skeptical.

"They should be sent here as soon as possible," Martin Beck said with conviction.

"Okay," Kollberg said. "Just one more thing."

"What?"

"Can I be dropped from this damn case from now on?"

"I think so."

After the telephone conversation, Martin Beck remained seated for a while, still deep in thought. But now he was more preoccupied with Kollberg and the hint of doubt in his voice.

Were these people really essential to the investigation of the murder?

Maybe not, but he had another, more personal, reason for his request. He'd never seen even a picture of either Broberg or Helena Hansson, and he was merely curious. He wanted to see what they looked like, talk to them, establish some kind of human contact and then see what his own reactions were.

Hampus Broberg and Helena Hansson were formally placed under arrest before Stockholm's Civic Court at five minutes after ten the following morning, Wednesday, July 9. They left Stockholm on the noon plane the same day, Broberg accompanied by a warden and Helena Hansson by a female prison guard and Åsa Torell, who was going to discuss joint investigation work with her colleagues in Malmö.

They landed at Bulltofta at a quarter to two.

22.

On the tip of Amager, immediately south of Kastrup airport, is Dragør. It's one of the smaller towns in Denmark, with about four to five thousand inhabitants, and now probably best known for its large new ferry harbor. In the summertime ferries shuttle between Dragør and Limhamn on the Swedish side, carrying all the Swedish cars traveling to and from the Continent. The ferries do a steady business even during the winter, mostly with heavier vehicles, trucks, buses and trailers. All year round housewives travel from Malmö to Dragør to buy tax-free merchandise on board and groceries, which are cheaper in Denmark.

Not so very long ago the little port had a reputation as a resort, and there was constant activity in the harbor, where fishing boats lay rail by rail.

As a health resort, Dragør had the advantage of being within commuting distance of Copenhagen. Now the proximity to the capital city is merely a disadvantage; the water off Dragør's piers and beaches is so polluted that it isn't suitable for either swimming or fishing.

The town and its buildings, however, haven't changed appreciably since the days when ladies lazily twirled their parasols on the beach promenade, carefully shielding their alabaster complexions against the ruinous rays of the sun, and along the shore gentlemen dressed in jersey bathing suits hardly flattering to their beerbellies, cautiously sampled the waters for their medicinal effects.

The houses are squat and picturesque, painted or plastered in a variety of gay colors, the gardens are verdant, smelling of berries, flowers and lush vegetation, and the winding streets narrow and often paved with cobblestones. The stinking automobile traffic that roars to and from the ferries sweeps past the outskirts of the town, and relative peace reigns in the old quarter between the harbor and the highway.

Summer vacationers still come to Dragør, despite the poor swimming. All the rooms in the Strand Hotel were taken on this Tuesday early in July.

It was three o'clock in the afternoon, and on the veranda outside of the hotel, a family of three was just finishing their late lunch. The parents lingered over a cup of coffee and a coffee ring, but the boy, who was six and whose name was Jens, couldn't sit still any longer.

He ran excitedly back and forth between the tables, constantly nagging his parents.

"Can't we go now? I want to look at the boats. Finish your coffee. Hurry up. Let's go now. Can't we go down to the boats now?"

And so on until his mother and father gave in and stood up.

Hand in hand, they strolled down toward the old harbor pavilion, which is now a museum. There were only two fishing boats tied up in the harbor—there were usually more—meaning that several had to be out in the Sound, catching mercury-contaminated plaice.

The boy stopped at the edge of the pier and began to throw stones and sticks into the muddy water. He saw several interesting objects bobbing against the side of the wharf, but they were too far away for him to reach them.

The ferry harbor was down the beach. Several cars were lined up on the large asphalt approach waiting for the ferry, which could be seen drawing closer out on the sparkling water.

The three vacationers turned and wandered slowly back along the pier and in among buildings and houses. They stopped on Nordre Strandvej and chatted with an acquaintance who was out walking his dog.

Then they continued along the road to where the houses ended and Kastrup airport began. There they turned off to the right and went down to the beach.

Jens found the wreck of a green plastic boat at the edge of the beach and played with it, while his parents sat in the beach grass and watched. At last he tired of this and went exploring for things that had been washed up. He found an empty milk carton, a beer can and a condom and then bitterly regretted showing his finds to his parents, who made him throw everything away again.

At the moment his father stood up and shouted at him, he caught sight of something intriguing at the water's edge. A box, it looked like. Maybe a treasure chest. He ran to pick it up.

His father took the box from him, of course. He screamed a little in protest but soon gave up. He knew it didn't do any good.

Jens' parents examined the box. It was waterlogged, and the black grainy paper, which had been glued to the thick cardboard, had come loose in some places.

But it wasn't dented, and the lid, which wasn't quite closed, seemed undamaged.

When they looked closer they could make out printing on the top:

ARMINIUS .22

And right underneath, in smaller letters:

Made in West Germany.

The box aroused their curiosity somewhat.

They opened it cautiously, so as not to damage the soaked lid.

The inside of the box was lined with polystyrene, compressed from the kind of plastic particles that get washed up in countless millions on the Swedish and Danish beaches on the Sound, the Baltic and the North Sea.

Two one-inch-deep profiles had been cut out of the white polystyrene block. One of them was in the shape of a revolver with a very long barrel; the other was less well defined, and they couldn't tell immediately what it was.

"A box for a toy gun," said the woman and shrugged her shoulders.

"Don't be silly," the man said. "There was a real revolver in this box."

"How do you know that?"

"It even says the make on the lid. An Arminius .22. And look here. This space is for an extra butt, so you can exchange it for one with a larger gripping surface."

"Uh," the woman said. "I think guns are horrible."

The man laughed.

He didn't throw the box away, but kept on carrying it as they walked up toward the road.

"It's only a box," he said. "Nothing to be scared of."

"But still," the woman said. "What if the revolver or the pistol had still been in there, loaded, and Jens found it and . . . ?"

The man laughed again and stroked his wife's cheek.

"You and your imagination," he said. "If the revolver had been in there the box would never have floated ashore. It's a pretty heavy number, a .22 like this. Besides, there couldn't have been a gun in this box when it was thrown in the sea. Nobody throws away an expensive thing like a revolver . . ."

". . . unless he's a gangster who wants to get rid of a murder weapon," his wife interrupted. "What if . . ."

She stopped short and yanked at her husband's sleeve.

". . . What if that's it? I think we should take this box to the police station."

"Are you crazy? And be laughed at?"

They started walking again. Jens ran in front of them; he'd forgotten his treasure box.

"Well, but even so," she said. "You never know. It can't do any harm. We'll go to the police."

The wife was stubborn, and the man, who'd had ten years' experience of it, knew it was usually easier to give in than to disagree.

And so it happened that a quarter of an hour later Police Sergeant Larsen in Dragør had his blotter ruined by a wet revolver box from West Germany.

23.

Whereas everything happened on Monday and something on Tuesday, nothing at all happened on Wednesday. Nothing that furthered the investigation, anyway.

Martin Beck had the feeling as soon as he awoke. That it would be a peculiar day.

He felt ill at ease and dissatisfied. He'd gone to sleep late and awakened early, with a leaden taste in his mouth and his head throbbing with unfinished trains of thought.

The same subdued mood prevailed at the police station. Månsson was silent and pensive, thumbing through his papers time and again and systematically crushing his never-ending toothpicks between his teeth. Skacke seemed discouraged, and Backlund polished his glasses with an injured look on his face.

Martin Beck knew from experience that lulls of this sort occurred during every difficult investigation. They could last for days and weeks and all too often could never be broken. The material they had to work on led nowhere, all their resources appeared exhausted, and all the clues reduced to empty nothingness.

If he'd followed his instinct, he would simply have dropped everything, taken the train to Falsterbo, lain down on the beach and let the rare Swedish warmth wash over him. The morning newspapers had reported water temperatures of 70°, which really was unusually warm for the Baltic.

But, of course, a Chief Inspector doesn't do that, especially in the midst of looking for a murderer.

It was all extremely annoying. He needed both physical and mental activity, but didn't know what to do. So he was even less capable of telling anyone else what to do. After a few hours of blatant inactivity, Skacke asked frankly, "What should I do?"

"Go ask Månsson."

"I already did."

Martin Beck shook his head and walked into his room.

He looked at the clock. Still only eleven.

Almost three hours till the plane bringing Broberg and Helena Hansson was due in Malmö.

For want of anything better to do, he called Palmgren's office and asked to speak to Mats Linder.

"Mr. Linder isn't available," the blond receptionist said lazily. "But . . ."

"But what?"

"I can connect you with his secretary."

Mats Linder was indeed unavailable. He had left for Johannesburg on the Tuesday afternoon flight from Kastrup.

On urgent business.

For the moment he wasn't even available in Johannesburg, in case anyone should have the absurd idea of trying to call him there.

Since the plane was still in the air.

It was uncertain when Mr. Linder would return.

Had the trip been planned?

Mr. Linder always planned his trips very carefully.

Said the efficient secretary authoritatively.

Martin Beck hung up and looked reproachfully at the telephone.

Hmm. The confrontation between Broberg and Linder just went down the drain.

Struck by a thought, he lifted the receiver again and dialed Aero-fragt's number on Kultorvet in Copenhagen.

Certainly.

Mr. Hoff-Jensen had suddenly been obliged to leave for Lisbon that morning.

It would be possible to reach him later at the Hotel Tivoli on Avenida da Liberdade.

But for the moment the plane was still in the air.

It was uncertain when he would return to Denmark.

Martin Beck conveyed the news to Månsson, who shrugged apathetically.

At two-thirty Broberg and Helena Hansson finally arrived.

In addition to the prison warden and an enormous bandage, Broberg arrived with his lawyer.

He didn't say anything, but the lawyer was not at a loss for words.

Mr. Broberg *couldn't* talk, since he'd been subjected to the most vicious kind of police brutality. And even if he'd been able to say anything, he had nothing to add to what he'd already stated in his testimony exactly one week ago.

The lawyer continued his prepared speech, now and then throwing murderous glances at Skacke, who was operating the tape recorder. Skacke blushed.

Martin Beck didn't, however. He sat with his chin cupped in his left hand and gazed intently at the man with the bandage.

Broberg was a completely different type from Linder and Hoff-Jensen. He was heavy-set, had red hair and coarse, brutal features. Squinty, pale blue eyes, a pot belly and the kind of head that would have sent him posthaste to the gas chamber if the late Lombrosi's criminological theories had been correct.

The man was simply loathsome to look at and was also ostentatiously and tastelessly dressed. You almost felt sorry for him, Martin Beck thought.

The lawyer felt professionally sorry for Broberg. He talked and talked, and Martin Beck let him, even though the man must have been repeating largely what he'd said to no avail at the court proceedings.

But the guy had to do what he had to do for the fat fee he would get when he eventually managed to have Broberg acquitted—or almost—and Gunvald Larsson and Zachrisson penalized for breach of authority.

And he wouldn't mind if that did happen. Martin Beck had long been depressed about Gunvald Larsson's methods, but had refrained from intervening, in the sacred name of loyalty.

When the lawyer reached the end of the saga of Brobergian suffering, Martin Beck said, still without taking his eyes off the prisoner, "Mr. Broberg, you can't talk then?"

A shake of the head.

"What is your opinion of Mats Linder?"

A shrug of the shoulders.

"Do you think he's capable of assuming responsibility for the company?"

Another shrug.

He examined Broberg for almost a minute longer and tried to catch the expression in his dull, unsteady eyes.

The man was obviously scared, but he also looked ready for a fight.

At last Martin Beck said to the lawyer, "Well, I gather that your client has been upset by the events of the past week. For the time being, maybe we should call it a day."

Everyone looked equally surprised—Broberg, the lawyer, Skacke and even the warden.

Martin Beck got up and went to hear how Månsson and Backlund were getting along with Helena Hansson.

He met Åsa Torell in the corridor.

"What's she saying?"

"A whole lot of stuff. But hardly anything you can use."

"What hotel are you staying at?"

"Same as you. The Savoy."

"Then maybe we could eat dinner together tonight?"

If they could, perhaps there'd be a pleasant end to this otherwise dismal day.

"It might be difficult," Åsa Torell said evasively. "I may have a lot to do here today."

She avoided meeting his eyes. Which was easy, since she didn't even come up to his shoulder.

Helena Hansson talked and talked. Månsson sat stock-still at the table. The tape recorder hummed. Backlund paced up and down the room with a shocked expression on his face. A death blow must have been dealt to his belief in the purity of life.

Martin Beck stood just inside the door, his elbows propped on a metal cabinet, and observed the woman while she repeated word for word what she'd said previously to Kollberg.

But now nothing was left of the semi-respectable façade or the thinly applied veneer.

In fact, she looked thoroughly unnerved and worn out. Just a whore, who'd got out of her depth and was scared to death. Tears trickled down her cheeks, and she soon started giving details of everyone and everything in her line of business, obviously in the hope that she would get off lightly.

It was all very depressing, and Martin Beck left as quietly and considerately as he'd come.

He returned to his room, now empty and even warmer than before.

He observed that the chair Hampus Broberg had sat in was moist from perspiration, both on the seat and the back.

The telephone rang.

Malm, of course.

Who else?

"What the he—what in the world are you up to?"

"The investigation."

"Just a minute," Malm said irritatedly. "Was it not understood, even quite clearly stated, that this investigation would be conducted as discreetly and efficiently as possible?"

"Yes."

"Do you consider a wild shooting match and a fight in the middle of Stockholm to be discreet?"

"No."

"Have you seen the newspapers?"

"Yes. I've seen the newspapers."

"How do you think they'll look tomorrow?"

"Don't know."

"Isn't it going a little too far for the police to pressure for the arrest of two people who are probably completely innocent?"

The Chief Superintendent had a point there, obviously, and Martin Beck didn't answer right away.

"Well," he said at last, "maybe it will look a little peculiar."

"Peculiar? Do you realize down there that I'm on the firing line for this?"

"That's too bad."

"I can tell you that the Chief of Police is just as upset as I am. We've been conferring for hours up in his room . . ."

Mules may ease each other's itch, thought Martin Beck. That had to be a quotation from Latin.

"How did you get in to see him?" he asked innocently.

"How I got in to see him?" Malm echoed. "What are you talking about? Is that your idea of a joke?"

It was well known that the Chief of Police was reluctant to talk to people. Rumor had it that some high official had even threatened to haul a fork truck up to the National Police Board and force the doors of the holy of holies in order to have a face-to-face conversation. However, the dignitary in question had a great weakness for giving speeches, both to the nation and to defenseless groups of his private army.

"Well," Malm said, "can you at least say that an arrest is imminent?"

"No."

"Do you know who the murderer is, but need more evidence?"

"No."

"Do you know what circles he moves in?"

"Not the slightest idea."

"That's absurd."

"You think so?"

"What in the world do you want me to say to the parties concerned?"

"The truth."

"What truth?"

"No progress."

"No progress? After a week of investigation? With our best men on the case?"

Martin Beck took a deep breath.

"I don't know how many cases I've worked on, but it's quite a number by now. And I can assure you that we're doing our best."

"I'm convinced of that," Malm said in a conciliatory manner.

"But that's not what I really wanted to say," Martin Beck continued. "Just that a week can be a very short time. It hasn't even been a week now, as you may know. I got here on Friday, and today's Wednesday. Some time ago we arrested a man who committed a murder sixteen years before. That was two years ago and therefore before your time."

"Okay, I know all that. But this isn't an ordinary murder."

"You said that before."

"There could be international complications," Malm said with a touch of desperation in his voice. "In fact, there already are."

"In what way?"

"Repeated pressure has been put on us by several foreign embassies. And I'm fairly certain that there are Security men from abroad already here. They're sure to turn up soon in Malmö or Copenhagen."

He paused. Then he said in a wavering voice, "Or here in my office."

"Oh, well," Martin Beck said consolingly, "they can't mess things up much more than Sepo, at any rate."

"The Security people? A man of theirs is in Malmö. Are you working together?"

"I wouldn't say that exactly."

"Haven't you met?"

"I've seen him."

"Is that all?"

"Yes. And only because I couldn't avoid it."

"We haven't received any positive information from them, either," Malm said despondently.

"Did you expect any?"

"I can't help feeling that you're taking this much too lightly."

"If that's true, you're wrong. I never take a murder lightly."

"But this is not an ordinary murder."

Martin Beck had a feeling he'd heard that before.

"You can't go at it any old way," Malm said, putting heavy stress on the words. "Viktor Palmgren was a celebrity, both here and abroad."

"Yeah. I gather he appeared in the weeklies every week or so."

"Hampus Broberg and Mats Linder are also prominent citizens."

"I see."

"You can't treat them any old way."

"Of course not."

"At the same time you must be very careful what you leak to the press."

"I don't leak a thing myself."

"As I told you last time, it could cause irreparable damage if certain of Palmgren's activities became public knowledge."

"Who would be irreparably damaged?"

"Who do you think," Malm said agitatedly. "The nation, naturally. This nation of ours. If it became known that members of the Government had been aware of certain transactions, then . . ."

"Then?"

"Then the political consequences could be devastating."

Martin Beck detested politics. If he had political views he kept them strictly to himself. He'd always tried to dodge assignments that might have political consequences. Generally, he offered no opinion when political crimes came up in a conversation.

But this time he couldn't help saying, "For whom?"

Malm let out a sound as though he'd been stabbed in the back.

"Do everything you can," he pleaded.

"Okay," Martin Beck said mildly. "I'll do everything I can . . ."

After a second he added, "Stig."

That was the first time he'd called the Chief Superintendent by his first name. And hopefully the last.

The remainder of the afternoon passed in a melancholy mood. The Palmgren investigation had bogged down.

However, it was unusually lively at the police station. The Malmö police force raided two brothels downtown, much to the indignation of the employees and to the even greater shame of the customers who'd been hauled in.

Åsa Torell had obviously been right when she said she'd have a lot to do.

He left the police station about eight, still feeling dissatisfied and vaguely worried.

His appetite deserted him, so there was no question of having a hearty *skånsk* dinner. He forced down a sandwich and a glass of milk, anyway, at the Mitt-i-City cafeteria on Gustav Adolf Square.

He chewed his food carefully and slowly. Through the window he studied the teenage vagrants, who were smoking hash and trading it for stolen records around the rectangular stone basin on the square.

No policemen were in sight, and the staff of the Bureau of Child Welfare must have had other things to do.

Eventually he strolled along Södergatan, diagonally across Stortorget and down toward the harbor. When he got back to the hotel it was ten-thirty.

In the lobby his eyes immediately fell on two men sitting in the easy chairs to the right of the entrance to the dining room. One of them was tall and bald and had a thick black mustache. He was also incredibly suntanned. The second man was a hunchback, almost a dwarf, with a pale face, sharp features and intelligent black eyes. Both were impeccably dressed, the mustachioed one in dark blue shantung and the hunchback in a well-cut pale gray suit with a vest. Both men had shiny black shoes, and both were motionless, staring vacantly straight ahead. A bottle of Chivas Regal and two glasses were on the table between them.

Foreigners, thought Martin Beck. The hotel swarmed with foreign guests, and on the flagpoles outside he'd seen at least two national flags he didn't recognize.

As he picked up the room key, he saw Paulsson come out of the elevator and walk over to the two men's table.

24.

Up in his room the maid had prepared everything for the night, turned down the bed, put out the bedside rug, closed the window and drawn the curtains.

Martin Beck turned on the bedside lamp and glanced at the TV set. He had no desire to turn it on and, besides, the programs were probably all over by now.

He took off his shoes, socks and shirt. Then he pulled open the drapes and opened out the double windows.

A faint breath of cool air, just barely noticeable, floated in from outside.

He propped his hands on the window sill and gazed out over the canal, the train station and the harbor.

He stood there for a long time in pants and fishnet undershirt and thought about nothing, on the whole.

The air was warm and unmoving, the sky filled with stars.

Illuminated passenger boats came and went; the train ferry bellowed in the harbor entrance. The traffic on the streets was almost nonexistent, and there was a long row of taxis outside of the train station with their vacant signs on and their front doors open. The drivers stood in clusters and passed the time of day, and the cars were painted in a variety of quite bright colors, not black as in Stockholm.

He didn't want to go to bed. He'd already read the evening

newspapers and he'd forgotten to pick up a book. He could go down and buy one, but then he'd have to get dressed again. Yet he didn't want to read either, and if he did, the Bible and the telephone directory were always close by. Or the autopsy report, but he knew it almost by heart.

So he stood there by the window and looked, feeling curiously alone and shut off. Totally of his own choosing, since he could have been sitting in the bar or at Månsson's home or in a thousand different places.

Something was missing, but he didn't really know what.

After he'd stood there for quite a while he heard someone tapping on the door. Very lightly. If he'd been sleeping or in the shower, he wouldn't have heard it.

"Come in," he said, without turning his head.

He heard the door open.

Maybe it was the murderer, striding in with his revolver raised, ready for action. If he aimed for the back of the head this time, too, Martin Beck would fall forward out of the window and, if he were unlucky, he would be dead before he was smashed on the sidewalk far below.

He smiled and turned around.

It was Paulsson in his houndstooth suit and his canary yellow shoes.

He looked unhappy. Even his mustache didn't seem quite as elegant as usual.

"Hi," he said.

"Hi."

"May I come in?"

"Sure," Martin Beck said. "Sit right down."

He went over and sat down on the edge of his bed.

Paulsson squirmed in his chair. His forehead and cheeks glistened with perspiration.

"Take off your jacket," Martin Beck said. "We're not too particular about formalities here."

Paulsson hesitated for a long time, but finally he began to undo the buttons on the double-breasted jacket and struggled out of it.

He folded it very carefully and laid it over the arm of the chair.

Under the jacket he was wearing a shirt with broad pale green and orange stripes. Plus a pistol in a shoulder holster.

Martin Beck wondered how long it would take him to get at the gun, if he first had to go through all that complicated unbuttoning process.

"What's on your mind?" he asked calmly.

"Uh . . . I wanted to ask you something."

"Go ahead. What?"

"You don't have to answer, of course."

"Don't be silly. What is it?"

"Well . . ."

And then finally it came, visibly after the exercise of a great deal of self-control, "Have you gotten anywhere?"

"No," Martin Beck said.

From pure courtesy he returned the question, "Have you?"

Paulsson shook his head wistfully. Lovingly stroked his mustache, as if it gave him renewed strength.

"This seems pretty complicated," he said.

"Or else it may be very simple," Martin Beck said.

"Simple?" Paulsson said.

Questioningly and incredulously.

Martin Beck shrugged.

"No," Paulsson said, "I don't think so . . . And the worst thing is . . ."

He broke off. With a hopeful glint in his eye, he said, "Have they been raking you over the coals, too?"

"Who?"

"Oh, the bosses. In Stockholm."

"They seem a little nervous," Martin Beck said. "What's the worst thing, you were going to say?"

"This is going to be a large-scale international investigation, politically complicated. With ramifications in all directions. Tonight two foreign security agents arrived. At the hotel."

"Those two characters sitting in the lobby a while ago?"

Paulsson nodded.

"Where are they from?"

"The little man is from Lisbon and the other one from Africa. Loranga Marcuse, or whatever it's called."

"Lourenço Marques," Martin Beck said. "It's in Mozambique. Do they have an official assignment here?"

"I don't know."

"Are they even policemen?"

"Security agents, I think. They introduce themselves as businessmen. But . . ."

"What?"

"But they identified me right away. Knew who I was. Strange."

Extremely strange, Martin Beck thought. Aloud he said, "Have you talked to them?"

"Yes. They speak very good English."

Martin Beck happened to know that Paulsson's English had serious shortcomings. Maybe he was good at Chinese or Ukrainian or something else that was valuable to the security of the realm.

"What did they want?"

"They asked things I really didn't get. That's why I bothered you like this. First they wanted to see a list of the suspects."

"So?"

"To tell you the truth, I don't have a list like that. Maybe you do?"

Martin Beck shook his head.

"Of course, I didn't say that," Paulsson said cunningly. "But then they asked me something I didn't get at all."

"What was that?"

"Well, as I understood it, but it has to be wrong, they wanted to know which people from the overseas provinces were suspected. The overseas provinces . . . But they said it several times in different languages."

"You understood correctly," Martin Beck said kindly. "The Portuguese claim that their colonies in Africa and other places have an equal status with the provinces in Portugal itself. Apparently they meant people—above all political refugees—from places like Angola, Mozambique, Macao, Cape Verde Islands, Guinea and so on."

Paulsson's face suddenly lit up.

"Well I'll be—!" he said. "Then I did hear right after all."

"What did you tell them?"

"Nothing definite. They seemed pretty disappointed."

Well, that was easy to imagine.

"Are they planning to stay here?"

"No," Paulsson said. "They're going on up to Stockholm. To talk to their embassy. By the way, I'm flying up there tomorrow, too. Have to report. And study the archives."

He yawned and said, "Better go to bed. It's been a tough week. Thanks for the help."

"With what?"

"These . . . overseas things."

Paulsson got up, put on his jacket and buttoned all the buttons with great care.

"Bye," he said.

"Good night."

In the doorway he turned around and said ominously, "I think this is going to take years."

Martin Beck sat still for two minutes. Then he grinned to himself, took off the rest of his clothes and went into the bathroom.

He stood under a cold shower for a long time, wrapped the bath towel around himself and returned to his place by the window.

It was quiet and dark outside. All activity seemed to have ceased, both in the harbor and at the railroad station.

A police car rolled slowly past. Most of the cab drivers had given up and driven home.

Martin Beck stood gazing out into the silent summer night. It was still warm, but he felt cool and fresh after the shower.

After a while he felt it was time to go to bed. Sooner or later it had to happen, after all, even if sleep still seemed far away.

He frowned at his pyjamas, which were lying on his pillow. They looked pleasant now, but would inevitably be sweaty and cling to his body when he awoke.

He put them in the closet. Folded the blanket neatly and put it away under the bed. Hung out the big towel on the drying rack in the bathroom.

Then he lay on his back in the bed, folded the sheet almost down to his waist and clasped his hands behind his head. He lay watching the ceiling, where the reflection from the reading lamp threw indistinct shadows.

He was thinking, but with neither precision nor concentration.

After he'd lain like that for fifteen or maybe twenty minutes there were more taps on the door. Very light this time, too.

Good God! he thought. Could he really stand more dribble about espionage and secret agents? Naturally it would be easiest to pretend to be asleep. Or was that neglect of duty?

"Okay, come in," he said with a sense of doom.

The door was opened cautiously, and Åsa Torell came into the room, dressed in slippers and a short white nylon robe, tied with a sash around her waist.

"You weren't sleeping, were you?"

"No," Martin Beck said.

After a moment he added foolishly, "You weren't, either?"

She smiled and shook her head. Her short dark hair shone.

"No," she said. "I just got in. I've scarcely had time to take a shower."

"I heard you had your hands full today."

She nodded.

"Yeah. Darn it. We've hardly eaten today. Just a couple of sandwiches."

"Sit down."

"Thanks. You're not too tired?"

"You don't get tired from doing nothing."

She still hesitated, with one hand on the doorknob.

"I'll just get my cigarettes," she said. "My room isn't more than two doors away."

She left the door ajar. He still lay with his hands behind his head and waited.

After twenty seconds she was back, closed the door soundlessly and padded over to the chair where Paulsson had been in agony about an hour before. She kicked off her slippers and drew her legs under her. She lit a cigarette and inhaled deeply several times.

"Oh, wow!" she said. "It's really been a helluva day."

"Are you beginning to have second thoughts about being a policewoman?"

"Yes and no. You see so much misery that you only heard about before."

She looked thoughtfully at her cigarette and continued, "But sometimes you do have the feeling you're doing a little good, too."

"Yes," he said, "once in a while."

"Did you have a bad day?"

"Yes, very. Nothing new or constructive. But it's like that a lot."

She nodded.

"Do you have any ideas?" he said.

"Huh-uh. How could I have, really? Except to say Palmgren was a bastard. A lot of people must have had good reason to hate him. What I mean is that maybe it doesn't have to be so complicated as some people seem to think. Revenge. Pure and simple."

"Yes, I've thought about that, too."

She fell silent.

When the cigarette was finished she lit another. She smoked Danish cigarettes—Cecil, in a green, white and red pack.

Martin Beck turned his head and looked at her feet, which were thin and gracefully arched, with long, straight toes.

Then he raised his eyes to her face. She looked preoccupied, and her eyes had a faraway look.

He continued to watch her. After a while she relaxed, lifted her head slightly and looked straight into his eyes.

Hers were big and brown and serious.

A moment ago she'd been preoccupied; now, suddenly, she was intensely present.

They went on looking at each other.

She put out her cigarette, and this time she didn't light another.

She moistened her lips and bit the end of her tongue. Her teeth were white, but slightly uneven. Her eyebrows thick and dark.

"Well?" he said.

She nodded slowly and said very quietly, "Well, sooner or later. Why not now?"

She got up and sat down on the edge of the bed.

She didn't move for a while. They still looked into each other's eyes.

Martin Beck freed his left arm. His hand brushed against her slim fingers. He tugged lightly at her sash.

"There's no hurry," he said.

She looked deep into his eyes and said, "Yours are gray. Actually."

"And yours are brown."

Åsa Torell smiled without parting her lips. Then she raised her right hand, slowly undid the knot, half stood up and let the robe fall to the floor.

He pushed the sheet away, and she sat down again, her right leg raised so that her foot rested against the left side of his chest.

"Have you thought about this before?" she said.

"Yes. Have you?"

"Sometimes. Once in a while during the past year."

They exchanged a few more words.

"Has it been a long time?"

"Terribly long. Not since—"

She broke off and said, "What about you?"

"Same here."

"You're good," she said.

"You are, too."

It was true. Åsa Torell was good, and he'd known it for a long time.

She was small but firm. Her breasts were small but the nipples were large, erect and dark brown. The skin over her midriff and abdomen was smooth and supple and the copious hair between her legs curly and almost coal black.

Her hand was lying spread out on his left leg and slid slowly upward. Her fingers were thin but long, strong and purposeful.

She was very open.

After a moment he moved his hands to her shoulders. She

changed position and lay on top of him—soft, deep and wide open and soon filled with him.

She panted in short, quick breaths against his shoulder and soon afterward against his mouth.

When she was lying on her back she felt very solid and secure, and her legs were strong around his back and hips.

When she left it had been light for a couple of hours.

She put on her robe and slippers and said, "Bye and thanks."

"Same to you."

Thus it had happened, and would never happen again. Or maybe it would.

He didn't know.

He did know, however, that he was old enough to be her father, even if that place hadn't been occupied for exactly twenty-seven years.

Martin Beck reflected that Wednesday hadn't ended so badly, despite everything. Or could it be that Thursday had begun well?

Then he fell asleep.

They saw each other again several hours later, at the police station. In passing, Martin Beck said, "Who booked you the room at the Savoy?"

"I did. But Lennart told me to do it."

Martin Beck smiled to himself.

Kollberg, of course. The schemer. Well, this time, anyway, he would never know for certain whether he'd been successful or not.

25.

At nine o'clock on Thursday morning the situation in the tracking center was at a standstill. Martin Beck and Månsson were sitting across from each other at the large desk. Neither of them said anything. Martin Beck was smoking, and Månsson wasn't doing anything. He'd used up his toothpicks.

At twelve minutes after nine, Benny Skacke made the first active contribution of the day by coming into the room with an enormously long strip of teletype in his hand. He stopped inside the door and started skimming through it.

"What's that?" Martin Beck asked.

"The list from Copenhagen," Månsson said dully. "They send out one like that every day. Missing persons, cars that've disappeared, things they've found, anything like that."

"A whole lot of girls who've run away," Skacke said. "Nine of them, no, ten."

"Well, it's that time of year," Månsson said.

"Lisbeth Møller, twelve years old," Skacke mumbled. "Missing from her home since Monday, drug addict. And she's twelve years old?"

"Sometimes they turn up here," Månsson explained. "Most of the time they don't, of course."

"Stolen cars," Skacke said. "A Swedish passport, issued to Sven Olof Gustafsson, Svedala, fifty-six years old. Confiscated at a prostitute's place in Nyhavn. His billfold, too."

"Drunken pig," said Månsson laconically.

"A steam shovel from a tunnel construction site. How can anybody swipe a steam shovel?"

"It's been done," Martin Beck said.

"Drunken pig," said Månsson. "Is there anything under guns? They usually come toward the end."

Skacke scanned down the listing.

"Sure," he said. "Several of them. A Swedish army pistol, 9mm, Husqvarna, has to be old. A Beretta Jaguar . . . Box for an Arminius .22, five boxes of 7.65 mm ammunition . . ."

"Stop there," Månsson said.

"Yes, what was that about a box?" Martin Beck said.

Skacke went back up the list.

"A box originally for an Arminius .22," he said.

"Found where?"

"Floated ashore on the beach between Dragør and Kastrup. Found by a private individual and left with the police in Dragør. Last Tuesday."

"Isn't Arminius .22 on our list?" Martin Beck said.

"It sure is."

Said Månsson, suddenly alert, his hand already on the telephone receiver.

"Yeah, sure," Skacke said. "The box. The box on the bicycle . . ."

Månsson energetically harassed the Copenhagen police switchboard. It took a moment before he was connected with Mogensen.

Mogensen had never heard of the box.

"No, I appreciate that you can't keep track of all that junk," Månsson said patiently. "But it *is* on your own damn list. Wait a second . . ."

He looked at Skacke and said, "What number is it on the list?"

"Thirty-eight."

"Thirty-eight. Three, eight," Månsson said into the receiver. "Yes, it could be important for us . . ."

He listened a minute. Then he said, "By the way, do you know anything more about Aero-fragt and Ole Hoff-Jensen?"

Pause.

"Yes, that'd be fine," Månsson said and hung up.

He looked at the other two.

"They're going to check it out and then call us back."

"When?" Martin Beck asked.

"Morgensen is usually pretty fast," Månsson said and returned to his reflections.

The call from Copenhagen came in less than an hour.

Månsson mostly listened. He looked happier and happier.

"Fantastic," he said finally.

"Well?" said Martin Beck.

"Well, the box was with their Technical Squad. At first the guy in Dragør was going to throw it away, but yesterday he put it in a plastic bag and sent it to Copenhagen. We'll get it on the hydrofoil that leaves the Nyhavn canal at eleven."

He glanced at his watch and said to Skacke, "See that a patrol car meets the boat."

"What did he know about Hoff-Jensen?" Martin Beck asked.

"Most everything. Evidently, he's well-known over there. A shady character. But untouchable. He doesn't make his crooked deals in Denmark. Everything he does there is legal."

"Palmgren's crooked deals, in other words."

"Right. And apparently they're big stuff. Mogensen said that both Palmgren's and Hoff-Jensen's names had figured in connection with illegal traffic in weapons and airplanes to countries that are covered by weapon embargoes. He knows that from Interpol. But they can't do anything, either."

"Or maybe don't want to," Martin Beck said.

"Quite likely," Månsson said.

He yawned.

They waited. There wasn't much else to do.

At ten to twelve the box lay on the desk.

They slipped it out of the plastic wrapper. Experience had taught them to handle such things with great care, even though this one had already received rough treatment and clearly had gone through many hands.

Martin Beck lifted the lid, put his fist to his chin and examined the molded sections for the revolver and the extra butt.

"Yes," he said, "you're probably right."

Månsson nodded. He opened and closed the lid several times.

"Opens pretty easily," he said.

They turned the box over and examined it from all angles. It was dry now and reasonably well preserved.

"Can't have been in the water too long," Martin Beck said.

"Five days," Månsson said.

"Here," Martin Beck said, "we've got something here."

He ran his finger over the bottom of the cardboard box, which had obviously been covered with paper. It had been soaked off by now, however, and was completely gone in places.

"Yes," said Månsson. "There was something written on the paper. Probably with a ballpoint pen. Wait a second."

He took a magnifying glass out of one of his desk drawers and handed it to Martin Beck.

"Hmm," Martin Beck said. "The imprint is visible. A 'B' and an 'S.' They show up fairly clearly. Maybe something else."

"Okay," said Månsson, "we have people who work with things a bit more precise than my old magnifying glass. I'll have them take a look at it."

"This revolver is, or rather was, a target weapon," Martin Beck said.

"Yes, I've gone into that. An unusual make, too."

Månsson drummed with his fingers on the table.

"Okay, we'll leave this with the Technical Squad," he said. "We'll have Skacke canvass the rifle clubs. And we'll go out and eat lunch. Not a bad division of labor, uh?"

"Sounds good," Martin Beck said.

"I can show you Malmö at the same time. Have you been in the bar at Översten?"

"No."

"Well, it's about time."

The Restaurant Översten is on the twenty-sixth floor of the Crown Prince Building. Viewing the city from its bar windows far surpassed Martin Beck's memories of similar experiences.

The whole city spread out below them, as if seen from an airplane. They gazed over Öresund, Saltholm and the Danish coast. To the north, Landskrona, Ven and even Helsingborg were visible in the startlingly clear air.

A blond bartender in a blue jacket served them minute steaks and cold Amstel. Månsson ate voraciously, then took all the toothpicks from the condiment rack, stuck one into his mouth and the rest into his pocket.

"Hmm," he said. "As far as I can see, it all fits together."

Martin Beck, who'd been more interested in the view than the food, reluctantly tore his eyes from the panorama.

"Yes," he said, "it looks like it. Maybe you were right all along. Although you were guessing."

"Guessing and guessing," Månsson said.

"Now we just have to guess where he is, too."

"Here somewhere," said Månsson with a leisurely gesture over his city. "But who could have hated Palmgren that much?"

"Thousands of people," said Martin Beck. "Palmgren and his cronies were ruthless. They crushed everyone and everything around them. For example, he ran a whole lot of different companies for longer or shorter periods of time. As long as they were profitable. Then when the profits weren't fat enough, they were simply closed down, and many of the people who worked there were just laid off without a cent. How many people do you suppose have been ruined just by 'legal' loan sharks like Broberg?"

Månsson said nothing.

"But I think you're right," Martin Beck said. "The guy has to be here, provided he hasn't left town."

"Or left town and come back," Månsson said.

"Maybe. Then it must have been unpremeditated. Nobody who'd planned a murder, and above all no hired killer, would ride up on a bicycle one summer evening with a target practice gun in a box on the package rack. Bigger than a shoe box, too."

The tall, blond bartender was standing beside their table.

"Telephone call for you, Inspector," he said to Månsson. "Will there be coffee?"

"It's the guy from the lab," Månsson said. "Coffee? Yes, please. Two calypsos."

Martin Beck caught himself thinking about the fact that Månsson was known at the restaurant. Would *he* be recognized at any restaurant in Stockholm? Maybe, from television and pictures in the newspapers. Then he thought about all the people who'd been mistreated and made to pay through the nose in Palmgren's scandalously bad apartment houses. He should really get a list of the tenants over the last few years.

"Well," Månsson said, "there had been a name on the bottom of the cardboard box. 'B' and 'S,' we could see that ourselves. The rest was hard to decipher. The guy at the lab found that, too. But he claims that there used to be a name there, probably the owner's."

"And what did he make it out to be?"

"B. Svensson."

The man who operated the target range looked thoughtfully at Benny Skacke. Then he said, "Arminius .22? Yeah, there's probably two or three guys around here who use that kind. I can't tell you right off who they are.

"Somebody who was here last Wednesday? I can't possibly keep track of everybody who shoots here. But ask the guy who's standing over there. He's been banging away there for ten days—ever since the beginning of vacation."

As Skacke walked over to the range, the man added, "Ask him how he can afford to buy so much ammunition, too."

The marksman had finished one round, reckoned his points and was in the process of pasting up black and white paper when Skacke approached him.

"Arminius .22?" he said. "Yeah. I know one at least. But he hasn't been here since the middle of last week. Good shot, too. If he'd use one like this instead . . ."

The man weighed his Beretta Jetfire automatic in his hand.

"Do you know his name?"

"Bertil something or other . . . Olsson or Svensson, I don't really know. But he works at Kockum's."

"Are you sure of that?"

"Yes. Some real lousy job. A janitor, I think."

"Thanks," Skacke said. "By the way, how can you afford to shoot up so much ammunition?"

"This is the only hobby I've got," the man said and shoved a new magazine into the pistol.

At the manager's cabin he was given a slip of paper with three names on it.

"These are the only Arminius owners I can think of."

Skacke walked back to the police car. Before starting the engine he looked at the list:

Tommy Lind, Kenneth Axelsson, Bertil Svensson

At the police station Månsson put a question to Martin Beck: "What are we going to do with the Broberg and Hansson duo?"

"Send them back to Stockholm. That is, if Åsa's done with her work."

"Yes, I'm done with what I came for," Åsa Torell said and looked at him with clear brown eyes.

The investigation now became routine. Two hours after they'd made inquiries at the police station in Handen the teletype machine spewed out the list of tenants in Palmgren's apartment houses.

It was in alphabetical order, and Martin Beck promptly put his finger on the right line:

Svensson, Bertil Olof Emanuel, lease terminated September 15, 1968.

"In other words, he got evicted," Månsson said.

Martin Beck located the number of Broberg's office in Stockholm. He dialed it, and a woman, who had to be Broberg's secretary, answered. Just in case, he asked, "Is this Mrs. Moberg?"

"Yes."

He told her who he was.

"Well, what can I do for you?" she asked.

"Mrs. Moberg, do you know if Mr. Palmgren closed down or discontinued any of his operations recently?"

"Well, that depends on what you mean by recently. Two years ago he closed down a factory that he had in Solna, if that's what you mean."

"What kind of factory?" Martin Beck asked.

"It was a rather small precision tool factory that made special machine parts. Springs and things like that, I think."

"Why was it closed down?"

"It was running at a loss. The companies that bought the parts must have built their machines or bought new ones, I don't really know. Anyway, there was no market for the products and instead of reorganizing production, they stopped manufacturing and sold the factory."

"And that happened two years ago?"

"Yes. In the fall of '67. I think he had a similar company that was closed down several years earlier, but that was before my time. I know about the other one because Mr. Broberg handled the liquidation of the firm."

"What happened to the employees?"

"They were given notice," Sara Moberg said.

"How many employees were involved?"

"I don't remember. But the papers are here somewhere. I can get them if you want."

"That'd be kind of you. I'd like to have the names of the employees."

"Just a minute," she said.

Martin Beck waited. Several minutes passed before she returned.

"Sorry," she said. "I didn't know exactly where the papers were. Should I read off the names?"

"How many are there?" Martin Beck asked.

"Twenty-eight."

"Did all of them have to quit? Couldn't they be transferred to one of the other companies?"

"No. They were all laid off. Except for one. He was a foreman and became a company janitor, but he quit after six months. Must have found a better job."

Martin Beck had found paper and pencil.

"Okay," he said. "Please read the names now."

He wrote while she read, but when she reached the ninth name, he raised the pencil and said, "Stop. Give me that last one again."

"Bertil Svensson, office worker."

"Is there anything more about him?"

"No, only that."

"Thanks, that's enough," Martin Beck said. "Good-bye and thanks for the help."

He went to see Månsson immediately.

"Here's the name again," he said. "Bertil Svensson. Laid off from a Palmgren company two years ago. He's an office worker."

Månsson turned the toothpick around with his tongue.

"No," he said. "A laborer. I talked to the personnel office at Kockum's."

"Did you get his address?" Martin Beck asked.

"Yes. He lives on Vattenverksvägen."

Martin Beck raised his eyebrows enquiringly.

"In Kirseberg."

Martin Beck shook his head.

"In Öster."

Martin Beck shrugged.

"Hmmph, Stockholmers," Månsson said. "Well, that's where he lives, anyway. But he's on vacation now. Started working at Kockum's in January of this year. Thirty-seven years old. He's divorced, apparently. His wife . . ."

Månsson dug around in his papers and pulled out a slip of paper with some notes scribbled on it.

". . . His wife lives in Stockholm. The accounts department deducts her alimony from his paycheck every month and sends it to Mrs. Eva Svensson, 23 Norrtullsgatan in Stockholm."

"Hmm," Martin Beck said. "If he's on vacation maybe he isn't in town."

"We'll have to see," Månsson said. "Maybe we ought to have a talk with his wife somehow. You think Kollberg . . . ?"

Martin Beck looked at his watch. Nearly five-thirty. Kollberg was probably on his way home right now to Gun and Bodil.

"Okay," he said. "Tomorrow."

26.

Lennart Kollberg's voice was full of foreboding when Martin Beck called him on Friday morning.

"Just don't tell me it has anything to do with that Palmgren case again," he said.

Martin Beck cleared his throat.

"I'm sorry, Lennart, but I have to ask you for a little help," he said. "I suppose you've got a lot of things . . ."

"A lot of things," Kollberg broke in irritatedly. "I'm short of people—like you, for example, and everybody else who ought to be here. I'm swamped with work. It's the same in town. Not even Rönn and Melander are there."

"I understand, Lennart," Martin Beck said softly. "But things have come up that put the case in a new light. You have to get some information on a man who may be the one who shot Palmgren. If worst comes to worst you could ask Gunvald . . ."

"Larsson! If the Home Secretary got down on his knees and asked him, he wouldn't be able to persuade him to work on the Palmgren case. He's had a belly full."

Kollberg quietened down and after a short pause he sighed and said, "So who is this guy?"

"Probably the same person we could've picked up at Haga terminal a week ago, if we hadn't screwed up. His name is Bertil Svensson . . ."

"Same as about ten thousand people in this country," Kollberg said caustically.

"Probably," Martin Beck said gently. "But we do know this about Bertil Svensson: he worked for a Palmgren company out in Solna, a fairly small precision tool factory, which was closed down in the fall of '67. He lived in one of Palmgren's apartment houses, but was evicted about a year ago. He's a member of a rifle club and, according to witnesses, used to use a gun that could well be the same model as the one Palmgren was murdered with. He got a divorce last fall, and his wife and two children still live in Stockholm. He lives in Malmö and works at Kockum's."

"Hmm," Kollberg said.

"His name is Bertil Olof Emanuel Svensson, born in the parish of Sofia in Stockholm, on May 6, 1932."

"Why don't you arrest him if he lives in Malmö?" Kollberg asked.

"We will, but first we want to find out a little more about him. We thought you could take care of that."

Kollberg sighed resignedly.

"Okay, what do you want me to do?" he said.

"He isn't in the criminal records, but find out if he's ever been picked up. Also find out if the social welfare agencies have had anything to do with him. Ask at the real estate office why he was evicted. And, last but not least, talk to his wife."

"Do you know where she is or shall I hunt for her, too? It only takes several weeks to find the right Mrs. Svensson."

"She lives at 23 Norrtullsgatan. Don't forget to ask her when she saw her husband last. I don't know what kind of a relationship they have, but it's possible he called or went to see her last Thursday. Can you do this as soon as possible?"

"It'll take all day," Kollberg complained. "But I don't really have any choice. I'll call when I'm through."

Kollberg hung up and stared gloomily at his desk, where maps, folders and reports lay every which way. Then he sighed, dug out the telephone directory and started calling.

A couple of hours later he got up, grabbed his jacket, shut his note pad and put it in his pocket. Then went down to the car.

As he drove toward Norrtullsgatan, he went over what he'd learned from his industrious session on the telephone.

Bertil Olof Emanuel Svensson hadn't come to the notice of the police until October '67. Then he'd been taken to Bollmora police station on a charge of intoxication. He'd been picked up in the entrance to the building where he lived and kept in jail for the night. From then until July '68, he'd been taken to the same police station five more times—once on another intoxication charge and four times for causing domestic disturbance, as it's called. That was all. There weren't any entries after July.

The Temperance Board had also been involved. On several occasions they'd been called to his home, by the landlord and by neighbors who claimed they were being disturbed by Svensson's drunken behavior. He'd been under supervision, but besides the two times he'd been held by the police, there'd been no reason to take action against him.

He hadn't been on any drunk and disorderly charges before October '67, and didn't figure in the Temperance Board's records before that date either. He'd got off each time with warnings.

The Svensson family had even come to the attention of the Bureau of Child Welfare. Complaints had been made by tenants in the same building concerning the treatment of the children.

As far as Kollberg could gather, the same neighbor was behind all the complaints to the various officials.

The children, who were then seven and five years old, were considered to have been left "to fend for themselves." They were poorly dressed, and the person who complained claimed he'd heard children screaming in the Svensson family's apartment. The Bureau of Child Welfare had made investigations, first in December '67, then again in May '68. They'd made several house calls, but hadn't found any signs of abuse. The place was not well taken care of, the mother seemed slovenly, the father was unemployed, and the family's finances were in bad shape. Nothing indicated, however, that the children were ill-treated. The older one got along well in school, was healthy and of normal intelligence, though somewhat shy and reserved. The younger child was at home with the mother during the day, but was sometimes left with a neighbor when the mother did some temporary job. The neighbor, who had three children of her own, described the child as lively, receptive and sociable and said she'd never shown any sign of poor health. In November of '68 the parents' legal separation had gone into effect. The children were still under supervision.

The Unemployment Office had paid out insurance to the family during the period from October '67 to April '68. The man had enrolled for job training and during the fall of '68 had gone through a basic course in mechanics at the Vocational Training Board school. In January of '69—the present year—Svensson had found employment as a laborer at Kockum's machine works in Malmö, where he'd then moved.

The Department of Public Health had made noise measurements on the Svensson's apartment in connection with the request for eviction submitted by the real estate agency. The noise—in the form of children screaming, people walking across the floor and water running—was considered above the acceptable norm.

That verdict applied just as well to the entire housing project, but no one seemed to take that into consideration.

In the month of June 1968 the Rent Control Commission reached a decision about the real estate agency's right to terminate the Svenssons' lease. The Svensson family had been forced to leave the apartment on September 1. No alternative housing had been found for them.

Kollberg had talked to the monster at the real estate agency. She was very sorry that they'd had to go as far as evicting the family, but there'd been too many complaints against them. Finally she said, "I think it was best for them, too. They didn't fit here."

"In what way?" Kollberg asked.

"We have a different class of tenants, if you know what I mean. We really aren't used to having, almost every single day, to call in the Temperance Board, the police, the Bureau of Child Welfare and God knows what all . . ."

"Then you reported the Svensson family to the authorities, and not the neighbors?" Kollberg had asked.

"Certainly. When you hear that things are not as they should be, it's your duty to investigate. One of the neighbors was very co-operative, of course."

He'd ended the conversation there, feeling almost sick with helplessness and disgust.

Did it really have to be this way? Yes, obviously it did.

Kollberg parked the car on Norrtullsgatan, but didn't get out immediately. He took out his notebook and pencil. With the help of his notes, he made the following list:

1967	*Sept.*	*Laid off*
	Oct.	*Intoxication (Bollmora Police Station)*
	Nov.	*Temperance Board*
	Dec.	*Domestic disturbance. Bureau of Child Welfare*
1968	*Jan.*	*Domestic disturbance (Bollm. P.)*
	Feb.	*Temperance Board*
	March	*Intoxication (Bollm. P.)*

April	Domestic disturbance (Bollm. P.). Temperance Board
May	Bureau of Child Welfare
June	Rent Control Commission's ruling on termination of lease
July	Decision on eviction. Domestic disturbance (Bollm. P.)
Aug.	—
Sept.	Evicted
Oct.	—
Nov.	Separation
Dec.	—
1969 Jan.	Moves to Malmö. Kockum's
July	Shoots V. Palmgren?

He studied what he'd written for a moment and reflected that this dismal chart almost cried out for a fitting title:

It never rains but it pours.

27.

Norrtullsgatan 23 was a seedy old building. After the stifling heat outside, it was surprisingly cool in the stairwell. It felt as though the damp chill of winter lurked in the walls under the flaking plaster.

Mrs. Svensson lived one flight up, and the door with her name, EVA SVENSSON, appeared to be a kitchen entrance.

Kollberg pounded. After a minute he heard steps from within and the rattle of a safety chain being unhooked. The door was opened slightly. Kollberg displayed his identification in the crack of the door. He couldn't see the person who answered, but heard a deep sigh before the door was opened.

Kollberg had guessed right; he stepped straight into a large kitchen. The woman who shut the door behind him was small and thin and had sharp, sad features. Her straggly hair had probably been dyed white some time ago, for the ends were almost white, with darker streaks higher up, changing to brown an inch from her scalp. She was dressed in a striped housecoat of sleazy cotton material with large, dark perspiration stains under the arms. The smell told Kollberg that this wasn't the first time she'd sweated in that coat since it had last been washed. She was bare-legged; her feet were stuck into a pair of terrycloth slippers of a nondescript color. Kollberg knew that she was twenty-nine, but would have guessed at least thirty-five.

"The police," she said hesitantly. "What's happened now? If you're looking for Bertil he isn't here."

"No," Kollberg said, "I know. I only want to talk to you for a while, if that's all right. May I come in?"

The woman nodded and walked over to the kitchen table, which was by the window. An open magazine and a half-eaten sandwich lay on a flowered plastic tablecloth, and a filter cigarette went on smoking on a blue-flowered saucer, which was already full of filter-tipped butts. Around the table were three chairs. She sat down and picked up the cigarette from the saucer, pointing to the chair across from herself.

"Sit down," she said.

Kollberg sat down and glanced out the window at a dreary back yard, relieved only by a carpet-beating rack and garbage cans.

"What do you want to talk about?" Eva Svensson asked, pertly. "You can't stay too long, because I have to pick up Tomas at the playground soon."

"Tomas," Kollberg said, "is the youngest."

"Yes. He's six. I leave him in the playground behind the School of Economics while I go shopping and do the cleaning."

Kollberg looked around the kitchen.

"You have another one, don't you?" he said.

"Yes, Ursula. She's at camp. On Children's Island."

"How long have you lived here?"

"Since last April," she said and sucked on the cigarette until only the filter remained. "But I'll only be allowed to stay over the summer. The old lady doesn't like the kids. Damned if I know where to go then."

"Are you working now?" Kollberg asked.

The woman threw the smoldering filter into the saucer.

"Yes. I work for the old lady we live with. That is, I get to live here in return for cleaning and cooking and shopping and washing and waiting on her. She's old and can't go down the steps alone, so I have to help her when she goes out. And other things."

Kollberg nodded toward a door across the room from the outer door.

"Is that where you live?"

"Yeah," the woman said curtly. "We live there."

Kollberg got up and opened the door. The room was approximately twelve feet by sixteen. The window faced the dismal yard. Beds lined two of the walls. Underneath one of them was a low bed that could be pulled out. A chest of drawers, two chairs, a rickety little table and a rag rug completed the furnishings.

"It's not too big," Eva Svensson said from behind him. "But we're allowed to be in the kitchen as much as we want, and the kids can play in the yard."

Kollberg returned to the kitchen table. He looked at the woman, who was now doodling with her index finger on the plastic tablecloth and said, "I'd like you to tell me how it's been for you and your husband during the last few years. I know that you're divorced or separated, but how was it before that? He was unemployed a rather long time, wasn't he?"

"Yes, he got fired almost two years ago. Not because he'd done anything. Everybody got fired because they shut down the company. It must have been losing money. Then he couldn't find a job; there just weren't any. No real job, I mean. He had a pretty good one before that. He was an office worker, but didn't have the proper education, and all the jobs he applied for went to someone who was better qualified."

Kollberg nodded.

"How long was he with this company before it went out of business?"

"Twelve years. And before that he was with another company

with the same boss. Palmgren. Well, maybe he wasn't the boss, but he owned the company. Bertil worked in the warehouse there, and later on he was a delivery boy, but then he was moved to the office of this company that was shut down. The other one must have been shut down, too."

"How long were you married?"

"We got married at Whitsuntide in 1959."

She took a bite from the half-eaten sandwich, looked at it, stood up and walked over to the counter and threw it into the sink.

"So we were married for eight and a half years," she said.

"When did you move out to Bollmora?" Kollberg asked.

The woman remained standing by the sink, picking her teeth with the nail of her little finger.

"In the fall of '67. We lived in a building on Västmannagatan before that. It was company housing, because Mr. Palmgren owned that building, too. Then he was going to repair the building and make offices out of the apartments, I think, and then we got to move into that new building he'd built. It looked a lot nicer, of course, but it was so far outside of town, and then the rent was really high. When Bertil got fired I thought we'd have to move, but we didn't have to. At any rate, not until later, and that was because of other things."

"What kind of other things?" asked Kollberg.

"Well, like Bertil drank," she said vaguely. "And the neighbor under us complained because he thought we made too much noise. But we didn't make any more noise than the other people in the building. Sound traveled really well, and you could hear children screaming and dogs barking and record players blaring, even if it was several floors below. We thought they had a piano above us until we learned that the piano was three stories up. And the kids couldn't play inside. Anyway, we were evicted last fall."

The sun had begun to shine into the kitchen, and Kollberg took out his handkerchief and wiped his forehead.

"Did he drink a lot?" he asked.

"Yeah, sometimes."

"What was he like when he was drinking? Aggressive?"

She didn't answer immediately. She walked back and sat down.

"He got angry sometimes. Because he'd lost his job and at the system and things like that. I got pretty tired of hearing that every time he'd had a couple drinks."

"It's claimed there were fights in the apartment sometimes," Kollberg said. "What happened then?"

"Oh, they weren't fights, exactly. We quarreled sometimes, and once the kids woke up and started playing in the middle of the night when we were asleep, and then the patrolmen came. Of course, we might have talked pretty loud once in a while, but we didn't fight or anything like that."

Kollberg nodded.

"Didn't you turn to the Tenants' Association when you were threatened with eviction?" he asked.

She shook her head.

"No, we didn't belong to anything like that. There wasn't anything to do, anyway, so we had to move."

"Where did you live after that?"

"I got hold of a one-room apartment for us to sublet. I lived there until I moved here, but Bertil had to go to a bachelor's hotel when we got divorced. Now he lives in Malmö."

"Hmm," Kollberg said. "When did you see him last?"

Eva Svensson drew her fingers through her hair at the back of her head, reflected a moment and said, "Last Thursday, I think it was. He came here real suddenly, but I made him leave after about an hour, because I had to work. He was on vacation, he said, and was going to be in Stockholm for a few days. I even got a little money from him."

"You haven't heard from him since then?"

"No. He must've gone back to Malmö after that, I suppose. I've seen nothing of him, anyway."

She turned around and glanced at the alarm clock standing on the refrigerator.

"I have to go get Tomas now," she said. "They don't like it if you leave the kids there too long."

She got up and went into her room, but left the door open.

"Why did you get divorced?" Kollberg said, standing up.

"We were tired of each other. Everything was such a mess. We did nothing but quarrel toward the end. And Bertil was home all the time, grumbling and feeling sorry for himself. I couldn't stand to look at him finally."

She came out into the kitchen. She'd combed her hair and put on sandals.

"I really have to go now," she said.

"Just one more question," said Kollberg. "Did your husband know the big boss, Mr. Palmgren?"

"Oh no, I don't even think he'd ever seen him," she said. "Palmgren sat up in an office and managed everything. I don't think he ever went to his companies. They were run by other bosses, sort of managers."

She took a string bag that was hanging on a hook by the stove and opened the kitchen door. Kollberg held the door open and let her walk out into the hall in front of him. Then he closed the door and said, "What newspapers and magazines do you read?"

"*Expressen* sometimes. Especially on Sunday. And *Hennes* and *Hela Världen* every week. Magazines are so expensive, I think. Why'd you ask?"

"I just wondered," Kollberg said.

They parted outside of the door, and he watched her walk away toward Odenplan, small and thin in her sleazy dress.

It was afternoon by the time Kollberg called Malmö to announce the results of his inquiries. During the last half an hour, Martin Beck had been pacing back and forth in the corridor, waiting impatiently for the call, and when it finally came he grabbed the receiver before the first signal had died away.

He started the tape recorder, which was hooked up to the telephone, and let Kollberg talk without interrupting him or making any comments. When Kollberg had finished Martin Beck said, "Good work, Lennart. Now I probably won't have to bother you any more."

"Okay," Kollberg said. "It looks like you've found the right guy. Now I have to go back to my work, but let me hear from you—to know how it went. Say 'hi' to the people who deserve it. Bye."

Martin Beck took the tape recorder with him to Månsson's room. They listened through the tape together.

"What do you think?" Martin Beck asked.

"Well," said Månsson, "the motive's there. First laid off after more than twelve years with Palmgren's company, then evicted by the same Palmgren and finally divorced into the bargain. And then he had to move away from Stockholm to get a job, a job that's socially and economically worse than the one he had before. All because of Palmgren."

Martin Beck nodded and Månsson continued, "Furthermore, he was in Stockholm last Thursday. I never really did understand why they didn't have time to pick him up at Haga terminal. If they'd just pulled that off, we would've had him when Palmgren passed away. It makes you mad to think about it."

"I know why they didn't make it," Martin Beck said, "but I'll tell you about it some other time. You'll be even madder when you hear it."

"Okay, save it," Månsson said.

Martin Beck lit a cigarette and sat in silence for a while.

Then he said, "There's something rotten about this eviction. It was apparently the real estate agency that put the various authorities onto him."

"With the help of a cooperative neighbor, yes."

"Who was no doubt also employed by Palmgren or Broberg or both. It's a fact that Palmgren wanted him out of the apartment when he didn't employ him any longer. In Stockholm an apartment like that is worth big money. Dirty money."

"You mean to say that Palmgren told his employees in the realty company to find a pretext for evicting him," Månsson said.

"Yeah. I'm convinced of it. Through Broberg, of course. And Bertil Svensson must've understood the connection himself. It's hardly surprising he hated Palmgren."

Månsson scratched the back of his head and pulled a face.

"No, that's true," he said. "But to go so far as to shoot him . . ."

"You have to remember that Svensson had been having a rough time for quite some time. When he began to realize that it wasn't just his own hard luck, but that he was being treated unjustly by one man or perhaps by a social group, his hate must have become an obsession. Practically everything was taken away from him bit by bit."

"And Palmgren represented just that social group," said Månsson and nodded.

Martin Beck stood up and said, "I think the safest thing is to send somebody out who can keep an eye on him for the time being, so we don't miss him again. Somebody who doesn't chase after little piggies on the job."

Månsson stared at him in amazement.

28.

The man whose name was Bertil Svensson lived in Kirsebergsstaden, close to the eastern city limit. The area is also called Bulltofta Hills or just the Hills, since, compared to the topography of the rest of the city, there are marked differences in elevation.

Living "out in the Hills" had always been looked down upon by the Malmö bourgeoisie, but many Kirseberg residents were proud of their section and enjoyed living there, even though their homes not infrequently lacked modern conveniences or were in general below average, since no one bothered to maintain or repair them. People who ended up in the poorest apartments either weren't wanted in the smarter residential areas or weren't considered to be in need of a higher standard of living. It was no accident that many of the foreign factory workers who'd come to Malmö during recent years lived in this area.

This was a working-class neighborhood, and few Malmö residents of the category that Viktor Palmgren, for example, belonged to, had ever set their foot there or were even aware that the area existed.

It was here that Benny Skacke rode his bicycle on Friday afternoon. He had instructions from Martin Beck to find out if Bertil Svensson was at home, and, if that were the case, to keep watch on him without arousing his suspicion. Skacke also had to communicate with Månsson or Martin Beck once every hour.

If all went well they were planning to arrest Svensson the same night; only a couple details were missing, Martin Beck had said.

According to what the man had told his employer and the rifle club, he should live on Vattenverksvägen, a street that cuts across Kirsebergsstaden from Lundavägen in the west to Simrishamn railroad in the east. From Lundavägen, the street sloped up to a hill, and Skacke preferred to get off his bicycle before he came to the crown. He walked his bicycle past the old, round water tower, which had been converted many years before into a residence. Skacke wondered if the apartments inside looked like pieces of pie. He recalled that he'd read a newspaper article on the scandalous sanitary conditions prevalent in the building, and that it was inhabited almost exclusively by Yugoslavs.

He left his bicycle on Kirseberg Square and hoped it wouldn't be stolen. He'd used black tape to cover the word POLICE on the frame, a cautionary measure he always took when he thought he should remain anonymous.

The building he was going to watch was an old two-story apartment house. He observed it for a moment from the sidewalk opposite. It had nine windows on the street, two on each side of the door and five on the floor above. There were also three attic windows, but the attic didn't seem to be lived in; the windows were thick with dirt and, as far as he could see, had no curtains.

Skacke walked rapidly across the street and opened the door. On the door to the right of the stairs he saw a piece of cardboard with the name B. SVENSSON printed on it with a ballpoint pen.

Skacke went back to the square and found a bench from which he could watch the building. He took out the evening newspaper he'd bought on his way from the police station, opened it to the center spread and pretended to read.

He had to wait only twenty minutes. The door opened, and a man came out on the sidewalk. His appearance fitted the description of the gunman at the Savoy fairly well, though he was shorter than Skacke had imagined. Even his clothes—a dark brown sport coat and lighter brown pants, a beige shirt and a tie with red and brown stripes—seemed to match the description.

Skacke kept his eyes on the man, but took his time. He folded the newspaper, stood up, put it in his pocket and began to follow the man slowly. He turned on a cross street and walked at a fairly brisk pace toward the prison at the bottom of the hill.

Skacke suddenly pitied the man walking ahead of him, wholly ignorant of how close the day was when he would be sent inside the grim walls of that ancient penitentiary. Maybe he was already confident he'd get away with it.

The man turned right by the prison and then left onto Gevaldigergatan, where he stopped beside the fence of the soccer field directly across from the prison walls.

Skacke stopped, too. A match was taking place on the grass field, and Skacke immediately recognized both of the teams— B.K. Flagg in red jerseys and F.K. Balkan in blue. It looked like a lively game was going on, and Skacke had nothing against staying to watch, but the man set off again almost immediately.

They continued out onto Lundavägen, and when they'd passed Dalhem Field the man in brown went into a sandwich shop. Skacke looked sideways through the display window as he walked past and saw the man standing in front of the counter. He waited in a doorway farther down the street. The man came out again after a moment with a box in one hand and a bag in the other and returned the same way he'd come.

Skacke could now afford to keep his distance, since he assumed that the other man was on his way home. As he passed the soccer field Balkan had just scored a goal, and a howl of joy rose in unison from the crowd, which seemed to consist mainly of Balkan supporters. A man with a small child on his shoulders was cheering vociferously, but Skacke didn't understand a word, since the man spoke Yugoslav.

The man he was shadowing went home, as he'd expected.

As Skacke walked past on the sidewalk across the street he could see the man take a can of beer out of the bag.

Skacke took advantage of the moment, went into a phone booth and called the police station. Martin Beck answered.

"Well?"

"He's back home. He went out just now to buy beer and sandwiches."

"Good. Stay there and call if he goes some place."

Skacke went back to his post on the bench. After half an hour he walked to a newsstand in the neighborhood, bought the other evening newspapers and a chocolate bar and returned to the bench.

Now and then he got up and walked up and down the sidewalk, but he didn't dare pass the window too often. It was dark now, and the man inside had turned on the light. He'd taken off his jacket, eaten the sandwiches and drunk two beers, and now he was moving back and forth in the room. Sometimes he sat down at a table by the window.

By ten-twenty Skacke had read the three newspapers several times, eaten four chocolate bars and drunk two bottles of cider; he'd had all he could take and was ready to scream.

Then the light was turned off in the room to the right of the door. Skacke waited five minutes, then called the police station. Neither Månsson nor Martin Beck was there. He called the Savoy. Inspector Beck had gone out. He called Månsson's home. They were there.

"Oh, so you're still out there," Månsson said.

"Of course, I'm still here. Should I have gone home, maybe? Why aren't you coming?"

Skacke sounded as if he were on the verge of tears.

"Oh," said Månsson nonchalantly, "I thought you knew. We're waiting until tomorrow. By the way, what's he doing now?"

Skacke gnashed his teeth.

"He's turned out the light. Probably going to bed."

Månsson didn't answer right away. Skacke heard a suspicious bubbling sound, a soft clinking and someone say, "Ah."

"I think you should do that, too," said Månsson. "Go home to bed. He didn't see you, for God's sake, did he?"

"No," said Skacke curtly, and hung up.

He threw himself on his bicycle and literally flew down the hill toward Lundavägen. Ten minutes later he was standing in the hallway outside of his room, dialing Monica's number.

At five after eight on Saturday morning Martin Beck and Månsson knocked on Bertil Svensson's door.

He answered the door in pyjamas. When he saw their identification cards he just nodded, walked back into the apartment and got dressed.

They didn't find a weapon in the apartment, which consisted of one room and a kitchen.

Bertil Svensson followed them out and got into the car without a word; he was silent the whole way to Davidshall Square.

As they went into Månsson's room he looked at the telephone and spoke for the first time.

"May I call my wife?"

"Later," Martin Beck said. "We're going to have a little talk first."

29.

The whole of that morning and a good bit of the afternoon Martin Beck and Månsson sat listening to the history of Bertil Svensson, who was now being held in custody. He seemed glad of the chance to talk, was anxious for them to understand him and looked quite annoyed when he had to take a break for lunch. His story largely confirmed their reconstruction and even their theories about the motive.

After he'd been evicted, forced to move, laid off from work and finally divorced, he would sit in his lonely room in Malmö thinking over his situation. It became clearer and clearer to him who was the cause of all his troubles: Viktor Palmgren, the bloodsucker, who lined his purse at the expense of other human beings, the big shot, who didn't give a damn about the welfare of his employees or tenants.

He began to hate this man as he'd never thought it possible to hate any human being.

A couple of times during the interrogation he broke down and began to cry, but soon pulled himself together and assured them that he was thankful for the opportunity to explain himself. He also said several times that he was glad they'd come to pick him up. If they hadn't found him, he said, he probably couldn't have held out much longer, but would have turned himself in.

He didn't regret what he'd done.

It didn't make any difference to him that he would be sent to prison; his life was ruined, anyway, and he didn't have the strength to start over.

When they were through, and there was nothing more to be said he shook hands with Martin Beck and Månsson and thanked them before he was taken to jail.

It was quiet in the room for a long time after the door closed behind him. At last Månsson stood up, walked over to the window and gazed out over the yard.

"Goddamn," he mumbled.

"Hope he gets a light sentence," Martin Beck said.

There was a knock on the door and Skacke came in.

"How did it go?" he said.

No one answered for a minute. Then Månsson said, "Oh, it was about like we thought."

"He must have been a cold-blooded bastard just to barge in like that and shoot the guy," Skacke said. "Why did he do it like that? I'd have gone to his house and shot him through the garden hedge when he was lying out in the sun or something like that . . ."

"It didn't really happen like that," Martin Beck said. "You can hear for yourself in a minute."

He wound back the tape on the machine, which had been running all through the interrogation.

"I think it's here."

He pressed a button, and the spools began to hum.

"But how did you know that Palmgren was at the Savoy at that moment?"

That was Månsson's voice.

"I didn't. I just happened to be passing."

Bertil Svensson.

"Maybe you'd better start from the beginning. Tell us what you did that Wednesday."

That was Martin Beck.

BS: My vacation had begun on Monday, so I was off work. In the morning I didn't do anything much, just messed around at home. Washed out some shirts and underclothes—when it's this hot you have to change pretty often. Then I had a couple fried eggs and some coffee for lunch, washed the dishes and went out shopping. I walked down to Tempo on Värnhem Square; it wasn't the closest store, but I wanted to kill some time. I don't know too many people in Malmö, just a couple guys from work, but it was vacation time, and everybody had left town with their families. After I'd done some shopping I walked back home. It was real hot, and I didn't want to go out again, so I just lay on the bed reading a book I'd bought in Tempo. It was called *Till Death*, by Ed McBain. It got a bit cooler in the evening, and at about six-thirty I rode my bike out to the rifle range.

MB: Which rifle range?

BS: Where I usually shoot. In Limhamn.

PM: Did you have the revolver with you?

BS: Yeah. If you want you can have it locked up in the club house, but I always take it home with me.

PM: Okay, go on.

BS: Then I shot for an hour or so. I can't really afford it. It gets pretty expensive with the ammunition and the membership fee and all, but you gotta have some fun.

PM: How long had you had the revolver?

BS: Oh, some time. I bought it about ten years ago, when I'd won a bit of money on the pools. I always liked the idea of shooting. When I was a kid, I always wanted an air rifle, but my parents were poor and probably couldn't afford one, even if they'd wanted to. But they probably didn't want to, either. The next best thing was going to the fairgrounds and shooting at those metal elks.

MB: Are you a good shot?

BS: Yeah, you could say that. I won a couple of contests.

MB: Well, when you'd finished shooting . . .

BS: When I'd done shooting I rode the bike back into town.

PM: What about the revolver?

BS: It was in the box on the carrier rack. I took the bicycle path along Limhamn's Field, then around the Turbine and past the museum and the courthouse. When I got to the corner of Norra Vallgatan and Hamngatan, I had to stop for a red light, and that was where I caught sight of him.

PM: Of Viktor Palmgren?

BS: Yes. Through the windows at the Savoy. He was standing up, and a whole lot of people were sitting at the table.

PM: You said before that you'd never met Palmgren. How did you know it was him?

BS: I've seen his picture in the newspapers lots of times. And once when I was going past his house he came out of the gate and got into a taxi. Oh yeah, I knew it was him.

MB: What did you do?

BS: In a way I didn't think about what I was doing. At the same time, I knew what I was gonna do. It's hard to explain. I rode past the entrance to the Savoy and left the bike in the rack. I remember I didn't bother to lock it—like it didn't make any difference any more. Then I, uh, took the revolver out of the box and stuck it inside my jacket. Oh, yeah, I loaded it first; nobody walked by, and I stood with my back to the street and sort of left the revolver in the box, while I put a couple cartridges in. Then I walked into the dining room and shot him in the head. He fell down onto the table. Then I noticed that the closest window was open, so I climbed through it and walked back to the bike.

PM: Weren't you afraid of being caught? There were other people in the dining room.

BS: I didn't think that far, only that I was gonna kill that bastard.

MB: Didn't you see that the window was open when you went in?

BS: No, I didn't think about it. I guess I hadn't counted on getting away like I did. It was only after I saw him fall and saw nobody was paying any attention to me that I started thinking about getting outa there.

PM: What did you do then?

BS: I put the revolver back in the box, and then I rode away over Petri Bridge and past the railroad station. I don't know the schedule for the boats, but I did know that the hydrofoils leave every hour, on the hour. It was twenty to nine on the station clock, so I rode over to the Butter Inspection Station and left the bike there. Then I went to buy a ticket for the hydrofoil. I took the revolver box along. I thought it was kinda strange that nobody came after me. When the boat left I stayed out on deck, and the stewardess said I had to go in, but I paid no attention and stayed out there until we were about halfway over the Sound. Then I threw the box with the revolver and the cartridges into the sea and went in and sat down.

MB: Did you know what you were going to do when you got to Copenhagen?

BS: No, not really. I could only sort a think a bit at a time.

MB: What did you do in Copenhagen?

BS: I walked around. And I went some place and drank a beer. Then I got the idea of going up to Stockholm to see my wife.

MB: Did you have any money?

BS: I had a bit over a thousand kronor—my two months' vacation pay.

MB: Okay, go on.

BS: I took the bus out to Kastrup and bought a one-way ticket to Stockholm. They said they'd tell me what plane I gotta fly on. Naturally, I didn't give them my real name.

MB: What time was it then?

BS: It was close to midnight then. I sat there till morning, and then there was a flight—seven-twenty-five, I think it was. When I got to Stockholm I took the bus from Arlanda to Haga terminal and then I walked home to the wife and kids. They live on Norr-tullsgatan.

PM: How long did you stay there?

BS: An hour. Maybe two.

PM: When did you come back here?

BS: Last Monday. I got to Malmö last Monday night.

PM: Where did you stay in Stockholm?

BS: At a kind of boardinghouse on Odengatan. I don't remember what the name was.

MB: What did you do when you got back to Malmö?

BS: Nothing much. I couldn't go shooting. I didn't have a revolver any more.

MB: What about the bicycle? Was it still there?

BS: Yeah, I picked it up on the way back from the train.

PM: I've been wondering about something. Before you saw Viktor Palmgren through the window at the Savoy, had you ever thought about shooting him? Or was it an impulse?

BS: I guess I must've thought about it before, but it wasn't like I planned to do it, exactly. But when I saw him standing there and I had the revolver with me, it hit me in a flash that it was the easiest thing in the world just to shoot him. From the moment I decided to do it I didn't worry about what would happen later. Right then it felt like I'd gotten the idea for the first time. But deep down I must've wanted him dead all along.

MB: How did you feel when you read the newspaper? You must have read the newspapers the next day?

BS: Sure.

MB: How did you feel when you realized he might live?

BS: I was mad at myself for making a bad job of it. I thought maybe I should've fired more times, but I didn't want to hurt anyone else, and it looked like he died right then, on the spot.

MB: What about now? How do you feel now?

BS: I'm glad he's dead.

PM: Maybe we should take a break. You need something to eat.

Martin Beck turned off the tape recorder.

"You can hear the rest later, by yourself," he told Skacke. "After I'm gone."

30.

Late on Saturday night, July 12 of this warm summer, Martin Beck was sitting alone at a table in the dining room at the Savoy.

He'd packed his suitcase an hour or two earlier and had carried it down himself to the reception desk. Now there was no immediate hurry, and he was considering taking the night train to Stockholm.

He'd talked on the phone to Malm, who'd seemed very pleased and repeated time after time, "No complications, in other words? That's excellent, just excellent."

Just excellent, Martin Beck thought.

The restaurant was comfortable and intimate, but rather splendid at the same time. Flickering candles on the tables were mirrored in the enormous silver tureens. The fitting complement of diners, conversing at a fittingly low level. Not so many as to be intrusive, nor so few as to make one feel lonely.

Waiters in white jackets. The little headwaiter, bowing and eagerly tugging at his cuffs.

Martin Beck had started off with a whisky in the bar and followed it with *Sole Walewska* in the dining room. With his meal he drank the house akvavit, which was flavored with secret ingredients and very good.

Now he was lingering over coffee and a shot of Sève Fournier.

It was all quite superb. Good food, good drink and attentive service. The summer evening outside of the open windows was dense and warm and pleasant.

Moreover, a case had been wound up.

He should have felt good, but it didn't look like it.

As it was, he noticed very little of what was going on around him. It was doubtful, in fact, if he was even aware of what he ate and drank.

Viktor Palmgren was dead.

Gone forever and missed by no one, save for a handful of international swindlers and representatives of suspect regimes in countries far away. They would soon learn to do business with Mats Linder instead, and so things would be, to all intents and purposes, unchanged.

Charlotte Palmgren was now very rich and practically independent, and as far as one could see, Linder and Hoff-Jensen had a brilliant future in store.

Hampus Broberg would probably be able to avoid another arrest, and a staff of well-paid lawyers would show that he hadn't misappropriated or tried to smuggle stocks out of the country or done anything else illegal. His wife and daughter were already in safety in Switzerland or Liechtenstein with fat bank accounts at their disposal. Helena Hansson would presumably receive some sort of sentence, but certainly not so severe that she couldn't set herself up in her former profession within the fairly near future.

There remained a shipyard janitor, who in the course of time would be tried for second-degree, maybe first-degree, murder, and then have to rot away the best years of hrs life in a prison cell.

Chief Inspector Martin Beck didn't feel good at all.

He paid his bill, picked up his suitcase and walked over Mälar Bridge toward the railway station.

He wondered if he'd be able to sleep on the train.

BLACK
AJAX

BLACK AJAX

GEORGE MacDONALD FRASER

Carroll & Graf Publishers, Inc.
New York

First Carroll & Graf edition 1998

Carroll & Graf Publishers, Inc.
19 West 21st Street
New York, NY 10010

Library of Congress Cataloging-in-Publication Data is available
ISBN: 0-7867-0553-1

Manufactured in the United States of America

CONTENTS

PROLOGUE

Galway, Ireland, 1818

The black man is dying, but neither he nor any of the other men in the barn suspects it. After all, he is quite young, and if the heavy negroid face is unhealthily puffy and badly scarred by old wounds which show oddly pale against the coarse dark skin, these are hardly fatal signs, and not unusual in his profession. He slumps, overweight and flabby, on a bench against the rough timber wall, a grimy blanket draped across his naked shoulders, an old hat on his woolly bullet head, and the hand holding a bottle of cheap spirits shakes visibly when he raises it to his lips, one of which has been split so deeply that it has healed into a permanent cleft running halfway to his chin. His arms are long and muscular, and though there are creases of fat overlapping his waistband, his sheer bulk gives an impression of formidable strength not yet quite gone to seed. His eyes are closed, and he is plainly tired, but not with a weariness that can be cured by rest; there may be no outward sign of deadly illness, but the pain in his kidneys and the ringing in his head are now continuous, and seem to him to be draining the spirit out of his big, hard-used body. A few years ago he was as famous in England as Napoleon; now he hardly remembers that time.

Squatting in the straw, watching him anxiously and now and then addressing him in low voices to which he responds with a grunt or a nod, are two men in the crimson coats and yellow facings of the 77th Foot. They are not typical of the British Army, for they, too, are black. They have been drawn to the barn by fraternal sympathy with the dying man, a sentiment not shared by the only other person in view, a small, rat-like Cockney shabbily dressed in a worn tail-coat whose buttons are either tarnished or missing, stained pantaloons, and a beaver hat almost innocent of fur. He is the manager, for want of a better

1

word, of the man on the bench, and is reflecting glumly that his protégé is the very picture of a beaten-up, broken-down, drunken pug who could (bar his sable skin) serve as a model for all those other prize-ring cast-offs from whom the manager, in his time, has scraped a meagre dishonest living, parading them from one country fair to the next, shouting himself hoarse with lies about their past prowess, thrusting them into combat with a bellyful of beer to batter or be battered by the local bully, and passing round the hat afterwards. It may be a far cry from the Fives Court or Wimbledon Common, from the hundred-guinea purses and the twenty thousand pound side-bets, but it usually pays enough to keep manager and man in food and drink as far as the next village or market-town.

Not that he expects much today, from the ragged, noisy crowd of yokels and urchins gathered about the makeshift roped square in the farmyard. Bleeding bumpkins, in the manager's estimate, never seen a shilling in their lives, living on pepper, potatoes and water, slaves to Popish superstition, and content to sleep in sties with their animals, if they have any. His one hope is the local squireen, easily recognisable because he wears boots and sits in a dog-cart above the throng, passing the flask with his cronies and flipping a farthing to the ancient fiddler scraping out a jig tune; with luck the bucolic potentate will be good, if not for cash, at least for a leg of mutton and a bag of spuds, provided the fight is a good and bloody one.

That depends, the manager is well aware, not so much on the local champion, a brawny, red-haired blacksmith who waits basking in the admiration of the gaping rustics, as on his own black fighter, whose behaviour this past month has been causing concern. Moody and with-drawn at the best of times, he has been going into long, trance-like silences, coming out of them only at the call of ''Time!'', when he has instinctively come to scratch with his fists up, moving in a slow parody of that lightning dance-step which was once the wonder of the Fancy. Twice he has been so sluggish that the despairing Cockney has had to throw in the towel against opponents too unskilled or lacking the strength to knock him out; once, he has come unexpectedly alive and smashed an opponent into insensibility in a matter of seconds. His manager can only pray that today he will perform somewhere between those two extremes and give the spectators their money's worth.

2

Assuming, that is, that he can be got on his feet and led out to
the yard, where the crowd is growing restive, the shrill Irish voices
demanding a sight of the famous black, the legendary American hero
whose feats once echoed even to this distant backwater, and who
remains sprawled and apparently comatose on his bench in the dim
interior of the barn. As the two soldiers and the cursing manager haul
him upright he mutters a complaint of noises in his head; they demand,
what noises?, but he cannot tell them. The manager becomes abusive,
and to their astonishment and alarm the battered black face, its eyes
still closed, smiles as though at some happy memory, for it is not the
angry Cockney snarl that he hears, but another voice, eager and excited,
from long ago, ringing down the years . . .

"You know how many people came to Copthorn? Ten thousand!
Ten goddam thousand, boy! An' they came on foot, an' on horses,
an' in carriages, to see Tom Molineaux, the Black Ajax — you! An'
when you meet Cribb again, there'll be twenty, maybe thirty thousand,
with the Dook o' Clarence, and Mistah Brummell, an' Lord Byron,
an' every bang-up swell in London, yeah, an' maybe the Prince his
own self! With half a million guineas a-ridin' on the fight — an' a
million dollars' worth of it'll be on *you*!''

Through the fog that clouds his mind, he hears it, and then it fades
to a whisper, and is gone. He opens his eyes and stands, swaying
slightly, steadied by the two soldiers, while the Cockney at the barn
door proclaims his fighter. As the raucous voice silences the spectators'
chatter, the black man closes his eyes again, wincing at the stabbing
pain in his lower body. Death is much closer now, but he is not aware
of its approach, and if he was he would not care. The manager's speech
has finished, the fiddler strikes up a lively march, the black soldiers
urge him gently forward, and he takes a faltering step. The scraping
of the fiddle is drowning out the noises in his head, then blending into
another sound from far away, the thumping of brass and a kettle drum's
rattle, growing louder amidst a tumult of distant voices, the murmur
of a great multitude, and the music of Yankee Doodle, stirring him to
action . . .

Soft grass under restless feet shod in black pumps and white silk
stockings with floral patterns. He skips on the damp turf, and a smirr
of rain is on his face and chest, shivering him with its chill, as he

3

moves forward into the winter sunlight, drawing the great caped coat closer about his shoulders. Out of the shadow, into the open, and the murmur of the throng swells to a great shout, Yankee Doodle rises to a crescendo, and now his feet are marching, the press of faces before him falling back to give him passage. White faces, all about him, smiling and grim, curious and jeering, hostile and laughing, fearful and admiring, marvelling and excited, and for a brief moment memory mingles with imagination in the mist of his mind, and he sees himself with their eyes . . .

The caped figure striding through the lane of people and carriages held back by the "vinegars", brisk burly attendants in long coats and top hats carrying horsewhips, his stride becoming a swagger as he shrugs off the cape to reveal the magnificent body beneath, the black skin gleaming as though it has been oiled, the jaunty head with its tight curls, the white silk breeches with ribbons at the knee and coloured scarf encircling the slender waist. He breaks into the shuffle of a plantation dance, laughing and waving to either side, a fine lady smiles from beneath the broad brim of her Mousquetaire and tosses him a posy which he catches, putting a flower behind his ear and bowing low over her hand before dancing on, blowing kisses to the roaring crowd as the faces retreat into shadow and the sound dies . . .

He is floating high above them, looking down on a vast human amphitheatre, thousands upon cheering thousands ranged about a great roped circle, and beyond them the rolling wooded English countryside is bright in the December noontide, with scattered bands of running people and carts and carriages and horsemen, all hastening to join the huge expectant throng whose every eye is turned on that black and white figure, no bigger than a doll far beneath him, striding ahead, arms raised and hands clasped overhead in the age-old salute of the prize ring. Within the circle he can see the roped square, and the little knots of men standing and crouched about it, the umpires by the scales, the bottle-holders and timekeeper, the vinegars patrolling the space between square and outer circle to ensure order, the gamblers' runners scurrying to and fro, and at one corner of the square a slim slight man, a Negro like himself but lighter in colour . . .

. . . whose eyes are glittering with fierce excitement as they come face to face by the roped square. The mulatto is muttering to him and towelling his shoulders vigorously against the biting cold, but the black fighter does not hear him. As he pulls off his waist-scarf and knots it to the ring-post all his attention is directed to the opposite corner where a man is standing clear of the rest, a tall white man with a rugged open face beneath crisp black curls, clad like himself in breeches and pumps, a man with the shoulders of an Atlas, massive arms crossed on his deep chest, heavy-hipped and long-legged, shifting slightly as he waits, rising on tip-toe and down again. He nods with a little smile, and as the black man raises a hand in reply his other self, back in the Irish barn, feels a strange peace settling upon him, a sense of contentment at the end of a long journey, and he realises with a growing wonder that the journey ended there, by that roped square long ago, when he looked across into the strong acknowledging face of the tall curly-headed man, nodding to him, and recognised, for the first and only time in his life, a companionship that was far beyond any bond of love or affection or loyalty that he had ever known, because it was of equals, apart and alone. He cannot explain it or even understand it, but he knows that the tall man feels it too, and he laughs in pure happiness as he snatches the hat from the top of the ring-post where his scarf is fluttering in the breeze, and sends it skimming over the ropes . . .

. . . to fall in the dust of the farmyard, startling a stray fowl which runs squawking wildly, and the red-haired blacksmith is rushing him, blue eyes glaring and arms flailing, and his feet shift and his body sways instinctively as he evades the attack. He knows he is too exhausted, in too much pain, to raise his hands or move his feet, yet somehow his hands are up, his feet are moving, and as the red-haired ruffian turns, the black left fist stabs into his face, and again, and yet again, and that is the last thing he remembers as the shadows close in, and then there is no more memory.

THE WITNESSES

THOMAS ("PADDINGTON") JONES,
retired pugilist and
former lightweight champion of England

Who knows what's inside a black man's head? Not I, sir, nor you, nor any man. You can't ever tell. Why? 'Cos they don't think as we do. They are not of our mind.

Now, I know there's them as says a white man's mind is no different, but I hold that it is. Take our own two selves, sir, if you'll pardon the liberty. You can see the thoughts in my eyes, and − how shall I put it? − yes, you can follow my feelings 'cross this broken old phiz o' mine, depending as I smile or frown, or set my jaw, or lower my blinds. Is that not so, sir? Course it is. And, begging your pardon, I can do likewise with you, pretty well anyway, though you're deeper than I am, course you are. Why, this very minute you're thinking, who's this cork-brained old clunch with his bust-up map and ears like sponges, to read my mind for me? Yes, you are! No offence, sir, but it's so, ain't it? Course it is.

Why's that, sir? 'Cos we understand each other, though you're a top-sawyer, as we used to say, and I'm an old bruiser, you're a learned man and I can barely put my monarch on paper. But we're white, and English, and of a mind, so to speak. Even with a Frenchman, with his lingo, you can still tell at first glance if he's glad or blue-devilled or bent on mischief, which he most likely is. It shows, course it does.

Not with your blackamoor, though. Not with the likes o' big Tom. Oh, he could talk, and make some sense, and do as he was bid (most o' the time), and put his case − but what was behind them eyes, sir, tell me that? What did he think and feel, down in the marrow of him? You couldn't tell, sir, you never can, with them −'less they're dingy Christians (half-white, I mean) like my pal Richmond, and even with him I could never take oath what the black half of his mind was turning over. And I knew him well, nigh on thirty year from when he beat

9

Whipper Green in White Conduit Fields, till he hopped the twig Christmas afore last. Poor old Bill, I fought him twice, and that's the way to know a man, sir, I tell you. Course it is. I milled him down in forty-one rounds at Brighton, I did, for a fifty-guinea side-stake – we were both lightweights, but he didn't have my legs (nor my bottom, some said, him being black), and he had this weakness of dropping his left after a feint. Well, what's your right hand for, eh, when a man leaves the door open thataway? I'd ha' done him at Hyde Park, and all, but I broke my left famble on his nob, you see, in the eighteenth round – see there, sir, the ring finger's crooked to this day. If it had been my right, I'd ha' stood game, held him off and wore him out with a long left, 'cos he didn't have the legs, as I told you, but when your left won't fadge, what can you do? Cost my backers a fine roll o' soft, my having to cry quits . . .

Beg pardon, sir, where was I? Ah, speaking of knowing Richmond's mind, as being half-black only. But big Tom, that was black to his backbone – no, a closed book he was. Not so much as a glint of natural feeling, as you might call it, in them strange yellow eyes of his, not even when he looked at you straight, which he seldom did. Head down, as if he was in the sullens, staring at his stampers, hardly a grunt or a mumble, that was his sort, as a rule. You'd as well talk to the parish pump or Turvey's pig, when the broody fit was on him. You'd wonder if he had a mind at all, or was dicked in the nob.

There were times, mind, when he would break out into the wildest fits, sky-larking and playing the fool like a jobbernowl or a nipper showing off with his antics, and other times, when he got in a proper tweak – in a tweak, sir? Why, bless you, angry, en-raged, in a fair taking – and you'd think, hollo, best stand off and look out, for it's a wild beast loose. But 'twas no such thing, sir, for all his oaths and roarings, it was only noise, sir, but no action. He knew he was lowly, you see, having been a slave in America, and I reckon that held him in check, somehow, as if he knew 'twasn't for him to show fight against his betters. Not even in the ring, you say? Ah, that was another piece o' cheese. He was seldom angry inside the ropes; simple or not, he knew too much for that.

Then again, I've seen times when he acted no more like a slave than you would. It's no Banbury tale, sir, he could be head high and to old blazes with everyone, even royalty in the very flesh, when he'd strut like a gamecock and look down his great flat snout like any tulip, the sauciest nigger counter-coxcomb you ever saw, and dressed to the nines, oh, the slap-up black Corinthian, he was! They laughed at first – but I seen the day when they stopped laughing, and no error.

But here's the thing, sir: even then, when he was in his high ropes, I could never fathom whether he was hoaxing or not, or queer in his attic, maybe. You could not tell what was stirring under that woolly top-knot, if anything was, or see behind those black glims, bright and bloodshot rotten as though he'd been all night on the mop – which he had been, often as not. If I had a guinea for every time I've seen him home, shot in the neck and castaway to Jericho, I'd be richer than Coutts, and that's a fact.

Drink did for him – drink and skirt. I never seen his like when it came to the chippers, and didn't they fancy him, just, for all his mug was more like an ape's than a human's, lips as fat as saveloys, his sneezer spread all over his cheeks, nob like a bullet, and coal-black ugly altogether. And not just the common punks and flash-mabs, neither, but your bang-up Cyprians, and Quality females, too, top o' the *ton* with their own carriages and mansions up west. They could not get their fill of him. Made my stomach turn to think of it, him stinking the way they do.

I reckon they were curious to know how a black man would be, so to speak, and I doubt if they was disappointed, for a more prodigious well-armed jockey I never did see, and as a trainer I've cast an eye over more likely anatomies than a resurrectionist. But 'twasn't only that; why, even the sight of him, sparring at the Fives Court, or walking in the Park, or best of all posing for that Italian statue-carver in Ryder Street, was enough to turn the best-bred of 'em into flash-tails, for bar his clock he was Apollo come to life, the finest, strongest, bravest body of a man you ever clapped eyes on. That was beauty, sir, "ebony perfection in the artist's eye", Lord Byron said.

Oh, if you could ha' seen him that day at Copthorn when he came dancing out to meet Cribb! That was the day, sir, the day of the Black Ajax, the Milling Moor in all his glory, shoulders like a Guardee and the waist of an opera-girl, trained to a hair with those great sleek muscles a-ripple under a skin that shone like a sloe, and light as

11

thistledown on the breeze. That was Tom, my Tom, for just an hour or so.

There will never come another like him, sir, I can tell you. I saw him on the peak, tip-top high, and I saw him in the gutter. I saw him rich and famous, and I saw him scorched and forgotten. Why, I saw him shake the Prince Regent's own hand, sir, and clink his glass of iced champagne punch while the noblest in the land clapped his shoulder all smiles – and I saw him face down in rags in a farmyard sty with the gapeseeds crowing each time he shot the cat, puking his innards out, so fat and used up he was.

A sad end to a sad story, you say? Well, I don't know about that, sir. I been in the Fancy man and boy for more'n fifty years, and they reckon I fought more mills than any boxer that ever came to scratch, and I lent a knee and held the bottle for as many more again. I was lightweight champion of All England. I stood up to the great Jem Belcher longer than any other did, giving him two stone, when he had *both* eyes, too! I've sparred with every champion of England since Mendoza – Humphries, Jackson, the Game Chicken, Gully, Cribb, and the rest of 'em. Nothing in Paddington Jones's record to think shame of, you may say . . . but I never had a day like Copthorn, sir, and I don't know many milling coves that did. *He* had that day, though, Black Tom Molineaux of America. The greatest day in the history of the game, a turn-up that they'll talk about as long as there's a prize ring. No, sir, I can't say his was a sad story, however it ended, not with that day in it.

I knew him as well as anyone in his life, I suppose. I trained him, and taught him, and seconded him, and nursed him (and cursed him, I dare say), and was as close to him as a man could be. But as I said, I never knew his mind, or what he thought truly of us, or of the Fancy, or of London that he came to a great black simpleton and yet was talk o' the Town afore all was done, or of England that cheered and jeered him, and loved and hated him – oh, and feared him, too . . . what Tom Molineaux thought of all of that, sir, I can't say. Who knows what's in a black man's head?

Did I say drink and wenches did for him? Well, that's gospel, sure enough, but when I think back on him I reckon pride did for him, too. I may not have known his mind, but I'll lay all the mint sauce in the

Bank to a sow's baby that he had pride in him for a belted earl, born slave and all though he was. You smile, sir? Well, I've said my say, and I tell you, he was a proud man, and paid for it.

What's that, sir? Was he the *best*? Ah, well, now it's my turn to smile. I'll put it this ways: Mendoza was no faster, Belcher was no cleverer, and Ikey Bittoon the Jew never hit no harder, to which last I can testify, having had three ribs stove in by him. In fine, sir, Tom Molineaux was as good as ever twanged – but the *best*? Bless you, there's no such creature, let the wiseacres say what they will. Why, sir? Because somewhere, and the good Lord only knows where, but somewhere, sir, there's always one better. Course there is.

LUCIEN-MARIE D'ESTREES DE LA GUISE,

gentleman of leisure,
Baton Rouge, Louisiana

It is simply untrue, whatever my more sycophantic admirers may say, that I insist on perfection in all things. That they should think so is, perhaps, natural, but that they should say so aloud is unpardonable, since it suggests that I am susceptible to flattery. No, I am fastidious, that is all, but I am well aware that perfection in anything is rarely to be found, even by such an assiduous seeker of the ideal as myself. This being so, I am content merely to insist upon the best — the very best, you understand, be it in personal comfort, wardrobe, feminine company, male conversation (I talk to women, of course, but I have yet to converse with one), horses, weapons, food and drink, amusement, or any other of those necessities and pleasures which gratify the senses of a cultivated man. And since I am noble, insistent, and rich, the best is usually forthcoming. When it is not, I withdraw. I remove, I take myself away, and if that is not possible, I endure, for as brief a time as may be, with good grace and perfect composure. It is not for one who bears the names of Guise and d'Estrees to do less.

Thus, when my American cousin, Richard Molineaux of Virginia, descends on my Louisiana estate, with the appalling demand that I accompany him to New Orleans to see his slave, "the best dam' fightin' nigra in the South" (his words, not mine) pit himself against another black savage, I decline with aplomb. Cousin Richard is not of the best. Indeed, it is hard to place him at all.

I say, with the insincere courtesy which kinship requires: "Give me the pleasure of your society here for as long as you wish, dear Richard, and by all means take your primitive to New Orleans to do battle, but do not ask me to be present. To a man of sensibility the spectacle of two gross aborigines mauling each other (to death no doubt) would

14

be painful in the extreme. I wish to oblige you in all things, as you know, but I cannot expose myself to that."

"Why, how you talk!" cries he, red-faced, and perspiring in my drawing-room. "Since when you tender o' niggers gittin' hurt, or kilt? I collect you kilt a fair few right here on yore own plantation —"

"Only under the painful necessity of discipline."

"Painful necessity, yore French ass! Yo' glad of an excuse to string 'em up!" cries he. He is of inexpressible coarseness, this Molineaux, being American of the English. It is true that I also am in the narrow legal sense American, but of France, which I need not tell you is a vastly different thing. We remain what we have always been, Frenchmen. The English, having no heritage of civilisation, become American without difficulty.

"An' 'tain't no necessary discipline that makes you git yo'self a front seat at the whippin'-house whenevah they's a comely yeller wench to be lashed!" bawls he, leering, and stamping his boots without regard for my Louis Seize carpet. "You jes' admires to see 'em a-squealin' an' a-squirmin' — oh, Ah knows you, Lucie! You got real dee-praved tastes, cousin!"

I invite him to sit, marvelling that my great-aunt should have married the grandfather of such a creature. "The necessary execution, occasionally, of one of my own slaves for disciplinary reasons, is something I deplore, since it is both expensive and inconvenient. The correction of personable young slave wenches at the whipping-house, artistically administered, is an aesthetic experience," I inform him. "But I do not expect you to appreciate the distinction. Be that as it may, my Richard, the privilege of watching your 'fighting nigra' display his disgusting talents is one which I shall be happy to forgo."

"Whut you talkin' 'bout? Ah thought you liked boxin'? Least, you never tire tellin' 'bout all the great champeens you seen in Englan'. Well, Ah got me a champeen, a nigra champeen, so now! An' he can whip any man 'twixt heah an' Texis, ye heah?"

If I shudder, do you wonder? How to explain to this oafish Richard, disdaining the apéritif I offer him and calling for his detestable "corn", that to compare his black barbarian to the English masters of *la boxe* is to compare . . . what? A plough-horse to an Arab blood, a drab to La Dubarry, a Dahomey idol to a Donatello? How to convey that

15

beside the speed, the science, yes, the beauty of an English prize-fight, the spectacle of his brawling brutes would be the crude beastliness of swine in a sty? An impossible task, so I do not attempt it.

If it should seem remarkable that I, an aristocrat of Louisiana, should not only know but admire to excess the pugilistic art, I must digress to tell you how this came about. During the late unpleasantness between France and England which ended so deplorably with the unnecessary catastrophe of Mont Saint Jean,* I had felt it my duty to unsheath the sword in my true country's service. After all, France is France, a Guise is a Guise, and mere accident of birth on the unfortunate side of the Atlantic cannot alter allegiance, or excuse a gentleman from discharging the obligations which blood and breeding impose. If I hesitated at all, it was at the thought of attaching myself to revolutionary upstarts, but I consoled myself with the reflection that others with lineage hardly inferior to my own had condescended to enlist in the armies which they commanded. In brief, we put the honour of France first, and the likes of Corporal Bonaparte nowhere.

Very well. Of my service I choose to say only that it ended with my being taken prisoner in '98, thanks to the mismanagement of our Irish expedition by a general who in civil life had been a vendor of rabbit-fur. *C'est la revolution.* Thereafter I passed some years in captivity in England. No need to speak of that curious country and its inhabitants, save to concede that they know at least how to behave to an enemy nobly born, and, my parole being taken for granted, I found myself a guest rather than a prisoner. And since their polite society is devoted to sport, I became acquainted with, and, I confess, fell under the spell of that great national pastime which they properly call the Noble Art.

At first, to be sure, the notion of watching the lower orders pummelling each other with their bare fists was repugnant. How could it be otherwise, to one whose training in personal combat had been confined to the épée, the sabre and the pistol, and whose whole being and temperament inclined to all that was refined and elegant, and recoiled from the vulgar and brutal? But it chanced that I had my first view of pugilism when I was conducted by Guards officers to an

* Waterloo

exhibition by the magnificent Mendoza, then past his prime but a master still, and was ensnared forever.

I saw, in the person of that amazing Jewish athlete, the embodiment of graceful motion allied to power, intelligence, and skill, and realised that here was the ultimate expression of the human body in action. Here was the beauty of the ballet wedded to the violence of the battle, the destructive force, unaided by any weapon, of Man the Animal, trained and controlled to complete harmony, terrible and sublime. I came, I saw, I marvelled at craft so complete that it seemed elevated to art.

This was mere demonstration, of course, sport without danger in which the Hebrew master and his partner displayed the shifts and feints and counters and bewildering nimbleness of foot which are the prime-to-octave of the prize ring. It was intoxication of the soul to behold. Only later, when I saw pugilists engage in deadly earnest, did I realise that it was something more, that here was Truth, the unleashing of man's deepest primordial instinct to destroy, to inflict pain, to wound, and to kill – but with a finesse whose delicacy would become the finest surgeon, and a dispassionate detachment worthy of the classic philosophers. In what other sphere, I ask, can the connoisseur witness and savour at length the slow torture, exquisitely inflicted, of one human creature by another, and experience the thrilling feral joy of the expert tormentor and the helpless protracted suffering and shame of the victim? Let no one deny to the English their share, however modest, of genius, for they have devised the purest form of cruelty, beyond the imaginings of clumsy Inquisitors or the pathetic de Sade, whereby man inflicts punishment, mutilation, agony, and humiliation on his own kind, gradually and deliberately, with the most subtle refinement, and calls it a game.

I do not box myself. I have aptitude enough for manly sport, and fence, shoot, and ride with more than ordinary address, but while I have indulged myself with dreams in which I possessed the prowess of a Belcher or a Mendoza, practising my art on impotent opponents, I recognise that this is beyond my power. I could not achieve "the best" – and even the best in the prize ring, where the difference between champions is a hair's breadth, must endure their portion of suffering. I do not share the peculiar English satisfaction of

17

experiencing pain while inflicting it. Sufficient for me to enjoy the art and the agony as a spectator.

To speak of this to my boorish Richard Molineaux would have been to expound Epicurus to a Hottentot. He had no thought beyond his "fightin' nigra" and his forthcoming triumph over another savage, the Black Ghost, the reigning monarch of what passed for prize-fighting in our southern states, a revolting parody of boxing more akin to the ancient *pankration*, in which the contesting slaves battered, kicked, gouged, tore, bit, and wrestled each other in murderous frenzy, frequently with fatal results. This Black Ghost, I was informed, had killed four opponents and maimed a dozen others, and was accounted invincible by the patrons of this loathsome butchery.

"Say, but jes' wait till ma Tom sets 'bout him!" exults my gross companion. "Why, that Tom, he the meanest, strongest, fightin'est buck in the country! He goin' chaw up this Black Ghost an' spit him all over the bayous, yessir! Ah tell yuh, Lucie, he licked ev'y fightin' nigra in Virginny, an' he tear the ears an' bollix offa that ole Ghost an' mash his face in like 'twas a rotten melon! He got fists like steel balls, and yuh couldn't fell him with a ten-pound sledge, no suh . . ."

And more, and more of the same in praise of his prodigy, until to quiet him I consent to view this behemoth in the slave quarters. I expect, from Richard's description, to see a giant of hideous aspect, with elephantine limbs, ponderous and clumsy, but no, to my astonishment here is a young black buck of middle height, hideous and primitive of feature, indeed, but shapely and well-made enough, as I see when he strips at his master's command. He stands square and stolid as a bullock, without sense. I bid him skip, and he shows agility, but no *élan*, no spirit, none of that eagerness mercurial that is the sign of the trained boxer. I bid him put up his fists, and he comes on guard like a novice, his hands before his face and his head bowed, as though in fear. I whisper to my Ganymede to strike him suddenly on the face with a cane. He flinches, but his feet do not move. *Bon appétit*, M'sieu Black Ghost, I say to myself, here is your repast, a mere dull lump of black flesh. But out of regard for Richard I observe only that his teeth are good and his skin smooth, without blemish or scar.

"Say, nevah no welts on nigras o' mine!" cries Richard. "'Fore Ah has 'em trimmed up we spreads a wet canvas on they backs, so

18

the cowhide doan' leave so much's a mark. But Tom doan' need no whip these days, do ye, Tom? No, suh, 'cos he's ma fightin' nigra, so gits the best o' pamperin' an' vittles an' wenches, ain't that so, Tom?''

"Yes, mass',' mumbles the black dolt, his head bowed.

"But you doan' git no pleasurin' yet awhiles, haw-haw – not till you done beat that ole Black Ghost into mush an' broke him up so he nevah fight no mo'! Then yuh gits all the pleasurin' you want – an' if you trim him *real* good, maybe Ah lets you wed wi' li'l Mollybird? How yuh like *that*, Tom?'' And my Richard cuffs him in playful humour, at which Tom shuffles and grins.

"Like dat right well, mass',' says he.

This astonishes me. "You permit your slaves to marry, then? My good Richard, why? They will breed as well without benefit of a sacrament which *Le Bon Dieu* never intended for such creatures. And consider, if you please, that to encourage sentiment of family among them is to sow discontent when they or their brood come to be sold apart, as may well happen.''

He puts out his great American lip. "Doan' breed nigras for sale. Ma nigras mo' like to family. Why, this boy Tom heah, he Tom *Molineaux*. He ma nigra, he bear ma name, take pride in bein' a Molineaux. 'Sides, he an' li'l Molly bin sweet on each other since they children, so's fittin' they should wed, now she's full growed.'' He cuffs the brute again. "You jes' itchin' for her, Tom, ain't that so? Well, you whup the Black Ghost, an' she's yo's, boy – in a real white dress, an' Ah give her a locket fo' a bride gift! Whut you think o' that, now? Say, Lucie, you like 'em yaller, don't ye! You gotta see her – hey, wheah that Mollybird?''

Knowing my Richard's taste in African flesh, I look to see some voluptuous she-ape, but am enchanted when Mollybird comes tripping from the women's cabins. She is perhaps fifteen, and of a delicacy to kindle the appetite of the most jaded, pale gold of skin and exquisitely slender, with dainty hands and feet, and great gazelle eyes in the face of a madonna. She approaches modestly, putting her hand into that of the boy Tom, and they smile on each other. And this fragile beauty is to be defiled by that hulking animal! An atrocity not to be contemplated.

"Ain't she the sweetest li'l wench?" crows my vandal cousin. "She virgin, too. Now, Mollybird, make yo' rev'rence to Messoor la Geeze, now!"

She makes her curtsey, and I see the fear start in her eyes when I beckon her so that I may caress her cheek. It is like silk to my fingers, and when I take a cachou from my comfit-box and place it tenderly between her lips that are like pink petals she trembles in the most delicious fashion. When I stroke her fine long hair and whisper in her ear what a pretty girl she is, and inquire of Richard what is her price, her terror is delightful.

"Why, Lucie, you ole dawg!" guffaws he. "Didn't Ah say yuh liked 'em yaller? No, no, ma boy, she ain't fo' sale! She promised to Tom heah — why, if he was to lose Mollybird he'd mope an' pine an' likely die on me! That's why I brung her f'm Virginny, to keep her close by him, fo' his comfo't. But not too close, hey, Tom? No honeymoonin' 'til you lambasted that ole Black Ghost!"

One does not haggle in the presence of slaves, so I say no more and put the delectable child from my mind for the moment. At supper Richard is his gluttonous self, and insufferably boisterous in his cups, pressing me to change my mind and accompany him to the fight next day, and boasting with intolerable noise of the punishment his protégé will visit on his opponent. I am courteously adamant in my refusal, which makes him sullen, and as the evening and his intoxication progress, I detect a change in my vainglorious cousin. He frowns, and falls silent from time to time, and scowls on his glass, and bites his nails — a cannibal at the table of de la Guise, but there it is.

Suddenly he explodes. "You know all 'bout boxin' an' fightin' men! You seen ma boy Tom — he's a prime figure, ain't he? He smash this Black Ghost feller, fo' sure, yuh reckon?"

I ask him, how am I to judge, who have seen neither fight, and he pours my Beaune down his uncomprehending throat. "That Black Ghost, he one killin' nigra!" he mutters. "They tellin' me he a reg'lar villain, got no mercy, beat the best fightin' nigras on the Gulf! An' Blenkinsop, whut owns him, they say he keep him caged up, in a cage with iron bars, an' shackled to boot! Say he cain't let him loose 'mong other nigras, even, for fear he tear 'em up in his rage! He ain't human, they sayin'!"

"My dear Richard, none of them is human. Vocal animals, as the Romans said."

His hand shakes as he fills his glass and soaks my table linen. "My boy Tom, he nevah bin beat! Why, he licked Matheson's nigra, that'd beat ten men, beat him senseless in twenny-two minutes, yessir! Matheson's nigra a real champeen, they say! Twenny-two minutes, an' cudn't git up to ma Tom!"

"Then why such anxiety?"

He licks his lips and drums his great fingers. "Black Ghost killed Matheson's buck two weeks back. Bust his neck in his two hands like 'twas kindlin'. Fight didn't last three minutes."

I assure him that form is not to be judged by such comparisons, and for a moment his fears subside. To revive them, I inquire what odds are being laid on this monster, and the stem of his glass is snapped between his fingers. His mouth works and his voice is hoarse.

"Five to one on th' Ghost," says he. "That's whut had me plungin'. Nevuh was sech odds! Ah cudn't resist, Lucie, Ah tell yuh!" His face is glistening as he turns it to me, red and staring. "Ah backed ma Tom to th' hilt!"

This becomes interesting. I inquire of figures, and he brims another glass and gulps: "Fifty-fi' thousand dollahs!"

I wonder, not at the prodigious sum, but at the folly of wagering it on an insensate piece of black flesh against a fighter of formidable repute whom, it seems, he has never even seen. I remind him of his confidence, so freely expressed but a moment ago, and he groans.

" 'Spose he lose! 'Spose he cain't whup the Ghost! The bastard kilt four men a'ready! 'Spose he kill ma Tom!"

"Why, then, my Richard, your enchanting Mollybird will be inconsolable, and you, dear cousin, will have lost an indifferent slave and fifty-five thousand dollars. What then? Your fortune, to say nothing of your acres at Ampleforth, are sufficient to bear such a trifling loss, surely."

"Triflin'!" bawls he, starting up. "Triflin'! Damn yuh, Ah ain't *got* it!" And another priceless piece of Murano workmanship is reduced to shards. "Ah ain't *got* hardly fifty-fi' thousand *cents*! Ah's ploughed, don't ye unde'stan', yuh frawg-eatin' fool!" My gratification at this unexpected news is such that I overlook the disgraceful term of abuse.

21

"Yuh think Ah'd wager a fortune Ah ain't got if Ah wasn't desp'rate?"
To complete my disgust, he begins to weep, slumped in his chair, this
pitiful article of Saxon blubber. "I tell yuh, Ah's owin' all aroun', the
bank, an' the Jew lenders, an' Amplefo'th bin plastered to hellangone
fo' yeahs, an' that dam' Gwend'line" — his wife, an impossible, gaudy
female of ludicrous pretensions and no pedigree — "spendin' like Ah
had a private mint — an' Ah's burned to the socket, Lucie! Ah's so
far up Tick River Ah cain't be seen, hardly!" He sinks his mutton
head in his hands. "Tom's *gotta* win — he gotta win, or Ah's turned
up fo'ever! Oh, Lucie, you ma friend, ma own cousin, whut Ah goin'
to do?"

A delightful spectacle, which I view with satisfaction, noting *en
passant* that whereas most men in drink are given to optimism, my
Richard in his maudlin state finds himself visited by spectres apparently
forgotten in his sober moments. That his terrors are well-founded I do
not doubt: the man is a fool, and a wastrel fool, I know, given to
reckless gambling, and extravagance in which his ridiculous Gwendo-
line, with her absurd notions of position, will have borne more than
her share. I am astonished only that in a few years he should have
dissipated a splendid fortune and one of the finest estates in Virginia,
and wonder if his misfortunes have reduced him to the point where
he will apply to me for assistance. But no, even in his abject state he
does not forget the obligations of gentility. His nauseous lamentations
are a mere confessional, for he is of that contemptible sort who find
solace in pouring out their miserable secret fears.

I see no immediate advantage to myself in his plight, but am moved
to alter my resolve not to accompany him to the contest which will
certainly prove his ruin. The spectacle of the gross Richard tormented
by desperate hope, his grotesque antics as he sees, in the destruction
of his vaunted "fightin' nigra" at the hands of the Black Ghost, the
utter dissolution of fortune and reputation, his dawning despair as he
contemplates the shame and degradation awaiting him, the loss of
honour and, it may be, life itself — no, that is an entertainment that I
shall assuredly not forgo. Indeed, it will afford me infinite pleasure,
and some compensation for his boorish denial to me of that ravishing
little octoroon, his pollution of my table appointments, and the affront
to my senses of his repulsive company.

My change of heart raises him from the abyss to raptures of gratitude, his pusillanimous nature finding comfort in a mere gesture of support, as though my presence at his debacle should somehow shield him from misfortune. He agrees readily to my suggestion that Mollybird should accompany us, which I assure him must inspire his champion. I do not add that her distress as her hero is thrashed to pulp will be as a sauce piquant to my enjoyment of the occasion.

The fight is appointed for the following evening, in the garden of one of the larger exclusive brothels of the Vieux Carré, an establishment familiar to me from my youth, when debauchery was an occupation, not an art. All has been arranged to delight the popular taste, with coloured lanterns among the trees to light the raised stage; couches placed for the more favoured patrons with row upon row of chairs behind for the sporting fraternity, and benches for the untouchables; buffets from which wines and delicacies are conveyed to the foremost spectators; an orchestra on the balcony plays the primitive plantation rhythms; black and yellow strumpets in the most garish of costumes flaunt their uncovered bosoms in parade about the stage, or lounge on the couches with the patrons; the bawds, hovering like so many bedizened harpies, despatch their choicest trollops to the richest clients; runners pass among the great crowd giving the latest odds and collecting wagers for the leading gamesters, who are seated at tables before the front rank; and on the stage itself the dancers of the establishment, stalwart young bucks and nubile wenches stimulated by the intolerable din of the musicians, perform measures of the most tedious obscenity to cries of encouragement and advice from the vulgar herd. I am deafened by noise, poisoned by the reek of cigars, offended by recognition from mere acquaintances who presume to greet me as I take my seat on a couch, and disgusted by the raffish abandon of the occasion. I resign myself, bidding Ganymede fan the fumes from about my person, close my ears to the guffawing and cackling of the mob, and am consoled to see that Richard, seated by me, is distraught and of that mottled complexion which in the bucolic passes for pallor, while Mollybird, crouched at his feet, trembles with anxiety. I smile and pat her shoulder, and she shrinks enchantingly.

Her fiancé, our admired Tom, has the appearance of a beast in the abattoir, grey of feature and twitching his limbs as he listens to a small nondescript who wears a brass earring and patters what I assume to be advice and instruction.

"That Bill Spicer, an English sailor," Richard informs me. "Knows all 'bout the Fancy, bin givin' Tom prime trainin', teachin' him the guards an' sech." He says it without confidence, and as I regard M'sieur Spicer, I share his pessimism.

A positive thunder from the musicians heralds the arrival of the Black Ghost, and, *ma foi!*, he is a spectacle, that one. He bounds to the stage like a hideous genie from a bottle, the image of that blacka-moor who ravishes princesses in the Oriental tale. He is a giant, a full head taller than Tom, stark naked, with great lean limbs and the torso of a Hercules, his whole body scarred with the wounds of his contests and the lashes of his overseers. He is terrific as he stalks the stage, grinning horribly and flaunting himself at the whores, flexing his mighty arms and rolling his eyes about him. His skull, from which one ear has been torn away, is small and shaved clean, so that it resembles a polished cannon ball. He booms "Ho-ho!" like an ogre as he makes his bow to his master, the corpulent Blenkinsop, and squats on his heels above Tom, baring the few yellow teeth remaining in his ghastly jaws, and spitting threats in an awful croaking voice.

"Po' li'l nigga-boy! Whyn't yuh run back t'yo' mammy? Cuz yuh stay heah, Ah gwine eat yo' ears an' yo' eyes and pull yo' tongue out yo' stoopid nigga haid! Yuh skeered, boy? C'mon up heah, yuh won' be skeered no mo', cuz yuh'll be daid!"

Blenkinsop's drivers make a great show of driving the brute back with their whips, to the cheers of the multitude, and I note with interest that Tom, who but a moment since seemed in a state of fear, is now at ease, shrugging and skipping a little as he waits his summons to the stage.

You must understand that these contests are conducted in the very crudest fashion. There is no question of referee or timekeeper or whip-pers-in to marshal the spectators, no weighing of the men beforehand, none of the ceremonial so dear to the true Fancy of the Ring, whereby the contestants are brought together at the mark for instruction and to shake hands, and without which no English mill is permitted to proceed for a moment. Why, there are no rounds or rules or even seconds. It is the pitting of wild beasts in an arena, without procedure, to belabour and maim as they wish until one is insensible or dead. As to the spectators, they are there to see a slave butchered as cruelly as may be, without proper appreciation of how the thing is done. There is no thought of style or grace or skill. The bully from the brothel bawls: "Fight!" and the savages tear each other to pieces.

Nor is there that moment of calm so striking in the true prize-fight, when the gladiators face each other at the mark. As Tom and the Black Ghost prepare for the assault the howling rises to a tempest, Richard bellows beside me, Mollybird hides her face at his knee, and in that audience of pandemonium only three are tranquil: myself, the stout Blenkinsop who lounges smiling as he sips his punch and fondles the slut on his knee — and the man Spicer, crouched by the stage, his bright eyes on the combatants. I feel, in that moment, an invisible bond with him: in that ignorant mindless mob who see only the monstrous spectral Goliath towering above the insignificant David, are he and I alone in noting the superb proportions of Tom's limbs, shining with health, the lightness with which he balances on his toes, the steady regard with which he watches his enemy? Spicer is softly calling: "Left hand, lad. Let 'im come to ye. Left, an' side-step. Distance, lad, distance."

It is good advice, and my opinion of this Spicer increases — but it proves fatal, for Tom, nodding that he hears, turns his head, and in that moment the Black Ghost, who has been mouthing and snarling taunts, leaps silent across the stage and with a lightning stroke of his mighty arm smashes Tom to the boards and is upon him, screaming again as he beats and tears furiously at his opponent. Tom breaks free and staggers afoot, but even as he rises the Ghost drives his knee into his face, and Tom stumbles like a drunkard as the giant belabours him without mercy. It is all he can do to retreat, shielding his head from those dreadful blows, the blood running down his face and chest, until another ponderous swing of that terrible arm hurls him to the boards, to be stamped and trampled underfoot. It is the end, before it has begun, think I, but he seizes the Ghost's ankle, tumbling him down, and grips him in a wrestler's lock. The Ghost howls and raves, but he cannot break the hold, and Tom has a moment to recover while my Richard shouts without meaning, the spectators deafen us with their cheering, the little Spicer's admonitions are lost in the uproar, and the fat Blenkinsop settles himself at more ease, laughing as he nuzzles his whore.

Now, it is not for me, who have seen Jackson and Mendoza and Belcher, and could describe every blow, every feint, and every parry of those masters, to record in similar particulars the progress of that unworthy gutter combat. In truth, I observe it only in general, my attention being claimed by the conduct of Richard and my yellow beauty, and the assembly at large as they behold the nauseating spectacle. For as it has begun, so it continues. Tom's respite is but temporary, for the Ghost escapes the lock by breaking his right thumb. The spectators shriek for joy as Tom, with one hand useless, stands helpless under the rain of blows visited upon him. Round the stage he is driven by that roaring black demon whose strokes fall on his body with such fearful impact that it seems his ribs and spine must be shattered. Did the Black Ghost but know how to use his fist, like a rapier rather than a hammer, all would be over in a few rallies. But he clubs with his huge arms, delivers savage kicks *à la savate*, tears Tom's hair from his head, rakes with clawing nails, and rends and bites when they close, with such ferocity that Tom falls repeatedly, and is twice hurled from the stage.

And the onlookers, then? They bay like dogs, exhorting the Ghost to maim, to kill, to gouge the eyes, to break the bones, to castrate. Men rise, eyes wild and faces engorged, aping with their fists the blows of the victor. Women white and black, their features like the masks of snarling leopards, squeal in ecstasy as the helpless flesh is pounded and the blood flows. My Richard waves his hands and rages blaspheming at his man to stand and fight, to smite the Ghost to perdition, and sinks back on the couch, his mouth trembling as with a seizure, groaning and all but weeping, a delightful picture of despair. The tender Mollybird shrieks and covers her face, but when Tom is hurled from the stage for the second time, and lies a bloody ruin before her, she casts herself upon him in a frenzy of grief.

"Stand clear, gel," says Spicer, and stooping sinks his teeth in the lobe of Tom's ear. He revives, but lies helpless as those nearest revile him, calling him a stinking coward nigger, urging him to resume and be slain, to afford them the sport of his torture, and the beaten hulk pulls himself up, with Richard bawling at him, and the man Spicer

26

snapping at his ear: "Left 'and! Left 'and! You ain't dead yet, lad! Stand away an' give 'im Long Tom! Go fer 'is peepers! Left 'and, d'ye hear?"

Tom hears, for he nods his head, the blood flying from his face, and regains the stage. The Ghost rushes yelling and flailing for the kill, and is brought to a halt as Tom thrusts out his fist at full length. It jars upon that devilish face and gives him pause, then he brushes it aside, beating with his great forearms, and again Tom topples from the stage and lies like one dead.

Mollybird screams and seizes Richard by the hand, begging him to give in. "Please, Mass' Richud, oh, please, doan' let 'im beat 'im no mo'! Please, mass', he dyin'! Oh, mass', take pity on 'im! He cain't no mo'!" I am touched, but Richard spurns her away, and runs raging at Tom, kicking him brutally in the side.

"Git up, yuh black bastard! Git up, damn yo' lousy hide! Fight, yuh carrion! Quit on me, will yuh? Git up theah, or by God Ah'll kill yuh!"

Spicer kneels by Tom's head, and again bites the ear. Again, it revives, but he can only shake his head, horribly slobbered with blood from the gashes on his cheeks.

" 'E's done, guv'nor," says Spicer, and Richard stands, his breath wheezing, speechless as he sees the death of his hopes in the battered carcase at his feet. Above on the stage the Black Ghost gibbers and struts in triumph, flinging up his hands, inviting the applause of the crowd who fling money and flowers and bon-bons to the stage. Blenkinsop approaches, lays a paw on Richard's shoulder, and commiserates.

"Reckon yo' boy cain't lay ma ghost, Mol'neaux! He used up, seemin'ly. You give him best, Ah reckon."

Richard does not hear him. He glares about him, at the gloating faces, at the Black Ghost prancing above, at the smug Blenkinsop who smokes his cigar and toys with his seals, smiling on his cronies. And Richard exceeds my fondest hopes, for in a voice hoarse with fury he stoops above Tom and shouts:

"You git up an' fight! You fight till you daid, ye heah! Or by the holy Ah give you a death'll last a week! Ah'll have you lashed, real slow, till ev'y drop o' black blood's dreened clear out o' yuh! Yuh heah me, yuh black swine! Git up, I say! Damn yuh! Fight, fight, fight!''

Mollybird swoons and I bid Ganymede place her on the couch beside me. The sensation of her slim shape within my embracing arm is infinitely pleasing, and as I put my flask to her lips I inhale the fragrance of her hair and feel the smooth skin beneath my fingers. I am of all men the least susceptible, but when her lids flutter and those wondrous eyes are revealed, and again I see the fear in their depths, it is too much. My desire conjures in my mind visions of ecstatic possession. I tremble in my turn as I picture her far from this sordid mêlée, in elysian surroundings to match her fresh loveliness, young, virginal, helpless, and adorable beyond expression. And I am inspired of a sudden, for as Richard raves, I see again what I have just seen upon the stage, my glance rests on the half-broken body of the man Tom, muttering feebly and shaking his torn head, while Spicer sponges his swollen face . . . and I pluck Richard by the sleeve, commanding him to be quiet.

"You wish to win this combat?" I ask. "You wish to save your fortune and your honour?"

He glares at me uncomprehending, his stupid red face bedewed with sweat, breathing like a bullock.

"If you do, you will cease these childish vapourings, and attend to me. I can put victory in your hand."

He looks from me to the stricken fighter and back again. He shakes his head in bewilderment, and stoops close to me.

"Whut you sayin'? Damn yuh, Lucie, you hoaxin' me? Whut yuh mean, Ah kin win? How, godammit? That black lummox is beat all to hell — look at him, blast yuh, ain't nuthin' goin' git him up again!"

"I assure you, my dull cousin, that if you do as I instruct, he will undoubtedly get up again. I believe he will win, but if he should fail, your situation can be no worse than it is at this moment — ruined, bankrupt, dishonoured . . . my dear Richard, you might as well be dead."

"Yo' crazy!" he cries. "Why, yuh lousy French pimp, yo' jes' tormentin' me, out o' spite!" He sobs and tears his hair, and I turn from him in distaste.

"As you please. Farewell, M. Molineaux. Enjoy your degradation. I shall."

He appears to be demented. He breaks again into insults, I sit aloof, and then à last he snarls at me:

"How, damn ye? Tell me! Whut I do, fo' God's sake! Whut yuh want, yuh dam' snake? Lucie, in the name o' Jesus, man, tell me!"

"You make a trade with me. You present to me, as a gift, this pretty toy for my amusement." I indicate the girl, who whimpers in most appealing terror. "In return, I show you the secret."

"She's yo's!" cries he. "Take the slut! Now, tell me – whut I do?"

I indicate his fallen champion. "Promise him his freedom."

At this there is sensation. They stare, they roar with laughter, Blenkinsop shakes his head and turns away, those out of earshot shout questions, they press forward about us, Richard makes to speak, is dumb, and stands amazed. I watch as the thoughts pass across his crimson face, he beats his temples in hesitation, and then with a curse flings away and kneels by Tom. His words are lost in the uproar. I am content to have Mollybird within my reach. I do not caress her, or draw her to me. I sit at my ease, waiting.

There is commotion about the stage, and Tom is coming to his feet, with the man Spicer giving support, and I hear Richard's voice raised in a different key of desperation.

"Free! Free, Ah tell yuh! Good boy, Tom – why, yuh ain't beat at all! Yuh ma fightin' nigra, sho' 'nuff, an' you be a free man, 'pon ma honour! Yuh heah me, gennelman, ma bounden word! Free, Tom, Ah vow!"

And more of the same, while Tom sways and paws at his bleeding wounds, and I wonder if the enjoyment of my new chattel is to be denied me after all. But I have seen what I have seen, for a brief moment, and Spicer has seen it, too, for he whispers urgently at Tom's ear, clenching his left fist, and Tom shakes his head in sudden resolution, sprinkling those about him with blood. He has had precious moments to renew his strength, and indeed there are those gamesters who cry that he has had too long a respite, and must forfeit the contest. But Blenkinsop laughs and shrugs, and the mob howl that it must be fought à l'outrance. The gamesters think of their gains, and the onlookers of Tom's torment to come, and the majority prevail.

Now I whisper in the ear of Mollybird. "Go to him, child. Inspire him with your love. Let him see the true reward for which he fights – your own self, his bride-to-be. If he wins, he is a free man, and what then? He can purchase your own freedom, and together you can live in sweet liberty. For I, myself, will put at his disposal the necessary funds, a tribute to his valour and loyalty! See, he raises his head, feeling returns to his eyes! His master offers him release – rush to him, *ma petite*, show him the greater prize within his reach! Animate him, then, renew his valorous ardour! But quickly, quickly – go!"

Ah, to capture forever the feeling in those glorious eyes! The fear, the amazement, the light of dawning hope, the springing tears of gratitude. She cries: "Oh, mass'!" and seizes my hand, pressing those tender lips upon it. "Oh, bless you, mass'!" My emotion is not to be described as, with a last look of adoration, she leaves me to hasten to her lover's side. Richard is urging him to the stage by main force, Spicer is pouring earnest instruction into his ear, and it is not for a slave-wench to intrude, but she calls to him, he sees her, and as she raises a slender hand I hear her voice shrill above the hubbub: "Free, Tom! Oh, Tom, free! You an' me, Tom! Free!" She is exalted, weeping, heedless of the guffaws and obscene sallies of the onlookers. Tom's vacant brute stare is turned on her, and as I see his bleeding mouth close like a trap and his indescribable features set in a mask of fury, I permit myself a moment of congratulation. If freedom is not sufficient inspiration to his dull mind, I have given him a little more. Perhaps the little that will turn the scale.

As he sets a foot on the stage, Spicer restrains him, and only in time, for the Black Ghost rushes at him like a steam train, his huge fists whirling like windmills. Spicer holds him still, and the Ghost, screaming with rage, gives back, beckoning him with taunts and curses, while the mob hurl abuse, deriding his cowardice. Spicer releases his hold with a sharp command: "Left, mind – an' break away!" The Ghost leaps to the attack, and out darts the left fist of Tom, full in the ogre's face. Tom retreats, the Ghost lunges, and again the left fist checks his rush – and again, and again, and yet again, and with each blow Tom moves away, while the spectators cry with astonishment at each stroke, the Black Ghost howls in fury and clubs in vain at his

30

retreating antagonist, and the little Spicer clutches the edge of the stage crying: "Circle, circle, keep away! Left 'and, left 'and!"

The onlookers are beside themselves with amazement and anger. This is not what they wish to see. This marches not at all. What, their champion, in full strength, held at bay? The poor victim, with his broken right hand dangling useless at his side, whom they had looked to see mangled and crippled for their delight, fighting at a distance, immune from the frenzied swings of the conqueror? They scream and curse, urging the Ghost to destroy the upstart, and the Ghost, maddened beyond endurance, rushes in wildly — to be met by that rapier fist, now on his temple, now on his eyes, now on his jaw, but ever checking his advance while his blows fall on empty air.

And I note, and marvel at, a phenomenon I have not seen since I left England. Obedient to the commands of Spicer, Tom delivers his blows and at once retires, back or to the side as seems best, in ungainly fashion. But as Spicer continues to cry: "Circle, circle!" his gait changes, as though by some instinct in his primitive brain. His heels lift, he moves on his toes, his shuffle becomes a dance, he finds a rhythm, his body sways from side to side. The Ghost must follow, screaming like a thing bereft of reason, rushing and flailing, only to encounter the relentless impact of that unerring fist.

You may know, or you may not, the potency of the blow that I describe. To the ignorant, it appears feeble enough, a stroke of defence to keep the attacker away. And so it is, but it is more. Not for nothing do the Fancy call it "the pride of British boxing". Oh, a Mendoza or a Belcher, had such been pitted against Tom that night, would have blocked and countered with ease, but the Black Ghost knows nothing of such arts. He is helpless against it, and learns the lesson that every prize-fighter knows, that the straight left hand, darting home again and again, is a fatal weapon of attack. From the trained man, striking with full power of body and shoulder behind the blow, never losing his balance, it is of stunning effect, sapping the strength of the victim, a stinging snake that robs him not only of vitality of body, but of mind also.

Tom is a mere novice, but against such a mindless animal his clumsy science suffices. Thanks doubtless to the tuition of Spicer, he has found the equivalent of the secret *botte*, that mythical thrust of fence which no swordsman can parry. But whence the instinct comes that prompts him to move in a rude semblance of what the Ring calls footwork, the shifting dance of the true pugilist, who can tell? For the many, it is learned by patient instruction and practice. To him I believe it is a gift of God.

Twice that night it betrays him. Once, slow to retreat, he is caught by a sweeping blow which fells him, but by good fortune the Ghost stumbles also, and Tom escapes. Again, missing with his left fist, he loses balance and is seized by those terrible hands. Let the Ghost but reach his throat, and all is lost, but in his unreasoning blood-lust the monster claws with his nails, and Tom wrenches free, his cheeks ploughed as though by talons.

And now the pendulum swings. The pounding left fist has done its work. The flesh about the Ghost's right eye is so swollen that it obscures his vision. In vain he twists his head, in vain tries to shield his other eye from that probing torment. Again and again the deadly fist strikes home, and now it is Tom who advances with each blow, and the Ghost who retreats. He cowers and cries out, his arms thrash in aimless fashion, he paws at the bloody mask of his face. But he cannot clear his sight, and there is no second to lance his engorged cheeks. The onlookers exclaim with savage delight — he is blind! Helpless he totters, and the cruel glee of the patrons knows no bounds as they urge Tom to destroy the tortured Cyclops. They bound to their feet, they rave and curse with the aspect of fiends. I see the whore of Blenkinsop, her comely little face distorted to that of a Medusa, her teeth bared and gnashing, her slim fingers rending her fan to shreds. At each blow her body shudders in ecstasy and she screams with laughter. Blenkinsop lounges and lights a fresh cigar, regarding the slaughter of his creature with sullen indifference. Richard is mad with excitement, beating his fists upon his knees as he bellows his triumph. Mollybird crouches beneath the stage, her hands clasped and her eyes closed, a charming study of maidenly devotion.

Spicer shouts a sharp command, and Tom directs his blows at the Ghost's body. They fall on the breast, the stomach, the groin, the kidneys, and the flanks. The Ghost wails in agony, falling to his knees. He rises, and is struck down again, and yet again. He crawls to the limit of the stage, imploring Blenkinsop, whom he can no longer see, to end his anguish. "Mass' Bob, Mass' Bob, make 'im stop! Cain't see, Mass' Bob! Ah's beat – mercy on me, Mass' Bob! Please, please, mass'!"

Tom, exhausted by his efforts, sinks to his knees and looks to Spicer. I note with interest the conduct of this English sailor. He frowns, and walks rapidly to Blenkinsop, plucking from his waist the blood-stained rag with which he sponged Tom's wounds. He presents it, but for Blenkinsop it has no meaning. He knows nothing of the pugilist's token of surrender. He calls instead to his drivers, who leap to the stage and lash the fallen Ghost with their whips, goading him to resume the contest. He tries to rise but cannot. He falls on his back, his head lolling over the edge of the stage, his blood coursing to the ground from a face that is a face no longer but a hideous crimson sponge.

Spicer casts down his cloth in anger, and nods to Tom to continue. Tom cannot rise. I see the great muscle a-flutter in his leg, and know that its use has deserted him for the moment. He pulls himself to the side of the Black Ghost, and gathers his strength for a last terrible blow directed at the upturned chin. Even through the din we hear the fearful crack as the spine is fractured at the neck, and as the Black Ghost's head hangs limp a deafening yell of delight rises from a thousand throats. I bid Ganymede bring the girl Mollybird to my house, and make my way to my carriage. Butchery, however detestable, I can view with a dispassionate eye, but slobbering expressions of gratitude from cousin Richard, before such a Gadarene assembly, are not to be borne.

SEÑORA MARGUERITE ROSSIGNOL,
lady of fashion
and independent means, Havana

Fact is, I don't much care to remember. 'Deed, suh, you'd be astonished
jus' how good I can be at *dis*-rememberin', specially when some
'quisitive stranger comes pokin' his nose in my private affairs, wants
to set it all down – for what? So you can lay an info'mation 'gainst me?
Pouf! Not these days, mister, not in this town. La Señora Rossignol is
re-spectable *an'* respected, as my good friend the Alcalde can tell you.
An' I doubt he'd take kin'ly to any Paul Pry seekin' scandal . . . to
squeeze money out o' prom'nent gennlemen, maybe? That ain't your
game? Well, then, I reckon you mus' be one o' those de-generates
that get all tickled up havin' a lady tell 'em the intimate de-tails of
her past, from her own ruby lips. Brother, have I seen my fill o' that
sort! What some men'll pay good dollars for . . . praise be. Not so,
you say? Oh, my apologies. So, mister, jus' what *do* you want?

Tom *Molineaux*? Me'ciful heavens! An' what in cree-ation is he to
you, may I ask? A subject of his-toric interest? My, my! Tom got
called plenty in his time, but that's a noo one. An' why might you
s'pose I know anythin' of his-toric interest 'bout him, or would tell
you if I did? Ah-h . . . you been talkin' to Lucie de la Goddam Guise!
Well, I trust you scrubbed real well with carbolic aft'wards. Pouf!
An' you want *my* side o' the story? Tom's story, you mean? Well,
perhaps I don't choose to tell. Why should I?

Your pardon? You are prepared to make me a gen'rous onner . . .
say it again, if you please . . . Honorarium? Suh, if that is some noo
kind of European perversion, I'd be 'bliged if you'd tell me what it
means, in simple American . . . *Payment*? For tellin' you 'bout Tom
Molineaux? Now, that I cannot believe! See here, my friend, if you
have been overhearin' loose talk an' have called 'pon me for some
pu'pose you are too bashful to confide straight out . . . well, I 'ppreciate

34

the flatterin' attention, but madam is not inclined these days, an' if I was, believe me, you couldn't afford it.

No, suh. I am not in need of capital, as you can see. Yonder coffee service is English sterlin' silver, my gown is pure China silk, f'm Paris, France — well, I thank you for the charmin' compliment — these fine furnishin's an' pictures an' all is bought an' paid for, as is the house; my maid, cook, an' footman ain't owed one red cent in wages, an' there is a drivin' carriage, *with* canopy, an' two horses in my stable, which you are kin'ly welcome to view — on your way out. Unless you choose to state your *real* business. Jus' so we und'stand one another.

My stars! You were *not* bammin' jus' now? You truly want to know 'bout that Tom? Well, that does beat all! Whatever for? I'd not ha' thought he was o' that much account. No one ever cared for him, hardly . . .'cept me, an' I knew no better. He made a name in *England*? Now, you do s'prise me. Oh, prize-fightin' . . . uh-huh, I guess he was good at that, if little besides. Well, it makes no neverminds what he did in England. He surely did hurt enough in America, him an' that . . . No, I b'lieve I do not care to remember.

My recollections are of the first impo'tance to you? Well, now, I can't think why they should be . . . oh, fo'give me if I smile, only I wonder do you know 'zackly what you are askin'? My recollections? La-la! My good suh, they are not what you are 'ccustomed to read in the ladies' journals. You 'ppreciate that, you say? Well, I 'ppreciate your candour, *I* mus' say! No, do not apologise. Like I said, we und'stand each other.

Well, now . . . I may not *care* to remember — but I do. 'Tis not the kind of thing a woman forgets, try how she may. Still, 'twill do no harm to tell now, I guess. I got over that mis'ry a long time ago, even if it did break my heart in pieces at the time . . . I had a heart in those days. So long ago . . . at Amplefo'th . . . when I was young in the sunshine . . . Oh, damn him! An' damn that worm de la Guise! You wouldn't b'lieve I could still feel the pain! Well, I don't — 'til some 'quisitive body plagues me to think on it!

I beg your pardon, suh. I fo'get myself. Quite in'scusable, what must you think? You have called 'pon me to make an inquiry, in genteel style, an' my outbu'st was most unbecomin'. Would you have

35

the kindness to pour me a glass of sherry f'm the cellarette yonder – an' kindly help yourself to refreshment. There is French brandy, an' aquavit', an' such. Jus' the smallest trifle ... I thank you. Now, let me collect my thoughts.

H'm, my recollections. Well, you shall have 'em plain, an' if they offend your delicate feelin's ... why, you shouldn't ha' come.

First thing, Tom Molineaux was a born fool. Strong in the arm, weak in the head, denser'n Mississippi mud. Even when I was little, I could see he had no mo' sense'n an ox. He was willin' an' kin'ly enough, an' I guess I took to him 'cos he took to me. Used to follow me 'round like a great hound puppy, f'm as early as I can remember. He was older'n me, but we used to play together, an' I had to show him how, at our games an' ev'ythin'. The older slave-childer used to make game of him, 'til he got bigger – an' then the boys took no more liberties with him, you bet, for he was prodigious strong an' could whip 'em three, four at a time. Yes, suh, he was one big likely nigger buck, an' ripe as a stud bull! Oh, my, I trust you will pardon the 'spression. Recollectin', I fall back into the common way o' speech. But that is what he was.

'Twas natural the gals all set their caps at him, an' he was fool enough to pay 'em heed, an' had his way with all o' them, but it was me he cared for always. "You my own true love, li'l Mollybird," he used to say. "True love!", I declare! Where he learned such words, I cannot 'magine. But he meant it, so far's he had sense to mean anythin', an' I b'lieved him.

One reason why he admired me to worship was I looked so different from the other wenches. They were common nigras, but I was what they called high yaller – yellow, you know, on 'ccount o' my white blood, an' fine-boned an' dainty. Ah, I was the sweetest, neatest little gold fairy you ever did see – well, I am not 'zackly plain in my prime, would you say, so you can imagine. The master's daddy, old Molineaux, used to call me Princess, never Mollybird, which is a real low plantation-wench name, if you like. Not my style at all, which is why I am Marguerite Rossignol, in case you wonderin'. Molly Nightingale, in French – Molly Bird.

So the older an' prettier I grew, the more Tom mooned after me, an' I dare say I used him somethin' shameful, as gals will. He was so in awe of me, an' the white people made me such a pet, he never dreamed to treat me like the nigra wenches. Once, when I's 'bout twelve, an' he was maybe sixteen, I teased him on to kiss me, an' like the born fool he was, he bragged 'bout it, and when old Molineaux heard, he was in such a takin' he had Tom triced up an' lashed 'til he couldn't walk. They told me I was never to even talk to him after, an' kept me in the big house in a chamber of my own, with a bed an' coverlet. Oh, I thought 'twas heaven! That was how precious I was.

Can you 'magine, it devoted Tom to me more than ever? An' I cannot think why, now, but I do believe it was bein' kept away f'm him that caused me to fall in love with him. I would see him starin' at my window nights, an' lookin' so melancholy, an' ev'yone knew he hadn't made so much as a whimper when they whipped him. I yearned for him then, as only a young girl can, ugly as sin tho' he was. Well, the other bucks were no better, or near so strong an' fine-bodied as Tom, an' what other men had I seen? It seems foolish now, but for three years I was in love with Tom Molineaux.

You think that hard to b'lieve? You see me here, the elegant lady of colour in her stylish salon, with her Paris gown an' fine complexion an' delicate airs, an' conversin' in that husky way the gennlemen so adore, ole-plantation-an'-la-m'dear — you s'pose I was this smart an' wo'ldly when I was fifteen? Pouf! I had no mo' sense'n a chicken. I was a simple little wench, an' Tom Molineaux was big an' strong an' kin'ly and gentle to me as if I was a ewe lamb. An' I loved him, strange an' all as it seems now. I have had some 'sperience o' the world since, and of men, an' I am no longer simple, but I am here to tell you that when a strong, brave man is fit to be tied for love of you, he is powerful hard to resist . . . when you are fifteen.

Would you be so kind as to make a long arm for that brandy on the cellarette? I have a fancy to somethin' mo' strengthenin' than sherry . . . deeply 'bliged.

Where was I? Ah, yes, it was when old Molineaux died that Master Richard made Tom a "fightin' nigra" an' began to match him 'gainst the bucks f'm other estates. I know nothin' of such things, but all the talk was that Tom was the meanest fellow with his fists in the whole Dominion, an' I was mighty proud of him, tho' I never saw him fight until . . . that night in Awlins. I didn't know what nigger-fightin' *was*, hardly, but I was glad for Tom, an' Master Richard makin' much of him, pettin' him an' givin' him fancy clothes an' sayin' he would be the mos' famous slave in the Southland.

Mos' nigras would ha' put on airs 'bove theirselves to be so tret by their masters, but not Tom. Truth to tell, he didn't have the gumption to get above hisself; he was jus' quiet, dull Tom as ever, an' I was the only thing could bring a light to his eye an' a smile to that big, ugly nigra face. Young Master Richard saw how 'twas with us, and gave Tom the freedom o' my company – an' *only* my company. "You want to pleasure yo'self, they's wenches a-plenty in the cabins," says Master Richard. "Mollybird she pure, an' stay that way. Maybe one o' these days, I let you have her, when yo' champeen nigra fighter of America. How you like that, Mollybird? You like this big go-alonger for yo' man?"

He would laugh as he said it, and cuff Tom's woolly head, and Tom would grin an' shuffle an' look on me like I was the Queen o' Sheba. I was grown enough to toss my head and look sidelong an' say nothin', like the white misses on their verandas, tho' I hardly knew what Master Richard meant 'bout Tom havin' me, or bein' my man. Oh, I knew what he an' the other bucks did with the wenches in the cabins, but I was the li'l Princess an' far above the doin's of the common slaves. My love fo' Tom was different; I yearned to have him with me, 'cos he was big an' brave an' would never let harm come to me, and if you'd asked me what I meant by lovin' him, I couldn't ha' said more'n that. I was innocent an' foolish an' fifteen, an' thought in fairytales. Nowadays I lay no claim to innocence or gi'lish folly, am three times as old, an' the only fairytales I read come in yellow covers . . . but I still can explain no better what I felt for Tom, then. Maybe it was true love, like he said.

Heigh-ho . . . yes, I think jus' a wee touch more brandy would be acceptable, when I come to think back on that night in Awlins. Master Richard had brought this little sailor-man to Amplefo'th, to brisk Tom up for 'nother fight, 'gainst a nigra called the Black Ghost. Ev'yone allowed it would be Tom's sternest trial yet, an' the sailor-man goaded him on to run an' leap over rails an' split kindlin', with Master Richard fussin' an' runnin' after them, an' the sailor-man cryin': "It's his legs, guv'nor! Got to make them legs like mainmasts!'' I remember he said that, over an' over, in that cracky English voice. I didn't know what a mainmast was, or what jumpin' an' splittin' wood had to do with prize-fightin'. I jus' found it all mighty amusin', but Tom didn't care for it. The sailor-man made him a big sack o' corn-husks an' bark, an' Tom had to whale at it with his fists, an' he liked that well. Master Richard had me down to the yard to watch him beat the sack, an' when Tom flagged, Master would point to me an' whisper in his ear, an' Tom would lay into the sack till it bu'st wide open. Lord, what a lovin' fool he was! An' I would clap an' cheer him on, an' feel the butterflies inside me as I looked on those splendid limbs a-gleam in the sunlight.

Yes, suh, indeed. You are f'miliar, I don' doubt, with those Greek an' Roman statues which are thought to show the ab-solute p'fection of the male form? I have viewed them, too, as well as – you may set this down – a great many livin' examples also, an' I am here to tell you that Tom Molineaux's was the most beautiful human body I have ever seen. M'm-h'm! Oh, his features were homely, like I said – fact, I can't recall many uglier – but that frame o' his was fit to melt a gal's legs f'm under. Talk 'bout heroic! Bein' young an' simple at the time, I did not rec'nise the feelin' I was feelin' then, tho' I can put a name to it now . . . but I shan't. Jus' say that if I'd been Queen Cle-o-patra an' seen him up fo' auction, the other bidders would ha' gone home dis'pointed.

It was that time Master Richard hinted 'bout Tom an' me bein' wed. Maybe he meant it, I can't tell. Mos' folks would say the reason he an' old Molineaux had been at such pains to keep a beautiful high-yaller gal virgin, was so they could get a real fancy price fo' her when she bloomed, 'round sixteen—seventeen, but I don' know 'bout that. They looked down their V'ginia noses at nigra-traders, so I can't be sure what they intended by me. All I know is what Master Richard said, an' I was the happiest l'il chucklehead in the state.

An' then the snake came wrigglin' in. M'sieur Lucie d'Estrees de la Goddam Guise, with his silk coat an' gold-topped cane an' eye-glass, fingerin' his dandy moustache an' scented like a female. He was Master Richard's cousin, an' we stopped at his fine house out by Pontchartrain the day before Tom's fight in Awlins. I was called to be shown off to him, an' had to hide my laughter, for I had ne'er seen such a picture of a popinjay, so bedecked an' ruffled an' languid fit to die. He looked old to me, so I guess he was forty, maybe, an' when he called me close to pet me I was still strugglin' not to laugh right out.

Then I saw his eyes, an' my laughter died inside me. They were sleepy and chill, an' as they looked me over, with that mean smile on his pretty little mouth, I fell a-tremble with fear, an' felt shamed and unclean somehow, to be so regarded. He stroked my cheek with his soft fingers all scented with rings on 'em, an' it was as though a slimy critter was leavin' its track on my skin. When he said, in that lispin' voice, how pretty I was, an' slipped a candy in my mouth, I near gagged it out, an' when he asked Master Richard what my price was, an' Master Richard said I wasn't for sale, I near swooned with relief. I could think of nothin' more horrible than to be owned by that mincin' exquisite with his gentle voice an' clammy touch and evil eyes. I didn't know why he was wicked, or why his gaze defiled me; I just knew he was vile in ways I couldn't understand.

You don't need me, thank God, to describe Tom's fight with the Black Ghost, an' I would not if I could. To me, a child, it was a first glimpse into Hell, with a chorus of yellin' fiends transpo'ted in cruel delight as they watched my love bein' tortured an' mangled by that monster. I stopped my ears an' eyes, an' thought I must go mad, an' when I saw his poor body broke an' dyin' (as I thought) on the ground, I threw myself on him wishin' only that I might die with him. Worst of all was to hear his own master, who I s'posed loved an' cared for him, threaten to have him killed by inches, an' to see Tom, all bloodied an' beaten, drag himself up again to be sacrificed.

Then the serpent de la Guise came whisperin' at my ear, lispin' of freedom for Tom an' me, an' how I might put spirit in him. Between my crazy grief an' wild hope I did as he bid me, with no thought of my fear an' loathin' of him. An' Tom won, I can't say how, for I could not bear to see it. Then I knew such joy – for he was free an' would make me free also. I would have blessed de la Guise an' kissed his foot in gratitude, but he went quickly away.

Ganymede, who was de la Guise's yellow valet, put me in a carriage with Tom, to take us back to de la Guise's house, for Master Richard was in such an ecstasy at his vict'ry that he must stay behind to celebrate, I s'pose, with his cronies an' such. I didn't care; I was with Tom, weepin' for happiness as I kissed his awful wounds an' comforted him, tellin' him of de la Guise's promise, an' how we would be free together – I, who hardly knew what freedom meant. Even Tom, dull Tom, knew more of it than I, for he put his great strong arm, with its cruelly broken hand, 'bout me, an' kept sayin' over an' over: "Free! Free! Free! Oh, li'l Mollybird, you my own woman now! My li'l princess, my true love!"

Yes, if there has been a moment in my life to call blessed, it was then, in that carriage rumblin' home to Pontchartrain, an' freedom.

They took Tom to the slave quarters to tend to his hurts, an' Ganymede gave me in charge of a tall mulatto woman who I guess was chatelaine. She turned me this way an' that, sniffed at my cotton dress an' old shoes as unfittin', and asked real cold when I'd bathed last. 'Twas only then, I think, that it came home to me that I was de la Guise's slave now, an' I shivered to think on't, 'til I remembered how kind he'd been at that awful fight. I was more scared of the mulatto woman's sour face an' bony hands, an' the big bunch of keys she carried like a jailer.

She gave me over to two black maids in dimitty dresses an' caps, such as I'd never seen, an' they took me upstairs to a room with a big bath on a tiled floor, an' washed me all over with scented suds. I felt like a princess then, an' thought I must be dreamin', in that wondrous house with its great hall an' sweepin' staircase an' lovely paintin's an' carpets an' marble columns such as I'd never 'magined. Why, I'd never seen a bathroom before, let alone thought to use one. Amplefo'th had seemed a palace, but it was a shack to this place, with all its luxur'ous appointments an' gilt furniture. It made me feel small an' frightened, 'til I remembered Tom was free, an' de la Guise would let him make me free, too.

After the maids had dried me I asked for my clothes, an' they snickered into their aprons an' said there was a fire in the room where I was to be taken.

"You ain't goin' need no clo'es tonight awhile, li'l honey gal," says one. "Nor no night-rail, neether."

"But don' fret yo'self," says t'other maid. "You'll get plenny silk dresses by'n'by, an' ribbons an' fal-lals, sho' 'nuff!"

When I saw the bed-chamber I was left speechless, it was so grand an' tasteful, in the loveliest soft colours, peach an' pink an' ivory, with a mighty four-post bed hung in silks, and mirrors ev'ywhere, so that I was put out to see myself bare wherever I looked, an' pulled the sheet from the bed 'round me. The mulatto woman came in, an' slapped me for makin' free with the sheet, an' bid the maids put it back. Now I was real scared, an' like to cry when she pulled me by the arm to a little window in the wall.

"Stand there," says she, an' slapped me again. "Keep yo' eyes open an' yo' mouth shet, or 'twill be the wuss for you, ye heah?"

I shook like a willow, for fear an' 'mazement as I looked through the window into another room that was set much lower in the house so that I was lookin' down into it, an' the folks in it were 'way beneath me. There was de la Guise layin' at his ease in a silk dressin'-gown on a chaise longue, smokin' his cigar, but what robbed me o' breath was the two white ladies on a couch nearby. One was yellow-haired an' t'other red, an' they were painted an' patched to admiration. I had never seen anythin' in the world so grand an' beautiful an' stylish. I thought they mus' be real princesses, or queens even, an' couldn't think why they didn't wear hardly any clothes at all. I'd never seen white ladies near naked before, an' was wonder-struck to see 'em so pretty an' soft 'neath their clothes.

The room itself was sumptuous, with walls lined with gold satin, an' furniture looked soft enough to sink into. There were paintin's on the walls of more lovely white ladies, an' near the fireplace smaller pictures of white men half-naked, standin' in poses with their hands raised as I'd seen Tom stand when the sailor-man had been 'structin' him. There was the sweetest smell of perfume, and I remember thinkin' (God help me!) that Heaven must look somethin' like that room, an' angels like those painted ladies.

Then a door opened down there, an' my heart leaped, for it was Tom, with that Ganymede. They had washed him clean of blood, an' though there was a plaster on his cheek an' on his brow that was swollen, an' his right hand was bandaged, it was a joy to see him walk steady an' like his old self. He was taken all aback to see the ladies there, an' I could have blushed to see them sit up smilin' on the couch, showin' off their bosoms before a coloured man, so bold. Tom stood confused an' put down his head, but I could see him givin' them a shot of his eye sidelong. De la Guise rose, very languid, an' looked at him, an' poor Tom stood mum, but couldn't keep from watchin' the white ladies.

"Well, Tom Molineaux," says de la Guise, "so you are a free man now. And right nobly you have earned your freedom. Who taught you this, eh?"

An' he let drive his left hand an' hit Tom smack on the mouth, an' laughed. Tom made a mumble, an' de la Guise said he had been well 'structed, but had much to learn.

"How will you live now that you are free?" asks he. "Will you be a prize-fighter?"

"Yes, mass'," mutters Tom. I could hardly hear him.

"But here you may fight only black men like yourself," says de la Guise. "Crude animals like the one you killed tonight." 'Twas the first I'd heard of the Black Ghost bein' killed, an' I gave a little cry. The mulatto woman twisted my hair an' hissed at me like a cat to quiet me. "If you aspire to be a true boxer, you must fight white men, and you can do that only in England, which is the home of the Noble Art." I doubt Tom had heard of England, for he was dumb.

Then de la Guise showed him the little pictures on the wall, sayin' that these were the great English champions. He called off their names, but I don't recall them, except one that stayed in my mind because it didn't sound English, but now bein' f'miliar with Spanish names, I b'lieve it was one such.

"Why, that man is half your size and weight," cries de la Guise. "But he could cut you to pieces in moments!" Tom looked at the picture an' growled somethin' I couldn't hear, an' de la Guise laughed an' claps his shoulder.

"Wait until you face such a man, you'll learn different. But do you know, Tom, whenever that man fights he makes one thousand dollars? Sometimes two thousand, five thousand, even. Why, in England they think more of him than of their King! You know what a king is, Tom?"

"Like in stories mammy tells," grunts Tom.

"Exactly so! Tom, you could fight like that man. You are strong and brave and supple. But you could learn only in England. Would you care to go to England, Tom?"

43

I could tell, from the jeerin' way he said it, an' the smile on those plump lips, that he was makin' game of him.

"If mass' say," mumbles Tom, an' de la Guise laughed, mockin'.

"No, no, Tom, if *you* say! Why, you are free, and your own master. Would you like to live high, and do as you pleased, ride in a carriage, wear fine clothes, like this robe of mine – feel, Tom, how smooth it is." Tom touched the robe like it was red hot, an' de la Guise spoke soft. "You could have white ladies, Tom, like these." He fluttered a hand, an' the two ladies got up an' walked over ever so lazy-like. One stood before Tom, smilin' an' poutin', an' t'other came beside him an' put a hand on his shoulder, an' they fairly did languish at him. I could not believe my eyes, white ladies with a coloured man.

"Do you like them, Tom?" says de la Guise. "I believe they like you very much. Eh, my dears?"

The ladies began to pet Tom an' caress him, an' the yellow-haired one was strokin' his arm, exclaimin' how strong he was, an' the other kissed his mouth an' clung to him. I was sick to my stomach to see white ladies so demean themselves, but de la Guise laughed and said he must not fear them, for they admired him and yearned to give him pleasure. Tom began to shake an' stare like a wild thing, an' then they left plaguin' him an' de la Guise asked him again if he liked white ladies. Tom stood dumb, gaspin' and all a-tremble, an' de la Guise struck him in the face to make him answer.

"Reckon so, mass'," says Tom, shakin' fit to die.

"Better than your little Mollybird?" asks de la Guise, an' my heart went cold as he glanced up at my window. Then he nodded to the ladies, an' they came close to Tom again, pesterin' an' cooin' like doves.

"Surely not?" says de la Guise. "She is waiting for you, Tom, in this house. Come with me now, and you may take her away, free, the two of you. I promised her you should have the money for her purchase." Oh, that soft, lispin' voice might have belonged to the fiend that tempted Jesus. "Or, if you please, you may stay here awhile with the white ladies. Choose, Tom. Which shall it be? One or the other. Sweet little Mollybird, or these loving white ladies?"

The mulatto woman had my hair in her grip, an' a bony hand 'cross my mouth to stifle my cry. 'Twas like a nightmare as I heard de la Guise repeat that vile, evil offer, an' through my tears I could only watch helpless as Tom, the poor mindless fool, went where his blind lust took him, an' let those white harlots embrace him an' draw him down unresistin' on their couch.

Must I tell you what I suffered in that moment? I think not. To say my heart broke – what does it mean? Yet 'tis all there is to say. Mollybird began to die in that moment, Mollybird the simple, trustin' little yellow gal. She's been dead many, many years now, her an' her broken heart, an' Señora Marguerite Rossignol, who has no heart, can say: what use to blame Tom Molineaux for bein' what he was? You'd as well blame a baby for crawlin' to a shiny toy. 'Twas no real choice that temptin' toad offered him, 'cos like a baby he didn't have a mind to choose with. Only a body.

I remember crouchin' by the bed, with the fire so hot to one side o' me, an' all cold on t'other, an' then de la Guise was in the room, speakin' to the mulatto woman.

"She saw and heard? Everything? Oh, excellent!" He went across to the little window, an' stood lookin' down, an' gave a little yelp of laughter. Then he turned to the mulatto. "Presently, have Ganymede pay those two, and put that animal into the street. Now go. I am not to be disturbed."

He came an' stood over me, still smilin' with those hateful snake's eyes, an' nibblin' at his lip. I was too numb with mis'ry to think even, let alone wonder that any man could be so cruel as make me see what I had seen.

"Poor little golden nymph," says he in that jeerin' lispin' voice. "So exquisite. So forlorn. Beauty, abandoned by the Beast. What would you? A brute has the appetites of a brute. But can she guess, I wonder, how great a favour the Beast has done to Beauty? What would freedom have brought her, with such a creature? What would her fate have been, eh?"

He bid me rise, an' I was too broke in despair to disobey, or even to shrink when he began to stroke my lips an' cheek with those soft slug fingers. Then he bid me walk 'cross to the door, an' back again, watchin' me with that gloatin' smile. "Perfection," says he, sighin', an' took my hands an' kissed them, an' at that I began to cry an' shake with fear at last, an' begged him to let me be, an' he began to laugh.

That, I think, is as much as I care to remember for you. No more is necessary, for I have told you all that I know of Tom Molineaux. The transfo'mation of Mollybird into Señora Rossignol, by that scented vermin de la Guise an' others, I am happy to leave to your 'magination. He was right, of course. I should be grateful to Tom. If he'd been true to Mollybird, there'd ha' been no elegant coloured lady, with her fine house an' servants an' carriage an' all, inquirin' of a gennleman visitor if he would care to partake of a service of aft'noon tea an' pastries ... If you'd be so kind as to draw the bell-rope yonder ... ?

CAPTAIN BUCKLEY ("MAD BUCK")
FLASHMAN,
late of the 23rd Light Dragoons

Black? What black? Ah, Molineaux, the fellow who gave Cribb pepper and a half . . . *that* black. Should think I do remember him. Made a rare packet of rhino out o' the brute, cost old Crocky and Jew King a fortune, wept all the road to Jerusalem, ha-ha! Aye, a sound investment, Black Tom, knew it the moment I clapped eyes on him, at the old Nag and Fish — the Horse and Dolphin,* you must know it, in St Martin's Street as you come off Leicester Square . . . no? Gone now, I dare say, but 'twas there I launched Tom on the road to Fistic Fame, as Egan would say, for 'twas my word that swayed Richmond, no doubt o' that. It was his ken in those days, where the sporting set was used to play cricket in the back field . . . oh, Alvanley, Sefton, poor old Berkeley Craven (blew his brains out over the '36 Derby, affected ass), Mellish, Webster, God knows who. I played a single-wicket match there once against Byron, the late poet. Odd fish, bit his nails, wore curl papers in bed to give his manly locks the romantic twist, got in a fearful wax 'cos I called him Sleeping Beauty . . . not a bad bowler, mind; not in Brummell's parish, but too good for me. No, boxing was my game — and milord Byron wasn't up to my snuff there, I can tell you, gamecock though he was. Small wonder. Why, I was the best amateur miller of the day, bar Barclay Allardice. I floored Cribb . . . once. Shan't tell you what he did to me . . .

Did I *know* Molineaux? Good God, man, I told you I *remember* him, but one don't *know* that sort of specimen. Nigger pugs, what next? Anyway, what the devil is he to you, whoever you are? Who let you in here, for that matter? You ain't a patient, are you? Or one o' those damned mealy brain-scrubbers? No . . . you don't have the

---

* Also known as the Nag and Blower, the Prad and Swimmer, the Prad and Pilchard, etc.

style to be barmy, and not sly enough for a pill-slinger . . . damn them all . . .

Ah, the Superintendent let you in, did he? And said you might talk to me? Burn his blasted impudence, never asked my leave – who the dooce does he think he is, my keeper? Aye . . . that's precisely what he *does* think, rot him. Well, let me tell you, sir, that my apartments are *not* to let, like most of 'em. I am one of a select band of gentlemen resident in this charming rural establishment because we have lost the battle with delirium tremens – temporarily, I hasten to add – and are in need of a breather between rounds, so to speak. We are here of our own free will, at exorbitant rates, have the freedom of the grounds, do not consort with the loonies, and . . . I say, you don't happen to have a drop of anything with you, I suppose? Flask, bottle, demijohn, something of the sort?

Ah, pity. We might have spent a convivial hour discussing thingummy . . . Molineaux, did you say? Interesting aborigine, that . . . don't suppose there's a man in England could tell you more of his doings, in *and* out o' the green fairy circle, than I . . . oh, the old pugs, to be sure, but their wits are addled, and fellows like Egan and Hazlitt would just rap a deal of romantic nonsense. They don't know the story of Barclay's gloves, or Joe Ward and the bullets, or how that ass Sefton came within an ace of challenging Prinny to a duel – yes, over Molineaux, I do assure you – or the indiscretions of Lady . . . ah, but we shan't mention names, what would they say at Almack's?

Yes, we could have had a jolly prose together . . . but I cannot abide *dry* discourse, what? So, good day to you . . . don't roll your eyes or laugh too loud on the way out or they'll clap you in the comic box before you can say "Bender!" Adieu, adieu . . .

What's that? You could call again after luncheon . . . with a spot o' lush, no doubt. My dear fellow, what a capital notion. Put 'em in separate pockets so that they don't clink . . . the attendants here have ears like dago guerrillas, 'tis like being in the blasted Steel . . . Better still, tell you what – see down yonder, past the trees, there's a gap in the fence that our turnkeys haven't twigged yet, much frequented by the local mollishers – personable young females of loose conduct, sir, who disport themselves with us wealthier inmates, for a consideration.

Gad, the state of the country! I shall be there at two, you can run the cargo in safety, and we shall not be espied or earwigged . . .

Damn you, did I say two o'clock or did I not? Already? Gad, how time flies. Well, thank God you weren't beforehand . . . You'd best be off, m'dear – here's a guinea for you. Tomorrow at six, mind . . . There she trips, my village Titania . . . sweet seventeen and goes like a widow of fifty. Don't look askance at me, sir, if you were in this bloody bastille you'd be glad of a tickletail yourself. Now, have you brought . . . oh, famous! Sir, you are a pippen of the first flight! Brandy, bigod, that'll answer. Fix bayonets and form square, belly, the Philistines are upon thee . . . Ah-h-h! Aye, that's the neat article. Sir, your good health . . .

Now, tell me, how did you get my direction in the first place? My *son*? 'Pon my soul, that was uncommon condescending of him; he don't use to oblige strangers, unless . . . didn't lend him money, did you? You married? Ah, you have a sister . . . oh, charming fellow, absolutely, quite the military lion, too. Taking her to see the hippopotamus, is he . . . and then to Astley's? I see . . . oh, couldn't be in better hands. No need for you to race back to Town . . .

Well, now, since we have time before us, I tell you what – ne'er mind questions, I'll recollect, and you can take notes. Capital . . . Now, you're too young, I take it, to remember London in the old days – in the French war, I mean, before the Regency? Just so. Well, if you're to understand about Molineaux, and how he came to make such an almighty stir, and so forth, I must set you right about that time. 'Twas as different from today as junk from Offley's beef. Free and easy and jolly, no one giving a dam, churches half-empty and hells packed full, fashion and frolic the occupations, and sport the religion. Boney might be master of the Continent, and Wellington hanging on by his eyelids in Spain, but they were the deuce of a long way from Hyde Park and the night cellars; the many-headed might be on short commons and the government in Queer Street, but when were they not, eh? A few sobersides fretted about morality and revolution, but since most o' the country was three-parts drunk, nobody minded them. The Town was on the spree, and we were "on the Town".

Hard to swallow, eh, for your serious generation, taking your lead

49

from our sedate young Queen, God bless her, and her pump-faced
German noodle – ah, there's the difference, in a nutshell! *You* have
the muff Albert, God help you, pious, worthy, dull as a wet Sabbath
and dressed like a dead Quaker; *we* had fat Prinny, boozy and cheery
and chasing skirt, in the pink of fashion as cut by Scott and approved
by Brummell. That's the difference thirty years has made. Your states-
men don't gamble or fight duels; there ain't one trace-kicker among
your Society women; royalty don't fornicate or have turn-ups at coro-
nations nowadays; and what noble lord trains a prize pug or flees to
France with the duns in full cry? Where are your dandy Corinthian
out-and-outers, dazzling the *ton*, sparring with the Black Beetles or
charging Kellerman's cavalry, breaking their necks over hedges, and
all for the fun of it? Or your peep-o'-day Quality beauties, with their
night-long parties, but fresh as daisies in Hyde Park by day? Or your
high-flight Cyprians, rising by wit and beauty from nowhere to enchant
the bucks and set the scandalised tea-cups rattling from Apsley House
to Great Swallow Street?

No, they wouldn't suit in this stale age, for they were a different
breed, male and female. I don't see the like today of Moll Douglas or
Caro Lamb, or Jane Harley – Lady Oxford to you, who had so many
brats by assorted sires they called 'em the Harleian Miscellany – or
dear Hetty Stanhope, even, who decamped to be a Turkish sultana, as
I recall. Women had style, then, as well as beauty. And men today
are so damned *sane* and proper, not like Camelford, who went to
France in disguise to try to murder Napoleon, or Jack Lade who married
a highwayman's wench, or my chum Harry Mellish who locked Clarence in the roundhouse and once lost forty thousand pounds on the
roll of a single dice, or the three Barrymores – Hellgate, Cripplegate,
and Newgate, so Prinny called 'em, and their noble sister was Billings-
gate, on account of her fishwife tongue. Aye, it was a different age,
gone now – and good riddance, you may think. But if it was wild and
reckless, it was alive, with spirits that England couldn't accommodate
today. It was ready for any kind of lark and freak, and to hail the likes
of Tom Molineaux as a nine-day wonder.

He wouldn't be that nowadays, I can tell you. Not to the modern
taste, any more than the bucks and beauties of his time would be.

Why's that, eh? I'll tell you why your age is different, and staid, and settled. It's 'cos you ain't had a good war in years; you han't peered into the abyss and looked death and ruin in the face. We did, with Europe under the Corsican's boot, the French at our gate, and Old England on the lion's lip. You may say now that the crisis was passed by '10 or '11, but we didn't know it. We'd just seen the finest force that Britannia ever sent overseas, forty thousand strong, wrecked at Walcheren, and our battered Peninsulars being driven back to Portugal. The devil with it, we said, we'll beat 'em yet, and whether we do or whether we don't, we'll eat, drink, and be merry, for 'tis all one. That's why England was full of sin and impudence, then.

No doubt you think our great concerns should ha' been Boney, or the Luddites, or when the King, poor Old Nobbs, would lose the last of his wits (such as he had), and whether Prinny would bring in the Whigs. Those are the matters treated of by bookworms and historians and fellows of that sort, who regard 'em as the burning topics of the day. Not a bit of it.

What d'ye think was the talk of the Town when I came back from the Peninsula in '09? Aye, I was invalided home after Talavera – that was the excuse, leastways, but the fact was I'd fought four duels in three weeks, and Old Hooky wouldn't stand it: swore I did our own side more harm than Victor. Damned sauce. I'd done the Frogs harm enough, and he knew it.

Talavera . . . Gad, that was the day. Who's heard of it now, the Spanish Waterloo, where the Peninsular war trembled in the balance? If we'd lost, Spain was lost, and perhaps the war; Wellesley would never ha' been Wellington, that's certain, and Boney would ha' conquered Russia. Talavera . . . heat, and dust, and bloody bayonets. Wellington vowed it was the most desperate fight he'd ever seen, with Victor outnumbering us two to one – aye, we proved that one Briton was worth two Frogs, that day. Good men, though, those same Frogs – d'ye know, there was a truce in the midst of the battle, when we and they watered our beasts together in the Portina brook, and exchanged snuff and civilities? Old Villatte, who commanded their cavalry, was there, and offered "King" Allan of the Guards his flask. King sluiced his ivories and shook hands.

"Thank'ee, *mon général*," says King. "Hot day, ain't it? Why don't you go home?"

"Après vous, m'sieur," grins old Villatte, and everyone burst out laughing, and our rankers and the French *moustaches* were swapping fills o' their pipes, and we cheered each other back to the lines.

Then they came at us like tigers, as only Frogs can, with "Old Trousers" thundering along a two-mile front, that huge mass of infantry tearing a great hole in our line. Fraser Mackenzie's Midlanders held on like bulldogs, it was touch and go, and then Victor let drive at our left flank below the Medellin Hill, and I thought we was done for.

"Now or never!" cries Anson. "Off you go, Ponsonby!" and away we went, 23rd Lights and German Legion, knee to knee against that huge tide of Froggy horse in the valley, with the trumpeters sounding charge. We were going full tilt when the hidden gully opened almost under our hooves, and "Hold on, Flash!" bawls Ponsonby, but my hunter was over it like a swallow, and the rest came jumping or tumbling after, and we went into their Green Chasseurs like a steel fist, sabres whirling and fellows going down like ninepins, such a turn-up as you never saw. There was a French square behind us, and great waves of their cavalry before, two hundred of our 23rd boys went down, but we scattered the Chasseurs, and then their Chevaux Legers and Polish Lancers broke over us like a tide, with those damned whistles in their helmets wailing like banshees. I took a lance in the leg and a cut on the neck – see here – but was holding my own till my poor little grey went down and some blasted Pole put a bullet through my sword-arm.

Time's up, Flash, thinks I, you won't make scratch this time, for what was left of us was being trampled underfoot, but they took me prisoner, along with a few others, and I was exchanged next day, leaking like a cracked pot. But they hadn't turned our flank, bigod, and our centre held, Froggy drew off with his bellyful, leaving seven thousand dead to our five thousand, Old Hooky ceased to be Wellesley and became Lord Wellington . . . and that was Talavera.

You know what came of it . . . we lived to fight another day, Hooky withdrew to Portugal, foxed Masséna with Torres Vedras, and held French armies in Spain that Boney could have used in Russia where he froze to death, France was beat – and all because the Light Brigade crossed that gully, perhaps. I like to think so, at all events; worth being skewered and trampled, what? In the meantime, I came home . . . now,

52

where the devil was I, before you reminded me of the Peninsula?

Ah, yes, I was asking what you supposed the buzz was in Town that autumn of '09? The war? The King's madness? The Cabinet? No such thing. The name on every lip wasn't Talavera or Hooky or Boney, but Mary Clarke – and I'll lay a million to a mag you never heard of her, eh? I thought not.

Ah, Mary! She was the sweetest little nesting-bird, and my first love 'fore I went to Spain – well, one of 'em. Shape of Aphrodite, sassy as a robin, and devoted to the study of cavalry subalterns – when she wasn't accommodating the Duke of York, that is. She was his prize pullet, you see, and we lesser lights (I was a mere cornet of horse then, but she was nuts on me) had to slip in at her back door in Gloucester Place like so many area sneaks. Gad, she was the bang-up Cyprian, though! Ten horses, three cooks, twenty servants, dined off a French duke's plate, and entertained like a bashaw's niece – York gave her a thousand a month, and you may believe 'twasn't enough. So dear Mary set up shop selling Army promotions, slipping the tickets for York to sign when he was too lushy or baked with her fond attentions to notice, I dare say. Oh, a prime racket she had, until some parliamentary pimp blew the gaff.

There was the devil to pay, York had to resign command of the Army, Mary was called to the Bar of the House and had 'em in fits with her sauce and sharp answers, and to crown all she threatened to publish York's love-letters. I saw some of 'em, and they were hot-house stuff, I can tell you. Cost the old calf's head ten thou' and a pension of four hundred a year to buy 'em back.

D'ye wonder that Mary Clarke was all the chat from St James's to St Giles? Mere wars and Commons votes weren't in it with her – or with Moll Douglas, the bird of paradise whom Mornington, Hooky's brother, had in tow when he went out as Minister to Spain. That set the tongues wagging at Almack's, for what made it worse was that Mornington's lawful blanket wouldn't divorce him or clear out of Apsley House. She'd been another bareback rider until Mornington married her; French piece, Gabrielle Hyacinthe de Something. Shocking taste in women he had. Whores, the lot o' them.

What's this to do with Molineaux? Why, to impress upon you what a light-minded crew of sensation-seekers Society was, ripe for any novelty — female, criminal or sporting for choice — and because it pleases me to hold forth at length while sampling this excellent drop o' short. So don't dam' well interrupt. We'll come to the Dusky Miller presently.

Speaking of sport, there was a mighty stink at Newmarket about that time, when two touts called Bishop and Dan Dawson were bribed to see that certain horses didn't start, so they blew arsenic into the water troughs, poisoned I don't know how many runners. They were grabbed, Bishop peached to save his neck, but it was the Paddington frisk for Danny, and half the turf set went down to Cambridge to see him drop, more than one noble lord, I'm told, heaving a sigh of relief when he died with his mouth shut.

Not that politics was altogether neglected in the clubs and drawing-rooms. Why, the day I landed there was a disagreement in Cabinet. Foreign secretary, Canning, an intriguing toad, if you ask me, with an eye on Downing Street, blamed the war minister, Castlereagh, for the Walcheren fiasco, and Castlereagh demanded pistols for two on Putney Heath. The pair of cakes missed each other altogether with their first shots, tried again, Castlereagh put a slug in Canning's leg, and Canning shot a button off his lordship's coat. I heard the news from Kangaroo Cooke, York's old aide.

"Bet you're glad they weren't alongside at Talavera," says he. "Still, they scored one hit, which is more than Tierney and Pitt could manage — and say this for 'em, it's a dam' stylish way to bring down a government."

Wasn't he right, though? Can't see Melbourne or Peel having the game to shoot each other, worse luck.

So, sir, there you have me, back in Town . . . and I can see the leery look in your eye as you hear me refer so familiarly to Society, with idle mention of nobility and royalty, and ask yourself, do I speak of what I know, or am I a rasher o' wind retailing second-hand goods? Yes, you do, damn your impudence, I know. You've cast about, I don't doubt, and are aware that the Flashmans are a smoky lot, not halfway up the tree nowadays. My son has the fame of his Afghan laurels, as I had mine in the Peninsula, but they don't last, and once the shine has gone, you're an unregarded relic of a disreputable age.

54

We ain't Quality, never were. Know what my father was? A slave-trader, making enough from black ivory to be a nabob, bought himself a house in South Audley Street and a place in the shires, sent me to Rugby, stumped up for my colours – but he was still trade, and if I was to cut my way into the charmed circle I must do it with my sabre. God knows I tried, at Rolica and Vimeiro, and scouting along the Douro, hunting glory, and in that charge at Talavera. I was "Mad Buck" when I came home, hero of the hour – aye, and *for* the hour – pointed out at Horse Guards, worth a hail-fellow from Clarence and a shake of the hand from Prinny, who swore he couldn't ha' done better himself, by George, sir, he couldn't . . . and wondered if I dare turn my eyes on the beauteous 'Lishy Paget – now she *was* Quality, and above my touch, but I had the style and the shoulders, and I reckoned the Flashman blunt wouldn't hurt.

Aye, but if you're a hero – and one who has cut his pigtail, mind – you must ride the rocket while it's ascending, for the stick'll come down at last. I pray God it never does for young Harry; with luck it won't, for he has a way with him, and the kind of fame that'll last a lifetime, even if he don't add to it, which he likely will. He don't know it, but by God I'm proud of him. He won his spurs clean, and he don't have that rum shadow that clung to me over my duelling – can't think why I was such a fire-eater in the Peninsula, but I was, and the hellish fact is that when you've been out a couple o' times you find a taste for it. Harry's a cooler hand altogether – why, the only time he stood up the young madman gave his man a free shot, and then deloped! I was never reckoned a funk, but damned if I'd ever have the pluck for that! Aye, I'm proud – as I shall tell him when . . . well, if he visits me. When you see him, you might . . . no, better not. Guv'nor in the blue-devil factory's best at a distance, eh?

I'll take some more of the red tape, if you please . . . thank'ee. And you may pour out that bottle of belch, too . . . To come to the point, when I came home in '09 I was a hero – and nobody. I'd been on the edge of the sporting set as a younker, before I went to Spain – sparred with Cribb, as I told you, took my wet at Stephen's and Limmer's, was reckoned a useful pradster at the Corner (no seat at the Monday dinners, though), lost a careful amount at Crocky's hell in Oxford Street, but was nowhere near Brooks' or Waitier's where the real gamesters played, and far outside the swim of the prime swells, the Four-in-Handers and heads of the Fancy.

As for the *ton*, the world of Society, I was nowhere. Too young, too unconnected, too unknown. The nearest I'd ever come to the top flight was to mount York's mistress unbeknownst, La Clarke aforesaid, and God knows I wasn't the only one to do that.

This won't do, thinks I, and pondered how I might make a "character" in Town, win my way into the clubs and salons, be a figure on the turf and in the Fancy, and, in fine, become a regular out-and-outer, a buck o' the first head, at home in Almack's and the Daffy Club* both, winning the lofty approval of the Town tabbies in the Park and pattering the flash in the Holy Land – and a mean, dicky ambition, you may say, but you ain't a young horse soldier with his glory all behind him whose father made his pile shipping blackbirds.

I knew it could be done, for while the West End was a damned exclusive place, it was easier to break in then, in those easy times, than it is now. Brummell had done it from nowhere – well, Eton – by being pleasant, and a top-notch cricketer, and looking just so through his quizzing-glass (usually at Prinny's neckercher), but he was a one-and-only, was George. You had to be *noticed*, and then admitted, and while some did it by high play, or writing poems, or toad-eating at Holland House, or inventing a new neckercher, or rattling the right dowagers, or even clambering round a room on the furniture without touching the floor, none o' these would ha' been my style – except the dowagers, and I didn't know any. But I had a stroke of luck – the damnedest thing you ever imagined, and before I'd been home a month I was in prime twig, top o' the mark, and "on the Town".

It was this way. Kangaroo Cooke, whom I mentioned just now, was a leading dandy, a Big Gun. We'd met, just, when I was a lad, and now I ran into him in Craig's Court, when I was settling up my Army bills. He proved to be a chum of Ponsonby, my old squadron commander, so nothing would do but he must dine me at White's, and

---

* Captain Flashman may well have known the Daffy Club a few years later, but not in 1809. It was founded, as an irregular drinking fraternity, at the Castle Tavern, Holborn, during the tenancy of Tom Belcher the pugilist, who did not take over until 1814. Daffy was gin, so called from Daffy's Elixir for infants, to which gin was occasionally added. The Four-in-Hand Club, a group of aristocratic drivers, flourished at the same time.

there, keeping my trap shut, my eyes open, and earwigging away, I heard a piece of gossip – dammit, I couldn't help but hear, for they were full of it, the prime scandal of the hour. As thus:

One of the leading bright sparks of the day was young Harry Somerset, Marquis of Worcester and son and heir to the Duke of Beaufort no less, a well-regarded flower of our nobility who was as sober and decent as his son was wild and wanton. The boy was nutty on skirt, though not yet come of age (they're the worst, you know), with a new charmer each week, until of late he'd fallen under the spell of one Harriet Wilson, a nymph of the pavey whose conduct would ha' made Messalina look like a nun. Not the usual muslin, you understand, but a notorious siren who'd been mount to half the rakes in Town – a fact to which young Harry was evidently blind, as often happens with young fools and older women.

Boys will be boys, to be sure, but what was bringing Beaufort's grey hairs round his ankles was that the idiot pup was babbling of marriage to this harpy, and at this rate breach of promise would be the least of it. There could be no buying her off, not with a whack at the Beaufort fortune in prospect, and no talking sense into the besotted Harry. Beaufort wanted to buy him colours and ship him off to Spain as aide to Hooky himself, but Harry wasn't to be budged; he was at Harriet's dainty feet, wouldn't hear a word against her, and Beaufort, no doubt seeing himself having to cough up almighty damages or become father-in-law to the Whore of Babylon, was at a nonplus. Either way 'twould be a hideous scandal. What the devil, the gossips asked each other, was he to do?

Well, I could ha' told 'em in no time flat, but 'twas no concern of mine, and it was only later, in idle meditation, that it struck me that whoever could detach the love-smitten younger Somerset from Circe's embrace must surely earn the undying gratitude of Papa, one of the highest and most powerful peers in the land, a kingpin in Society, a Biggest of Big Guns, and the answer to a toad-eater's prayer. A duke's a duke, dammit, only one rung below a Prince of the Blood. It would have to be managed without expense, opprobrium, or the least breath of inconvenience to His Grace, but the dodge I had in mind was right as a gun, and promised a fine gig as well.

So I dug out my recently discarded regimentals and sauntered forth in full fig to call on La Belle Harriet at her crib in Mount Street (aptly named). My tale, earnestly delivered with becoming emotion, was that a comrade, Toby Wilson, had expired in my arms in the Peninsula, whispering: "M'sister . . . dearest Harriet . . .", and here I was in the hope that she was the sister referred to. In which case, my heartfelt condolences, and with them those little keepsakes which I had culled, with a manly tear, from his pockets – a snuff-box, rings, seals, baccy-pouch, and a pipe with a Saracen's head on the bowl, raked out from the rubbish in my attic.

Whether she swallowed it I've never been sure, and I doubt if she could tell you herself, for all her attention was taken with the dashing dragoon in his tight pants, bowing his stalwart six feet and fairly bursting with boyish admiration. That at least was genuine enough on my part, for she was an opulent beauty with a bold eye and a loose lip, not more than twice my age, and there was more cloth in her turban than in the rest of her deshabille.

In any event, dear old Toby was never mentioned again, and within an hour my youthful innocence had succumbed to the wiles of this practised enchantress. I ain't claiming it as a conquest, by the way, for I doubt if anything with whiskers could have escaped her when she had an hour to spare, and I'd no call to employ the family gift for seduction beyond an artless blush, a gasp of adoration, and letting her have her head. Afterwards, to be sure, I regarded her with calf-like worship and pleaded for a return, which she was pleased to promise for the following afternoon. In my juvenile passion I anticipated this by boarding her again on the spot, and left her in a state of sweet collapse, vowing to call again on the morrow at five precisely.

Next morning I scouted about and learned by inquiry that Harry Worcester's haunt of the day was the old O.P. tavern in Drury Lane, a theatrical ken kept by Hudson the song-smith, where the younger *ton* were used to look in for coffee and musical diversion of an early evening. That suited admirably, and I went home and wrote a note: "Oh blind, oh trusting! H.W. betrays you! If you doubt it, repair to her directly and behold Shameful Truth unveiled! A Friend", super-scribed and sealed it plain, and instructed my man, a seasoned artful dodger, to deliver it incog to the O.P. at five on the nail.

You can guess the rest – young Somerset, with blood in his eye, bursting in past a swooning abigail to discover his inamorata and your humble obedient rounding the last bend, so to speak. He let out a howl they must have heard in Lambeth.

"By God, it's true!" bawls he, nearly in tears, and damned her in violent terms, of which "Traitress!" was the least. What she said I don't recall, and he turned on me, crimson with fury and hurt pride. I had my britches on in a trice, in case he offered assault, but he knew how to bear himself, I'll say that. Good-looking lad, he was, and straight as a poker.

"I shall call you out!" stammers he. "Whoever the hell you are!"

"Over this bit o' soiled muslin?" says I. "Talk sense, lad. You'd find yourself fighting half London."

"Damn you!" cries he, and whipped his glove across my face, very dramatic. "My friends will wait upon you!"

"You'll wait a dam' sight longer," says I. "My lord, I was out half a dozen times in the Peninsula. I don't have to prove myself cub-shooting."

He went pale as chalk. "Dastard! Coward! I'll cane you in the street!"

"Try it, and I'll put you across my knee," I told him. "Now go home, you silly fellow. She ain't worth it. Be thankful you found out in time."

He wasn't a fool. You could see him struggling with his self-esteem as he looked from one to other of us. Then he fumbled out his purse and flung it on the bed before her.

"Take that, you . . . you . . ." He was choking mortified. "Oh, I am well served for a fool!" To my utter astonishment, he turned to me again. "Your pardon, sir. I struck you a coward's blow, and I am sorry for it." And then he burst into tears and stalked out, which marred the gestures, rather. Still, not bad for seventeen.

Save for one startled squeal, dear Harriet hadn't uttered a sound, but now, when I suggested we resume our romp, she spoke at some length, in terms which would have shamed a fishwife, and tried to rake me with her nails. I grabbed my duds and fled, pursued by abuse and flying crockery, leaving her to mourn her lost love, or her failure to nap his guv'nor's rent, more likely.

I toddled round to White's without delay, and sent my card in to Kangaroo Cooke. When he came down I drew him aside.

"I'd be obliged, colonel, if you would present my compliments to His Grace of Beaufort, and give him my assurance that he need feel no further anxiety over Lord Worcester's relations with a certain female person. A complete and final breach has taken place."

Kangaroo looked like a cod with a moustache at the best of times, but now he fairly gaped, and demanded what the dooce I meant.

"Not another word, sir," says I. "Pray deliver my message, and you may add that the matter has been managed with every discretion. Nothing will be heard from either party, and I believe that if His Grace renews his offer of colours to his lordship, it has every chance of acceptance."

"Buckley," says he, "what the devil have you been up to?"

"Let us say," I told him, "that I have had a word with the young man, and that he now sees where his duty lies. No, sir, I cannot in honour say more. I am delighted to have been of service to His Grace. Good evening, colonel."

I left him goggling, and as I'd expected young Harry Somerset removed himself from Town and the curiosity of the *ton* without delay, departing for the Army in Spain where, I'm happy to say, he distinguished himself as Wellington's galloper. I was less gratified, though, when Kangaroo buttonholed me on Piccadilly to tell me that His Grace of Beaufort sent his compliments, hoped to make my acquaintance at some convenient time, but regretted that this could not be for the present, owing to His Grace's many engagements. "Discretion, what?" says Kangaroo. "Never fret, he's damned obliged, I can tell you."

Well he might be, but I thought it dam' shabby; I'd looked for a word of thanks from the Duke himself, at least, but I didn't know how things were done, then, and was suitably dumfounded when there arrived a note from the leading Society female of the day, the queen of the cream of the *ton*, the Countess of Jersey, enclosing (I couldn't credit my senses, and it fluttered from my trembling fingers to the floor) a voucher for Almack's.

You can't conceive what that meant, so I'll tell you. Almack's was the holy of holies of the polite world, the innermost circle of the Upper

Ten Thousand, the pinnacle of Society, where only the favoured few could hope for admission. Why, ambassadors, generals, chaps with titles and pedigrees a yard long fairly clamoured and intrigued and toadied to be let in, and grovelled for a nod from the female dragons who ruled beneath its famous chandeliers. This was the club where Wellington himself was turned away for being improperly dressed, hang it all, not above one in fifty of the exclusive Guardees could cross the threshold – and mere Captain Flashman, late of the 23rd Lights, had a voucher. It was beyond belief.

Plainly Beaufort, God bless him, had hit on the finest (and least noticeable) way of rewarding me for my services, and had said a kind word to Lady Jersey, and she (as I learned later) had had me pointed out in the Park, and been pleased with the view. She was a remarkable creature, "Queen Sarah", undisputed leader of the Diamond Squad though she was still in her twenties, devilish handsome and mistress of forty thousand pounds a year, but renowned as the most affected, talkative, and downright uncivil woman in England. Her word was law at Almack's, and while I dare say my looks and bearing had something to do with my being sent that heavenly, precious voucher, I don't doubt she'd also done it to spite some other hopeful.

I made my debut with Kangaroo doing the honours, leading me across that glittering floor to the charmed half-circle where Sarah sat, plumed and ridiculously regal, with her court of grand dames, many of 'em unexpectedly young and pretty, and bursting with blue blood. It was like being presented to the Empress of Russia. She stirred her fan and looked me up and down, icy cool.

"I am told that they call you Mad Buck, Mr Flashman," drawls she. "I wonder why?"

"I am told that they call your ladyship Sweet Sally, marm," says I. "But I don't wonder at all." And before she could wither me for this effrontery, I gave her my gallant grin. "There, marm – now you know why they call me Mad Buck."

It could have cost me my voucher then and there, and for a moment she was at a loss how to take it – and then, d'ye know, she absolutely blushed with pleasure and laughed like a schoolgirl. Fact was, for all her airs she had no notion of proper behaviour, and was so used to being toadied that a saucy compliment from a devil-may-care soldier

61

took her unawares. I believe she decided that I was a "character", and might be indulged, so while others were given their formal name or title, I was "Buck" to her thereafter, and she, the toploftiest tabby of them all, was well pleased to be "Lady Sal", but to me alone. I offered her no other familiarity, I may say; she wasn't that sort.

So that was how I arrived "on the Town", and came to mingle with the upper crust, was welcomed from Almack's and Boodle's to Bob's Chophouse and Fishmonger's Hall,* received the nods from White's window and had my own stool and tankard in Cribb's Crib, and while never aspiring to be a Tulip, much less a Swell (for I dressed plain and expensive, à la Brummell, to impress Sweet Sally and the drawing-room mamas), was known as a regular out-and-outer, a Corinthian of the sporting sort, a flower of the Fancy who would fib with peer or pug . . . and best of all, I danced with 'Lishy Paget under the chandeliers, all those old country dances that she loved, Gathering Peasecods and Scotch reels, which were all the crack then, before the waltz came in . . .'Lishy of the flashing eyes and chestnut hair, dancing in a dream through those few golden years until she was taken from me, so young and lovely still, and full of life . . . and what did Society or Almack's or any of it matter then . . . ?

Damn your eyes, if I choose to grow maudlin in my cups it's not your place to sigh like a flatulent sow. Your own fault for pressing booze on me . . . come along, man, fill up. No doubt you feel you've been the soul of patience, listening to my social triumphs – and if you still think I've been telling rappers you may go to Almack's and look at their books, blast your impudence. It's in King Street, but I believe they call it Wilkins' or some such name nowadays; gone to the dogs, I dare say, like everything else.

Now, since I've educated you in the ways of that world of my long-lost youth, as a needful eye-opener, I'll tell you what you wish to know of Black Tom Molineaux, and how he brought the prize ring

---

* William Crockford (1775–1844), founder of the famous gaming club, began life as a fishmonger, and is supposed to have established himself as a professional gambler early in the century when he and his partner in a "hell" won £100,000 in a 24-hour sitting. "Fishmonger's Hall" was the name applied to his various establishments, including the palatial building in St James's Street which he eventually opened in 1827.

a fame and lustre it had never known before, and mayn't again. Aye, he did that ... he and one other. Tom Cribb of Bristol.

You'll have heard that after Broughton, who was the first true Champion nigh on a century ago, the Ring fell into disrepute. All kinds of sharps and ruffians came in, crosses were fought, and decent folk stayed clear of it. Two men rescued it, Dick Humphries and Dan Mendoza, splendid fibbers and straight – tho' there were those that said it was wonderful how Mendoza would come to life after the Jews had cried up the odds on his opponent. But they were my boyhood heroes, those two, Danny especially, for he was the first fighter to get up on his toes and move. Gentleman Jackson did for him, by ruffianing that had nothing genteel about it, and in their wake came three of the best that ever stepped up to the scratch: Hen Pearce, the Game Chicken; John Gully, who became an M.P. after Reform and is a name on the turf nowadays; Jem Belcher, who was the living spit of Boney and might ha' reigned forever if he hadn't lost an eye playing rackets.

Their battles, and Jackson's setting up his pugilistic academy, raised boxing to the heights and made it the first sport in England, patronised by royalty, talked of in every club and ken and cottage and great house from John o' Groats to the Land's End. The world of fashion took it to its bosom, why, even the Almack's tabbies murmured the odds on Maddox and Dutch Sam behind their fans, and admired the prints of Gregson, the Lancashire Giant, although only the faster Quality females attended the mills. No one could call himself a Corinthian who hadn't taken Jackson's lessons or sparred with the leading pugs, the noblest in the land sponsored the top men and backed 'em with fortunes, whenever a good mill was mooted the whole Town would be agog over the two men, their weights, their conditions, their records, who was training 'em, what were the odds, when would the office be given – for it was outside the law, you know – damme, I even heard Pearce and Gully coupled with David and Goliath in a sermon at St Margaret's. The whole nation was united in the Fancy, and took pride in it as showing the best and bravest of Old England.

The war had much to do with that, you know. Well, 'twas natural enough to compare the mills with the sterner battles abroad and see in the pugs the stuff that had held the French at bay so many years. I remember Clarence, our late king, holding forth for the hundredth time about the set-to between Gully and Pearce, which fell in the same month as Trafalgar.

"Was not one an echo of t'other?" says he. "Damme, I say it was! Could anyone doubt, who saw those two noble fellows at blows, that we were better men than the French or the Spaniards or the dam' Danes an' the rest o' that continental rabble? No, sir! Why, sir? 'Cos we learn from our cradles to fight like men, not like back-stabbin' dagoes or throat-slittin' Frogs. They have their stilettoes, we have our fists. We fight clean, sir, an' hard, an' don't cry quits while we can stand on our feet! Why, sir? 'Cos we're Englishmen, an' boxin's our game, an' makes us what we are, an' be damned to 'em!"

They cheered him to the echo, which encouraged the dear old muffin to recollections of his own pugilistic prowess.

"Man ain't a man till he's put his fists up, what? Why, I was a midshipman of fourteen, damned if I wasn't, an' this marine, fellow Moody, says: 'King's letter-boy, are ye? Papa's little letter-boy, more like'. Did I sport me rank, hide behind me blood? No such thing. Would ha' thought shame. 'Put 'em up,' says I, an' off came our jackets, an' bigad, didn't we fib each other, just! Blacked his eye, an' he tapped m'claret, shook hands, best o' friends after. That's our way, damme – an' why we'll beat the beggars out o' sight! 'Cos o' the good old game, gives us bottom, makes us men, damned if it don't!"

Blowhard stuff, you'll say, in the vein of scribblers like Egan and Hazlitt and the rest who liken our pugs to Achilles and Hector and Nelson, and compare a mill for the Championship to Waterloo or the Nile – but strip away the bombast and you'll find a grain of truth. The schoolboy who feels bound to face up to the bully for his manhood's sake, and puts up his little fists when he *knows* he's beat and all hope's gone – well, when he sees the French bearskins coming over the hill, he remembers, and finds in himself something that holds him steady for longer than those Frenchmen. I know *I* did, and I wasn't alone.

You may laugh when I say that the spirit that brought Cribb to his feet, half-dead and blind with his own blood, was the same spirit that kept men at their guns at Trafalgar and held the gate at Hougoumont . . . well, wait till you've faced the likes of Cribb, *and* been in a battle, and then laugh all you've a mind to.

Speaking of Cribb brings me to Molineaux, for each was the making of the other. At the time I speak of, early in '10, a year had passed since Cribb had beaten Jem Belcher for the second time, and was undoubted Champion. There was no lack of first-class men, but he'd thrashed the best of 'em – Maddox, Belcher, Gregson, Bill Richmond the black, as well as second-raters like Tom Tough and Ikey Pigg – and the question was: where was a challenger to be found? There were those who thought Cribb invincible, not without cause, for even the wisest heads could not remember a fighter so designed by nature for his work, or blessed with so many virtues. Close on six feet and fourteen stone, strong as a bull, he could shift like an opera-dancer when he chose, and to see him in the ring was to understand why boxing is called the Art of Self-defence, for his style was to mill on the retreat, letting his man come to him – and then out would flash those terrible fists, so fast you could barely see 'em move. No one ever hit so hard, they said, but what endeared him to the Fancy, above all his speed and science and cleverness, was that he never knew when he was beat. Only one man, George Nicholls, had ever licked him, over fifty-two rounds when Cribb was younger, and even Nicholls himself could never tell how.

So Cribb was king, and like to remain so, on that spring evening when I toddled down to the old Nag and Fish for cricket and a heavy wet with some of the sporting men – Sefton and Craven were there, I remember, and Goddy Webster, Lady Holland's boy, who was Caro Lamb's prime favourite, and Moore the poet, and Monk Lewis, I think, and of course Bill Richmond himself. He'd been a slave in America, brought to England by some general or other, and a tip-top lightweight in his day, though near fifty when he met Cribb, who was stones heavier and stronger, and Bill had spent an hour and a half running away from him; now he was well retired, and ale-draper at the Nag and Fish, but was to the fore in all the Fancy's doings.

I was looking out near the wicket where Goddy Webster was batting when he said: "Man Friday, what?" and I saw this rum-looking cove at the edge of the field, apart from the other spectators. He was black as the ace o' spades, dressed like a scarecrow, with a bundle on a stick over his shoulder. After the game, Richmond, being a man of his own colour, went and spoke with him, and presently came into the tap, grinning all over his face. We asked him what was up and he burst out laughing.

"See that black boy yonder? Come all the way f'm America, jes' to see me. Ye want to guess why, gen'men? He's a millin' cove, seemin'ly, wants I should make him a match."

"Why don't ye?" says Craven. "He looked a likely chap enough."

Bill rolled his eyes in wonder. He was a droll, well-mannered fellow, pale brown of skin and long in the head, as different from the other nigger as could be. "Oh, he's likely, sho' 'nuff. Big, strong boy. Thing is, he *knows* the match he wants made, an' ain't 'bout to take any other. You want to guess who he wants to fight . . . Cribb!" He slapped his thighs, crowing, and we shouted with laughter. Sefton said we should have him in, and take a rise out of him, but Richmond shook his head.

"Be 'bliged if you leave him be, my lord, 'Tain't but a simpleton, don't know the time o' day, shouldn't make game of him. Ain't got a penny in his puss or a thought in his head. Ain't et in a while, neither, an's gettin' outside a rump steak in my kitchen this minute. Guess I'll give him a shakedown, maybe take him to the Garden tomorrow, get him porterin' work." That was Richmond all over, and why he was so well-liked.

Monk asked the fellow's name, and Richmond spluttered and gave a comical look at Sefton.

"Kind o' familiar, seemed to me. Why, it's Tom Molineaux!"

"What?" cries Sefton, whose name was Molyneux. "Why, damn his impudence, where the devil did he come by it?"

At this everyone roasted Sefton, wondering what dusky charmer he had favoured, and wouldn't he visit the kitchen to greet his American child? Moore offered to write a poem, "The Black Prodigal's Return", and there was great merriment. When the company dispersed I chanced to glance in at the kitchen door, and there was the cause of their mirth, hunched over the table shovelling grub into his ugly black phiz and swilling it down from a pint-pot, grunting and gulping as though he hadn't seen peck for a month. Must get this one a voucher to Almack's, thinks I.

There was a fly buzzing about his plate, and he flapped at it once or twice with hands which were uncommon small and neat for a man of his size. I was about to pass on when he muttered a curse at the fly's persistence, and as it shot past his head his hand whipped up and caught it . . . and I stopped where I was. As he wiped it off on his threadbare coat, he spied me, and dropped his eyes, glowering.

"Catch another one, my boy, can you?" says I, and he looked blank, with his great blubber lips hanging open, but as another fly buzzed above his head he made a snatch — and there it was, crushed in his pink palm. Well, well, thinks I, and sauntered in, seating myself on the edge of the table. He shot me a wary glance of his bloodshot ogles and dropped his gaze.

"I hear you're a milling cove, Tom Molineaux," says I. "Now then, how many men have you fought in the United States?"

His reply was a mumbling growl I could hardly make out. "Ah whupped fo'teen, fifteen, mebbe."

"All niggers, I'll be bound. Who was the best of 'em?"

He licked his lips. "Black Ghost, Ah reckon. He kilt fo', five men, they sayin'." He shot me another leery look. "He busted ma hand. Ah busted his neck." He looked a likely enough murderer, and I believed him.

"And you have come to England to fight Tom Cribb. Why?"

He kept his gaze on the table. "They sayin' he the bestest. Champeen, whupped ev'y millin' cove in Englan'. Ah whupped ev'y nigra fighter in 'Merica." And now he lifted that woolly bullet head and looked me in the eye. "Guess Ah whup Tom Cribb now." No brag or bounce, you understand. He said it plain, and then put down his head again.

"Well now, Tom," says I, pretty mild, for I guessed he would dub his mummer if I laughed or took a high tone, "that's as may be. Many good men have tried and failed, you know. Why d'ye suppose you're better than they?"

He wriggled in his seat, and scowled, like a stubborn child. "Ah's the bes' millin' cove they is. Better'n Tom Cribb or anybody."

Bill Richmond came in just then, and cried out to see Molineaux seated. "Why, you lubber! Git your ass out that chair when cap'n talks to you, ye hear? Who you think you are, to set before a gen'man? Git up, damn your black hide!"

Molineaux got up, with no good grace, and I winked at Richmond.

"Why, mind your manners, Bill! This is the fellow who means to floor Cribb, you know. We must show him respect . . . and see what he's made of, eh?"

"Why, cap'n, he ain't but a dummy!" cries Bill, and then, seeing what I was about, he grinned and nodded. "Oh, yeah! We sho'ly must! Now, then, boy, shuck off your coat. Lively now – an' put your hands behind your head!"

Tom glowered, but did as he was bid. Richmond took a pot from the table, as though to drink, and dashed it all of a sudden over his cracked boots. Tom jumped back, too late.

"You ain't too quick!" scoffs Bill, and threw the pot at him. Tom dropped it. "No, sir, you ain't quick at all! Now, boy – make a fist, hold it right there!" Tom obeyed, goggling, and Bill snatched my cane and lashed him over the knuckles. Tom howled and hopped, wringing his hand.

"What you do that for, man?" cries he.

"Oh, my goodness!" cries Bill. "Did I hurt your poor little hand? Oh, mercy me, I'm so sorry!" He stepped up and hit Tom in the breadbasket, doubling him over. "Did that hurt, too? Oh my, oh my! Yessir, boy, you surely are in prime twig to beat Tom Cribb! Why, he'd be shakin' in his shoes if – "

"Ah wasn't ready!" bawls Tom.

"Oh, I should ha' told you!" cries Richmond. "Tom Cribb, he'll write you a letter, tellin' you when he's goin' to fib you! It's a rule in these parts, so black chawbacons don't git took unawares!" He slapped Tom back and forth. "Put your head up, boy, when I talk to you! An' you think you're a millin' man, hey, a prize-fighter?"

"Ah's a fighter!" roars Tom, looking monstrous, and yet in awe of this fiery browbeater half his size. "Ah won my freedom fightin'! Won fiffy-fi' thousan' dollahs, beatin' Black Ghost, an' my master set me free."

"Well, 'magine that!" cries Bill, in mock amazement. "You mus' be one hell of a fightin' terror, Tom Molineaux!" He stepped back, slipped off his coat, and squared up. "C'mon then! You show me! Sport your fives, boy! Fall to, an' let's see how you goin' to beat Cribb!"

Tom looked in such a bait that I expected a wild rush, but he stood glaring murder at Richmond, and then shook his head.

68

"Ain't fightin' you," says he sullenly, and I saw his eyes stray to the table and the leavings of his meal. "You call me what you please, don' make no matter." He stooped to pick up his coat. "Ah thank you fo' the vittles."

Richmond let out a snort. "What's matter, boy, you skeered o' little ol' Bill?"

"Ain't skeered o' nobody," growls Tom. "Ah guess Ah be steppin' on."

I took a hand then, and not only because I wanted to see what this strange blackamoor was made of, and whether his feet were as fast as his hands. It was damned odd, but I'd taken a fancy to him. He'd taken blows and dog's abuse, but wouldn't raise a hand to the man who'd fed him – a man, by the way, who could ha' chopped him up in no time, but Tom didn't know that. He thought he was sparing Richmond, and as he put on his ragged coat and looked about for his stick and bundle, I'll be shot if he didn't look half-dignified, which is an odd word to use about a great black booby, but 'twas the case.

"Hold on, Tom," says I. "Mister Richmond wishes to take your measure."

"Ah knows that," says Tom, head down again. "Ah's 'bliged to him."

"God bless me!" cries Bill.

"I'd like to measure you myself, Tom," says I. "Spar a round with me?"

He looked up, and I'll swear there was terror in his eyes as he rolled them at me. "You a white man!" says he.

"So I am, and so is every fighter in England, bar Bill here. You'd best learn to fight white men, if you hope to meet Cribb, for he ain't going to change colour to suit you. Never fear, I can box. Come now, let's see what you can make of me."

But he didn't care for it above half. "You gen'man," mutters he, and I saw that the notion of hitting "massa" was too much for him. "Ain't fightin' you ... cap'n," says he, shaking his head, so I gave Bill the wink again, and he heaped insults on the brute, taunting him, squaring up and slapping him, and finally planting him a facer, and at that Tom tossed his coat aside and squared up in turn, but – which I

thought odd — with no sign of anger. Take care, Bill, thinks I, he may
not be such a johnny raw after all, and if he catches you with the brute
strength of those mighty arms and shoulders, you'll feel it.

I needn't ha' fretted. It was Mendoza to a chopping block, for old
as he was Richmond was one of the prime scientific millers of the
day, and Tom was dished from the start. His only ploy was to shoot
out his left, fast enough, stand dumfounded when Bill stopped or
slipped it, and then put in a right cross that came from Chelsea by
way of Green Park. He knew no more of in-fighting than the town
clock, and when Bill feinted and planted a one-two in his guts his
astonishment was comical to see. He was slower on his pins than a
Shire horse, and while he had some rudiments of footwork he had no
notion of setting himself to counter.

Bill went easy, weaving on his toes and hitting where he chose, but
once Tom caught him with a left which came in at his fly-catching
speed. Bill floored him for that, and twice again, and Tom began to
thrash like a windmill, at which Bill commenced to rag him in earnest,
with fist and tongue.

"My, boy, you sure can mill!" Whack! "You must ha' been the
talk o' the ol' plantation!" Whack! "You went down the cowpens
with massa an' chewed the bollocks off the Black Ghost, lawks a
mercy!" Whack! "An' massa set you free, land sakes, Jemima, 'cos
you bust up some ol' crippled nigger you could ha' knocked down
with a good fart!" Whack! "An' you think you can *fight*!"

Tom went wild at last, and rushed him, and when Bill ducked,
damme if the great bullock's fist didn't smash through the panelling
as if 't had been paper. He was mad with rage, so Bill fibbed him with
three hard lefts to the nob and a right upper-cut, and down he went
with his senses knocked half out of him. I told Bill to give him a
shove in the mouth, and he gulped it down and sat on the floor with
his head in his hands. Bill clapped him on the shoulder and came
across to me, rubbing his knuckles.

"Guess Cribb can sleep o' nights, cap'n," says he, looking droll.
"Hey, boy — you still set on bein' a prize-fighter?"

D'ye know what the clown replied? I couldn't believe my ears. He
sat there, all of a heap, head bowed, and growled: "Ah *is* a fighter.
You floored me, but you din' hurt me. An' we wasn't holdin' or

throwin', neether. An' Ah was tired. When Ah's rested, Ah trim you up good. Then Ah whup Tom Cribb.''

Richmond was knocked all of a heap between mirth and anger. ''Well, blow me! Why, ye great black lummox, ye couldn't whip a kid's top! My stars, cap'n, did ye ever hear such sauce? Why, you jack puddin', you, ye never even touched me! Ain't that so, cap'n?''

''He did, though, once.''

''Aye – once! Didn't rattle my ivories, even!'' He turned angrily on Tom. ''You want to be a miller, boy – which you ain't – you best learn not to talk like a rasher o' wind! Here, git up off o' my floor – if you ain't *too tired*, that is!''

Tom took his hand and got up, looking damned sour and troubled. I saw how it was; he'd never met a boxer before, and his thick head couldn't take in the novelty. He scowled at Bill like a spoiled infant.

''You got a lot o' tricks,'' growls he. ''You don' fight. You . . . you jus' . . . full o' tricks!'' He couldn't describe what he didn't know, you see.

''Tom,'' says I, ''d'ye think you could learn Mr Richmond's tricks, as you call 'em? If he was to show you, eh?''

Bill stared at me open-mouthed. ''What's that, cap'n? You ain't thinkin' I could *make* somethin' of him, surely? Why, he'd never be above third-rate!''

''Take off your shirt, Tom,'' says I, and he did. ''Now, then, Bill, how many peel as well as that? Ain't he made to be a miller?'' For I'd never seen likelier, shoulders and arms of a blacksmith, but neat in the waist.

''So's half the coal-heavers in Deptford!'' cries Bill. ''That don't make a millin' cove, cap'n, you know that!'' He shook his salt-and-pepper head in impatience. ''What d'ye *see* in him, cap'n?''

I couldn't ha' told him, any better than I can tell you now. God knows 'twasn't skill, for he had none, hardly. The broken panel testified that he could fib uncommon hard, supposing an opponent ever let him, his left had been fast enough to catch Richmond once (which had mortified Bill, I knew, though he never let on), and I believed him when he claimed not to be hurt – I doubted if much could damage that black nob, which might ha' been solid bone for all the sense it

71

contained. All that didn't amount to snuff in his favour, yet I felt there was *something* in him, if only that the great ignorant booby, a freed slave, mark you, had made his way, the Lord alone knew how, across the ocean to a foreign land to try his hand at the impossible. It was an infant reaching for the moon – no, a Yahoo in search of the Holy Grail, if you like. To see him there in Richmond's kitchen, glowering mumchance with his ragged shirt in his hand, mumbling about "whupping Cribb", when a retired pug of fifty-odd, who'd never been more than middling useful, had just made him look like a looby ... why, it was laughable. Whatever could have inspired his ridiculous dream? The pathetic thing was that he believed it. Most folk would have said he was dicked in the nob ... or that I was.

"He's got beef, Bill," says I, "and bottom, I dare say. Enough to earn him a few bob against the make-weight bruisers, if he was trained a little."

"An' where's the good in that, I should like to know?" scoffs Bill. "Anyways, who says he's got bottom? He's a nigger, ain't he? Cap'n, there's butchers an' draymen an' 'prentice boys, an' tailors even, that'd fib him to death! Damme, Ikey Bittoon's faster on his pins, an' he couldn't catch up wi' the mutes at a funeral! 'Sides, I got the ken to mind; I can't waste time on black hobbledehoys."

"Then get Paddington Jones. He'll train him if anyone can. I'll see him right, and pay this chap's board, too."

He looked at me quizzy-like. "You mean it, cap'n, don't ye? Well, ne'er mind the board. A few quid'll do for Pad, though why you should blow away your blunt beats me." He looked at Tom, and sniffed. "He might win ye a guinea in side-bets against some drunk farmer, naught better. What d'ye think the likes o' Randall or Tom Belcher, aye, or Baldwin or Dogherty would do to him, eh?"

"I can't say, Bill," I told him. "But I doubt if they can catch a fly on the wing. And I'm certain sure they don't think they can beat Tom Cribb."

PADDINGTON JONES,
resumed

Now, as I told you, sir, Tom was a bad 'un to manage, but my oath! he was a prime pippen to train. I've said it afore, and I say it still, of all the scores I handled and coached and held the bottle for, there never was one that was a quicker study – as a fighter. Not that he was sharp in the mind; as I've said, he was a right jobbernowl when it came to using his noddle, but if ever a man carried his brains in his fists and feet, Tom did. I knew it, too, soon as I felt him out at half-arm. Course I did.

I'll never forget that day; it was the strangest thing. I was taking my wet in the Coach and Horses, which was Jem Belcher's ken in Frith Street, that he went to after he gave up the Jolly Brewer, and what d'ye think we were cracking the whid about? Why, *the want of good heavyweights*, and not a star in the sky to compare with Cribb – and 'twas in that very moment I had the summons that was to put me in the way of Tom Molineaux! What d'ye think o' that, sir? I remember Jem's very words:

"I'll be hanged if there's one fit to *spar* with Cribb, even, since I gave over my belt! Why the pick of 'em, Gregson and all, would turn tail if my Trusty so much as barked at 'em!" Trusty was his dog, you understand, that he had of Lord Camelford. "By God, if I'd my two eyes, I'd back myself against any fourteen-stone man in the kingdom!"

No one denied it, but said "Aye, aye, Jem, you're right there!" for all knew how bitter Jem was over his dead ogle. Mind you, I'll not say he was wrong; if he'd had both eyes when he met Cribb, well, I'd not ha' cared to live on the difference between 'em. He could never find his distance, you see, with one peeper gone, as he found when he challenged Hen Pearce and was done in eighteen rounds. That was when Gully, you know, said Belcher couldn't ha' beat Pearce if he'd had *four* eyes, and I reckon 'twas that jibe that resolved Jem to challenge Cribb – aye, twice he tried, and twice he lost. Well, sir, a man should know when his day's past, ain't that so? Course he should.

He took it very ill, did Jem, him not being above twenty-eight when he fought his last battle, and on the day I speak of he was sour as a crab, running over all his old victories, even his brawl with Joe Berks at Wimbledon Common the day I fought Ikey Bittoon – d'ye know, sir, we set to in the shadow o' the gallows where Jerry Abershaw, the great bridle cull, was a-hanging in chains! You don't see that sort o' decorations at sporting matches these days! "Aye," cries Jem, "and Abershaw's corp could show more game than half of today's millers, damned if it couldn't! There's not a good heavy man left in England, depend upon it!"

That was the very second, sir, that I had word that Bill Richmond was looking for me. "Whose dog's dead?" thinks I, and toddled down to the Prad and Swimmer, and there was this great black cove in the yard, stripped to the buff, lifting the four-stone weights one-handed, sir, as if they was straws. Damme if I ever see a finer specimen.

"Cap'n Buck thinks we can make a miller out o' him," says Bill Richmond. "What d'ye say, Pad?"

"I shouldn't wonder," says I. "If he fibs as well as he peels he'll do some mischief."

"Ha!" says Bill. "Well, he fibs like a casualty, and above par at that. I think the Cap'n's apartment's to let myself, but 'Get Pad Jones', says he, 'and I'll pay the shot', so there ye are."

Well, Tom and I put on the mauleys, and in two minutes' sparring I knew three things. He couldn't box, he couldn't move – and he had hands as fast as Dan Mendoza at his best.

"Well, now, blackee," says I. "Put off the gloves and let's see ye dance." I had to say it four times afore I could get it into his head what I wanted, and then blow me if he didn't dance a hornpipe! I asked him where he'd learned it, and he says, off an English sailor in America.

"A rare teacher he must ha' been," says Bill. "I seen heifers could dance better. What are ye about, Pad? He won't do, am I right?"

"Oh, he'll do," says I. "But what he'll do, or how far, we'll have to see." Truth was, sir, I could feel my innards singing as they hadn't done in ten years and more, when I first saw Jem Belcher at work in old Bill Warr's dining-room at Covent Garden. He was seventeen then, was Jem, and just come to Town, and damned if he didn't floor old Bill, who was one of the nimblest shifters in the game, half a dozen times. 'This 'un can go with any man in the kingdom!' says Warr — well, I couldn't say *that* of Tom, not by a mile, but just the speed o' that left hand, sir, was enough for me. If the rest didn't follow, then I was a Dutchman. I told Bill then and there I would take the lad in hand.

"The Cap'n ain't the only one with a 'For sale' sign on his shap," mutters Bill. "Very good — we'll give him the regular diet. Out on the road, under the mattresses, hefting the hammers, but if you think you can teach him to guard and counter, God help you, 'cos I can't."

"You keep your hammers and mattresses both," says I. "He's strong as a bull already, and he don't need no purges nor draughts neither. Any fat on him'll sweat off with a bit o' breathing. Now, Bill," I told him, "you mind the tap, I'll mind the boy. Send us out those two big glim-sticks from the kitchen, will ye?"

He gave me a rum look, but presently the little scrub-girl, Betty, brought out the candlesticks, fine heavy articles nigh on three feet long, and I strapped 'em on Tom, one to each leg. While I was about it, Betty stood admiring Tom as though he were the Lord Mayor come to visit, and I thought, aye, you won't be the only one, my gel, and sent her packing. She was a little wisp of a thing, with a face as dirty as her apron, but she fair glowed at Tom, and when he smiled at her with that great ugly grin of teeth, she laughed right out and scampered inside.

"Now then, Tom, let's see ye dance the hornpipe," says I. He hadn't said a word, but now he glowered at the glim-sticks.

"Cain't dance wi' sech things," says he, growling sullen.

"Yes ye can," says I. "Ye want to be a miller, don't ye? Then you'll mind what I say, and do as I bid you, no matter what. So stir your hopper-dockers! Come, now — caper!"

You see what I was after, sir? If a man's slow on his pins, you make him walk and run and dance encumbered, no matter how clumsy at first, until he can move as quick with the weights as he did without 'em. Then, when you take them off, you'll find he's twice as fast as he was before. Tom wore them glim-sticks hour in, hour out, but never so long as might injure him. He did not like it, though. Why, he set up such a roar, but I kept him at it until he was like to drop. Then I took 'em off him, and give him a good rub down with the oil, and set him to the hornpipe again; he was stiff for a moment, and then did he not dance! He saw the virtue of it, and laughed as he danced, clapping his hands and larking the way they do.

Well, sir, I'll not weary you by telling all the tricks I was at to improve his speed. After a day or two, when I had him moving more like the thing, I marked the ground and had him skipping from mark to mark, back and forth, on his toes, till he could find the marks blindfold – that's the beginning of footwork, you see, sir. We did it with the glim-sticks and without, and he came more nimble by the day.

You might think, being slow of mind, that he'd be patient, but not he. By and by he tired of skipping and dancing, and taxed me to fight with him, so I gave him a little breathing with the gloves, to show him what a clunch he was. He couldn't touch me, and I hit him where I pleased, not hard enough to sting – not his body, leastways, but his mind, for I called out where I would plant my hits before I made 'em. By George, he did not care for that, sir! If you had seen that glaring black mug and them yellow eyes, you'd ha' wished a wall between you, and I took care, expecting him to break into rage and come tearing at me. But did he? He did not. Aha, thinks I, here's a step for'ard. I sat down with him, and put my arm round his shoulders – as far as I could reach, that is, and didn't he stink, though?

"Tom," says I, "you ain't a miller at all. You can't fib me, and you couldn't fib little Betty, hardly. You don't stand proper, you don't move proper, you don't hit proper, and you don't know what guarding or countering is, neither. Well, Tom, that won't do."

He shook my arm off, sudden-like. "You jes' full o' tricks, like Mass' Richmond!" cries he. "You don' fight, no more'n he do!"

"It's a fact, Tom," says I. "But it should not be, ye see. You're bigger and stronger than me and Massa Richmond – why, you should mill me down in a minute. Well, now, Tom, I'm going to show you how. 'Twill be hard work, Tom, but by the time I'm done wi' you, why, you'll knock me off my legs in a moment – and Massa Richmond, too. I promise you that, my boy. What d'ye say now, eh?"

He sat there, sweating and stinking, looking like a black fiend o' the Pit. "An' Tom Cribb," says he.

That was the first I'd heard of Cribb, for Richmond had kept mum, and it fair took the wind out of me. And d'ye know, sir, that was the first I studied him, like, to see what he was about. It was enough to make you laugh, and I nearly did, but by the grace o' God I didn't. You asked me, you remember, what was in his mind, and I said I couldn't tell, which is the truth. But I knew then, sir, there was something beyond my ken, so I didn't laugh, nor pull a face, nor say him nay.

"Why, yes, Tom," says I. "And Tom Cribb."

D'ye know, sir, that was the best thing I ever did for him? That was when we took the road to Copthorn. I see that, now, tho' I didn't at the time.

'Twas when the work began, and all, I tell you. How long does it take to make a milling cove? Forever, some would say, but I say it depends what's in him. It was in Tom, in the heart and soul of him – and in that body, believe me. Wi' that kind o' stuff, sir, it don't take long, as you shall see.

I taught him the guards – Harmer's, and the sloper, and Broughton's, and when he'd some notion of those, I showed him the Bristol, and Mendoza's. All of 'em – with wooden billets strapped to his forearm, the glim-sticks being over heavy. And so to off-fighting and in-fighting, and countering and milling on the retreat, with down-cuts and upper-cuts and quick returns and hitting past, and the long left hand that he favoured over all.

Sir, it was a joy. He had the aptitude, and learned more in a week than most in a month. Fact is, he was a natural. Course he was, and once he'd twigged the secret of moving feet and body and hands together – well, sir, it's a fine thing, to see a fighter taking shape before your eyes. And such a fighter as I knew him to be. Jem, thinks I, you talk of the lack of heavyweights, but I've got one growing under my hands, I have, and so help me he will astonish you!

You may judge of my feeling when I tell you that after the first week I brought my traps down to the Dolphin and lived in, to be near him. It was up at five each day, to exercise and dance and practise footwork; beefsteaks, tea and toast at eight; then the guards until noon – he had a great fancy to Mendoza's guard, which is a stiff chop at your opponent's straight left, see, with your right hand which you then turn into a blow at his neck; two or three o' those and your enemy's left arm's nigh broke; mine was so black and blue I had to muffle it. Toast and bacon at noon, a sleep, boxing and beating the bag, steaks and beer for supper, and into bed by nine; he throve on it.

I kept them all out o' the yard by day, except Richmond, who would come to watch us now and then, but said not a word except: "He'll need picklin' " – his knuckles, you see, had never been toughened, so we had him sleeping in gloves soaked in brine, and painted the knuckles wi' spirits and turpentine to harden 'em. Very small his hands were, which is a rare boon in a fighter, for when he fibs all the power bears on a small point, and the hands don't damage so easy as they would if they was large. Good hands, sir, small but strong in the fingers is best; if a man's hands break, he's done, be he never so fine a miller. Look at Tom Spring, as prime a heavyweight as ever was, but broke his hands on Langan and never fought again. Course he didn't.

I told you Bill Richmond said not a word when he watched us breathing, nor interfered with my methods. But I could see his feelings change by the day, as Tom improved, tho' he never let on. Fact is, sir, he couldn't believe his eyes, and I reckon he felt his innards stirring, too, like mine. I seen he was itching to take a hand, so one day, after about three weeks it would be, I said he should try Tom out himself, and he did – but with bare knuckles, sir, no mauleys.

"What's this, Bill?" says I. "You don't want to harm him, surely?" Fact was, I didn't care to think what Tom's fast hands might do to Bill, if he planted a wisty one. Yes, sir, he had come on that much.

"I'm going to see what he's made of," says Bill.

Now, sir, I must tell you that Richmond was as clever a mechanic as any, old and all as he was, and he went at Tom as though there was a thousand guineas in it. Tom was taken fair aback, and milled on the retreat, but Richmond was fast enough to fib him three or four good 'uns, and tapped his claret; Tom just shook his head and Richmond fibbed him again, and cut him over the eye. I was astonished, and ready to step in, when Bill shouts:

"Did it hurt, then? Here's another for you!" and lands a flush hit on his nob. "You think that's hurtin', don't ye! You don't know the meanin' o' hurt!'' And fibs him again, left and right. "Ye think I'm fibbin' you? Depend upon it, boy, when Tom Cribb fibs you, 'twill be as though you was hit by a hammer! That man can strike the bark off a tree with his bare hands, d'ye know that?''

"Ah b'lieve it when Ah sees it,'' says Tom, guarding away, but not countering or trying to hit past.

"Oh, my, you'll *believe* it!'' cries Bill. "I won't give odds you'll *see* it!''

He bore in again with the same resolution, and they rallied, but Tom had his measure now and stopped and guarded with fair science, still not countering or hitting inside or over, but always on the retreat. D'ye know, sir, Bill could not hit him! Yet half a dozen times, I'll swear, Tom could have planted him a good one, but held his hand. Bill must see he's fighting shy, thinks I, and I reckon he did, for after a rally he stepped back and looked at Tom ever so hard, and then bade me look to Tom's eye, which was sporting the ruby. It was little enough, so I plastered it, and sent Tom away to lie down.

"Well, Bill,' says I. "What cheer?''

"So help me God,'' says Bill. "I thought my arm was clean broke.'' He showed me his left wrist, all bruised and swollen. "That was the Jew's stop he was givin' me! You taught him that? He learned that? Pad,'' says he, "I swear to God I never saw his right hand move – but didn't I feel it, just! An' I came out to roast him, to test his game!''

"Well, you fibbed him a few,'' says I. "He took 'em well. He's game enough.''

"I don't know that,'' says Bill, shaking his nob. "Nor do you. You've brought him on, I don't deny, an' he defends better'n I ever thought to see. But I'm played out, I ain't strong enough to hurt him, nor are you. Can he take his gruel, Pad, tell me that!''

"Make him a match,'' says I. "Cropley the coal-whipper, maybe, or Uncle Ben Burn. They'll feel him out.'' But he wouldn't have it, saying Tom was not ready for Cropley, and Burn would be no proper test. "He ain't but a Fives Court messenger,'' says Bill. "I want a nuller that can fib the head off a stone statue, but private-like, not in a regular mill. I want to see what Tom can take, 'fore we let the Fancy see him.''

Then I knew, sir, that Richmond had high hopes of Tom.

"Tell ye what," says he. "We'll give him a breather wi' Dutch Sam."

If he'd said "wi' Tom Cribb" I'd ha' been no more astonished, for Dutch Sam, though past his prime, was reckoned still the hardest hitter in the game. He wasn't more than a lightweight, either, but that right hand of his was a grave-digger, as I knew to my cost. I'd been beat a few times, but Dutch Sam was the only fibster who ever put me to sleep.

"Walk-er!"* cries I. "If Tom ain't ready for Cropley, how the dooce d'ye reckon he can face Sam, that nigh killed Cropley? And ye saw what Sam did to Medley last month only!"

"You ain't heedin' what I say," says Bill. "I ain't about to *match* Tom wi' him. See here, Sam's retired, an' he's bushed, and for a twelve-month now he's been trainin' on blue tape – but he can still fib hard as ever. If we tip him some spangles, he'll go a few rounds wi' Tom, and find out what bottom he has."

It was not my place to argue, so next day I smoked Sam out at the Hole-in-the-Wall, Randall's place in Chancery Lane.† Sir, I never seen a drunker Jew, and not a feather to fly with, as Bill had prophesied. We had to bring him down to the Nag on a hand-cart, and when we'd got him three parts sober wi' coffee and toast and his head in a bucket, Bill won him wi' the spangles aforesaid and the promise of lush unlimited.

"Thtrike me dumb, I'm your man," says Sam. "Oo's the wictim?"

"Now, Mister Elias," says Bill, "here's what you do. I've a nigger out yonder, an' maybe he can take gruel, an' maybe he can't. You bore in at his belly, hard as you can, but if you touch his neck or phizzog you'll never drink in my tap again, see?"

"Truth me for that, Bill," says Sam, sporting his daddle. "I'll thtartle the black rathcal, thee if I don't. Vot 'appens if I break hith ribth?"

---

* "Walk-er!" A term of disbelief and derision, from John ("Hookey") Walker, an early time-and-motion expert whose reports were so frequently challenged by workmen that "Walker!" came to signify a tale not to be trusted. (See Dickens' *A Christmas Carol*.)

† This tavern and its proprietor achieved immortality from their mention in the most famous example of boxing literature, Hazlitt's essay, "The Fight". It was at the Hole-in-the-Wall that the writer "got the office" about the contest between Bill Neate, "the Bristol Bull", and Tom Hickman, "the Gasman", on December 10, 1821.

"We'll risk that," says Bill. "Just steer clear of his figurehead, an' no upper-cuttin', mind."

Well, sir, they set to wi' the mauleys, and I was a-tiptoe to see how Tom would fare with a real fibber. Sam had science, and made play at first, feinting at Tom's head, drawing him in, and then stepped inside and planted him a one-two to the body, as hard as he knew. Tom doubled up, and if Sam had used his invention it'd have been hard on the black, but he held off, and Tom came back at him game enough, and planted him a facer with that quick left, which made the Israelite blink. He bore in again at half-arm, slipping Tom's left and stopping his right, and gave Tom three or four severe winders. Tom gasped, but did not bend, and before Sam knew it Tom hit him clean off his feet with a wisty right. They set to again, and yet again and again, with Sam closing and hammering Tom's breadbasket cruelly, and each time Tom floored him with blows to the head. At the last time of asking Sam sits up and says:

"S'elp me Cot, if 'e doth that again I'll upper-cut hith black nob off, tho I will! My old muvver didn't raithe me to lothe all me teeth a-rattlin' a darkie'th belly to no purpothe! Gi' me a ball o' fire afore I forget methelf an' beat hith clock in!"

Bill reckoned he'd served his turn and earned his wet, and sent him into the tap while we looked to Tom. Even with the mufflers, Sam had bruised his middle and flanks, but when we asked if he hurt, he shook his head. I gave him a good kneading with the oil and sent him in to rest. Bill was drumming his fingers and looking at the sky, with a light in his eye.

"We can't tell whether he's got bottom 'til he's been in a proper mill," says he, "but, by God, Pad, if he can take Dutch Sam's best ... why, I don't know but what he may do!"

"So think I," says I. "Mind you, Bill, he's green yet. Sam got inside as he pleased."

"Why, Sam has science," says he. "Fifteen years' worth. Tom's had less'n a month, man! I tell ye, Pad, if I thought ..." Then he laughed, sir, and shook his head, and said ne'er mind what he thought, but to work with Tom as before, and take him out on the road each morning.

"Run him down Chelsea way first thing, buy him his breakfast at

Don Saltero's,* an' bring him back by the Green Park an' St James's. Have him buy half a stone o' plums at Kelsey's each day, an' then along Piccadilly an' home,'' says Bill, grinning leery-like, "but keep your mummer closed, an' if anyone asks who he is, give 'em his name, an' naught besides.''

"He'll eat no bloody plums while I'm training him!'' I said, and Bill winked.

"Nor will he, old Pad. The maids can have 'em, just so Tom buys 'em.''

Can you guess what he was about, sir? Why, he wanted Tom to be noticed, and wondered at, to set the Town talking of this mysterious black cove who ran through the West End each morning all muffled up in a greatcoat, buying plums at the fashionable fruiterer's, with the well-known Paddington Jones at his elbow. Oh, he was a fly file, was Richmond, for he knew that the more they saw of Tom, and the less they knew of him, the more they'd be piqued, and when the time came to make a match, the greater would be the interest among the Fancy, and the bigger the side-bets and subscription purses. He was a nigger with a head on him, was Bill.

So I ran Tom to Chelsea and back daily, and didn't the heads turn as he trotted through the Park, and up St James's? There weren't many of the Quality afoot at that time o' day, but I knew the word'd spread, and sure enough we had a prime stroke of luck on the third day, for just as we turned out of Kelsey's shop, with Tom hugging his bag o' plums, out of one o' the clubs steps the Prince of Wales, with Colonel Harry Mellish and old Mr Sheridan and others, who'd been at play all night by the look of 'em.

"God save us, what's this?'' cries the Prince. "Jones, Jones, who the devil's that blackamoor? Aha!'' says he, "he's a miller, damned if he's not, eh, Sherry? Well, Jones?''

"By your highness's leave,'' says I, "he's a friend of Bill Richmond's new come from America.''

---

* James Salter, servant to Sir Hans Sloane, set up as a barber and coffee-house proprietor in Cheyne Walk, Chelsea, in 1695. Part of his shop was a museum of curiosities presented by Sloane and others, and although this collection was sold off at the end of the eighteenth century, the premises continued to be used as a tavern, and retained the old name of "Don Saltero's'' bestowed on Salter by one of his patrons, possibly Richard Steele. The building was pulled down in 1866; it was on the site of 18, Cheyne Walk.

"Ye don't say! Why, then, he's a miller for certain! By God, but he's black! Eh, Sherry? Blackest thing I ever saw in my life, what? And a damned stout fellow, too, I'll be bound! What's his name?"

"Tom Molineaux, please your highness," says I.

"Molineaux, eh? Well, how d'ye do, Master Molineaux, glad to see you!" cries the Prince, and holds out his hand. I nudged Tom, and he took it – and you'll think me soft, sir, but I was the proudest man in London that moment. Not just for Tom, you know, but for Old England – for how many foreign kings' sons would take the hand of a common man, and a black at that, so free and easy, with the finest in the land looking on? Yes, sir, I was right proud.

"When will he fight, Jones?" says the Colonel, who was a keen blade of the Fancy. "Where's the turn-up to be, eh? Who'll he fight – Gregson? By George, George, he looks man enough for Gregson, don't he?"

"Hold up . . . Molineaux?" says the Prince, and squints at Tom. "No connection to Sefton, I suppose? The Earl, ye know? His name's Molyneux. Not black, though . . . is he? Sefton ain't black, Sherry? No, no, damme, course he's not! Damned ugly, mind you, but not black." They all roared with laughter, while Tom stood there with his head down, right out of his bearings, for while he'd no notion who they were, he could see they were nobs such as he'd never encountered in his life. One of the gentlemen asked what was in his bag, and when he showed the plums, damned if they didn't pile into the fruit, saying they were the most refreshing article, and just the thing for a dawn thirst. Mr Sheridan had one, as big and red as his own conk, but the Prince said they'd give him the wherry-go-nimbles, and he'd liefer not, but thanked him, and if you could ha' seen Tom grin then, sir, 'twould ha' done your heart good. All o'er his face he grinned, to see such jolly, kindly gentlemen – d'ye know, I doubt if white men had ever spoke him so before, and he was dazed by it, but happy, too.

"He'll fight Gregson, though, won't he?" cries Mellish. "It must be the Giant, eh?"

"Will ye mill Gregson over, Tom?" says the Prince. "Damned if ye won't! What? What?"

Tom hadn't said a word, but now he grinned wider than ever.

"Ah's goin' beat Tom Cribb," says he.

My stars, you should have heard 'em then, sir! Some laughed, and some cried that he'd do it, too, and the Prince laughed loudest of all, and wished him well, and I wondered if St James's had ever seen such a sight before, the noblest in the land cracking the whid with a black prize-fighter and pecking his plums, and all as cheery as could be. I wished they'd stash it, mind, for Tom in his simplicity might easy ha' given offence, so I begged the Prince's leave to brush, in case Tom should take cold, and he let us go with a wave and a kind word.

A fair crowd had gathered, and among them two bucks with a pair of Cyprians in tow, decked-out flash mots who goggle-eyed Tom as he ran by. I saw his head turn, but thought naught of it until we were padding it over Princes Street, when I asked him what he'd thought of the company, for I was eager to hear what he'd made of the Prince.

"Fat gen'man real kindly," says he.

"Fat, curse your impudence! Who're you to say so, ye sooty marvel? You'd best mind your trap, my boy. Well, what more?"

He gave a rum grin, leery-like. "Mighty fine ladies in London. Real sweet an' pretty, sho' 'nuff," and chuckled deep down.

"Never mind that! You keep your mind on your work, d'ye hear? They weren't no ladies, neither," I told him, and he said he guessed not, and rolled his eyes, ho-hoing. If he'd been white, I'd have dressed him down sharp, for the last thing a training man needs on his mind is skirt, but him being black I never thought he'd dare. That was all I knew.

I wondered what Bill Richmond would make of our encounter with Royalty, but he was all for it. "Dutch Sam'll pass the word, an' all," says he, well pleased. "A regular mouth, is Sam. Aye, it'll be all the buzz on Town presently." Which it was, more than we guessed, for the Earl of Sefton, hearing that the Prince had coupled his name with Tom's, and some similar pleasantry having been made before, swore it was more than enough, and damned if he wouldn't call him out. He was in his proper high ropes, but his noble friends persuaded him it was all slum, so he dropped it, but wouldn't notice the Prince for a month.

Now I told you, sir, that Tom was rare to train but bad to manage, and so he proved that very night. I was used to dorse on a mattress in the tap, and woke to the sound of thumping and scuffling out by the back, where the maids slept – Nance, a big country fussock who was forever sporting her juggs at the customers, and Flora the tap-girl, and little Betty the slavey. We're being screwed, was my first thought, so I took a cane and crept out. There was squawks and creaks from the maids' billet, so I opened the jigger wary-like, and damme if Tom wasn't atop big Nance on the bed, wi' his backside going like a fiddler's elbow, and Flora stark by the bed, hissing at 'em 'twas her turn, and Nance was like to play him out.

I didn't use no circumvendibus, but laid my cane across his rump, and he shot off Nance like a rocket and let drive a right that would ha' knocked me to Hanover Square if it'd got home, which I took care it didn't. I was so wild, sir, that I never minded his size or strength, but lammed into him with my cane, going for his giggling-pin, and that sent him skipping. I slammed the jigger and loosed my wrath on the girls, calling 'em such names as I think shame on now, dirty puzzles and crummy butters and that they should be fly-flapped for the whores they were. Nance was a right trollop, and gave me sauce to my face, but Flora was all whine and weep, snitching on Nance who she said had edged Tom from the first, and they'd been strapping this week past. Poor little Betty lay mum as a mouse in her crib; well, I didn't blame *her*.

Bill must not know of this, thinks I, for he'll set the wenches out of doors for certain, and be at odds with Tom; 'twill be misery-go-round and likely adieu to the promisingest heavyweight I've seen in years. So I gave the girls toco and stern warning, for all the good it would do fat Nance, snickering and tossing her head, and went out to Tom in a great rage.

"What d'ye mean by it, ye black golumpus? D'ye think I sweat and train you for *that*, damn you?"

Did he look down, or show humble, or even glower? Not a bit of it. He stood cool as a flounder, looking down his flat snout at me, bare naked and bold as brass.

"Ain't but pleasurin' maself. What's it to you?" says he, and gave the meanest grin, gibing at me. "Ah like wenches, 'speshly white meat, an' what you goin' do 'bout that, Mister Paddin'ton Jones?"

If you'd heard him, sir, you'd ha' been dumbstruck as I was, for I'd never known the like from him. Oh, he'd grumbled and shown stubborn now and then, when I'd worked him too hard, but that had been childish sullens, where this was bold-staring impudence, with a tilt to his head, daring me. I was so wild, sir, I near took the cane to him, but he came up on his toes.

"Best not, Pad," says he. "You git pepper if ye try."

'Twas the way he said it, sir, not with a growl or a jeer or a threat, even, but calm and almost gentle, that told me he was a changed man. I haven't the gift of words to explain the difference, but he wasn't sullen slow Tom to be bidden no more; he was giving me eye for eye as an equal, him that had been so lowly, and 'twas God's truth that he could ha' given me pepper if I'd squared up to him. Whether 'twas flooring Dutch Sam, or meeting the Prince, or having his way with Nance, or knowing his own strength and the science I'd taught him, I can't say, but summat had changed him; perhaps in that black brain of his that I could never fathom he knew that Molineaux the miller meant as much to me as he did to Tom himself. I saw I must take a new tack with him.

"Well, Tom," says I, and tossed the cane aside, "I see ye're an even bigger born fool than I always thought. You want to be a fighter, don't you – d'ye think you can spend your strength on sluts, and fight? Why, ye black ninnyhammer, you'd be too baked to toss your chap over the ropes! And you talk of meeting Cribb!"

"I kin beat Cribb, don' you fret! Wenchin' don' do me no hurt. Fo' white fighters, mebbe, but not fo' me. The mo' wenches I has, the better ma trim, see?"

"God damn your thick nigger skull!" says I, getting warm again. "Ye think ye know better than I, that's trained more pugs and fought more mills than Abraham's grandfather? Why, ye clunch, wenches are worse poison for a miller, black or white, than booze! But if you think contrary, why, tell Bill Richmond in the morning, and he can kick your black breech into the street, where you belong!"

"No, he won', neether," says he, and there was more cunning than sneer in the grin on his ugly phiz. "Bill Richmond countin' on me. So's you. You ain't goin' spoil things, cryin' rope on me to Bill jus' 'cos I give Nance an' Flora a li'l futter."

I all but planted him one then, sir, pepper or no, for the brazen black effrontery of it. Did you ever hear the like for sauce, and presumption? – for I swear I never did. But I held back, for two could play his game.

"Bill's counting on you, is he? Well, perhaps he is and perhaps he ain't, and I'd not find out if I was you, Massa Tom! Maybe he'll be content to spend his blunt and peck and booze on a dunderhead that thinks he can mount every mollisher from here to Peckham, and *still* stand up in the ring. But not I, Tom. Good-night to you."

I was turning away when he growls: "What you mean?"

"Why, I'm giving you up, Tom. You may be worth someone's while, but you ain't worth Paddington Jones's, d'ye see? Not unless you give your solemn oath to steer clear o' skirt. And I don't know as I'd believe you if ye *did* give your affy-davy. Well, it's a pity. You see, Tom, with me, you might ha' got within arm's length of Tom Cribb. Without me, you'd best go for a porter at Covent Garden, if they'll have you."

"You ain't the on'y trainer!" cries he, but by then I was in the tap, seeking my mattress. Sure enough, after a few moments I heard his footstep in the dark. I swear I could hear him thinking.

"If I was to do like you say," growls he. "Give my word, honest. You wouldn't gi' me up?"

"Why, no, Tom. Give me your bounden oath, and all's bowmon."

So he did, and if I didn't believe a word of it, no matter, I'd put him in place, which was necessary, sir, if I was to handle him. I had my doubts, after that night, whether he *would* ever come within reach of Cribb, but he was right in one thing: I was counting on him to do me some credit, and had no wish to cry off at halfway.

I kept my mummer shut to Bill next day, and put Tom through his running and training as before. He shaped well enough, for all his fornications, and within the week was in prime trim as ever. I slept with one eye open, I can tell you, but 'twas quiet as a crypt, and I could tell from the sulky looks of Nance and Flora that Tom was holding to his word, thus far leastways.

Captain Buck Flashman, who'd persuaded Bill to give Tom a run in the first place – ah, you knew that, sir, course you did – was used to stop by at the Nag occasional, to see how Tom shaped, and now he and Bill had me go a few rounds with Tom in the mufflers, but at full stretch. I was hard put to it, sir, I can tell you, and glad to keep my distance, for when it came to holding and throwing I was a babby to him. He cross-buttocked me twice, grinning to show he was going gently, and his in-fighting was tip-top; I never knew a right cross come in so fast.

Captain Buck took my place, and if Tom had held off with me, he did no longer. He bore in hammering, and Captain Buck, for all he was a prime amateur, could do nothing with him. Twice Tom floored him, the last with a down-cut to the neck that dazed him well beyond time, and the Captain pulled off his mauleys and shook hands.

"He's a slasher," was his verdict. "Well, who shall it be, Bill, for he must have a match, that's certain. Cropley? Maltby? George Cribb?" This was Tom's brother, sir, game but of no account. "Not Gregson, though; he ain't ready for that, what? Who's best for him to beat?"

"The Bristol Man, Burrows," says Bill straight out. "He's big, an' game, an' not too clever. An' I know who'll second him."

"What's that to matter?" asks the Captain.

"A good deal," says Bill, looking sly and giving me the wink. "I got my reasons, cap'n. Trust me for that."

WILLIAM HAZLITT,

essayist, critic,

and journalist

"I would not miss it for the salvation of mankind," said Lord Foppington when he heard that Lady Teaser's case was to come before the Lords, and so said I to myself as I left the Holborn Castle on the fine evening of Monday the 13th of July and set my course for Leicester Square. For mine host, the incomparable Gregson, having served me a dish of the mutton-chops for which his hospitable board is justly famed, and whispered me "the office" that the scene of next day's action would be Tothill Fields, where the dark powers of Africa would contend with the sturdy force of our own Gloucestershire, I exclaimed: "I'll be hanged if I don't go directly to view this American prodigy of Richmond's, and whet my appetite for the battle." My education was so far wanting that, though well versed in the lore and language of the Fancy, and ever eager for the conversation of those students and professors of the green fairy circle, *I had never seen a fight*, but now, having heard in Bob's house that the celebrated Elias (known as "Dutch" Sam from his preference for the "juniper", so Toms tells me) had been down to the Horse and Dolphin to test the newly come Black Ajax, and had pronounced him "a rum 'un to fib" (which translates as a formidable fellow), I was resolved to see this portent in the dusky flesh, come what might.

It will be a battle royal, thinks I, and hugged myself in anticipation, for if this Molineaux can win "golden opinions" of such a fearsome gladiator as Dutch Sam, of whom Cropley said that he had rather stand half an hour's milling from Tom Belcher than five minutes of the Jew's punishment, then, I told myself, he should be worth an early rise and a hasty breakfast to see. He is reputed a *hammering fighter*, and his Bristol opponent the gamest of the game, so it will be Hannibal against Scipio "and damn'd be him that first cries 'Hold, enough!' "

Oh, ye philosophers and critics, who hold with Suetonius that the pen is mightier than the blade, spare a thought for those whose weapon is the humble fist. Disdain not the honest pugilist who fights with Nature's arms as beneath your notice, but consider that when he *fibs his adversary's nob* or causes his claret to flow upon the turf, "making the green one red", he strikes with the spirit and bravery of his fore-fathers at Crécy and Agincourt, and inflicts no hurts one-tenth as deep as you with your acid judgments and corroding pens.

But enough of reflection. I was going down Long Acre, wishing I had some companion to share my enthusiasm and the fantasies of sporting discussion, when I saw ahead of me a tall robust man with a swinging stride, heading west. I know that one, thinks I, and coming up with him saw that it was indeed Mr Gully. I blessed my luck to have encountered of all men the one acknowledged the best judge of the Noble Art, and pressed him to come with me. I was determined, I said, to form my opinion of the African beforehand, and hear what the amateurs had to say, to see how our judgments were borne out in the ring. He laughed, and said the opinions of the amateurs were not worth stale snuff. "They think because the black is two inches shorter and so many pounds lighter, it may tip the scale, but that's nothing to the fighting men," says he. "The Fancy have no imagination. They judge of what has been, and can't conceive of what is to be. The Bristol Man has won a mill or two in the West Country, while the black, I'm told, has not yet been out, so the leg-men cry up the odds against him, and the amateurs take fright. It is all gammon; wait till they come to the mark."

I took this to heart, for Mr Gully is the most cool and sensible of men, with an unbiassed discretion, and no slave to his passions in these matters. I asked was he not curious to see Molineaux beforehand, and he smiled and shook his head, saying he would wait till he was within the ropes. I told him Dutch Sam's opinion, and he said Sam was a comedian. – "But for all that, you can take his word for a fighter's bottom against all the prejudices and pedantic notions of the Fancy." Richmond would not risk Captain Flashman's money if it were not *a sure thing*, he added. "What! Is Mad Buck behind the

Moor?'' said I. "That must put a damper on the Bristol faction,
surely.'' He seemed to doubt this, saying their loyalty would last while
the odds were on their man, whoever his opponent's patron might be.
We shook hands, agreeing "to meet at Philippi", and I went alone to
the Horse and Dolphin, primed with the best opinion in the world, and
ready to share it with each and every. It's the devil for any one to tell
me a secret, or share his thoughts with me, for if they are worth
repeating, they are sure to come out. The public ear is too great a
temptation to me.

There was a great press in Richmond's parlour, and a prodigious
noise, some singing, some discussing the house's beef pies and porter,
and all talking of the fight. A large fellow with a bottle nose was
holding forth that Molineaux, being new to the country, must be at a
disadvantage from the London air and his change of diet from America,
where black men were given nothing but roots. Dismal talk in Richmond's house, and not to the liking of his listeners, so I told them air
and diet had nothing to do with it. "You have no imagination," says
I to Bottle Nose. "You judge of what has been, and have no conception
of what is to be.'' "There's profundity, d—d if it isn't!'' cries another.
"You're a student of Kant, sir, don't deny it. What'll you have, brandy
or champagne or anything at all?'' A little man in a corduroy weskit
waxed facetious over Kant and *cant*, which delighted the many at
Bottle Nose's expense, who swore he would not stand it, and offered
to stove in the ribs of any man in the place. This is not what I came
for, thinks I; jollity and mirth by all means, but I'll see the black or
forfeit my head. Accordingly I made my way through the press,
"sweaty nightcaps" and all, and by the exercise of some agility won
through to the yard behind, where the object of my quest came in
view, displaying his manly form at the weights, to the admiration of
the Corinthians.

Ladies, you have never seen an African warrior! The poor person-
ations of fancy, the sooty figures of Astley's or Drury Lane, are but
caricatures, vain pantomime imitations when compared with the reality.
The black boys who proffer your morning chocolate, or keep your
train from the muddy cobbles, are pygmies to the Anteas who now
dwells at the Horse and Dolphin. This is the Noble Savage tamed, yet
not so tame that he will not strike terror in the boldest who must meet

him in the ring. Molineaux indeed is no giant in height, but his shoulders are those of Atlas, his limbs are glossy ebony perfection of grace and power, his carriage a model of primitive nobility. True, his features are homely. As Toms might say, *they would stop the clock*, but their mobility is remarkable, changing from a smile "to dazzle the eye" to a terrible aspect that would become Prester John in majesty enthroned.

> So frowned the mighty combatants, that hell
> Grew darker at their frown.

"Confound me if I ever saw an uglier dial." Thus Bottle Nose at my elbow, who it seemed had either followed me in disgust at finding no challengers in the tap, or perhaps because they were too many. "Well," says he, "when the Bristol Man has improved his looks for him, he may still drive a profit scaring crows." There's a nice conceit, thinks I, and would have advised him not to dismiss the black's chances for being two inches shorter and a few pounds lighter, when all conversation was brought to a stop by Egan's asking the black hero how he would treat Burrows the Bristol Man in the morning. Sooty Tom gave a great grin and said he would knock the wind out of him so hard he would be glad to get back in his *burrow* again. This amused the groundlings, whose laughter inspired Molineaux to caper and rain blows upon the fibbing-bag, saying he would rattle his ribs so – and so! – and so!

"It ain't manly, it's not fighter-like," says my Bardolph of the Bottle Nose. "If he is so sure (which he can't be) the less said about it the better." I believe Richmond thought so, too, for he is one "that bears his sable honours meekly". He took Black Tom by the arm, saying he must go to bed, and they bade the company good-night to great cheering. "Well, confidence is half the battle," said the wit in the corduroy weskit. "Aye, but only half," said Bottle Nose, "and he may get a rare drubbing in the other part of it. The black's a bag of wind." "He may *blow* your chap back to Bristol," says the weskit. "Let him vapour and swagger all he likes," contends Bottle, "your best men are always the most modest, and I'll lick anyone who thinks otherwise!" The other, who knew well how to enrage and placate by turns, kept his antagonist adroitly in play, until the discussion became general, whereupon all returned to the parlour to pass the night in "loud and furious fun".

Having satisfied my curiosity by seeing the Moor, and wishing to compare my impressions with those around me, I joined readily in their debate, first as interlocutor and presently, with the warmth of Richmond's hospitable fire and the soothing potency of his rum shrub, as attentive auditor. There is no contentment so complete as that which comes from convivial company, a topic of mutual interest, comfortable surrounds, and a sufficiency of pleasant but not too inebriating refreshment, the whole compound being given a *teinture piquante* by the reflection that we would be better in bed. My lodgings seemed unconscionably distant, the streets between might be alive with pads and buz-gloaks, Oliver I was certain must be out of town, and had not my dearest Sarah cautioned me against the night air which she was sure must give me a chill? Thinks I, I'll be hanged if I stir a foot, when I can pass the night here among these good companions, and if their conversation and mine host's fire become too heated, there's the back parlour where I can lie snug and peaceful as if I were at Winterslow, and be on hand to join the Moor's caravan for Tothill Fields in the morning. Why, there shall be no need of early rising, and I'll break my fast at leisure upon Richmond's best!

And so to bed (on the back parlour couch) I went presently, and dreamed of grinning blackamoors who grimaced and glared their adversaries to submission, and woke with sunshine on my face. I peeped out to find the main parlour empty but for a maid who scrubbed the floor. "What, no one up yet?" "Why, sir, master's up and gone these four hours past, with Black Tom to the fight, and the gentlemen with them." "What, gone! and I, like Enobarbus, have made the night light with drinking, and slept day out of countenance? It will all be over and done by now!" She was sure it would be, and that Tom must have won, having all the prayers of the fair sex of the Horse and Dolphin riding pillion on his dusky shoulders, and her own three-farthings which Mister Jones had promised to wager on him at judicious odds.

I cursed my folly and ill-luck together. This is what comes of late hours and eye-water, and listening to the babbling of fools without imagination, says I. Seeing the little slavey's alarm at my outburst,

I said, well, one hope disappointed is enough for the day. "Let me see, if Tom has milled over his man, and the odds were, say, six to one against him, your three-farthings will have brought you fourpence-ha'penny – I'm sure that's right – which with your stake will be fivepence-farthing. But if he has taken a melting, why, my dear, you're off Point Nonplus. Here's a shilling to cover your loss, if loss it be, and if you would win favour in the eyes of Heaven, the next time a gentleman sleeps in of a fight morning, then do thou strike and spare not, and he will bless thee, child, as one waking to Gabriel's trump."

She ran away with her face in her apron, but taking the "bob" with her. I went in search of traffic for Peck Alley, as Toms would say, my mind running on "Lilliput chickens boil'd, and hams that flit in airy slice" as consolation. But I'll see a fight one of these days, I vowed, "or aile lig i' the grund for it", which at least will spare me the vexation of waking to dashed hopes in Richmond's back parlour.

CAPTAIN BUCKLEY FLASHMAN,
resumed

Tom's first fight, against Burrows the Bristol Man – lord love you, 'twas no fight at all. A formality, sir, a spectacle, arranged by that most prudent of managers, Bill Richmond. What's that – was it a cross? Burn your impudence, no such thing! D'ye think I'd touch a queer mill? That'll cost you another bottle o' red tape for effrontery. A cross, indeed!

No, my green companion, I mean that once Richmond knew he had a promising chicken in Molineaux (at my prompting, you recall), he made sure the lad was seen to advantage in his first bout. Which meant choosing the right opponent for him to beat: some hulking lout who didn't know cream from cider but had won a few mills out o' Town, and would be strong and stupid enough to endure a sound thrashing and show a fine gory figurehead afterwards – science ain't in it with blood when it comes to raising cheers from the mob, you see. The Bristol Man answered to perfection; he was the victim, Tom the executioner. But there was naught smoky about it. 'Twas cut-and-dried inevitable, that's all.

Confound it, don't ye know that's how a fighter's name is built, by choosing good matches that he's sure to win, and catch the Fancy's fancy, eh? If he starts underdog, so much the better for him – and for profit. Richmond was fly to that, bragging Tom's prowess while admitting the Bristol Man's advantages of weight and height, and seeing to it that word got about from Dutch Sam how in breathing Tom he'd been warned to steer clear of his upper works – aha, said the wiseacres, that must be the nigger's weak spot. Consequence? Seven to four on the Bristol Man the night before the fight, with Bill sighing and wagging his foxy grey head as he took the bets. As Molineaux's patron I was bound to back him handsomely, so I spread a few hundred judiciously among the legs, and looked forward to further investment at the ringside. Oh, they don't call it the Noble Art for nothing!

95

In truth, though, money was the least of it for me. If anything was needful to confirm me in the front rank of the sporting *ton*, 'twas to be sponsor to a top-notch pug, and I'd seen enough on my visits to the Nag to be sure that my first judgment of Tom had been sound. Pad Jones had brought him on famously, and while I doubted he'd ever be in Cribb's parish, I knew he'd do me credit.

I took my own way to the ground that Tuesday morning, though, for while some Corinthians were used to drive their fighters to the field, and make a great proprietary show, it always looked dam' vulgar to me, and we Flashmans are devils for good taste. I was sure Richmond's caravan would go by Whitehall and Parliament Street to catch the public eye and join with the common herd coming over the Horse Ferry, so I tooled my curricle sedately through the Park to James Street, and who should be on the corner of Castle Lane, hunting for a jarvey and getting nowhere, but Pierce Egan. Better than the town crier, thinks I, for while he wrote the sorriest stuff, he had the public ear and would puff Tom far and wide.*

I took him up, and he made a desk of his hat on his knee and scribbled as we bowled along past the Artillery Ground.

"Hark to this, Buck," says he familiarly. "'Unknown, unnoticed, unprotected and uninformed, the brave Molineaux arrived in England'. How's that for a lead paragraph, eh?"

"Masterly," says I. "Leigh Hunt must look to his laurels."

"But who *is* Molineaux, that's the point? Richmond is close as an oyster, and Blackee himself don't gab to be understood. Pad Jones says he was a slave in America – is it so?"

I told him it was, and how Tom had won his freedom.

"Oh, that's rare! 'Broke the shackles with his iron fist...'" says

---

* Pierce Egan (c.1774–1849), was the most famous boxing writer of his day. His *Boxiana*, a collection of pugilists' biographies and reports of fights, was a bestseller in 1812, but was outstripped by the huge success of *Life in London* (1820–1), which gave to the world Tom and Jerry – not the cat and mouse of the 1940s cartoons, but their originals, Jerry Hawthorn and Corinthian Tom, who, with their friend Bob Logic of Oxford, explored the fashionable, theatrical, sporting, and seamy sides of the metropolis. Egan's success excited considerable jealousy among rival writers, and while his racy, freewheeling prose, heavily laced with slang and cant, delighted his readers, it and Egan's reputation were to suffer at the hands of later critics. For all that, he holds an unchallenged place among reporters and historians of the ring, and *Boxiana* remains a classic in sporting literature.

he, pencil flying. "Here, though, we must play up the African warrior. His father wasn't a chief, I suppose? No? Well, I have it! ... 'Descended from a warlike hero, who had been the conquering pugilist of America ...' H'm ... what the dooce brought him to England, d'ye know?"

"Wants to be champion, I believe."

"Ye don't say! I must have Cribb's opinion on that ..." Scribble, scribble. " 'Britain attracted his towering disposition ... left his native soil in quest for glory ... raging seas were no impediment to his heroic views ...' There's a happy phrase, I think ... 'Now offers himself, a rude, unsophisticated savage –' No, come, that won't do. 'Stranger', I think, not 'savage' ... mustn't alarm our fair readers. Aye, 'Now offers himself to the patrons of that manly sport which instils valour in England's hardy sons and gives stability to the national character ...' Capital stuff!" says Pierce. "Now, then, no secret you're his patron. Why, Buck?"

"Born a slave," says I. "My family's always been dead against it. Grandfather spent his life ... ah, helping niggers to better themselves. Well, there you are." I gave a modest shrug. "Don't need to play that up, though."

" 'Patron of freedom!' " cries the Grub Street oaf, scribbling like a thing demented. He was babbling about "a dusky hand stretched out to tear the fistic laurels from Britannia's brow" when we rolled into Tothill Fields, which was a sizeable meadow in those days, 'tween Chelsea and the river. This being a minor mill, there was no outer ring or stage, but several hundred were gathered about the ropes, and groups of people were hurrying down from the Horse Ferry Road. There were a number of carriages already there, and among their occupants were Saye and Sele, Alvanley, Sefton (come to see his sooty namesake uphold the family honour, no doubt), Cripplegate Barrymore, and various Four-in-Handers. I raised my whip to their hails, and wheeled in by the ring, the commonalty cheering and making room.

Tom was by the ropes, wrapped in a greatcoat, with Richmond and Pad Jones, and at the other corner stood the Bristol Man, Burrows, stripped and sporting a torso and arms that would have done Hercules credit, a great tow-headed ruffian grinning all over his yokel face as he spoke to his second – and when I saw who *that* was I bore up sharp, I can tell you. Richmond had made a point, you remember, of the Bristol Man's having the "right" second . . . no, no, I shan't name him, just yet. Richmond meant it for a surprise, and so do I.

"Not a beak in sight," says Egan, hopping down. "Well, it ain't a big enough turn-up to disturb the peace. Hollo, there's Crocky! Well, old fellow, what price, then?"

"Five to four Bristol," says Crockford, tipping his tile to me and leering all over his pasty face. "G'day, captain. Here's Lord Barrymore offerin' a thousand 'gainst your black. What's your pleasure?"

"At those odds I'll take it all," says I. "Why've they dropped?"

"They've seen your man," says he, and I saw that Tom had shed his coat, and the mob were craning to look and gasping in excitement. "Ah," says Crocky, all knowing, "they've seen some blackamoors before, but none like that, I'll lay!"

Damme, he was right, for Tom shone in the morning sun like an ebony statue, flexing his splendid arms, and when he skipped it was like some savage war dance. The mob cheered, and Crocky shook his head.

"Evens in a moment, at least. Aye, I thought so − three to two Molineaux! You was just in time, captain!"

The legs were racing about, crying the late odds and jotting in their readers, as the two men ducked through the ropes and took their handlers' knees. There was no weighing, as at the big mills, but Jackson called out Tom at thirteen two, and the Bristol Man unstated. When they came to scratch, and it was seen how large Bristol bulked against Tom, and half a head higher, the odds went back to evens, and Crockford laughed as the legs scampered harder than ever.

Then Jackson called for silence, and the two shook hands and squared off, Bristol planted like an oak, Tom dancing on his toes − and in the hush over Tothill Fields I could hear my heart racing. Oh, I knew it was Tom's fight, but how would he play, how would he shape? When you see your fighter primed and ready, for the first time, you're bound to swallow hard and grip your knees. Jackson nodded to the time-keepers, called "Set to!" and they went at it.

Well, they breed game men in Gloucestershire, and had need to that morning, for I never saw a more one-sided melting. Tom made no play at a distance, but bore straight in at half-arm and used the other's body as a drubbing-bag. Burrows could make nothing of him, clumsy and flat on his feet as Tom danced in and out, hitting where he chose and pounding his ribs. His fists went like steam-pistons, too fast to be seen, and when Bristol put in a counter, Tom either took it without wincing or slipped it with ease, hardly bothering to guard or stop. In thirty seconds he scored the first knock-down, doubling Bristol up and flooring him with a muzzling right that travelled a bare six inches. That was Burrows's epitaph, for every round ended alike, Tom flipping him to the body and practising on his nob till he fell. Burrows was game; he rushed, and was nailed by Tom's left; he tried to hold and throw, and got handfuls of air for his pains.

It was the plebs's delight, a scientist butchering a clod who was too brave to give in. By twenty minutes Bristol's face was a bloody swamp, by the half-hour he was reeling like a soused sailor, but fib as Tom might he could not put the brute away. Time and again the rounds ended with Bristol bleeding on the grass and crawling back to his second's knee, but at every call of "Time!" he would come staggering back to scratch, spouting gore like a fountain, but grinning and trying to raise his fists. Tom knocked him into the ropes, and he hung there helpless, but when Tom appealed to Jackson – and got a rare huzza from the mob – the Bristol Man heaved up again, and it was nigh on an hour before he went down for the last time, and lifted a hand in surrender. Tom had not a mark on him, but I saw Pad Jones making earnest examination of his fists, which must have been the sorest part of him.

Then it was all "Hurra for the black!", with hats in the air and a surge of people about Tom clapping his shoulder, vowing he was a slasher and a pounder and God knows what. He and the Bristol Man flung their arms about each other, Pad Jones tried to get Tom into his coat, Bill Richmond nodded like a man well content, and Tom embraced 'em both and began to caper, beaming and chortling with his arms in the air, skipping in that plantation dance-step that would soon be known all over Town. I beckoned him, and he pranced over to the curricle with Pad and Richmond at his heels.

"Well done, Tom, my boy," says I. "How are you?"

"Say, Ah's fit's a fiddle, fresh an' easy, Cap'n Buck!" cries he, with the sauciest grin. Hollo, it used to be "Cap'n", or "Mass' Buck", with a respectful bob, but what the devil, he'd just won his first mill, and in slashing style, too. "Say, but he weren't nuthin', nuthin' at all! Reckon Ah fibbed him down real good! Hey, Pad, am Ah a miller? You bet Ah am! What you say, Bill Richmond? You bring on yo' Gregsons an' yo' Tom Belchers, an' Ah show you! Yeah, bring on yo' Tom Cribb!"

"Ye think so?" says Richmond, with an odd glint in his eye. He looked back at the ring, over the heads of the cockneys cheering about the curricle. "Tell ye what, Tom, you jus' rest here wi' the Cap'n awhile. He'll give you a seat, won't ye, sir? Up with you, now. You jus' set right there, boy, an' keep your eyes on Pad an' me, 'cos we got somethin' to show you."

I didn't know what he was about, but Richmond never did anything without good reason, so I let Tom sit by me, swathed in his coat, full of brag and ginger, begging a swig of the "cool Nantz" from my flask, toasting me familiarly as "Cap'n Buck!" and so uncommon pleased with himself, as he waved to the mob and whinnied his infectious black laugh, that I couldn't take offence. Farewell to our humble, shuffling sambo, I thought, and why not, for he's a figure now, for all the man he's thrashed is no more than a stalwart pudding.

Cripplegate limped up, snarling his congratulations like the charming loser he was and swearing our wager had been at evens, not five to four. I didn't heed him, for a strange scene was being played before my eyes. The crowd were dispersing, the stakes and ropes being removed, and Jones and Richmond were approaching the little knot of folk round the Bristol Man, who sat on the grass counting his teeth through a mouth that was like a gaping wound, while his bottle-holder sponged the blood from his shattered face.

His second stood by, turning as Richmond and Pad approached; he smiled and held out his hand; then his face fell and the hand was withdrawn.

They were too far to be heard, but Richmond was shouting, and suddenly he slapped the second's face and squared up − and in a twinkling the second shot a left at his head, and Bill was sent sprawling. Pad Jones dodged in, letting fly a fist. The second slipped it almost lazily, and as Richmond jumped up and bore in on his other side, the second upper-cut him and in the same moment his other fist knocked

Jones clean off his feet. It was over in an instant, the two of 'em grassed, and the second shrugging and turning away to see to his principal.

Beside me Tom grunted and half-started up, staring as Richmond and Jones climbed to their feet and came back to us, Richmond none too steady and Pad nursing his peeper.

"You see that, Tom?" cries Richmond, out of breath. "You see what that big cove did to me an' Pad, swattin' us off like we's flies? Did ye see his hands move, 'cos I swear I didn't!" He felt his jaw tenderly. "Damme if he ain't loosed a couple o' my dice! Well, I wanted you to see that, Tom, so you can study that man, that big good-lookin' file wi' the curly hair, who put down two 'sperienced millers without shiftin' his feet, even! 'Cos he's the feller you came 'cross the herrin' pond for, my boy! That's Tom Cribb."

It was no news to me, of course, but now I saw what Richmond had been at. He'd picked the Bristol Man as Tom's adversary because he was a prime chopping-block, but also because he knew that Cribb, being from Bristol, always turned out to lend a knee to a fellow-townie, however humble; that was Cribb's sort. And Richmond had picked a quarrel (some gammon about a foul blow, I believe) so that Tom should have a glimpse of the Champion at work.

"So there ye are," says Bill. "You seen him, but, boy, you ain't *felt* him! Well, what d'ye say now?"

Tom's great lips had gaped at the mention of the name, and he frowned as though puzzled to see the man at last. "That Tom Cribb?" growls he. "The Champeen of Englan' – that him?"

"The one and only," says Pad.

Tom stared for a moment, and then looked sly, glancing sidelong and rolling his eyes in comical fashion.

"Well, my-my!" crows he. "So that's Tom Cribb! Why, he looks a right nice feller. Ain't you 'shamed, Bill Richmond, pickin' on a quiet 'spectable gen'man like that? Ain't you larned no manners?" He gave his deep darkie chuckle. "Well, Ah guess *he* larned you an' Pad, silly ol' men, baitin' a champeen thataway! Oh, oh, oh!" cries he, giving a great shudder and clasping his coat about him. "Cap'n Buck, Ah's catchin' cold a-settin' here! Cain't we go home, Cap'n Buck, an' leave these foolish pe'sons 'fore they starts mo' brawlin'?

Ah's powe'ful cold, cap'n, Ah's a-shiverin' suthin' painful!'' And damned if he didn't contort his grotesque face in a mighty wink at me.

''Damn your eyes!'' splutters Richmond, struggling for speech, at which Tom fairly cackled with mirth, and I judged it best to wheel the curricle away and remove this eccentric insolent nigger before Bill, stamping in fury, burst his bounds. Damned if I knew what to make of Molineaux and his antics (and still don't) but as we threaded our way through the multitude streaming towards the Horse Ferry, and I was preparing to shout the starch out of him, he forestalled me with another of his plantation guffaws.

''That Bill Richmond! Tryin' to skeer po' li'l Tom wi' that foolishness! Aimin' to teach the sassy nigguh a lesson, ho-ho!''

''Not before time, I think! Now, see here, Tom—''

''Why, Cap'n Buck, Ah knowed 'twas Cribb f'm the fi'st!'' He was grinning like the dam' sunrise. ''Ah see his picksher on the wall in that Don Saltero's cawfy-house, din't have to ask who 'twas, 'cos 'tis bigger'n all th'other spo'tin' pickshers. An' the way he eyed me today when Ah's millin' the Bristol Man — he studyin' me real close, Ah see that.'' He exploded with mirth. ''Hoo-hey, an' ol' Bill gits hisself floo'ed for nuthin', an' Pad gits a shiner!''

''I'll be damned!'' says I, astonished and trying not to laugh. ''Well, ye've seen Cribb with his hands up, at all events. You can thank Richmond for that.''

''Din't tell me nuthin','' says this amazing aborigine. ''Allus knowed Tom Cribb mus' be a top-notchah, 'thout seein' him flip Bill an' Pad so easy. Big man, fibs real sweet. Sho', Ah seen him.'' He waved to the cheering louts running behind as we bore up towards the Greycoat School, and settled back with a contented sigh, black phiz beaming. ''An' he's seen *me*.''

So that, my industrious inquirer, was his first fight, and I trust you've sense enough to see that the change it wrought in Tom was a sight more remarkable than the mill itself. It was like taking the hood off a hawk: he'd stood up in an English ring, against a white pug, tested his skill and strength, heard the screaming worship of the crowd, and got thoroughly drunk with bounce and conceit. More than that, he tasted the first fruits of victory in hard money ... but I'll tell you about that when you've done your duty with the brandy . . . fill up, man, I won't dissolve!

There was a mighty crush at the Nag to toast his triumph: the swell crowd with Alvanley, Sefton, and Mellish to the fore, lesser lights of the Fancy, and the raggle-taggle hoping for free drink from the winning patron. Richmond, half-sour-half-pleased at Tom's showing in the ring and his antics afterwards, handed him the subscription purse of forty guineas, to which I added a cool hundred − I cleared three thou' in stakes on the fight, and Bill a hundred or two − and our sable hero was so moved that he danced before the counter, snapping his fingers and singing a darkie jubilee, to wild applause. Then he spread the rhino on the table, roaring to the customers to admire it, tucking flimsies into the bosoms of the tap-wenches (all of whom had backed him with their ha'pence), and calling for drink for the company. I put a stop to that, reminding Bill it must be to my account, and damme if Tom didn't claim priority until Bill spoke a sharp word in his ear, at which he had the sense to pocket his blunt with a show of boisterous comedy that still had a gleam of defiance in it.

There was no damping him, though. When Egan quizzed him, scribbling away, about the Bristol Man, our gladiator dismissed him with a wave, and announced that he was ready to back himself with his newly-gotten winnings against any pug, light or heavy, in the country. "They sayin' Mistah Jem Belcher an' Mistah Gregson retired!" cries he. "Guess they knows what's good for 'em, but ifn they gits tired ale-drapin', Ah's heah!" Dutch Sam was "on'y a lightweight, an' Ah reckon he's too well 'quainted wi' this already!" sporting his right to renewed cheering. "What's that? You say Mistah Tom Cribb was at the mill today? Well, lan' sakes, think o' that! He ain't heah now, is he, 'cos Ah'd sho' like to interdooce maself!" Both fists flourished, with great grinning and eye-rolling, and the welkin fairly rang. The Corinthians laughed, the common herd hurrah'd and raised their pots, the Cyprians pressed about him, and one bold painted trollop begged to feel his biceps, squealing with admiration. Tom stood like a beaming black colossus in the midst of it, planting smacking kisses on the titters who clung to either arm, detaching himself only to quaff the magnum of fizz which Alvanley had presented; he did it by clapping the bottle to his lips and draining it, while the mob cheered and stamped, and having gasped for breath, demanded: "Can Tom Cribb drink thataway, hey?"

"Wonderful what a good mill can do, eh, cap'n?" says Pad Jones.

"Dam' nigger mouth!" growls Richmond. "To hear him ye'd think he'd beat Broughton!"

"Why, Bill, it's but fighter's talk," says Mellish, who had come to our corner. "He's only a black child, man, after all."

" 'E ain't that childish,' says Pad, and I saw he had a grim eye on Tom and the mollishers, who were now paying attention to Tom's thigh muscles and screaming when he demanded, with roaring ho-ho's, to return the compliment.

"Bit of a mutton-monger, I shouldn't wonder," laughs Mellish. "Well, Pad, you'll just have to prime him with raw eggs, stout and oysters, what?"

Then Sefton called for silence, and pledged Tom as "the newly-come American hero" who had made such an auspicious entry to the English ring, and must, he did not doubt, add lustre to the laurels of our grand old game – which I thought damned handsome of him – and the toast was drunk with three times three. Sefton shook his hand, and I heard Richmond curse under his breath when Tom took it, bold as you please, man-to-man, and clapped Sefton on the shoulder (at which my noble earl raised an eyebrow, with a glance at his collar to see that Tom's sooty daddle hadn't creased Scott's best superfine). I saw Alvanley's lips twitch, and Mellish muttered "I say!", while Richmond ground his teeth.

You see, there was a nice etiquette in the Fancy, where the highest in the land were on terms with the pugs – why, they drank together, and sparred together, and gossiped together, easy enough, in a way that foreigners with their rigid distinctions could make nothing of. But there was a line that neither ever crossed. The Quality never condescended, and the pugs never presumed; each respected the other, and kept his station. Tom, blast his impudence, treated Sefton as an equal, and I knew, from the cock of his woolly head, and the look in his bloodshot eye, *that he knew better*. Dammit, he knew what he was, and what Sefton was, and he'd seen enough at the Nag and Blower, where the classes mingled, to know how peers and pugs conducted themselves. But his victory, the plaudits, and the consciousness of what he, Tom Molineaux, was and might become, had gone to his head altogether. I'd seen the beginnings of this intoxication after the mill, in his familiarity to me, his amusement at Richmond's expense, his roaring and bragging celebration, and now in his "Why, that's fine, milord, that's jus' fine!" as he slapped Sefton on the back. Richmond could have killed him, and I resolved to be elsewhere when he spoke his mind to our cocksure gladiator, for I guessed he'd get only sauce in return, and 'twould do my dignity no good to be on hand. So when Sefton and the other swells took their leave, I too brushed, leaving Tom to his boozy revels among the mollishers, Richmond preparing to pitch into him, and Pad Jones looking decidedly blue.

The fact was, I didn't mind. I'd got unto myself a fighter who'd be the talk of the Town, and if he chose to give himself airs or kick up larks, why, the Town would talk all the more. A prize pug, and a black one at that, who tweaked the Quality by his presumption, would be a novelty, and a refreshing one – not least to me, for when you've had to scheme your way into the *ton* it's capital fun to see those who were born to it having their fine feathers ruffled. I promised myself some quiet amusement in parading Tom through the haunts of sporting fashion – well, I might be his backer, but I wasn't to be held accountable for his manners.

If soldiering teaches you anything, it's to lose no time, aim high, and strike boldly, so before bedtime I sent a note to my old cricketing acquaintance, George Brummell, begging his assistance in a toggery matter, which I was certain must fetch him. Sure enough, he rolled up to my rooms in South Street at eleven the next morning, exquisite as always, yawning and demning the dem' dawn, and I drove him round to the Nag, confronted him with Tom, and told him what was afoot.

"Gad's me life!" says he, dropping his eye-glass in disbelief. "You want my advice in rigging out *that*? Buckley, have you no mercy, dammit? At this time of day, too, without warning! Richmond, a glass of brandy! I feel quite loose!"

"He ain't that frightsome," says I, although Tom was showing the effect of his night's mop, red-eyed and shocking seedy. "And you won't find a finer figure for a swell case anywhere, I'll be bound. Which shall it be, George – Scott or Weston?"

He choked on his brandy. "It's a dreadful dream," says he. "Curse me if curried lobster ever passes my lips again." He took another shot of his glass at Tom, who was glowering like Apollyon. "No, begad, he's real! *Quel visage!* My dear Buckley, are you mad, or castaway entirely? Who in his right mind could present that monstrosity to Weston or Scott?"

"Nobody but Brummell," says I. "Come, George, forget his phiz and consider the rest of him. Why, he's a snyder's delight. Anyway, it's for a lark. And Scott would tog out a Barbary ape if you gave the word."

"A happy comparison," says he, but his lips twitched; he was all for fun, in his quiet way, and the kindest soul alive. "But I'll be shot ere I drive down the Grand Strut with him." He hopped down, shook hands with Tom, complimented him on his victory – trust George to be beforehand with the whiz – and walked slowly round him, quizzing up and down. "Dam' fine leg, but those Guardee shoulders will need accommodation. Aye, Weston, I think; his sleeves are altogether inspired these days, and we'll catch him while the fit lasts."

So to Weston we went, and such was the power of George's name that they never blinked an eye. Under his supervision they measured and chalked and pinned and jotted their notes, and Tom, who had been so full of buck the day before, stood mute and wary in their midst, while Brummell discussed collars and pockets and buttons, and how the pantaloons must fit like a skin and yet give complete freedom of movement, to which Weston's minions nodded and exclaimed in reverence as though it had been the Sermon on the Mount. I stood it for about an hour, by which time George's coat was off and the floor was knee deep in paper and bolts of cloth, and one little snyder was in tears and ready to fall on his scissors. I suspect they were still at it by candlelight, and to some tune, for when they screwed him into the duds next day Tom was the bangest-up Corinthian you ever saw. The coat was a marvel of pale grey superfine – I'd thought a red or blue would have suited, but Brummell swore there wasn't another rig of that peculiar grey between Soho and the Serpentine.

"Except his Royal Highness's," says the snyder-in-chief, in a voice of doom.

"Cut by Scott, so it don't signify," says George. "Now, then, the neckcloth ... Waterfall, Mail Coach, Osbaldeston – no, demned if I don't make him one of my own! The Molineaux, begad! Ah, Tom, Tom, you'll live in song and story!''

That was a sight, Beau Brummell, the dandy of dandies, arranging Tom's neckercher, folding and twitching and stepping back to consider before adjusting a crease just so, and that dreadful blackamoor map grinning above the snowy linen. For now that he had grown used to being in a tailor's shop (where I'll swear he'd never been before) he was back in his cheerfuls again, craning to observe his reflection and giving little chuckles of pleasure. And didn't he cut a figure, just, for if Nature had played him scurvy in the feature department, she'd done him proud beneath the neck; I never saw a frame better designed for the snyder's art, with those splendid shoulders and neat waist, and when he stood forth with Weston's superfine showing never a crease, his white pantaloons tight to perfection, the top boots gleaming, and George's creation billowing beneath his chin, the minions were in raptures, and Brummell admitted that he might very well do.

"Demned if I ever saw a neater fit beneath the shoulder," drawls he, "and that's the sticking point, eh, Weston? Very creditable, quite in the – good Gad!''

He went pink, for in considering the rig-out he'd fallen into his critical pose, head back, one foot forward, and tapping a finger on his chin – and damned if Tom wasn't doing likewise. Like all blacks, he was a born mimic, and 'twas the most comical sight to see those two immaculate figures viewing each other identical, the pale fine-featured Corinthian head on one, and the grinning black savage on t'other. George threw up a hand in surprise, Tom did the same, George turned to me, Tom followed suit, and George burst out laughing.

"I'll be demned! I say, Buckley, don't for any favour give him an eye-glass, for if he sports it at our swells I swear there'll be a revolution! And no hat, mind, or the effect will be spoiled. Now, he's all yours, my boy! I'll leave you to stump the pewter. Well done, Weston! Good day to ye, Tom, and keep your chin clear o' that neckercher!''

Tom swept him a most elegant bow, crying: '' 'Bliged t'ye, Mistah Brummell!'' and preened himself before the mirror, turning this way and that to admire the hang of the tails, and all as to the manner born. I had the deuce of a job to get him out of the shop.

Native sense warned me that I'd be best not to exhibit my protégé in the Park at the "bitching hour" of five, when all the Quality turned out to see and be seen. Ten years later, in the Tom-and-Jerry days, when the vulgar horde had come West with a vengeance, and the Park was a jamboree of both nobility and flash, dukes and tradesmen, town tabbies and trollops, it would have suited, but not in the war time. The Park then was exclusive to the *ton*, and the commonalty kept clear of it in the afternoon when the titles promenaded in fashionable array to gossip and sneer, the bucks on their bits of blood and the ladies in their vis-à-vises. The gargoyle frontispiece of blackamoor Tom, attired in Weston's finest, would have been decidedly *outré* in that company — I shuddered at the thought of encountering Queen Sarah and her Almack's Amazons, and having my great piccaninny beaming and crying: "Halloo, gals!" So I tooled the curricle discreetly along Park Lane, or Tyburn Lane as my guv'nor used to call it, and into the north end of the Park about noon, when the more select females would still be at their toilettes, and most of the traffic was of the sporting set. I wanted Tom to be seen, you understand, but not so much as to draw frowns.

He was in capital spirits at first, well pleased with his new togs, beaming affably to the carriages and riders, admiring the fine trees, and exclaiming at the cows and deer browsing by the walks. He attracted much attention, the riders reining up to stare and the carriage females all a-titter and turning their heads. I acknowledged acquaintances, but didn't stop to chat, content to let Tom bask in the world's regard, which he did in gallant style, nodding and waving, and telling me this was "real supernaculous".

After a while, he seemed to smile and wave less often, and by the time I wheeled in at Tattersall's Corner he had fallen silent, brooding at his boots. I thought the sight of the Horse Capital of the World, with all its colour and bustle, might revive his interest, but no such thing. It was an auction day, and the enclosure and club-room were crowded with the horsey *ton*, the bucks and squires with their grooms and tigers, and the great press of jockeys and touts and blacklegs, all come to gossip of turf and hunt and view the four new Persian prads just come from Asia, and wag their heads over the bidding; it was lost on Tom, although he was still the focus of all eyes. I made him known to a few, and he barely grunted; when I pressed him to a glass of arrack and a sandwich, he shook his head; young Dick Tattersall (they call him Old Dick nowadays, by the way) came down from his table all smiles, for he was a keen amateur miller, and anxious to meet the new aspirant, but all he got from Tom was a nod and a mutter.

I couldn't think what was troubling the brute, but seeing he'd make few friends in his present dumps, I put him aboard again and made for Piccadilly. He continued blue as ever, even when we passed Old Q's house and saw a sight which I was sure must gladden the heart of a lickerish nigger: two of the prettiest little angelics, dressed as Corinthians, hats on blonde curls, sporting their shapes in tail-coats, tight breeches, boots and all, tripping down the steps flourishing their canes and giggling. I remarked on them to Tom, explaining that Old Q was notorious for peculiar debauchery, and the two little winkers had undoubtedly been putting him over the jumps that morning; the surly oaf didn't even look at 'em, so I wheeled into Half-Moon Street and pulled up, out of all patience.

"What the devil's the matter? Confound it, I fig you out to the nines, drive you through the Park, show you the sights, and ye're as lively as a dead trout. What's wrong, man?"

"Nuthin'," says he. "Wan' to go home."

"What the dooce for? Look here – what's cast you down? Out with it, rot you! What's amiss?"

He sat hunched in his magnificent coat, clenching his fists, and suddenly burst out in a furious growl:

"They's laffin' at me! Damn 'em, why's they laffin'? 'Cos Ah's a black man all dressed up? Ah seen 'em, in the Park, an' 'mong the hosses yonder! They's all a-laffin', makin' mock o' Tom Molineaux!" I'll swear there were red sparks in his eyes. "Say – that why you had me decked out in these fancy duds, Mistah Brummell an' all, so they make game o' me? That yo' joke, Cap'n Buck?"

Vent your heat on me, and you get it back with interest. "Damn your eyes, don't dare take that tone to me! Laughing, were they? And who the hell are you, curse your impudence, that your betters can't laugh if they choose? Count yourself lucky they *do*, d'ye hear? What d'ye expect, when they see a nigger decked out like the Prince Regent, scowling his black head off? See here, my boy," says I, "I gave you

109

a swell case to be noticed, to be talked about, because a fighter who ain't in the public eye is nobody, d'ye understand? And I haven't lodged and fed and trained you and brought you on so that you can have the vapours when I show you to the Town!''

"Whut call they got to laff?'' roars he, turning on me. "Ah ain't a . . . a scarecrow! Nor a dwarf, like in a show!''

"Ain't you, now? Well, I'm damned! No, you ain't a scarecrow or a dwarf, you're a black pug too big for your blasted breeches! And you're *my* pug, d'ye hear? Now, Mister Tom Molineaux,'' says I, drawing breath and temper, "I've been dam' good to you, because I thought you had something in you, and might make a show in the ring — but if you don't care for it, and are so almighty proud that no one can even look at you, and *smile*, bigod! — why, then, you can get back to the gutter where you belong! Well?''

Would you believe it, he wasn't done yet. "Ah ain't goin' be laffed at!'' cries he. "They wasn't laffin' yes'day, when Ah mollocated that big lummox! 'Cos o' this, ain't it?'' He seized the skirt of his coat and shook it.

"Tear that, and so help me God I'll take this whip to you!'' I was near speechless with fury. "Let it go, d'ye hear? Jesus, man, d'ye know what it cost?'' It was past belief, a nigger pup with sensibilities, and I at my wits' end to put sense and reason into him. If I'd not had an interest in his future, I'd have kicked him on to the pavement, shiny buttons, Brummell's cravat and all. I tried a line that I thought might serve.

"If folk laugh at you, laugh straight back at 'em, blast you! Aye, consider, when they laugh, how you'd serve 'em in a mill! Think of that, hey? Damn my blood if I ever knew such a fellow! Now, look alive, for I'm taking you to a place where I swear you will *not* be laughed at — not by anyone who signifies, leastways. Sit up, can't ye, and look as pleasant as you know. Smile, you black fool!''

He stared at me a long moment, mutiny and murder in his eyes, and they did not change as his thick lips twisted in a grin fit to frighten the French. He nodded, and I whipped up, and presently we rolled into Berkeley Square, where I made the circuit twice to test his conduct. The saunterers and promenading ladies stopped to quiz him through their glasses and stare sidelong, and true enough, there was as much disdainful amusement as curiosity in their looks, but the delicate bloom by my side must have taken my words to heart, for he bore it with the lordliest air, reclining at ease and only glancing to right or left, ugly but serene with Brummell's creation billowing beneath his chin. You're hatching something, you bastard, thinks I, but at least his sullens had passed for the moment. I turned the curricle east and we came by the quieter streets to our destination, not far from the Nag and Blower.

You've seen Blake's famous picture of the Fives Court? It's a nonsense, to be sure, for it shows every great miller and name of the Fancy that ever was, all assembled together (which they never were – why, they even have Molineaux himself, posed and peeled for a bout, and elsewhere Hen Pearce, the Game Chicken, and Bill Warr, who were dead and buried side by side at St Pancras years before Tom came to London), but the general view is right enough. The Fives Court was to boxing what Tattersall's was to horse society: the hub of the universe. Here the Fancy would congregate in the great barn of a building with its galleries and boxes overlooking the roped stages; here the challenges were given and the matches made, the wagers laid and taken, the disputes settled and the benefits held; here you might see the Prince of Wales in hearty discussion with Gentleman Jackson or Bill Richmond; Dutch Sam or Mendoza sparring on the stage while Paddington Jones or John Gully explained the finer points to young Lord Palmerston; Big Bob Gregson, who fancied himself a poet, having his verses conned by Byron himself; Egan in warm dispute with Hazlitt; and everywhere the great buzz of form and weight and training, and who was coming forward among the younger men, or declining among the older, and fight, fight, fight! All gone now, most of 'em leastways, into the shades and Blake's picture.

As soon as we entered the Court Tom's behaviour was put to the test. Every head turned, and while for the most part the pugs regarded him with shrewd appraisal, there was no denying the looks of the Quality. Amusement, disbelief, contempt, and even disgust were written on every lordly face as they surveyed the nigger in his finery, so outlandish with that grotesque black phiz and woolly pate; there were stifled guffaws, and an outraged whisper of "Weston, bigad, or I'm a Dutchman!" Oh, aye, they were a damned ill-bred lot, the Georgian bucks, beneath their polish – no consideration at all for me, you'll notice, whose man they were sneering at. Much I cared – and neither, seemingly, did Tom, for he kept the indifferent countenance he'd shown in Berkeley Square until Gentleman Jackson (who hadn't earned the name for nothing), came forward to take his hand and bid him smiling welcome, reminding him that he'd umpired the fight the day before, and leading him off to make him known to the millers.

I looked about for Richmond and Pad Jones, whom I had warned to be on hand. Bill was scowling like a Moor at Communion.

"That's Mister Brummell's handiwork, I guess! Well, cap'n, pardon the liberty, but I don't like it. That's one nigger who's blowed up high enough already. Cribb's here, did ye know?"

Sure enough, he was, cracking with his Bristol cronies.

"What of it, Bill? Are you afraid Tom will challenge him?"

"I'd not put it by him!" cries Bill. "What I'm 'fraid of is that Cribb'd accept!"

"It might suit if he did," says Jones, thoughtful-like. "He ain't fought in a while, an' Tom's in prime condition."

"Prime condition?" scoffs Bill. "Your arse in a bandbox! He's beat one third-rater, a bloody farmer wi' two left feet, an' you say it might suit! Talk sense, Pad! Cribb'd swallow him whole!" He glared in Tom's direction. "What for you had him figged out thataway, cap'n? He looks downright foolish!"

I told him I had heard already on that subject from Tom himself, and had put him in place.

"Yeah?" says Bill doubtfully. "By your leave, cap'n, I'll bear up yonder 'fore he does any mischief!" And off he went to take Tom's elbow as our novice was borne by Jackson to Cribb's circle and the momentous presentation took place. I drew near, all eyes and ears, in tune with the rest of the company, for Tom's avowed intent in coming to England had been well advertised by Egan, and I didn't doubt that his bragging had reached Cribb's ears.

D'ye know, 'twas the oddest thing: I believe they liked each other from the first. They made a grand pair, face to face, Cribb the taller by a couple of inches, florid and handsome in his sober broadcloth, Tom with his vast shoulders and trim waist set off by Weston's coat, the long legs muscled like whipcord in the dandy pants. If he'd been impassive before, he was bobbish enough now, paying no heed to the covert smiles about him.

"How-de-do, Mistah Cribb," says he, grinning.

"Glad to know ye, Mister Molineaux," says Cribb soberly, and they shook hands, lightly enough, no crushing.

"Come a right long way to . . ." Tom paused ". . . to shake yo' hand."

Cribb inclined his curly head. "Obliged to ye, I'm sure."

"Mister Cribb was second to the Bristol Man yesterday," says Jackson.

"Ah know that, suh," says Tom, beaming at Cribb wider than ever. "You did right well to keep him at scratch so long."

Cribb, ever a man of few words, said: "He's game."

"He sho'ly is," says Tom. "Jus' kept a-comin'."

Cribb nodded, quite deliberate, and smiled. "Thaat's the way," says he, in that deep West Country burr, and you could have heard a pin drop as they stood eye to eye, measuring each other, calm and steady. In that long moment, I'll swear, they were away in some place of their own, the Fives Court and the company forgotten, and at last Tom began to chuckle, a gentle bubble of darkie laughter, and Cribb, who wasn't given to mirth as a rule, grinned back at him – and that was when I knew that each liked what he saw, for as one they shook hands again as easy as could be, and now Jackson was steering Tom to another group, with Richmond hovering like a nervous hen, and Pad Jones let out a long breath.

"Bli'me, cap'n, I'd not ha' been surprised if Tom had planted him a facer! If ye'd heard him last night, swearin' how he'd beat the blood out o' Cribb's carcase when they met, an' see him now, civil as you please. Tell ye what, cap'n, ye never know wi' a nigger, do ye?"

Indeed you don't, thinks I. Within an hour I'd seen him in so many moods: cock-a-hoop with his new duds, in black fury at being laughed at, silent and thoughtful after I'd dressed him down, and now cheery and at ease with Cribb of all people, when I'd half expected him to challenge the Champion on the spot, and be set down for his pains, but he could not have borne himself better. But I still had the uneasy notion that he was reining in, remembering the sidelong sneers and mocking glances, and biding his time to show 'em that Tom Molineaux was more than a ludicrous black clothes-horse. His opportunity came in an unexpected way.

In case you don't know about Gentleman John Jackson, I'll tell you – in return for another shove in the mouth . . . thank'ee. He was no ordinary pug, but decently born and educated, and since he'd resigned the title won from Mendoza fifteen years before he'd done more to raise boxing from the gutter than any man before or since. The noblest in the land frequented his academy in Old Bond Street to learn the Noble Art at his hands, and he was on terms with them all; he was boxing's arbiter and authority, respected for his genteel style as much as for his ringwork – and at that he was still formidable, at the age of forty-two. He'd downed Mendoza in ten minutes, was a lightning hitter, but renowned above all for his defence, of which he gave occasional demonstrations with his famous "handkerchief trick".

This was worth going to see. He would put his right foot on a handkerchief, stand with his hands down, and offer a guinea to anyone who could plant a hit on his unguarded head; they mustn't strike his body, and he mustn't move his foot from the kerchief. No one had ever taken a guinea off him.

Well, this day one of the Corinthians begged him to show the trick; Jackson laughed and shook his head, saying he was too old, but they pressed him, and at last he dropped his handkerchief, took his stand, and invited the young millers to try their hand.

It was laughable, and wonderful. Man after man stepped forward, squaring up and setting themselves, while Jackson stood with his thumbs in his pockets, and at each sudden blow he would duck or sway aside or pivot on that fixed right foot, and the fists would strike nothing but empty air. Straight lefts, muzzlers, crosses, half-arm digs, down-cuts or upper-cuts, the smiling face would avoid them all, and the pugs sweated and swore and thrashed away while the company roared delighted applause.

None of the leading men took part, of course, and when some fool called on Cribb to try his luck he didn't trouble even to shake his head. Then some mischievous ass cried for the blackamoor to show his paces, at which Richmond shouted angrily that he'd do no such thing, and Tom grinned and said (with a glance at Cribb, which the Champion ignored) that he'd come to England to *fight*, not spar. That

114

had them clamouring louder than ever for him to essay a blow at Jackson – hoping the dressy nigger would make a fool of himself.

"Come on, blackee! Jackson won't hit back, you know!"

"He ain't as big as the Bristol Man, neither!"

"A sight harder to fib, though – maybe blackee don't care for that!"

"Can't bear to crease Weston's coat, is that it?"

Some rascal cried out that these black fellows had no game at all, and another shouted "Swell togs, but no *bottom* to his breeches, what?" which provoked roars of mirth. Richmond rounded on them, begging them to let the man alone, and Jackson, frowning, called out: "That will do, gentlemen!" which drew murmurs of agreement from the better sort. The swell rowdies wouldn't leave off, though, and Richmond appealed to me to step in, which I might have done if I hadn't been curious to see what Tom would make of their taunts and sallies – would he hang his head or bang theirs together? He did neither, but only grinned his most innocent darkie grin and turned to the group who were loudest in baiting him.

"Any o' you gen'men got a hunnerd guineas says Ah cain't touch Mis' Jackson's upper works?"

That silenced them, until one, a red-faced tulip with a sprigged weskit and striped stockings, swore it was a sham, and the nigger was putting up a bluff.

"Sho' 'nuff," says Tom, leering like Cousin Corntossle. "But Ah's game. Is you gen'men game? Or cain't you 'fford the hunnerd guineas?" And the grinning scoundrel stroked Weston's immaculate lapel and looked down his nose at the striped stockings.

"Damn your impudence!" cries the tulip, but in the face of Tom's challenge, and the mirth of the crowd, he had no choice but to confer briefly with his cronies and then cry, very well, a hundred guineas you can't plant one on Jackson's head.

Tom gave him a jaunty bow and turned to Jackson who was regarding him with puzzled amusement.

"Be 'bliged if you let me try to touch you, Mis' Jackson," says Tom, shaping up. Jackson hesitated only a moment before stepping back on to his handkerchief. "No favours, mind," he warned. "Very good – set to!"

Tom gave a little shuffle, feinted with his right, and out shot the

115

left, missing by a whisker as Jackson ducked. He raised a brow in appreciation, and then he was swaying and shifting and pivoting as Tom rained left hands at him; one of them brushed his hair, but none got home. I took a glance at Cribb and saw him intent, murmuring something to the man at his elbow. Tom tried again, one-two, without success, and the rowdy bucks let out a delighted crowing.

"'Tain't the Bristol Man this time, blackee!"

"Ask him to stand still, why don't you?"

"I say, mind Weston's cuffs!"

Tom stepped back, glowering, and I wondered if we were about to see an outburst of temper, but then he bore in again, driving wild blows at Jackson's head which the master slipped with ease.

"Why not kick, like a Frenchman!" bawls the red face.

"You'll have to be sharper than that, nigger!" cries another.

Tom paused, breathing hard, and gave a sudden gasp, clasping a hand over his heart. He swayed, distressed, Jackson started forward in concern — and Tom's left shot out and tapped him ever so gently on the brow. Jackson's mouth dropped open in amazement; he looked down quickly and saw his right foot was still on the handkerchief. A great buzz of astonishment arose, and one of the rowdy bucks yelled "Foul!" Tom, standing straight now, with no sign of unease, asked: "Did Ah touch ye, Mis' Jackson?"

"You touched me," snaps Jackson, looking dam' grim at being hocussed. He fumbled out a guinea, but Tom shook his head.

"Ah di'nt win yo' guinea fair, Mis' Jackson. Ah cou'nt win it if Ah tried all day, you know that." He gave a great hoot of laughter, pointing at the rowdies. "But Ah sho' won their hunnert guineas! Ain't that so, gen'men?" He rolled his eyes, looking comical. "An' yo' right! Gotta be real sharp — speshly if youse jus' an iggerent nigguh!" He slapped his thighs, and the whole assembly went into peals of laughter, jeering at the rowdies who, with an ill grace, handed over the shekels — Richmond saw to that. In a twinkling all was changed, fellows exclaiming at the shrewd way the black had fooled his mockers, others clapping Tom on the back, even Jackson smiling and shaking his head. Cribb stood and watched, impassive as ever, until Tom, beaming with mischief, turned towards him and called out:

"Mistah Cribb any mind to stand on hank'chieves?"

There was a roar at that, instantly hushed. Cribb glanced at Tom and then said quietly to Richmond:

"Tell your man there are three or four prime heavyweights wi' their eyes on my title. When he's bested one of 'em, he can talk to me." He nodded to Tom, pleasantly enough, and went off, to a chorus of approval, and judging it a satisfactory afternoon's work, I beckoned Tom and we went also.

BILL RICHMOND,

former slave, retired pugilist,
inn-keeper, manager and fight promoter

Truth to tell, I never cared for Captain Buck Flashman above half. Didn't trust him, neither. Oh, sure, he took up Tom Molineaux where I'd ha' given him the go-by, but 'twasn't 'cos he saw a champion in him, whatever he says. No, sir, Tom was but a toy, or a pet poodle, to the Captain, something he could show off 'round Town, and cut a figure among the *ton*: "Here's my black miller, ain't he a caution?" That was Cap'n Buck's style, to be topsides wi' the Fancy, and get noticed at Tatts and the Fives Court and Limmer's Hotel. You see, Cap'n Buck wasn't that much of a swell – oh, he knew the sporting set, and Brummell was his friend (but who *wasn't* Brummell friend to, he was the amiablest man alive), but I heard for a fact the Cap'n was blackballed at Boodle's club, and wasn't even thought of at White's or Brooks's, where the real Quality gathered. Never could figure how he was received at Almack's; queer start, that was. Course, the ladies liked him, well set-up fellow that he was, the commoner sort 'specially, Sal Douglas and those. He had the name of a real ruttish buck, and the Mayfair mamas wasn't pressing him to call, exactly, 'specially the Pagets, whose gal he married, later on – Gretna Green 'lopement, that was, with old Paget killing his cattle all the way to Scotland to catch 'em, but he came too late. Her brothers would ha' called him out, but Papa wouldn't have that. Said 'twas bad 'nough, losing a daughter, he didn't figure to lose his sons as well. So I heard. You see, Cap'n Buck had killed Lord knows how many who'd called him out; sharps or barkers, 'twas all one, he was the killingest gentleman 'round.

How come an old darkie ale-draper knows all these Society goings-on? Bless you, sir, when you mind a ken like the Horse and Dolphin, you hear it *all*, high and low, and I mean *all*.

118

Anyways, that's why Cap'n Buck took up Tom. He was jealous as sin to cut a dash howsomever he could, and Tom was just a means to that end, as I said. D'ye know, I don't believe the Cap'n cared all that much whether Tom *won* his mills, even, or what matches we made for him, or how he trained on (or *didn't* train, more like), just so long's he made a show and set the tongues a-wagging. That was what counted wi' the Cap'n – that and picking up heavy money in side-stakes from the gudgeons. He did right well out o' Tom that way. But he never had feeling for him – not like Pad Jones, f'instance. Pad really cared for Tom. Me? Well, now, sir, I tell ye, I loved him . . . and I hated him. No, I don't hold hate in my heart for him now. Just can't ever forgive him, is all.

There was a real mean streak in the way Cap'n Buck tret him, though. Oh, he was as nice as pie on top, but he served him some right cruel turns. The business o' them gloves of Cap'n Barclay's, that was just for mischief and malice – I'll tell you o' that presently. And when Tom kicked up shines, and wouldn't rouse himself to train, or mind what Pad and I told him, and would get hisself lushy three days at a time, or gallivant wi' the whores and mollishers – why, a word from Cap'n Buck would ha' brought him to heel, but when Pad and I begged him to say it, he would just laugh and put us by. That ain't no kindness, is it?

My 'pinion is that he looked on Tom as a raree show, and took pleasure in seeing what he would do next, him being a real dense nigger new-come to London and all at sea. It was like baiting a bull, the way he'd push Tom forward so he looked ridiculous; I reckon he wanted to see how Tom would act, and didn't care if it hurt him or no. 'Twas the meanest thing. Poor Tom had no more sense'n a china orange; he was just a great babby, and you know what a babby wants, sir, sure ye do. He wants folks to like him, and Tom figured if he made a name as a miller, why, ev'yone would like and admire him, and when they didn't, or laughed at him, he couldn't think of any way to win their regard but to play the fool. And that he did, and the Cap'n edged him on, I believe – and that's the best reason I don't care for Buck Flashman. He made Tom Molineaux a real comic nigger. Tom Molineaux that was the best and bravest black man that ever toed the scratch, and did what no black man ever did before. He did it all by his own self, sir, with Pad Jones to guide him, and me a little – but no thanks to Cap'n Flashman. No, sir, no thanks at all.

The meanest trick he served Tom was after the fight wi' the Bristol Man, when he had Brummell fig Tom out in Weston's swellest case o' clothes, and paraded him 'round Town and the Fives Court. Well, you know what happened, and how Tom took a rise out o' Gentleman Jackson – lordy, when I think o' the harm that might ha' done, if Jackson hadn't *been* a gentleman, top to bottom! And putting him in Cribb's way – mister, my heart was in my mouth for fear he'd get sarsy with Cribb, and gall him into a match. Oh, Pad'll tell you he'd ha' held his own, but I say he'd ha' taken such a thrashing from Cribb as might ha' sickened him permanent. He needed 'sperience, sir, he needed *pain*, he needed to learn to *take* gruel as well as give it, afore he was ready for Cribb. He needed two-three turn-ups wi' *real* millers, not hay-gobblin' hicks like Burrows.

Cap'n Buck wouldn't have it, though. When we came back from the Fives Court, he says:

"Well, my boys, that went famously! We'll have our hero in the ring with Cribb before the year's out, or my name's Bonaparte! Didn't ye hear him? 'When he's bested one prime heavyweight...' That's as good as to say that if Tom whips the likes of Dutch Sam or Caleb Baldwin, Cribb will meet him. He daren't refuse – nor will he want to! He knows that after today all the buzz will be of the Black Ajax, the Milling Moor, and Cribb ain't the man to shirk a challenge, never fear!"

"Beg pardon, cap'n, but that's what I do fear," says I. "Tom needs a few good mills behind him first –"

"One, Bill, only one! Now, who shall it be?"

"Well, sir, I say more'n one, but to begin with Pad and I reckon that a match wi' Tom Blake would suit."

"What, the old sailor? Damme, is he still *alive*? Come, come, Richmond, we must do better than that! The fellow's older than Buckhorse's grandmother!"

"He's touchin' forty," says Pad, "but age don't matter wi' him. He's strong, he's clever, he did for Coachman Holmes, and they don't call him Tom Tough for nothing. He stood toe to toe wi' Cribb for a good hour –"

"Well, so did Bill here!" laughs Cap'n Buck.

"No, sir, I did not. I ran away from him as best I could. Blake didn't, and if Tom can take his gruel *and* floor him, he'll have done right handsomely."

"Handsomely enough to go against Cribb! Capital!"

"No, cap'n, handsomely enough to go 'gainst some other good man, and then maybe another . . . and then Cribb."

"Oh, stuff, Richmond! Why, didn't Jones say he was ready to see Tom go against Cribb *now*? Ain't that so, Jones?"

"I spoke hasty," says Pad. "Bill's right – two or three good mills, and he'll be ready for Cribb."

"What a pair of old women you are, to be sure! Well, he can fight your Tom Tough for all I care – and then Cribb will meet him, you'll see!"

It nettled me to hear him laugh and take it so light. "And if he does, cap'n – and gives Tom a proper hiding 'cos he ain't ready?"

"Luck o' the game!" laughs he. "Win or lose, he'll have had his chance, won't he?"

You mean he'll have served your turn, thinks I, swaggering 'round Town with "your black fighter". Let him take a good drubbing and you'll drop him like a hot brick. He was no Camelford or Alvanley, to stand by a beaten fighter, or I was mistook. I said as much to Pad, and he smiled, quite serene.

"Tom ain't going to be a beaten fighter, Villem. He's going to be Champion, given time and hard graft. And don't you heed the Cap'n – I mind the training, you make the matches, and if Cap'n Buck don't like it he can go and break wind in Bunhill Cemetery. We'll do very well without him."

And we might ha' done, sir, if the Cap'n had let Tom alone, but he didn't. Figging him out like a nonpareil once wasn't enough; he had to take him driving in the Park again, and to the races, and the theatre, and parade him 'round Mayfair, and what with all o' that, and late suppers at Bob's Chophouse, and gaming at Fishmonger's Hall, and parties with Cyprians and flash doxies, Tom was in a fair way to being the spoiledest nigger you ever saw – and worse. Nothing kills a miller faster'n lush and strumpet, and thanks to Buck Flashman, Tom was getting his fill of both.

121

I let it go for a week, and then told the Cap'n plain that it must stop.

"What?" cries he. "He wins a fight for you, and you'd grudge him a few days' frolic? Shame on you, Richmond, where's the harm in it?" Laughing, as I said.

"The harm is, cap'n, that I've made the match with Blake, four weeks from today, one hundred guineas a side in your name, and unless Tom goes into hard training directly, 'twill be no match!"

"Gammon!" cries he. "Why, he can beat Blake and four like him!"

"No, he can't, cap'n, 'cos I won't let him try. If he ain't in condition to fight, I'll forfeit."

"Not my money, ye won't! He'll fight, I tell you!"

"Not wi' me in his corner, sir," says I, and 'fore he could tell me I didn't have the only knee in the world, *I* told *him*: "And not wi' Pad Jones, neither. I know Pad, sir. He's a serious man, and he'll wash his hands of Tom 'less you make him give over these high jinks and hooraying 'round the Town."

"Will he, though? Well, you may tell Master Jones that he ain't the only trainer in the Fancy," says he, grinning. "Barclay Allardice is to try Tom out, did ye know? Ah, that makes you think! Come, come, Bill, let's have no more of this! Tom's a spry young buck, full of sap! Why, you're a nigger yourself – you know how it is with him. Let him play a little, we'll see he's in prime twig to meet Blake, I promise you!"

"Cap'n, it ain't just the training. Why, Tom is but a child, and the indulging you're giving him'll be his ruin! We got to keep him in hand, sir, don't ye see?"

But "You fret too much, Bill," was all the change I got, and a sly wink as he told me that he was presenting Tom to Barclay Allardice at Jackson's Rooms next day, and why didn't Pad and I come along to see the fun?

I put no stock in his hints, for I knew Captain Barclay (as Allardice was used to be called) too well to believe that he'd train a pug just to oblige Buckley Flashman – let alone a pug who passed his nights on the mop wi' Charlotte the Harlot. He was a Scotch gentleman, an Army officer, and the best amateur miller and foremost athlete of the day. Walking was his great joy, prodigious distances he covered in record times, wagering on his self, and in those crazy days there was no want of mad gambling men ready to lose their money to him – a thousand miles in a thousand hours for a thousand guineas was one of his bets, and he won it, too. Never was a man in finer trim – or so skilled at putting others in condition; he knew more about training fighters than Pad or Jackson, even, and made a point of trying out every promising chicken.

I told Pad what the Cap'n had said, and he laughed. "Buck Flashman's a rasher o' wind! Barclay trains them as he wants to train, but he won't touch Tom – what, a Yankee, and black to boot! He'd as soon train Boney!''

Still, Pad and I determined to be at Old Bond Street next morning, and when Cap'n Buck came by to take up Tom in his curricle, we tailed on behind – the two of us padding the hoof while Tom rolled in the rig like a lord, and Cap'n Buck made game of us, asking Tom wasn't it prime to have running footmen? So help me, he sure knew how to ruin a nigger.

Every swell in creation was at Jackson's for the set-to, with the Duke o' Clarence at their head, all chaffing and taking their mellow drains. Captain Barclay hadn't shown yet, and while we were waiting Cap'n Buck took Tom to the pigeon-holes where the mauleys were kept – and did something, out o' pure dam' mischief as I believe, that turned the course of Tom's life. Just a little practical joke, of the kind Buck Flashman loved, but oh, mister, what came of it!

Now, as you know, in practice set-to's both men wore the mauleys, or mufflers, big padded gloves so that nobody got hurt. But folks in the know were aware that Captain Barclay had a pair of special gloves on the top shelf for his own use; he had taken gobs o' stuffing out of 'em, so they was half as heavy as the regular mauleys, which meant that Barclay's blows had twice as much force and pepper as his opponent's. Real Scotch trick, I reckon. Maybe he figured, being an amateur setting to 'gainst professional bruisers, he needed all the 'vantage he could get, but anyway, that's what he was used to do.

Well Cap'n Buck knew all about the special gloves, and damme if he didn't lace 'em on to Tom, and put another reg'lar pair on the shelf in their place, with a wink to Pad and me to show what he was at. Presently, in bowls Barclay, and after the how-de-do-your-highness

and compliments, he goes to the pigeon-hole and takes out the mauleys.
I saw him start, and examine 'em real close, and look 'round to see
if his special pair had been mislaid, and then he saw Tom was already
wearing 'em. Cap'n Buck was looking at the ceiling, innocent-like but
fit to bust – and I don't mind telling you, sir, I had to look away not
to smile, seeing Barclay hocussed with his own Greek work, for of
course he dassn't say a word for very shame, but must put on the
reg'lar mauleys and make the best of it.

Well, 'twas the worst of it, and no mistake. He was a fine young
miller, six feet and springy, with the handsomest figurehead – and
didn't he take care of it, just, for if Tom had got home on his conk
with the light gloves there'd ha' been more claret on the floor than on
the sideboard. Consequently was, Barclay had to mill on the retreat,
which wasn't his style, and Tom, finding his long left didn't fadge, took
to closing and smacking the body real hard – the big looby couldn't tell,
you see, that he was wearing light mauleys: lace mittens or bolsters,
'twould ha' been all one for what he knew. So he bore in and lammed
away, never guessing how he was hurting his man, and didn't Barclay
dance! He was clever on his feet, though, and I could ha' wished the
gloves had been equal, for he was a rare test o' Tom's agility.

What pleased me most was that a week's bouncing and bucking
hadn't taken the edge off of Tom's speed hardly; he shifted real nimble,
flipped well at half-arm, and chased Barclay to desperation. "This
can't last," says Pad, and sure enough Tom danced in, feinting high,
and planted a one-two to the body that would ha' kilt a mule, and
down goes our gallant captain with a couple o' busted ribs – "and
well served," whispers Pad, "for a sneaky Sawney brogue-beater, him
and his skinny mufflers!"

There was huge outcry and wonder when they saw he was hurt,
with Cap'n Buck roaring concern, and damning Tom for his violence;
they were all agog that a man in mauleys could do such damage, and
the Duke swore he was the most hammering fibber in the nation. His
stock went up summat peculiar with everyone 'cept Barclay; when
they'd strapped him up pale and pained he took Tom's hand right
enough, but with no charity in his busted bosom, I could see.

"You fib dam' hard for a sparring-match," says he, pretty sour.

"I hopes I din't hurt ye too much," says Tom, 'pologetic.

"Hurt? I'll be on the braid o' my back for a week!" snaps Barclay, while Cap'n Buck was all consolation, trying not to whoop. Oh, he was mighty amused, but his jape made Tom an enemy for life, for I reckon Captain Barclay never forgave him for giving him such a basting 'fore all his swell friends — and no good came o' that.

You may guess that Tom was no easier to leash in after this bout, either. He figured he must be the fatalest fibber since Goliath, and when Pad and I told him 'bout the light gloves, he wouldn't believe it, said we was just trying to cry him down.

"You jus' jealous 'cos Ah floored him so quick'n easy!" cries he. "Best amateur miller in England, and how long he stan' up to me — two minutes, mebbe? Din't stand, neether — run like a skeered hen, never touched me, an' Ah nailed him good! Don' gi' me no gammon 'bout light mauleys! Why, but fo' them mufflers Ah might ha' kilt him — an' Ah wasn't tryin', hardly!"

I got so wild, listening to his brag, I couldn't trust myself to speak. 'Twouldn't ha' done a pinch o' good — he never minded me, not then or ever, and you know why, sir? 'Cos I was black, like him. Any heed he paid, 'twas to Pad or Cap'n Buck — and only one o' them give him good advice.

"Ne'er mind Barclay," says Pad. "He ain't a match — but Blake *is*, and if you're to stand up to him in a month's time you must put body and mind in order, d'ye hear? No more booze, no more chippers, no park-sauntering and coming home wi' the lark. Ye've had a week's fun wi' your fine new acquaintances — I won't call 'em friends, for that they ain't —"

"They real kind to me, whatever!" growls Tom.

"Is that so?" says I. "Even when they's laughing at you?"

He glared at me. "They quit laughin' when Ah took a rise out o' Gen'man Jackson! They wasn't laughin' when Ah melted that buck Barclay! They real polite to me, you bet! An' 'tain't like back home, neither, where ev'y white man 'spects you to git out his way, an' shoves you offa the sidewalk ifn you don', no suh! Over heah it don' make no nevahminds if yo' black or white — lissen, they don' got no slaves in Englan', you know that?"

"They ain't got no cotton nor baccy in England, neither!" I told him. "And they real kind to dogs and horses. Why, you big jackass, you're just the latest toy in the shop, don't you see? By and by they'll get tired o' you, and your big black ass'll be shot off Piccadilly so fast it'll change colour! You think 'cos they pay you heed now, that they your *friends*?''

"What *you* know, Bill Richmond?" scowls he. "Nobody goin' git tired o' me! White ladies sho' ain't gittin' tired – wore out, maybe, but not tired, haw-haw! Real 'portant ladies like Miss Janey Perkins, what's an actress – she had me in her bed –"

"Janey Perkins is a two-bit whore! Like all the rest of 'em!"

He gave me a real mean sneer. "How'd *you* know? Ah ain't seen no white ladies callin' on *you* lately! An' she ain't no whore!"

Pad says, quiet-like: "Whore or not don't signify, Tom. I'll put it plain. You meet Blake in four weeks. You won't be fit to meet him, or the village lush, if you're goin' twenty rounds wi' Janey Perkins or any other wagtail every night o' the week. Now, you can choose, Tom. I don't train mutton-mongers. Which'll it be?"

That sobered him; he had respect for Pad, and I guess knew how much he owed him. He laughed kind of sulky-like, but came round in the end, saying he'd only wanted a bit of fun, and it hadn't done him no harm, look how he'd crumpled up Barclay, hey? Pad said nothing, but set him to work on the weights and fibbing-bag, bed at nine sharp, steaks and small beer, and running at four of a morning when the streets was empty.

He took it wi' no good grace at first, and Pad and I had to look sharp to keep him from straying, which ain't easy in a hostel, with spirits to hand and lusty gals like that Nance and Flora. We physicked and purged him to damp his Adam, and slept wi' one eye open, but I suspicioned, from Nance's smirks, that Tom was somehow finding occasion to climb aboard now and then; I'd ha' turned her out, but Pad said let it be, Tom was training into good trim and in better spirits by the day, so keep all comfortable.

'Twas the best luck that Cap'n Buckley was out o' Town at the time, so Tom had no one to edge him on to mischief. I told you the Cap'n was mad nutty on the Paget gal, and she on him, so her folks had whipped her off to Bath, and then to their country seat, 'round Oxford somewheres, to get her beyond his reach, I guess. It didn't answer, for he was hot-foot to Bath, and then to a village near the

Paget place, so he could moon under his lady-love's window clandestine, until old man Paget took him for a poacher one fine night (so
he said), and filled his arse wi' buckshot. That kind o' thing never
discouraged the bold Buckley, but the Paget chit took fright for his
life and bade him back to Town, where he was so busy consoling
himself with Sir John Manners's young wife (for being a devoted
swain didn't stop him mollishing, ever) that he had no time for Tom
bar a look-in at the Nag now and then.

That was just fine, and by the week o' the Blake mill Tom was in
the primest twig. His skin was sleek and his eye clear, his speed was
such as Pad couldn't touch him, his knuckles was like teak, and when
we took him to the Fives Court for a spar wi' Dutch Sam, why, anyone
could see the Jew was nowhere. Tom Blake came to watch, wi' Cribb
at his elbow, and when 'twas over Blake says: "Well, was he ever so
good, 'twill be only one hiding more, and at any rate I'll find out what
stuff is in him."

"Villem, take note," says Pad. "Blake's beat 'fore he starts – and
Cribb's alive to our Tom. Let him win well o' Tuesday, and you may
have a tilt at the championship when you choose."

"Not 'less I'm sure he can win it," says I, for I tell you, sir, I was
mortal scared of matching him wi' Cribb too early. Yet watching him
'gainst Dutch Sam, I hoped and wondered, for I knew I was seeing
the best heavy man in England bar Cribb his self. "One thing at a
time, Pad. Let's wait 'til Blake's hollered 'nuff."

Pad went easy wi' Tom in the last week, lest he be trained too
sharp, and we tried to keep him clear o' the Fancy crowd that packed
the tap day and night, for the Town was on fire wi' the fight and eager
for a glimpse of "the Black Colossus", as Egan called him. The
sporting Corinthians pressed in to shake his hand, and their Cyprians
were not backward; I never saw more skirt preening and ogling 'round
a prize pug. That dam' Janey Perkins the actress was foremost wi' a
bevy of her theatre titters, all come to squeal and kiss him for luck.
Janey was one of your real fancy doxies, painted and feathered like a
Mohawk and twice as noisy, clinging on Tom's arm with her dairies
in his face and laughing her hoyden head off.

"That's the very thing to keep his mind on his work!" snaps Pad.
"Damnation, she'll have him hotter'n the town bull!" But either Tom

was seeing sense for once, or the physick was working, for he was civil and modest as a new curate, thanking her kindly and begging to be excused.

"My eye and Betty Martin," says Pad. "Pious as Paul he is, but I know what the bastard's thinking. Damme if I don't stick a wedge 'neath his door tonight and stand sentry under the window. The sooner he's snug in Canterbury the better." Janey was cooing at Tom's listener, but Pad hustled him away, leaving her squawking and crying good luck after him.

We'd spoke rooms at Canterbury for the night 'fore the fight, which was to be at Margate. Cap'n Buck and Blake's patron, a sporting baronet named Breen, had agreed it must be out o' Town, for with all the buzz and interest the London beaks would have been down on us, and naught spoils a mill more than having to hare 'cross the county line, fighters, handlers, spectators, ring-posts and all, with half Bow Street on your heels and Bond and Reed men waving their damned warrants. Margate was a close secret known only to us and Jack Randall, who'd give the office on Monday evening, in time for the Fancy to troop down to Margate during the night. It was no joke, sir, in those days, to arrange a turn-up in peace and quiet.

We jaunted down to Canterbury on the Monday in a closed rattler, Tom with a shawl over his mug so that no one would know he'd left Town. Cap'n Buck stayed behind for the moment to fool the magistrates, and we kept Tom close and had supper in our chamber at the inn. We settled in early, three in the bed wi' Tom in the middle, and a happy man I was, sir, to see his black pimple on the pillow when we doused the glim. 'Tis ever the same afore a fight; you've slogged away to get your man in trim and watched over him like a new bride, and there he is, nice and natty, and you think all's bowmon and so to Nod. Next I knew was Pad swearing in the dark and firing the glim.

"Who's prigged the mutton?" says I, half-asleep.

"Mutton's the word, or I'll eat my boots!" roars Pad. "The bugger's hopped the wag! Out, Bill, and after him!"

Tom was gone, and the jigger ajar, so we bundled into our clothes and tumbled downstairs and into the street. How the deuce he'd slipped his cable without rousing us, I couldn't figure, any more than why he'd done it.

"Why, to kick his heels up!" cries Pad. "I knew he was too holy and humble by half, I should ha' had darbies on him! Damn that slut Perkins for firing him up! What's o'clock? Jiminy, nigh on four! The black villain's had time to cover every nun in Kent and drink his self daft in the bargain!"

"Not the night before a mill, surely?"

"A lummox like him, what does he care? Come on, Canterbury ain't so large. If we bustle we'll nap him afore he's foundered altogether!"

We cast about through the dark streets, and came on a pilot who steered us to the likeliest dives and family pannies. We gave a good gun to two or three without success, and at last struck home at a likely flash-ken where they were keeping it up to some tune, with dancing and song and nobody sober. "Blow me, if it ain't another lillywhite!" was the cry when they saw my colour, so we knew Tom was about, and sure enough there he was abovestairs, in bed wi' three nightingales – three, sir, on my oath – and half castaway in the bargain. I near burst into tears, and Pad was raging; we dragged him out in his shirt, with the sluts screaming and the flash coves and queans belowstairs laughing and cheering as we hove him out, but what with his weight and him stumbling in drink, we had to hire a hurdle to get him back to the inn. We threw him in a chair, blowing like a whale and muttering to his self, and a pitiful horrible sight he was.

I was nigh heart-broken, for never would he be fit to fight that day, but Pad ground his teeth, white as wax.

"He'll fight if I have to kill him first!" says he, and slapped Tom right and left, which no more than made him blink. "Salt and water," says Pad, and we held his great pug nose and dosed him to bursting. He came to and shot the cat from the window, howling to wake the dead, and then we sent for coffee and dosed him again. He was grey-green by this, and weak as a kitten, so we bundled him into bed and let him sleep three or four hours, when Pad roused him out, smacking him about the head while I worked at his neck and shoulders.

We had him half sober by noon, and tried him with some bread and milk to put peck in him at the least, but he flashed the hash again, and sat with his head in his hands.

"Ma haid hurts," groans he. "Lemme be, Ah's awful sick."

"Ye'll be sicker yet when Tom Tough sets about you," says Pad.

"D'ye hear that? In two hours you toe the scratch, damned drunken dog that you are! Now get up and walk, ye pig!"

We had to heave him to his feet, and Pad kicked him till he stumbled up and down, with a whine or a groan at every step. Pad drove him on with blows and curses, but never a word of why he'd sneaked out to the sluts and daffy, for it didn't signify now, when all that counted was to get him well enough to climb through the ropes at Margate. Soon after twelve we tried him with thick gruel, and he kept it down.

"Get the beasts put to," says Pad, and when I had seen to it we took him by a side-door to the yard, with a blanket over his head, and spanked off for the coast.

Half-past one was the appointed hour, and I doubted if we'd be in time, for the road was thick with rigs and people hurrying to the fight. Tom sat a-sway with the blanket about him, and devil a word of sense to be had from him, while Pad put salts to his nose, which made him weep, and presently he came to and looked about in a daze.

"Where we goin'?" says he, and when Pad told him he let out a wail and lay back with his eyes closed, whimpering that he was powerful sick. We were close by the ground now, and could hear the shouting of the crowd, and fellows by the coach spotted Tom within, and set up a great cry that here was the black at last.

Tom blinked and sat up, fresh as a two-day corpse. For a moment I thought he'd cat again, but he hung his head and muttered: "Ah's sorry, Pad! Ah's so sorry!" and wept.

"Hang your sorrow!" says Pad. "Sit up, d'ye hear? Look alive, damn you! I never brought a blubbering pug to a mill before, and I ain't about to." Tom mopped his face with the blanket, and gave a great grunting sniff. "Now see here, Tom Molineaux," says Pad, and gripped him about the shoulders, "you're a fool and an ingrate and a damned black pest, but you're the best fighting cove on earth this minute, d'ye hear me? If ye feel sick 'tis no wonder, for you're half-drunk, but drunk or sober you can floor Tom Blake, mind that!"

'Wha's ingrate?" mumbles Tom, looking owlish.

"Christ, he can hear anyway!" says Pad. "Can he see, that's the point? Get the shades down, Bill, while we dress the brute! God help us if they see him like this!"

We got him into his breeches and stockings and pumps, wi' the scarf at his waist, and I sponged his face while the roar of the impatient mob grew louder, and Cap'n Buck banged on the door and looked in, damning our eyes. He looked out again fast enough when he saw Tom's state, and I thought, that's the last we'll see o' you this day, my loyal patron. Tom sat slumped and sleepy, humming a darkie song.

"Can ye stand?" asks Pad, and Tom stood, more or less. Pad looked at me. "If he can walk to the ring and be floored, well, 'tis a defeat. But if he cries off drunk, he's ruined. Tom – can ye walk, lad? Can ye put up your fams?"

Tom said not a word but a great belch of wind, nodded hard, and came on guard, but mighty confused.

"Well enough," says Pad. "Out ye go, then, head up, walk brisk and steady! Bill, lay hold on his elbow!"

There was a great yell when Tom appeared, with the blanket well over his head, and you bet I was at his side while Pad followed wi' the towels and bottles. A great press crowded in, cheering and staring. "Here comes the black! Huzza for the nigger!" The vinegars heaved away to make a lane to the ropes, which gave us the excuse to go slow. Tom didn't stumble, but I could feel him shudder, and he gave sad little moans, ducking his head 'gainst the strong sea-breeze which had the lookers-on clutching their tiles and capes, and that I guess stopped 'em noticing what a rum state he was in.

There was no stage, just forty-forty grass inside the ropes, and Blake at one corner, all six feet and fifteen stone of him; for all his forty years he looked to be in fettle, no spare fat, chaffing with his seconds, Cribb and Bill Gibbons, and jigging up and down a sight more nimble than I liked. Cap'n Buck was nowhere to be seen, but Breen was to the fore among the Quality, with the ladies in the open rigs craning to see, and behind them the great dark spread of the crowd, seven thousand strong (so I heard), and in the distance the sound of the sea.

"Never a bloody magistrate when ye want one," growls Pad, and it would have suited just fine if the bailiffs had stopped the mill that minute, for when I took the blanket from Tom's head he was grey and peaky as ever, and horrible bloodshot. Gully, who was to umpire, called the men to the scales.

Sir, if my salvation depended on't, I couldn't tell you what they weighed, for I was having conniptions that Tom'd fall off o' the scale.

When Pad gave him the hat, he looked owlish and set it on his head, and everyone laughed, thinking he did it in fun.

"Throw the dam' thing in the ring!" whispers Pad, so he did, and all but tumbled over. I pushed him through the ropes and gave him my knee 'fore he fell down, and so help me Hannah he sat like a sack o' grits, eyes closed and grunting something peculiar.

"Ah's goin' be sick!" whines he. "Oh, sweet pityin' Jesus, ma po' haid!"

Every eye was turned on him from that great wall of faces, someone said the nigger was trained off, and the cry went round among the legs, "Six to four Blake!" Gully called 'em to scratch, I heaved Tom up, and he ambled for'ard somehow and stood swaying with his head down while Gully read the articles.

"Pad, I don't believe he knows where he's at," says I.

"No matter," says Pad, "so long as he knows what he's here *for.*"

They shook hands — leastways, Blake did, grabbing Tom's daddle, eyeing him cautious-like — and when Gully called "Set to!" ye could see Blake was shy, having seen Tom at work, for he circled away and looked leery under his brows, and Tom turned with him, blinking his eyes and blowing out his cheeks, with his hands half-up.

"Lord love me, he's goin' to spew again!" mutters Pad. "Oh, God, if Blake hits him in the belly!" But Blake was still wary, weaving his great knotted fists; whenever Tom swayed, Blake flinched, but then he bore in, planting a smart one-two. Tom staggered, and would ha' gone down, but Blake, getting bolder, closed at half-arm, pounded his ribs, and planted him a tremendous facer, flush on the trap. And it's God's own truth, sir, Tom all of a sudden came alive, head up and eyes wide open, and hollered: "Damn yo' skin, what ye do that for?"

He hadn't been shamming drunk, I swear, for he still looked 'mazed and foolish. No, he'd been the foxedest nigger all day, and still looked like to puke, but that facer braced him somehow, and when Blake tried another one-two he blocked the one, slipped t'other, let go a shaky left, and moved away. He wasn't steady, but his feet were going at last, and he circled, head a-shake, and Pad let out a whooping sigh, for now Tom was milling on the retreat, guard well up. I don't say he was in his senses, and he was greener than black, but he was *eyeing*

132

his man, and when Blake led off he blocked it easy, feinted, and side-stepped on his toes, daring Blake to come to him.

"Thank God!" says Pad. "Oh, land him another facer, Blake, and s'help me he'll be stone-cold sober!"

Blake tried it, but Tom stepped outside and in again, smacking him the first real blow he'd struck, a right chopper down his face. Blake tried to close, but Tom's left was stabbing his nob like a piston, and when Blake tried a left of his own, Tom flipped it away and nailed him a down-cut to the neck. "Bravo, Mendoza!" bawls Pad, and as Blake stumbled, down came the right again, the rabbit-blow, driving him to his knees. He was up in a trice, waving to Cribb as he went to his corner, while Tom came to my knee, rubbing his eyes like a man coming to.

Pad sluiced him wi' the bottle, but Tom took it off o' him and drained it dry.

"Gi' me mo'!" croaks he. "Oh, lawdy, but Ah's dry! Oh, ma po' haid!"

"How are ye, Tom?"

"Bloody sick," groans Tom. "Ah got sech a mis'ry in ma belly! Oh, gi' me 'nother drink, Pad, 'fore Ah burns up!" He clapped the bottle to his mouth. "Oh my, oh my! Oh, Ah's hurtin' sumpn cruel!"

"Where?" cries Pad. "Where did he hurt ye?"

"Not him, the mollishers! Oh, Lawd, three on 'em, Ah's clean wore away, awful sore!"

"Well, it can't be the clap, not yet," says Pad. "Ne'er mind if ye're sore! How's your innards?"

"They's b'ilin' sick," whimpers Tom. "Oh, my, was Ah lushy! Say, was that the fust round?"

"It was, and that's Tom Blake – Tom Tough, so keep your distance 'til ye're in condition to box, d'ye hear?"

"Ah kin box!" gasps Tom. "But Ah ain't 'bout to. Ah's tired an' sick, got to put him down quick, Ah reckon. Oh, ma haid!"

And damme if he didn't step out, pretty groggy, for the second round, standing flat-footed while Blake planted him two or three flush hits on the head to shrieks of excitement from the mob, and then Tom fetched him the most tremendous smash to the jaw that sent him flying through the ropes. I never saw a faster punch, sir; one instant Blake was boring in, the next he was sprawling, and Tom came to my knee, holding his belly. Pad was in a fury, telling him to mill on the retreat, to shift and cut away, for the hits that Blake had planted had been reg'lar melters. Tom made nothing of 'em.

"He don' make me dizzy, but daffy does. Cain't skip 'round, Pad, or Ah tumble down sho'. Guess Ah kin ruffian him, though."

And that, sir, was 'zackly what he did, for the few rounds the fight lasted. He just *let* Blake hit – and Blake was a real punishing fibber, mind, strong and savage – but for every blow he planted Tom gave him back two, and they were grave-diggers. He chopped Blake's arms nigh to pulp, 'til his guard was feeble, and fibbed him head and body, no science, but brutal hard. One time he took Blake in chancery, and mangled him so hard I wondered the man came to scratch again; he was a fearsome sight, upper works cut all to pieces, but Tom, for all the smashing he'd took, showed nary a mark.

Pad was like to despair, seeing the man he'd trained to so much science hammering in like any coal-heaver. Not me, tho', for Tom had taken real gruel in his turn, first I'd ever seen him eat, and minded it no more'n snowflakes. That warmed my heart; I'd always known he had strength, but now I knew he had bottom, too.

With five rounds gone in as many minutes and his figurehead like the knacker's yard, Blake got chary of standing toe to toe and began to box – oh, he was a prime miller, sir, as fly as brave, and now Tom must move and chase to come at him. He was getting soberer by the minute, as his footwork showed, but Blake was no Bristol Man to be pommelled at will. Bloody and busted as he was, he milled well on the retreat, guarding as best could wi' his bruised arms, and try as Tom might, he could not put in a finisher. That, and the distemper of his head and guts, made him peevish, and he started hollering at Blake to stand and fight.

"You beat, Tom Blake, why'nt you quit? You want Ah should chase you clear 'round Kent county? Give over runnin', dammit! Fight, cain't ye, or cry 'nuff!"

Blake milled away backwards, saying never a word, but not so the crowd. They didn't like it 'bove half, and roared at Tom to dub his mummer and finish him, 'stead o' jibing at a beat man. They yelled at Blake to stand game and not give best to a saucy nigger, and from that they turned to abusing Tom in earnest, telling him to take his dam' tongue and his black carcase back to the States. The whole company took up the cry, and called him an ape and a savage and a low-down slave and I don't know what, hissing whenever he got in a blow, and I began to fear they would rush the ring. Fact was, they couldn't abide to see a white man thrashed by a black – a *good* white man, I mean; they hadn't cared a fig when Tom hammered the Bristol Boy, but Blake was a different article. He was a first-run heavyweight, and if Tom could whip him, why, maybe he could whip all the way to the championship, d'ye see?

That was when it all changed, I reckon, in that sixth round. Yes, sir, that was when England began to fear Tom Molineaux. He wasn't the laughable darkie, the raree show, ever again after that. They commenced to fear him, then – and to hate him. Every blow he struck, they bayed like hounds, the whole crowd heaving ahead and cursing 'til I thought the vinegars must be trod under and the ring broke in. When Tom milled down Blake's guard and knocked him clean off his gams with a wisty left, there was a shout to bust the heavens, and if Gully hadn't raised his arms and roared 'em down, they'd ha' broke the ropes for sure.

"Fair play, there! Fair play!" cries Gully, and they held off, but the jeers and yells came thicker than ever. Tom stared 'round, all bewildered, and when he came to my knee, he asked:

"What's a matter? What Ah done wrong? Why they 'busin' me thataway, like Ah was fightin' foul or sumpn? Ah's fightin' fair, Bill! Ain't Ah, Pad? Sho' Ah is! What they want o' me?"

"Get away, ye black bastard!" yells someone, and "Be off, ye dirty nigger!" I never knew such a storm of 'bomination, they was so wild, fists shaking and cussing him the vilest names, although the Quality was silent for the most part, and the better sort trying to hush the people, but I saw a couple o' ladies that joined in the outcry. Gully waved his arms in vain – and then the rummest thing happened I ever saw in the ring, while Tom sat nigh weeping on my knee, begging me to tell him what to do.

The timekeeper called, and when I pushed Tom up to scratch he was fearful to go, but went when Gully beckoned. That was when the hats and clods o' turf and even brickbats began to fly into the ring, and one knocked Gully's hat off, and while he was scrambling for his tile Tom was alone, wi' the lumps hailing down 'round him. Then Cribb, who'd been putting Blake on his feet, left him and came for'ard his own self to the scratch, and at that you can bet the brickbats stopped, and the yelling also, 'sif someone had taken the crowd by the windpipe. Cribb took his stand maybe a yard from Tom, but didn't say a word or glance at him even, only stood there and looked 'round, real slow and grim, eyeing the crowd. Someone cried a cheer for the Champion, and there was a few huzzas, but he never minded 'em, just stood regarding the people this way and that, and the cheers and cries faded down to a whisper, 'til that whole assembly was as still as in church, and all you could hear was the wind and distant sea. Then Cribb said a word to Gully, gave Tom the littlest nod, and went back to his corner and sent Blake to the mark.

Ye know, sir, I have to own that I never liked Cribb all that much, can't tell why. But I never saw a man I respected more.

Gully called "Set to" in such a silence the crowd might ha' been asleep. Tom didn't want to, what wi' being still confused wi' drink and sickness and the baiting they'd give him. That was the first time I'd seen him scairt, sir. He'd never known such hate before, the screaming faces and shaken fists, and if he could ha' run I believe he would. What stirred him at last was when Blake, wi' the blood caked on his face and body and his eyes nigh swollen shut, came stumbling at him wi' his fists up, and the legs crying "Any odds the black!" Even then Tom went for him only half-hearted, but Blake was too weak to stand, and one little left put him down again.

He came out, though, for the eighth round, and landed Tom a facer, croaking: "There's for 'ee, blackee!" Tom bored in, and planted him a real churchwarden's right that knocked him arse over ears. Cribb and Gibbons did what they could, but at the half-minute he was still sound asleep, and Gully took Tom's famble and cried: "Molineaux the winner!"

And that, sir, is how Tom Molineaux, woozy wi' daffy and collywobbles and half the strength drained out o' him by a night's fornicating, beat Tom Blake, the game Tom Tough, in twelve minutes or there'bouts, and I swear if there was a less popular man in Kent that day, he must ha' had leprosy. There was hissing and booing, but less'n before, for they gave their voices to cheers for Blake. Gully put 'round a hat for him, and when he was come to the swell division they crowded 'round to clap him on the shoulder for his bottom, and plenty he had o' that. He came lurching and grinning to shake Tom's hand, and swore he'd never been milled so hard, and the crowd cheered wi' might and main, so they might ha' been cheers for Tom, too, for all you could tell.

There was one there, though, to give him a bravo and a slap on the back and all smiles, and guess who that was, sir – why, Cap'n Buck Flashman, to be sure! Not so much as the tip o' his whisker had I seen 'til then, when the fight was won and his man cock o' the walk, but now he was full of delight and great action, crying how proud he was, and what fettle, Tom? and bidding Pad and me rub him down 'fore he took cold. 'Twould ha' been a different tale if Tom had tumbled down drunk in the first round, you bet. The Cap'n shook hands wi' Breen and the Corinthians, who were bound to congratulate him, and then led Tom to a tilbury where Lady Manners was set so that she could smile on him and touch his hand wi' the tips o' her dainty fingers, aye, and look him over wi' a lazy smile that I didn't care for 'bove half. Alvanley and Mellish, who were the best o' the bucks, shook Tom's hand also, and Lord Sefton called out to all that would listen: "He's a dam' stout fellow, I say, a damned stout fellow!"

Tom stood, head down and silent, while the Quality praised him, and the commons looked on grinning but liking him no better. Pad and I would ha' had him away to the carriage, but he shook his head, and damned if I knew what to make of him. He wasn't scairt no more, nor sick for what I could see, but his teeth were set hard, and he kept shooting little looks sidelong, at the bucks, and the crowd, and the legs that were paying or collecting, and all the confusion 'round about.

"Gi' me a guinea," says he, so I gave him the flimsy, and he went to where Gully had the hat they'd put 'round for Blake, and dropped the flimsy in it. Now, sir, I thought 'twas just kindness, but I don't think that no longer. It was policy, sir, such as I'd not ha' credited him wi' thinking of. For he had that grinning look, now, and when those closest, who saw what he'd done, cried bravo and well done, he threw off the blanket round his shoulders, and held up his hands to the crowd.

"What the dooce is he about?" wonders Pad, and Cap'n Buck began to call out to him. Tell truth, sir, I wondered if the drink was still at work in him, for he waited 'til the buzz o' the crowd was stilled, and then he called out:

"Lawds, an' ladies, an gen'men! Ah am Tom Molineaux of Virginny, in th'United States of 'Merica, an' mebbe Ah's the best millin' cove in the hull o' Creation – an' mebbe Ah ain't! Ah got ma own 'pinion on that, an' you got yo's. You seen me fight a real game man today, a real prime miller. You make o' that what you will. Ah's in England to do ma best, to fight fair, an' to stand up to any man who'll come to scratch wi' me. An' whether Ah win or whether Ah lose, you good people goin' to gi' me fair play, 'cos they ain't no people in the whole world as good an' spo'tin' as the people of Ol' England, an' you know yo' good ol' game o' prize-fightin' mus' have the best, an' by golly Ah's goin' see that you gits it! An' the Lawd bless you all, an' you take care! An' God save the King!"

No, sir, he was not drunk, he was not distempered, nor had he gone queer in the attic, though you might ha' thought so if you had seen our phizzes – Pad wi' his mouth wide as a cod's, and Cap'n Buck struck dumb, and the Quality a-stare at this astonishing address from the black figure in his white breeches, alone in the ring. He gave a little bow, and walked back to us, and someone – I guess it might ha' been Sefton – cried "Bravo!", and the Quality clapped and cried: "Well said, the black!" and in a moment there was a great sighing noise that burst in a storm of cheers, and hats were flying into the air, and handkerchieves waving, and someone struck up "Marlbroug", and in a moment they were hollering it out, "For he's a jolly good fellow, and so say all of us!" They were all 'round him, grasping his hands, and slapping his shoulders, and I swear he took more punishment in those few moments than ever he got from Tom Tough. We had to fight our way to the carriage, wi' the vinegars clearing a way, and Cap'n Buck calling for three cheers and a tiger.

We got Tom inside and closed the blinds, but the mob tore 'em away and beat on the coach, yelling and cheering. I was all concern for him, for 'twasn't natural or like him at all, sir, to speak as he'd done, before all those folk, who'd never spoke out in all his life before, not public, I mean. He looked tired to death, lying back 'gainst the cushions, while Pad poured him a tot, and outside the people had unyoked the horses and were dragging the carriage along.

Pad gave him the dram, and he sipped and coughed and waved it away like 'twas nauseous to him, which was no wonder. Then he opened an eye and gave us a sleepy little smile slantendicular.

"Them people likin' me a little bitty mo' now, you reckon?" says he.

TOM CRIBB,

former heavyweight Champion of England,
retired publican

Truth to tell, master, I did not rate the black high. Well, there I were mistook. Now that I'm an old 'un, I can confess it. Yet, if I held him over cheap, 'twere natural enough. A man can only judge as he sees.

He'd beat Burrows. Well, who could not? He'd licked Tom Blake, but old Tom at Margate weren't half the man as I'd beat five year afore at Blackheath, when I were but a younker and Blake were in his prime. Ah, he were Tom Tough in them days, I can tell 'ee. Dead on his pins after an hour's stern milling, but still he came back at me. And rattled me all o'er the shop 'fore I put him down.

When he met Molineaux he were older and stouter and slower by far. The spirit were gone out of him, too, I reckon, or he'd ha' stood game longer than he did 'gainst a man who didn't fight well above half. Some said the black had been training on daffy and doxies, and had come to the ring half-soused, and that were the reason he showed so little style. I know naught o' that; he seemed sober enough at the end on't. But whatever o' that, 'twere no great mill. They flogged each other for five rounds, no science, no quarter, and when Blake went in his shell, Black Tom could not pry him out. Strength and youth did it at last. A hammering youngster thrashed a tired oldster. But I saw naught in the black to trouble me.

'Deed, I'd thought better of him when I'd watched him spar wi' Dutch Sam. I see then he could shift right sharp, guard well, and fib hard and fast, but he showed little o' that 'gainst Blake, only slogging. I said to Bill Gibbons: "This chap's one o' them as is champions wi' the mufflers, but half-starters when they come off." See, master, 'tis one thing to trip about the Fives Court showing off your feints and dodges, wi' naught at stake, but another to stand bare-hand in earnest wi' a sixteen-stone bruiser who aims to smash you, and *everything depending upon it.* Many a brave man fights wary then, not 'cos he lacks bottom but 'cos o' the burden of knowin' 'tis now or never.

I've felt it. Why, I've sparred wi' big Bob Gregson, him they called the Lancashire Giant, and gone full tilt and fancy free, and if he planted me a melter, what then? It cost me naught, being only a breather 'tween friends. But when I faced that same Bob at Moulsey, an October day cold as January, knowing his weight and strength and that one false step and my title would be o'er the hills and far away, ne'er mind Mr Methuen's stake money and the side-bets, and all them years o' rough milling gone for nothing ... ah, that's a different thing, master. But only them as has been there, knows that.

So when I thought Molineaux might be a half-starter, 'twasn't that I doubted his game. I told Gibbons: "He's a likely chicken in practice, but he's raw in the ring. He han't found his feet yet, and p'raps ne'er will. Whether or no, he'll never be a match for me."

'Twere no boast, master, but my belief, and most o' the Fancy thought likewise. Well, we was wrong. He had more in him than met the eye, of skill and fighting sense – and none was wronger than them as supposed he lacked bottom. I was not one o' those. I'd looked him in the eye.

After the Blake set-to, all the buzz was: when would I meet the nigger? I said naught to that. 'Tweren't my place, as Champion, so I turned a closed listener to the rashers o' wind in my public, and let my chums answer: "What, has Blackee challenged, then?" For that he had not done, and I knew why: Richmond and Pad Jones was unsure o' their man still. "Letting I dare not wait upon I would," says Pierce Egan. "But come, Tom, what d'ye say to all the talk?" I knew better than to open my gab to that one.

But talk there was, and louder it grew as time went by 'til it seemed all Lunnon could think o' naught but the 'mazin' black, and how would he fare 'gainst me. Buckley Flashman led the chorus, vowing to see his man Champion 'fore the year was out, tho' by all I heard the black were more partial to racketing wi' Cyprians and punishing the lush than putting his self in trim for a mill. It did not damp his conceit, tho', bragging how he'd take me to task. Never to my face, mind you; he steered clear o' the Union Arms, and kept his boasts for the Corinthians and pint-snappers at the Prad and Pilchard.

141

I ne'er minded it. I'd seen for myself that Molineaux were a jolly cove, full o' fun and antics as the darkies are, and cared not what he said. 'Twere all gammon to make Richmond's customers laugh, and no harm to me. Why, if brags won mills I'd ha' lost every fight afore it begun!

But if I paid no heed to the nigger's swaggers, or the loose patterers, there was them as did. 'Twould be some weeks after the Blake mill that Jackson, with Gully and Gregson, came to my parlour, all mighty sober-faced.

"Tom," says Jackson, "will ye fight the black?"

I asked him if a Johnny Newcome wi' a mill and a half behind him had the right to bid for my belt before the likes o' Belcher or Gregson himself.

"They ain't bidding," says Gully. "Besides, ye've beat 'em both. No one's challenged you in two years, nor like to."

"Well, let the black challenge, then," says I. "He talks a-plenty, from what I hear, and Richmond, and Buckley Flashman. They know where to find me."

"True enough," says Jackson, "but with all the gossip, and Molineaux strutting about Town, and Richmond's sly hints, and you saying ne'er a word . . . why, the buzz is that Molineaux's itching to fight – but you're not."

All three on 'em was eyeing me wary-like, to see how I took that.

"Then they's fools and liars that says it," I told him. "And you know it, John Jackson."

"Aye, he knaws it," says Gregson, "but the noodles that gabs i' the cloobs dawn't knaw it. They're sayin' ye're blate, man."

"Are you saying it, Bob?"

"No such thing!" says Jackson, mighty sharp. "But you know Richmond. He ain't your best friend, and if he can drop a word against you, he'll do it, and twist it to his advantage – the louder the buzz, the more profit to him and the legs when the match comes off. Why, 'twill be the biggest thing the Fancy's ever seen!"

"And not only the Fancy," says Gully. "Tom, I'll be plain with you: 'tis the talk of the nation. They think more of this fight than of the war in Spain – this match that is not made, and they want to know why. I was by the House today, and heard ten mentions of Cribb and Molineaux for every one of Boney. Not a Member or a lord but asks when the fight is to be. 'What's Cribb about? Is he shy o' the black, or what?' D'ye know who spoke those words, Tom?'' He tapped me on the chest. "Aye, as reported to me by a peer o' the realm? The King, no less.''

"Aye, even Owd Nobbs is askin', 'alf-daft an' a' as he is!'' growls Gregson. "Tha's boond to meet him, Tom lad.''

I said here was a great pother over one black Yankee.

"That's the point!'' cries Jackson. "A black Yankee – that's why folk are in a fever that ne'er gave boxing a thought before. Deuce take it, there are school-teachers in Newcastle, and doctors in Aberdeen, and misses in parsonages – aye, and dowagers in Almack's, all wi' their heads together whispering: 'A foreigner ... a black man ... Champion of England?' That's the question, Tom, and there's soldiers in Spain and jacks in the Channel Fleet asking it, too! And but one man on earth can answer it, or prevent it!''

I'd never known Jackson, that was so genteel and soft-spoke, to be that warm afore. Bob and Gully was nodding to every word.

"I'm Champion,'' says I. " 'Tain't for me to challenge no upstart.''

"Right you are,'' says Jackson, "but if I put it to Richmond, in public, that he must give over all his gas, and the darkie's, and write a proper challenge, or be published all o'er Town, the pair of 'em, for braggarts and hang-backs (Egan'd see to that!), and if Richmond writes such a challenge ... will ye take it up, Tom? Aye or no?''

Put plain that way, 'twere food for thoughts, and I'll tell ye what they was. I'd no fear o' the black ... nor much wish to meet him. I hadn't milled in two year, my parlour were giving me a goodish living, I had my name and fame, and had put on flesh and were comfortable. There'd been talk o' retirement and benefit, and I did not care if I ne'er did more scrimmaging than were needful to pitch rowdies into the street. I had no inclination to defend my title 'gainst a swaggering black pug. But, master, ye can see how 'twould ha' been for my credit and good name had I refused. So I made no bones of it.

"Two hundred guineas a side, and a purse of a hundred,'' says I. "Twenty-four-foot ring, grass or stage, yourself to stand umpire, and Buckley Flashman may put up his man any day 'twixt now and the year end. I'll meet him.''

"Thank God!'' cries Jackson, and wrung my hand. "But 'twill be

Richmond, not Flashman. He's given over the black, I believe.''

"I heard that," says Gully. "What's to do?"

"Some falling-out or other, it makes no matter. Tom, this is famous! Why, this match will be the greatest – aye, and the richest! – that ever was!"

"Four to one Cribb, or longer," says Gully. "But, Tom, no need of an early match, once 'tis made. Take time to train up."

They was eyeing me again. Jackson said he was right, two years was a long time idle. "The black's in training, and has fought two mills this summer. Best breathe yourself for a few weeks."

"In training, is he?" says I. "In the flesh-market, from what I hear."

"Even so, he's got five years on you, Tom, and raw or not, he's nimble and strong," says Jackson. "Oh, if I'm a judge he's not up to your mark, nor ever will be, but ... well, you know better than to take any man lightly. What d'ye scale now ... sixteen or over? I'd give yourself a month ... or more. Eh, John?"

Well, master, 'twere good advice, but it irked me, I tell ye. I guess I'd had my fill o' this wonderful nigger, as if he were Jack Slack and Mendoza all in one skin, and I must sweat like any novice to be up to him. I'm a patient, easy cove, but to have Gully and Jackson, of all men, as solemn as old wives o'er my condition, put me out of all liking. I'd ha' given 'em a short word, but for big Bob.

"Mak' it December!" cries he. "An' nivver glower at me, Tom Cribb! Tha's fatter'n a Christmas goose, ye owd booger! See noo, man – I'll be layin' a hoondred pun tha puts the darkie doon inside ten roonds, an' I dawn't want to lose me brass 'cos tha's got a belly like a poisoned pup an' it takes thee twenty! So nivver glower, I say, but get thasel' oot on't road!''

What could I do but laugh wi' him, and all the heartier 'cos I knew he made sense. For all that, I thought little o' the black.

JOHN DOE,

alias Richard Roe,

footman to Belinda, Lady Manners,

wife of Sir John Manners, Bt

Let us speak low, sir, if you please. Walls, you know, has ears. Now, sir, do you pledge me your solemn hoath, your bounden word as a man of honner, that my hidentity will remain forever hanonymous? Not the least 'int to a living creeter as I 'ave spoke to you? I must hinsist on your haffy-davy, sir, or it is no go at all! Not a word shall pass my lips hotherwise, nary so much as a syllable! Why, if 'twas to be known as I 'ad blowed – confided, like – 'twould be my perfesshnl ruin, no less. Loyalty and trust, sir, is the sacred hemblems of our vo-cation, and 'im as breaks that trust, sir, disgraced 'e is, cast into houter darkness, and not a bloody 'ope of a sittywation thereafter. And I tell you, sir, not one word would I dye-vulge, hunder *torcher*, heven, if conscience did not compel me. That is the fact, sir; 'tis conscience alone as does it. The blunt would not tempt me, sir, not hif 'twas ten times the sum you hoffer – and very generous and 'ighly hacceptable, to be sure, but conscience is the thing.

It 'as cost me dear, believe me. I 'ave wrestled with my very soul, sir. But when I think of the trust as *she* broke, the betrayal of the 'usband she swore to love, honner, hobey, and all of that, I can keep silence no longer. Not that 'e was a whit better, but that's by the way. For 'tis a wife's sacred dooty, is it not, more'n an 'usband's? But 'er, what did she know of dooty, for all 'er fine hairs, and treated us in the servants' 'all like muck, she did, and 'ad no more dooty in 'er than a halley-cat! And with a nasty, low nigger and all!

You do give your word, sir, on your honner? Very good. You'll keep the same, I know, being a gentleman, a real hout-and-houter, as I seen soon's I set heyes on you, if you will forgive my a-saying so. We learn, sir, in the perfesshn, to tell Quality from common, do we not? I should say we do!

Well, then, in your ear ... *it — is — true* ... what you been told. Lady Manners was the paramour of the black pugilist Molineaux! There, now! 'E was not the first or honly, I can tell you, but the honly *black* man, you hunderstand, and 'ow she came to lower 'erself that far, well, sir, it fair leaves me speechless. Oh, there is many a fine lady of the *ton* as gives 'er wedded lord a pair of hantlers, as the saying is (and I could tell you, aha! but that is not in our bargain, so mum), but none I ever 'eard tell of as would stoop to de-grade 'erself with the likes of that ... that sooty monster! It passes thinking of, sir. But Lady Bel, she did, more shame to 'er. It is gospel; I seen 'em at it, an 'orrible sight, and fair turned my stummick.

I blame Sir John, partly. Very loose, 'e was, a right rake, and let 'er go 'er own ways so long as she gave no cause for scandal. Why, she'd been hon and hoff with more gentlemen than I'd care to count, and all the Town knew when she took up with that Mad Buck Flashman, but that was not hout of the way in Society in them days, I grieve to say. Sir John did not deign to let on, 'im being proper bred, and 'aving 'is own muslins to mind, but I say 'e did wrong, sir, wrong as could be, to turn a blind heye to the blackamoor — and hif, as some said, 'e did not twig, well, 'e hought to 'ave done.

It was this way, sir. Lady Bel, being young and topsides with all that was fast and fashionable, always 'ad a heye to the gladiators, and was seen at the mills a sight more often than was becoming, to my mind. Low ruffians is what they are, sir, and hought to 'ave been beneath the notice of 'er and hother young Quality females. Bad enough, you may say, when the pugs is white, but when I seen her at Margate, after Molineaux 'ad beat that Blake creeter, and was presented to 'er by Captain Flashman (as should 'ave known better, 'im being a hofficer), and 'ad the himpidence to kiss 'er 'and with them great lolloping lips, and the glowing look she give 'im — well, sir, I tell you I thought shame for 'er sex! To see 'er, that was so finickal and dainty, a-smiling on that black reeking savvidge, more like a hanimal than an 'uman 'e was ... well, sir, you may picter my feelings.

I feared the worst, then. Did I not say to Mister Jessup, our butler: "She'll 'ave 'im, Mr Jessup, or I'm mistook." "What, the black?" says he. "Never! A lady of 'er sensibilities — himpossible! Besides, she is a-lashing the laundry with Captain Flashman, is she not?" "Even so," says I, "you mark my words, Mr Jessup," and I was proved right, sir.

This I will grant 'er, that she 'ad that much discretion, or cunning you might say, to 'old off until Sir John was gone down to Northamptonshire for the 'unting, and she could pursue 'er clandestine hamours hunremarked, by 'im leastways. By that time the black was all the crack, 'aving been matched to meet the Champion, and was fêted and petted something sickening by all the sporting *ton*, and not them halone. Mr Carlisle, a professor gentleman, hemployed 'im as a model for teaching hanatomy, 'im being a specimen of the nigger breed, I dare say, and they 'ad 'im a-posing among them Greek statues of my Lord Helgin's and all – stark naked disgusting at a guinea a time for all the gentlemen to view, and would you believe it, sir, they exhibited 'im special to *ladies* also, and 'im in a britch-clout as would not 'ave made a pocket 'andkercher!

I never saw nothing so vile 'orrid, sir, not in all my days, as that beastly creeter, all shiny black and a-bulging, rolling 'is heyes and grinning, and the ladies letting on as they was comparing him to the statues – I knew what they was comparing, and it was not no lump of Greek marble, neither! I was that mortified I could not think where to look, and me misfortunate to be the honly man there hamong Lady Bel and 'er fine friends, all a-quizzing of 'im and whispering behind their muffs.

"Do you know, my dear Georgina," says Lady Bel, "that for the first time I believe I understand Desdemona's partiality."

"Oh, fie, Bel!" cries 'er friend. "Do you not recollect how the play ends?"

"I was thinking of the earlier acts," says Lady Bel, sly-like, and at that they all burst out a-tittering, and vowed she was the wickedest thing. Desdemona was a lady wedded on a man of colour in a play, you see, Mister Jessup told me.

Lady Bel beckoned the hattendant that was there, and spoke with 'im sotter votchey, and tipped 'im a flimsy, and then – it is the shameful truth, sir, I tell no lie – he bade the black go in behind a screen, and Lady Bel and the Honnerable Georgina went round about it, and after a moment come out again, Lady Bel with 'er lazy smile like a tabby that 'as been at the cream, and t'other one blushing and in whoops. You never saw nothing so brazen, sir, the pair of 'em.

147

Need I tell you what followed, sir? I must on haccount o' conscience, though it makes my 'ead swim to think on it. 'Twould be a week after, my being hindisposed by some crab meat at supper, that I harose about one of the morning and caught young Halbert, the junior footman, and the boot-boy, on the backstairs in their night-shirts. I hasked what was the meaning of it, but dubbed close they was until I took a cane to the boy, and 'e sang loud enough then, that Lady Bel 'ad the Hafrican habovestairs in 'er chamber, and Halbert and 'im was habout to spy on 'em from 'er ladyship's boodwar, as they 'ad done many nights past.

"You lying tyke!" cries I. " 'Ow dare you slander your mistress, you young 'ound, you? I'll not leave a hinch of skin on your breech for this!"

But my 'eart misgive me, sir, that true it was, and young Halbert swore to it, 'ow 'er ladyship's habigail – one of them French 'ussies, all paint and hinsolence – was used to leave the area door hunlatched of a night, and that coloured scoundrel was hupstairs by one and hout by six, reg'lar as clockwork, "and Lady Bel and the habigail both a-playing ballum-rankum for 'im, ain't it so, 'Erbert, we seen 'em ever so often, didn't we?" 'Im and that scamp 'Erbert was grinning and sniggering, sir, they thought it the primest gig, filthy little brocks.

Well, I was at a loss what to do, sir, as you may himagine, but not wishing to believe the worst without I 'ad seen for myself, I hordered the boy to bed and bade Halbert to conduct me, and went and hobserved through the crack of 'er ladyship's boodwar door. And I would cut out my tongue rather than say it, sir, but conscience compels – there was that monstrous blackamoor stallion a-setting naked on 'er lady-ship's own bed, laughing and clapping 'is paws while Lady Bel and the habigail, with not a stitch between 'em, was a-dancing and a-flaunting of theirselves at 'im, and the candles all lit, and then the pair of 'em set about him, squealing like wild things, and carrying on for hever so long, and that 'orrid black fiend . . . no, sir, I can say no more, but they was at it, I can tell you, and never did I think to see Christian females so habandoned. The things they done, sir, and that *he* done, well, I was like to puke, and would 'ave tore myself away, but young Halbert was not to be budged, and 'im with the tail of 'is

148

shirt crammed in 'is chops to keep from laughing hout loud, 'e was that shameless.

So there it was, sir, as I 'ad seen with my own heyes, and naught for it but to hinform Mr Jessup, for with that Halbert and 'Erbert already in the know, 'ow was we to keep it from the hother servants, and then 'twould be the gossip of the 'ole world. Mr Jessup was that took aback, 'e needed a ball o' fire to set 'im right, and then said, very stern, it was 'is dooty to see for 'imself, such a scandal, 'e could not credit without 'e saw the same. So 'e did, the next night, and come down hafter an hour or more, and the sweat a-running off of 'is brow, sir, like water. 'E plumped down in 'is chair, all a-tremble, and sent Halbert straight to the cellar for a bottle of the old Nantes, to settle 'is self.

"By goles! I seen a deal in sixty year, and thought to know as much as befits a Christian, but that man o' colour is like nothing in nature!" says 'e. "God 'elp Tom Cribb!"

"God 'elp 'er ladyship, you mean!" cries I.

"John Doe," says 'e, "she needs no more 'elp than Potiphar's wife! Jezebel was a babby to 'er, a hinnocent! She's run mad, pleasuring mad she is! It's that," says 'e, "or the nigger's bewitched 'er!"

"Must we give our notice to the steward?" says I. "We are perfesshnl men of reppitation. Can we abide in this 'ouse as she 'as turned into an 'eathen bagnio? We must think of our good names, Mr Jessup!"

That gave 'im to consider, sir, right enough. "Eight and thirty years 'ave I served Sir John, and 'is father afore him. Where would I find another sittywation, at my time, tell me that? No, John, we must not be 'asty. Why, what would be said, what scandal might not harise, if the likes of you and me, perfesshnl men as you say, was to 'op the wag sudden-like? Besides," says 'e, mighty solemn, " 'tis not our place to judge our betters, whatsoever their conduck. That Lady Bel," says 'e, taking a long pull of the Nantes, and shaking 'is old grey noddle, "beats anything in the Bible, I do believe, or them wicked Roman hempresses of yore. As for the black fellow, I would not 'ave credited such. It is the tropic sun as does it, I reckon."

Well, sir, what was we to do, 'cept our hutmost to prevent such scandalous goings-on coming to the ear of the vulgar public? "We can stop the gabs of young Halbert and the boy 'Erbert, at all events," says Mr Jessup, 'tho 'ow 'e was to do that was beyond me, but 'e 'it on a prime notion. A long 'ead on 'im, 'ad old Jessup. He summoned 'em, stern as a judge, and told 'em that heven to *talk* of the 'orrors they 'ad witnessed would make 'em parties to unnatteral vice, which was a capital hoffence. I don't know as Halbert, who was a dodgy 'un, believed 'im, but 'Erbert fell a-blubbering, and both swore to keep their mummers shut.

But hothers knew, sir. The black, you see, was in training for 'is match with the Champion, and 'is people must 'ave twigged to 'is hassignations with my lady, for twice of a morning, nigh on six, the time when the habigail was used to let the nigger out at the area door, there was a man a-waiting, a lean likely villain in a round shap and black coat. Mr Jessup, who was a follower of the Fancy, swore it was Paddington Jones, the bruiser as 'ad charge of Molineaux – and if you ax me how Mr Jessup come to be at the back winder at that time o' day, sir, I cannot say, but I 'as my suspicions 'e was doing more spying than sleeping, and at 'is hage, too. Howsomever, Molineaux and the man Jones fell a-bickering in the very street; I 'eard 'em myself the second time, such habuse and filthy words as would 'ave scorched your ears, sir, afore they goes off together.

Now you may wonder at it, sir, but all the time she 'ad been de-grading of 'erself with the black by night, Lady Bel 'ad been spry as a starling by day, driving hout with Captain Flashman and 'er friends, receiving and paying of 'er calls, seen about Town and the smart shops and the theatre and Halmack's, all quite the thing. I hattended on 'er as dooty demanded, and I fair marvelled at the brass fore'ead of 'er, I did. I should tell you, sir, she was the most delicate and refined creeter to look upon, hever so fair and fresh-like, with the sweetest manner and them wide blue peepers, butter wouldn't 'ave melted, and such a taste in dress as ravished the *ton* haltogether. 'Twas a privilege to wait hupon 'er, and made me right proud – until that hugly blacka-moor, I never could hesteem 'er the same after, I could not. I would see 'er a-languishing on the Captain's harm, laughing with 'er fine friends, hinnocent as day, and think to myself, woe hunto you, my lady, your sins will find you hout one o' these days, or I'm parson's pig. And so they did, sir.

How Captain Flashman got wind of 'er goings-on, I know not.

P'raps by way of Paddington Jones or some hother of the black's people. Nor I wouldn't put it past that French habigail, a sly malishus trollop with more hairs and graces than 'er mistress, and the wickedest tongue. Anyways, sir, came a daybreak when I was in the kitchen at my morning wet, and Mr Jessup come in a huge fluster with his wig like an 'en's nest, and fair dragged me to the back winder, and who should we see but the Captain 'is very self, jumping down from 'is curricle, and the prads steaming like boiled flounders. Still 'alf-dark it was, but we could see as the Captain 'ad black rage writ all over 'im, pacing up and down in a passion and thrashing 'is whip on 'is boot.

" 'E's twigged 'em!" says Mr Jessup. "By goles, John, we'll see murder done, so we will!"

"I'll run for the charlies!" says I.

"You'll not!" cries 'e. "I would not miss this for a seat in the Lords!"

Just then we 'eard the habigail a-tittering on the stairs, and in a moment hout comes the nigger from the area door. The Captain spoke never a word but laced straight into 'im with 'is whip, lashing 'im something cruel, and the blackamoor took all hunawares and staggering and bellowing loud enough to fetch the beadle, and the Captain red as fury.

The black 'ad with 'im a little toy bird in a cage which I knew for 'er ladyship's, and guessed she must 'ave give it 'im, and it fell and broke on the cobbles. "Ma present!" hollers Molineaux. "You done bust ma present, damn ye!" – you know the way they talk, sir. " 'Tis all broke to smash!"

"I'll break more than that, you black son of a bitch!" cries the Captain, laying on, but Molineaux caught the lash away from 'im and dealt 'im such a leveller as I thought would 'ave killed 'im.

"The grave-digger!" cries Mr Jessup, and danced on 'is wig. "There's pepper, by goles!"

But the Captain tore off 'is coat, and flung it in the gutter, such a swell case, sir, as though 'twere a rag, and fair flew at Molineaux with 'is fists, calling 'im bastard and worse. The black sprang away, waving 'is fists and laughing, daring the Captain to come on, and so 'e did, sir, and they struck and mauled heach hother like madmen, the Captain swearing and the blackamoor laughing and taunting 'im, and Mr Jessup was beside 'isself, 'opping hup and down that hexcited, crying: "That's for 'is nob! Go for 'is bread-basket! Foul, foul, by goles! Now, now, the one-two!"

I know nothing of milling, sir, and despises it for a nasty brutal business, but heven I could see as the Captain was no match for the beastly grinning savvidge, and sure enough Molineaux beat 'im all hover the street until 'e tumbled down and lay there, the blood on 'is lips and stark murder in 'is heyes. If there 'ad been a sharp or barker to 'and, sir, Molineaux would 'ave lain dead on the hinstant. But the Captain did not get up again, and Molineaux cries: " 'Ad enuff, hey? Why, you ain't some chicken, Captain Buck! You's no better at fightin' than Lady Bel says you is at —in', you poor white trash!"

I 'umbly begs pardon, sir, but them was the words 'e used. I could scarce believe my hears, from a low coloured rascal to a hofficer and gentleman born, the disgrace of it. I felt hutterly hashamed, I did. And then, what do you think – the blackamoor picked up the Captain's coat and wiped 'is 'ands hupon it, and threw it down and went a-strutting off, guffawing like a bull calf. The Captain, 'e said not a word, but got hup presently and hinto 'is curricle and drove away – and then, sir, ah then! We 'eard a winder bang shut hover'ead, and 'er ladyship and the habigail laughing and hexclaiming habovestairs! What do you think of that?

Captain Flashman never came to the 'ouse no more. Nor did the nigger, nasty beast. We was well shot o' that one, but I regretted the Captain, sir, a proper hopen-'anded gentleman 'e was. Mr Jessup said, funning like, that 'twas a shame, for 'e would 'ave liked to see 'em box a return match, but I do not share 'is 'umour, sir. To my way of thinking, the reppitation of our 'ouse 'ad been polluted, sir, the honner of Manners 'ad been blowed upon by that dirty black creeter.

What, sir? I 'ave hexplained much as was 'idden from you? Why, I am much gratified to 'ear you say so, and glad to 'ave been of service . . . oh, my dear sir, thank'ee, deeply hobliged . . . most generous indeed! And I 'ave your word my name will not happear . . . ?

PADDINGTON JONES, *resumed*

How could I give him up, sir, I ask you? If't had been any other miller, I might have washed my hands and bidden him good-day, but with Tom . . . I could not. No, not if he'd drunk the cellars dry, boxed the watch, and covered every moll from the Chelsea waterworks to Shadwell Dock — which he tried to do, Lord knows, and I was nigh on desperate when he took up with that high-flying slut Manners, for he was in her bed the best part of a fortnight. But I'd come too far with him, you see, and turned him from a clumsy looby into as fine and fast a heavy man as ever I knew, and how could I say farewell to all o' that within a month of him fighting for the Championship of England? Tho' when he rolled up to breakfast ho-hoing how he'd thrashed Buck Flashman, I'll own I thought 'twas out of my hands, and the end of him.

Richmond was near out of his wits. "Ye know what'll come o' this?" bawls he. "You infernal black fool, they'll have ye in the Roundhouse afore noon, for assault, and in the Spike Hotel for the next six months!"

"Ah don' b'lieve so," says Tom, sporting his ruffles with Weston's fine coat slung over his shoulders like any shawl. "Ah don' b'lieve Cap'n Flashman goin' to tell the beak: 'Oh, please yo' honour, this heah is the niggah whut mounted ma mistress an' whupped me in the street'. Ah cain't heah him, 'zackly!" He gave a great splutter of laughter. "Say, whut's fo' brekfuss, Flora? Ah's been exercisin', an' mighty sharp set!"

Bill was that angry he could hardly speak. "Damn you! An' what in God's name you goin' to do for a patron now!" was all he could say.

"Git any number o' patrons," says Tom, cool as you please. "Lawd Sefton back me in a minnit. Or Mistah Mellish, or Alvanley, or thee Mark-wess o' Queens-burr-ee!" says he, rolling his eyes. "Why, whut's a matter, Bill Richmond, you worrit 'bout the two hunnerd guineas? Git two thousan', easy. Say, Flora, how 'bout two o' yo' big juicy rump steaks, the way Ah likes 'em?''

"Get out!'' yells Bill. "Get your black ass out o' my house!'' He was raving, sir, and I thought he would fly at Tom, who sat back on the bench like a dandy in a club and looked him up and down, pitying almost.

"You ain't puttin' me out, Bill,'' says he. "Now, why'nt you let me git ma brekfuss in peace, then me an' Pad'll git out on the road, an' then Ah'll whale the bag an' limber the weights, so I'll be in fettle to dee-molish Tom Cribb? Huh? That's yo' style, Flora, broil 'em up, gal!''

There was nothing to say to him, for 'twas all true. Buck Flashman daren't charge him, for his credit's sake, half the bucks of the Fancy would be ready to back him, and neither Bill nor I would give him up now – as well he knew, the grinning black villain – not with the prize in reach, and the dream like to come true. For this I'll say, 'spite all his gorging and mollishing and going to bed at cock-crow castaway foxed, aye, and brawling with the charlies and being haled before a magistrate who let him go with a caution (being a follower of the Fancy, I dare say) – for all o' that, sir, he was out on the road with me at peep o' day, and worked and sparred and trained like any Trojan, he did, and all his whoring and hurrawing seemed to have taken no more out of him than a ten-mile trot. Any other pug would ha' been burned to the socket, but Tom Molineaux was of different metal. Course he was. I don't say he throve on loose-living, or that he could not have been sharper and stronger still, but I *do* say that in those last weeks before Copthorn he was moving as well and fibbing as hard as I could have wished, for all that he was still haunting the kens by night, on the mop and in the saddle.

We never saw hide nor hair of Flashman after his turn-up with Tom, and it took Bill Richmond all of three days to come out of his sullens, but there was no lack (as Tom had guessed) of sporting men ready to stand the stake, and the purse might have been subscribed a hundred times over, for the fight had caught hold of the Town, aye, and the country, like a fever. I never knew the like, sir, 'fore or since: Crocky reckoned there was a cool five million laid out in wagers, such a sum as had never been known for any mill or race or sporting contest whatever, the papers were full of it, Egan was predicting that Cribb would be tried as never before, the Corinthians were sporting their "Molineaux" bands all over St James's, the milliners were doing a great trade in black dolls with woolly heads which were all the crack with the Quality kidlings, ladies were wearing little Yankee flags with their stripes and stars, Tom was cheered to the skies when we took our runs in the Green Park, the old Nag and Blower was crowded like a Tyburn scragging day and night, Bill was fretful 'cos Tom was still a stone heavier than he liked at fourteen two, and I was wore to a shadow, sir – I swear I never sweated so hard for my own mills as I did for that one.

Happy, tho', for I was beginning to *hope*, not least 'cos Dutch Sam and Mendoza had taken to dropping by our ken, to watch Tom at work, and even to spar with him. I knew what that meant: the Jews were taking note of our man, and fixing their odds according. It had been five to one Cribb, but that soon narrowed 'til you might get two to one; on Guy Fawkes they were offering ten to one that Molineaux would not stay with Cribb fifteen minutes, but by the month end 'twas seven to four only, and few takers. The word had gone out that the black was shaping, and the excitement rose ever higher – save for Tom, who was placid as a pond in summer, 'cos he *knew* he would beat Cribb, and told the world the same. 'Twasn't gas, either; he was that cocksure. I did not mind, sir; a man who truly believes he's about to win is a surer bet than any head-shaker.

It was too much for Richmond, tho'. He was in terror not only over Tom's carry-ons, but about that same confidence, which he judged ignorant folly.

"Give over yo' goddam braggin' fo' jus' two minnits, an' lissen to me, will yuh?" says he, all darkie-talk in his excitement. "You reckon Cribb's yo' meat – but you don't *know* him, you ain't seen him fight, even! I've fought him –"

"An' he trimmed you up good!" chortles Tom.

"Dam' right he did – me an' ev'yone else! An' you know why – why he's champeen of England? Not jus' 'cos he's the fastest, strongest, cleverest pug ever come to scratch – oh, sure, you c'd be as strong an' as fast, mebbe even as clever, tho' I doubt it – but, brother, that ain't the half! You've never *been* where Cribb's *been*!"

"An' where might that be, pray?" says Tom, yawning.

"Flat on yo' back!" roars Richmond. "With yo' innards beat out, an' both eyes closed, and half yo' ribs busted, an' yo' hands all broke, an' nuthin' in the whole world but mis'ry an' pain! *That*'s where Cribb's been!" He stamped and took a turn about the yard and stuck his phiz into Tom's, glaring. "An' *that*'s when Tom Cribb gits up an' starts to fight! *That*'s why he's champeen! 'Cos he don' know the word 'quit'! It ain't just that he's trained mind and body – they's a little bit sump'n mo'." He took a breath, and put his hand on Tom's shoulder, quiet and weary. "An' Tom, boy, I don't know if you got it. But we sure as hell goin' find out. Now, you do sump'n for me? You have a dish o' tea, and git in your bed by nine? An' don't stir out 'til six – will you do that for me, Tom?"

For once Tom heeded him, but I guess 'twas just humouring, for next night he was up to his shines again with Janey Perkins and the rakes at the Coal Hole. I had long since given up reproaching him, but in the last fortnight I tried a different tack to rein him in: I let up on his training, in part 'cos I didn't want him trained off on the great day, but also I knew 'twould give him to think, if I showed indifferent. Sure enough, when I didn't rouse him out to run, and left off our sparring, he came frowning to know why. I shrugged and said it didn't signify, now, he might train solus if he liked – d'ye know, sir, he did that very thing, *and* took to turning in by nine! I watched him closer than he knew, for any sign of the crotchets, or nerves, or clogged bowels, but come December the seventeenth he was in prime twig, a stone too heavy, maybe, but as fit to fight for his life as he ever would be.

The next day, Tuesday the eighteenth, would see it settled, and I was that tired, sir, as one is when all's done that can be done, and you must abide the moment. All the months of graft were behind us, the Bristol Man, and Tom Tough, and Buckley Flash, and Tom's racketing about Town, and all the rebukes and swearing and passions – they did not amount to snuff now. I could ha' slept for a week, but put on a good face for Tom's sake. Bill was grim as a Turk, that long pepper-and-salt noddle would have set well on a churchwarden – the truth was, sir, the man was frightened out of his wits, both for his fighter and the money he'd laid out with the legs, more than a few hundred, I believe, and he'd put up the stake guineas himself, which didn't signify in rhino, being less than half a monkey, but showed he wanted no obligation to patrons. I had not bet myself, not out of fear, nor superstition, but, to put it plain, sir . . . I did not know. Word was that Cribb had trained steady and would strip at about fourteen and a half – overweight, like Tom, so you might take your choice between 'em.

The mill was set for Copthorn Common, which lay about thirty miles from Town, hard by East Grinstead in Sussex. Gully and Richmond had chosen it as being close to both Kent and Surrey, so that if the magistrates got wind there would be two counties to bolt to, but it was labour lost. He'd have been a bold beak that sought to queer *that* fight, with the whole world agog; they'd have tarred and feathered him, I dare say. Lord lu'mme, we could have set up the ropes in Hanover Square! But Copthorn suited me, for it meant an easy coach the day before, and a quiet night in new quarters, which keeps your man occupied and free of care.

But quiet it was not, sir, for the inn was packed to the eaves, like every house for miles around, and seemed to be uncommon full of Bristol men, bawling five to one Cribb, ten to one the black would fall within fifteen minutes, *hundred* to one he would not last the hour. Oh, come, Pad, thinks I, have you not the game to back a man of your training to stand up a quarter hour? And a hundred to one is too good to lose any day. So while we were at supper in our chamber I slipped down and sought out Abe Moss, one of Jew King's legs, a known file that would not dare welsh, and laid ten on each count. I felt the better for it, as backing my own man, and told Tom what I'd done. He laughed and thanked me, with his ear cocked to the Bristol boys singing below. You know the air, sir, course you do, "Down in the Valley Where She Followed Me", but these were the words:

> Oh, say have you heard
> Of the handsome young coal-heaver
> Who down at Hungerford
> Used for to ply?
> His daddles he used
> With great skill and dexterity,

Winning each mill, sir,
And blacking each eye!
(*Omnes*)
A true Briton from Bristol,
A rum 'un to fib,
He's the Champion of England,
His name is TOM CRIBB!

Our Tom was set at ease, picking his teeth and smiling. "Say, they sho' like that man, don' they? Well, Ah hope he's lissenin', 'cos 'tis the last time. Tomorrow night they goin' be singin' 'bout *me*.'

Richmond, who had been looking middling sour, and had made nothing of his peck, grunted that he'd better not count on it. Tom was used to his blues by this time; he laughed and asked what ailed him, he knew we were sure to win.

"That don't mean they'll be singin' songs about it," says Bill.

"Why, how you talk!" scoffs Tom. "Ah'll be they new champeen – sho', they'll be singin'! Din't you hear 'em huzza me on the road today? They likes me – say, Ah bet they likes me a sight better'n that dull dog Cribb this minnit –"

"Oh, yeah?" cries Bill. "Well, 'bout the sixth round tomorrow they ain't goin' be likin' you one dam' bit, an' you best know that!"

"What you mean, sixt' round – ?"

"By that time," says Bill, "all them as bet you wouldn't stay the fifteen minutes will have lost their money." He poured himself another shot o' the red, took a pull, and glowered at Tom. "An' the gashly 'spicion will be sinkin' in that you just 'bout liable to hand Cribb the lickin' o' his life. An', brother, you won't have a friend in the world! 'Cept me, an' Pad here – an' I ain't all that sure 'bout him, either."

I thanked him for that, and Tom set up a great jeer, but Bill shouted us down. What with worry and waiting, he'd been punishing the pot, and was cut enough to be quarrelsome.

"Don't tell me how pop'lar you are!" says he. "I read Pierce Egan, an' it don't signify two megs! You better get one thing in that thick nob o' yours, Tom Molineaux – you ain't fightin' only Cribb tomorrow. You fightin' England! An' that's a tall order, boy! Go ask Bonaparte – he ain't makin' that much progress at it!"

Tom looked at me with his mouth open, for he could make nothing of it. "England? Bonaparte? Pad, whut he talkin' 'bout?"

"Nix," says I. "Cheese it, Bill." For he was alarming me, sir, troubling Tom that way. It was God's truth what he was saying, and all the more reason for not saying it and upsetting his man. But maybe he was trying to prepare him, for he took another long drain and slapped the table.

"What I'm sayin' is that there ain't a solitary soul in this country that wants you to win!" cries he. "You think 'cos they cheer you, they're *for* you? Oh, they likes you well enough – the way folks like a li'l piccaninny, 'cos he's cute and full o' capers, and makes 'em laugh . . . and he's harmless!"

"Bill, will you stow that talk?" says I, and laid hold on him, but he shook me off, and went rattling on, while Tom sat bewildered and angry.

"See here, Tom Molineaux, the truth is they don't believe you got a hog in hell's chance of beatin' Cribb! So, sure they'll cheer ye . . .'til they find out how wrong they were. And then, brother, you'll smell the difference! Remember how they hissed and cat-called when you were whippin' Blake at Margate? Well, that weren't nothin'! Tomorrow it's Cribb, and the title – and they love their fight game, and they invented it, and they think they *own* it! You think they'll admire to see a sassy loudmouth nigger take it away from them – from Cribb, that they think's the finest man alive, over Lawd Wellin'ton, even? A *black man*, Champion of England?"

"Damn your eyes, Bill, will you leave off?" says I, for while 'twas truth, as I told you, 'twas doing Tom no good at all. He heaved up on his feet.

"You mean they try to cross me? Bust in the ring?"

"I ain't sayin' that," Bill told him. "Jackson's umpire, and he's square. No, they'll give you fair play – and no more. Just don't give 'em a chance to cry 'foul' –"

"Bill, ye're God's own bloody fool!" says I. "Is this any talk to a man on the eve of a fight? Don't heed him, Tom, he's three sheets in the wind! Now, come to bed, do, and let's have no more of this foolishness."

Truth was, I was too mad to stay, sir, and hoped Tom would follow me to the bed-chamber and leave Richmond to grouse and booze by himself. I might soothe and settle him then. But he did not turn in for a good half-hour, when he seemed well enough, quiet-like, but content seemingly, so whatever else Bill had to say could have done no harm.

BILL RICHMOND, *interpolated*

Guess I must ha' been lushed well 'bove par, to talk as I did that night. Truth was, mister, I was played out with the time dragging by, and the Cribb folk belowstairs singing and bragging, and my dark doubts and fears for the morrow, when 'twould be all to play for, and that poor fool Tom would find himself tried beyond anything his ignorance could imagine. He thought he was a fighter, but he didn't know what *real* fighting was, mister, not then. The wiseacres'll tell you one mill is like another, but 'tis not so. There's a breed of men, and Cribb was one of 'em, apart from the rest, and a fight for the Championship is like no other set-to. Tom was trained, 'spite of his devilment, as well as Pad could do, well trained – but he was not *prepared*, mister, and I knew it. That was why I sluiced down the juniper more than I should – me that was never castaway in my life, hardly. My hopes went up and down with the liquor, I guess, and 'twas when they were highest and I could picture him fibbing Cribb to hell and glory, that it came on me to warn him how the Fancy would turn on him when they saw their Champion beat at last. 'Tis a terrible thing for a fighter when the mob turns against him; it can beat him in turn. He'd tasted a little of it, with Blake, and it had scairt him; tomorrow would be ten times worse, and better he should know it now, I reckoned, than in the twentieth round.

'Twas hard hearing for him, on the eve of the fight, and I don't wonder Pad flew up in the trees. But I was glad he chived off in a pet, for not in a thousand years would I ha' said in his presence what I told Tom Molineaux that night.

Pad slammed the jigger just as I was telling Tom he'd have fair play enough from Jackson and the other gentlemen, and that Cribb had never fought foul in his life. That calmed him pretty good.

"Then Ah don' need no more'n that," says he. "Ah beat him, Bill, sho' 'nuff. Ah *knows* Ah goin' beat him."

"Just so you don't leave no room for argument 'bout it," I told him. "Just mind that Cribb'll keep coming, and if you want to win you better put him away cold, so he don't come round 'til New Year's."

"Colder'n a clam on an ice-cake!" cries Tom, grinning fit to bust ... and just the sight of him then, mister, I could ha' wept. To see him so young and eager and rarin' to be at it – I don't know why, but it set me to remembering, and to saying what I'd not ha' said in Pad's hearing – or any other man's, white or black.

"Yassuh, colder'n a fish's ass!" says he.

"Well, you do that, Tom," I told him, "and you'll have won a whole heap more'n a prize-fight. Or a championship, even."

"Why, whut you mean, Bill?" asks he, and I could ha' bit out my tongue, for 'twas a deep thing I'd never thought to tell. I said 'twas nothing, but he pestered at me to find out what it was, over and over. "Do tell, Bill! Whut mo' will Ah win? Whut else?" So I reflected, and it seemed maybe 'twas fit and right to tell him, and could do no harm, and might do good.

So I told him ... about my own early life, when I was a slave back in Cockold's Town, on Staaten Island, in the old colony times. My mammy and me were owned by a reverend, name o' Charlton, and he sold me, or gave me, I don't rightly know which, to an English general, Earl Percy. It was the time of the revolution, when the British lost the colonies, and General Percy brought me to England when he came home.

"Well, Tom [I told him], that English general was one o' the most important men in England, and in time became Duke o' Northumberland. Yes, sir, he was a big man, but more'n that, he was a *real* man. He gave me my freedom, and an education, and had me taught a trade, 'prenticed to a cabinet-maker up north, in York. He taught me boxing, too, and a whole lot besides. You see, Tom, I'm half-white, what they call dingy Christian, and back in New York they used to say I was half-nigra, half-*human*. That was when I saw that white folks didn't believe black folks were really *people*, or part o' the human race. Well, Earl Percy, he didn't think that way at all.

"The day he gave me my freedom, I told him how grateful I was, and d'ye know what, Tom, he near tore my head off, and cussed me for thanking him. 'Ye don't owe me a dam' thing, William!' says he. 'It is I, and my countrymen, who owe you an apology, for having held

162

you in bondage! It is a crime for which we will pay dearly, I believe, but what little I can do to right the wrong I have now done, in your case. But don't thank me – don't *dare* to thank me, d'ye hear?'

"Well, I didn't know what to make of him; I was just glad to be a free man, whatever he said. He wasn't alone in England, though, for they took 'gainst the slave trade, and 'bolished it, and I guess some day they'll make others take 'gainst it, too, and that'll be the end on't. But 'twasn't just slavery he hated, it was the way black folks were tret, and looked down on – half-human, you see. 'It makes my blood boil! You are a man, as I am!' cries he, and you should ha' seen him, red-faced and raging! 'But, dammit, you must *prove* it, William – prove it in their very teeth!' And that was why he trained me to be a miller.''

"Whut's that to do wi' it?" says Tom.

"He wanted me to be Champion of England, Tom, and he told me why. Oh, he'd studied 'bout it, real hard. 'Your people will not always be slaves, William,' he told me, 'but they will always *think* like slaves until one of them wins – not buys, or steals, or has given to him – but *wins*, fair and square, some thing which the white man believes belongs to him alone. The Championship of England is such a thing. You may think it a small thing, a mere prize of sport, and therefore of no account, but believe me, William, I know my race and kind, and I tell you, when a black man wins it, he will have changed the world.' "

Tom sat wi' his mouth open, and I don't know what he thought. Maybe 'twas in one ear and out t'other, he was that simple. But I guess maybe he had a small inkling, for he nodded, real slow, and then he frowned, and shook his head.

"But . . . but you nevah won the champeenship," says he.

"No, Tom, I didn't," says I. "But I reckon I found me a black man who can."

BOB LOGIC, Esq.,

student, sportsman,
and former pupil of Tonbridge School, Kent

Did I see the set-to between Cribb and Molineaux? I should just think I did. 'Twas the most famous thing! I was twelve, and my two best chums and I had broken bounds the day before, to see the great mill at all costs, "for it will be the fight of the century," says I, "and worth any number of gatings and floggings." "The mill of the *century*, which has still nine-tenths to run?" says Jerry. "Oh, that's Bob's *logic*, I suppose. Well, I'm with you, at all events." Tom cried aye to that, so we cut out on the Monday, and the dickens of a wet odyssey we had of it to Sussex, for the rain fell like stair-rods twenty-four hours together, and unless you were by the outer ring you might (says Tom) as well have been on the sea front at Deal in a Channel gale. The rain *de*scended, and the fog *as*cended, for there was twenty thousand about the ropes, and all steaming like so many bowls of bishop. "Why, this air is as clear as Bob's *logic*," says Jerry, "you would think they were all blowing clouds together!" "Not a bit of it," I told him, "for there's nothing *smoky* about this mill, you'll see."

It was uncommon fun, I can tell you, for we wheedled lodgings with an old dame at Grinstead, having put together five bob from our pocket dibs to pay the score, and then hey, for Copthorn! with a breakfast of chops and cucumber and ketchup inside us. It was five miles through mud knee-deep, the whole vast throng ploughing ahead like grenadiers, the road so churned that all the rattlers and gigs and chaises that had brought the sporting men from Town had to take to the fields, and over the ditches and smash through the hedges – Jerry swore he counted fifty rigs fast in the plough, and we were caked with clay to our middles, and still raining to drown Noah.

Oh, if you could have seen it – the swells in their curricles and phaetons, whips cracking like muskets, four-in-hand Corinthians with more capes than Africa, the chestnut men tending their braziers, the pie-men and pedlars and ballad-mongers with Gregson's latest, the puppet-stalls where Punch beat the baby and was crapped by Jack Ketch, farmers on cobs and plough-horses even, yokels and clerks and tradesfolk and a parson trying to hide his collar, and all as merry as mice despite the rain and cold, united towards one glorious goal – the fight! It was like all the great fairs that ever were, with Astley's thrown in – why, there was even a chap on stilts, much admired for he could see over the heads of everyone.

"We must get to the fore if we're to see anything of the mill," said I. "The *four*?" cries Tom. "Well, we must use our *fives*, Bob, or we'll be at *sixes* and *sevenses*!" This inspired us to pursue our way to the outer ropes with alacrity, and being small and nimble we fetched up among the great circle of vehicles which the bucks had made about the green fairy circle, and there were the vinegars parading with their whips, and the legs and Jews already at work by eleven o'clock, crying their odds, counting their change, and bilking the flats whose blunt was flowing "like the golden stream of Pactolus," says Jerry. "Oh, hang Ovid!" cries Tom, "but, since you mention it, we *Midas* (might as) well put a couple of bob on Cribb, eh?" But all our pockets were to let by now, which was as well, for the flashmen and leery coves were thick about us. " 'Ware priggers, you fellows," says I. "Secure your ticker, Tom, or the dummy-hunters will have it." "Well said, Bob," cries Jerry, "Tom had best *watch* out, or he'll lose *time*!" Tom tried to work up a jest about our being "*Cribb*'d, cabin'd and confined", but we gave him nothing but *black* looks.

A tall swell on a curricle must have overheard us, for he asked where we came from. We said Tonbridge. "Why, you scamps, you've slipped your cables, I'll be bound!" laughs he. "Well, up you jump! I'm an old Rugby boy myself, but I'll be hanged if you don't see the fun in style!" He was a real tip-top blood, with splendid black whiskers and togs bang-up to the nines. We mounted up, you may be sure. "This is a rare spec," says I. "Why, sir, it is as good as a box for the pantomime!"

Mr Jackson was on hand at twelve precisely, smiling and tipping his tile to the assembly, and had the vinegars marshal the vehicles at the foot of a hill to one side of the ring to shield the gladiators from the elements. Our host was a dab with the ribbons and tooled the curricle into place to a nicety. The hill was thick with people, more hundreds coming by the minute, crouching together against the rain, but making such a roaring hum of noise, says Jerry, that he could hardly hear himself think!

And now a band struck up on the far side, playing martial airs, and there was a great cry as the scales were carried within the outer ring, a sure sign that the hour of battle drew nigh. Never was such excitement – and now, to a mighty cheer, comes Molineaux, attended by his black pal, Richmond, and the famous Paddington Jones. "My father saw Richmond fight," says Tom, and our Rugby Corinthian asking against whom, Tom says: "Why, sir, against the London mob, when he defended Lord Camelford the time the people attacked him for not lighting his windows to celebrate peace with Boney." "Why, that's ten year ago nearly," says our host. "Aye, Richmond was one of Camelford's knights of the rainbow at that time." Meaning a black servant in gaudy attire, which was double Dutch to me then, but I didn't care to ask.

Molineaux skipped and danced and beat his arms to keep from shivering in the icy blasts, but presently saluted the crowd to applause, bowing and grinning and blowing kisses before shying his hat into the ring and retiring to peel.

"I say, Buck," cries one of the swells to our host, "this weather won't suit your darkie one bit."

"He ain't my darkie," was the rejoinder.

"Ye don't say? I had not heard. Well, if Cribb don't finish him, the ague will. Why, he'll be chilled *white*."

"No, he won't," whispers Jerry. "For you know, Bob, that for all he's *black*, Molineaux is reckoned a regular *green* 'un, and his pal Richmond, we're told, is a knight of the *rainbow*, so if Cribb should do his opponent up *brown* and tap his *claret* so that he *yell*-ers, why, I shouldn't wonder if he doesn't end up quite *blue*-devilled."

I would have pitched him out for this sally, if it had been my curricle, but just then there was a roar to split the heavens and drive the rain back on high – for here came Cribb the Champion, doffing his hat to the crowd before dropping it quietly over the rope and going off in turn. "Cheer, boys, cheer!" cries Jerry. "We must hollo ourselves *dry* in honour of the Bristol Achilles, the famed Black

166

Diamond, ere he does battle with the dusky Roscius for the honour of Old England – and afterwards we'll *wet* our whistles in celebration!''

But nothing exceeded the acclaim which was to follow, the band striking up ''Yankee Doodle'' and ''Heart of Oak'' as the two heroes stood forth, stripped for the fray, and approached the scales together, Cribb a half-head taller than his opponent, stalwart and erect, his body white as snow, Molineaux glistening black in the rain, the drops hanging on his woolly head like dew on a hedge – oh, never was there anything so fine, and I thought to myself, let Vicesimus Knox* flog me to death for this lark, or expel me to the moon, I don't care, for I'd not be elsewhere now for all the treasures of Arabia, and never, never shall I forget what these old eyes, that were once a wondering schoolboy's, saw that day, with twenty thousand voices ringing in my ears as the white man and the black stood up together before the finest, noblest, bravest mill of them all . . .

* The Rev. Vicesimus Knox (1752–1821) was headmaster of Tonbridge School from 1778 to 1812.

PADDINGTON JONES, *resumed*

My one fear that day, sir, was the weather. It was starvation bitter and the rain lashing, which could not ha' been fouler for Tom. I chafed and rubbed him and clapped on the oil, and muffled him in a greatcoat when they went out to the scales, but even so he was shivering and hissed between his teeth. "Ah's 'bout froze, Pad," says he, and I set him to skip and slap while they put Cribb on the scale.

"Fourteen stone, three pounds!" cries Jackson, and as he stood up they put the rule on him. "Five feet ten and one half inches!"

"Too heavy by a stone," mutters Bill Richmond. "And in the wrong place, thank God! Look at his waist, Pad!" And sure enough there was a lip of flesh where he ought to been trim, sure sign that he'd shirked in training. He looked well for all that, easy on his feet and his skin like silk; I never see Cribb stripped but my heart came into my mouth.

Tom took the scale at fourteen stone two, and there was laughter when they measured his height, for there was two inches of black curls on his nob, which made him seem taller than his five foot eight and a quarter. "God, if we could only ha' taken another eight pounds off o' him!" groans Bill, but I didn't mind that, for being shorter he was more compacted than Cribb, and when I gave him a last chafing my heart settled again, for it were like rubbing black marble, and I could feel him quivering to be off.

"Take your corners!" says Jackson. "Four to one Cribb!" yells a leg, "Five to two the Champion within the quarter!" roars another, "God bless ye, Tom!" says Richmond, the mob set up a great blast of noise, and I slipped inside the ropes and knelt to make a knee. Tom sat upon it, staring across the ring, where Joe Ward was doing the like for the Champion. Cribb looked back and gave Tom a little nod, and I felt him start ever so slightly on my knee, but when I touched his pulse 'twas steady.

Jackson had read over the rules to them under shelter, so now he

168

beckoned 'em up to the mark, and the shouting swelled to a great roar as Cribb stepped forward.

"Tom," says I, "this is what ye came from America for. Go and take it, lad." I'd thought hard what to say, sir, what advice would be best at the very last, and them was the words that came out. He came off my knee and stepped to the mark, and Jackson brought 'em face to face. Cribb still looked calm enough, but Tom's face was like a mask. They shook hands, and my innards gave a leap as I saw what no one had given a thought to – that Tom's reach was a good two inches shorter than the Champion's.

"Are you ready, Sir Thomas?" calls Jackson, and Apreece looked at his repeater and cried: "Time!"

HENRY DOWNES MILES,
editor of Pugilistica *and*
PIERCE EGAN, *author of* Boxiana

ROUND 1. The combatants put themselves in attitude, eyeing each other with the most penetrating looks. For a moment a solemn pause ensued. A little sparring, and Molineaux put in a right-handed body blow. Cribb smartly returned right and left on the head, and one for luck on the body. Molineaux closed and Cribb threw him.

ROUND 2. A furious rally, heavy blows exchanged. Cribb's did most execution, being thrown straight forward, while Molineaux struck with astonishing power, but little judgment. Cribb planted a tremendous blow over his adversary's right eyebrow, but which did not knock him down, he only staggered a few paces. Cribb shewed the most science, although he received a dreadful blow on the mouth, and exhibited the first signs of *claret*. 4 to 1 Cribb.

ROUND 3. Sparring. Molineaux attempted a blow on Cribb's nob, but the Champion parried it, and returned a right-handed hit under the Moor's lower ribs that laid him on the earth. Still 4 to 1.

ROUND 4. Molineaux rallied, when the Champion delivered a severe hit on the face that levelled him, the ground being wet and slippery.

ROUND 5. An excellent round, both rallied in great style. Molineaux's blows were short, Cribb returned with spirit, but the Moor knocked them off. A rally at half-arm followed. Desperate milling for half a minute. They closed, and Molineaux fibbed very dexterously in Dutch Sam's style, but at length fell. The Knowing Ones were lost for the moment, and no bets were offered.

ROUND 6. The Moor planted a blow upon the nob of the Champion, who fell from the bad state of the ground.

ROUND 7. Molineaux rushed in, and Cribb put in a violent blow to the forehead by which he picked up a handsome "rainbow" and went down.

ROUND 8. Both had been taught discrimination and discovered each other's powers. Cribb found that his notion of beating Molineaux off hand was truly fallacious; he was mistaken in his ideas of the Black's capabilities who rallied in prime twig, notwithstanding the severe left-handed hits which were planted on his nob. Cribb began to adopt his famous retreating system. The men rallied desperately. Molineaux fell, but Cribb appeared weaker than his opponent.

ROUND 9. Gallantly contested. The battle had arrived at that doubtful state that the betters were puzzled. Molineaux gave such proofs of gluttony that 4 to 1 now made many tremble that had sported it. Both appeared dreadfully punished; Cribb's head was terribly swelled on the left side. Molineaux's nob was also much worse. On Cribb's displaying weakness, the *flash-side* were full of palpitations. Molineaux rallied, bored in, and by a strong blow through the Champion's guard brought him down, evidently much exhausted. The Knowing Ones looked queer; Cribb had been fighting too fast. Spectators, panic-struck, began hastily to *hedge-off* while others better informed still placed their confidence in Cribb.

ROUND 10. The conceit by this time was tolerably taken out of both combatants; their faces were hideously disfigured. Molineaux bored his opponent to various parts of the ring. Cribb kept knocking the Moor about the head, but he seemed to disregard it. For full two minutes hits were exchanged, greatly to the disadvantage of Cribb. They both went down.

ROUND 11. Courageously contested. Molineaux brought Cribb down.

ROUND 12. Cribb put in a severe hit on the body. Molineaux returned on the head and fell.

ROUND 13. Molineaux received a severe facer from Cribb, but went down from the force of his own blow. 6 to 4 Molineaux.

ROUND 14. The Moor went furiously in. The Champion was levelled.

ROUND 15. Cribb planted a blow over the guard of the Moor, which occasioned a most determined rally, no shifting, but giving and taking till Molineaux was knocked down from a hit on the throat.

ROUND 16. Rallying, but Molineaux went down from fatigue. Evens.

ROUND 17. Cribb still continued his shy plan. Molineaux evidently had the advantage and not only gave Cribb a desperate fall, but fell upon him. Betting very shy, anybody's battle.

ROUND 18. The Champion planted a severe blow on the body. Molineaux returned a hit on the Champion's head, who hit the Moor off his legs but fell from his own blow. Both exhausted.

ROUND 19. To distinguish the combatants by their features would have been impossible. It was astonishing, the determined manner in which these heroes met – Cribb, acting on the defensive, was got by Molineaux against the ropes with both his hands, and held Cribb so that he could neither make a hit nor fall. While the seconds were discussing the propriety of separating them, which the umpires thought could not be done till one of the men were down, about two hundred persons rushed from the outer ring, and it is asserted if one of the Moor's fingers was not broken, it was much injured by some of them attempting to remove his hand from the ropes.

All this time Molineaux was gaining his wind by laying his head on Cribb's breast, and refusing to release his victim; when the Champion by a desperate effort to extricate himself was run down to a corner, and Molineaux having got his head under his arm, fibbed away most unmercifully, but his strength not being able, it otherwise must have proved fatal to Cribb, who fell from exhaustion and the severe punishment. The bets were now decided that Molineaux would not fight half an hour, that time having expired.

ROUND 20. Molineaux brought down Cribb by boring and hitting.

ROUND 21. Cribb planted two blows on the head, which Molineaux returned and the Champion was thrown. The well-known *bottom* of Cribb induced his friends to back him 6 to 4.

ROUND 22. Of no importance.

ROUND 23. The wind of both appearing somewhat damaged, they sparred. Cribb put in a blow to the left eye, the Moor gave Cribb a severe hit to the body and threw him heavily.

ROUND 24. Molineaux began with considerable spirit. Some hits were exchanged and Cribb was thrown. Betting tolerably even.

ROUND 25. The Champion endeavoured to put in a hit on the left eye, but the Moor warded it off and knocked down Cribb.

ROUND 26. Both trying to recruit wind and strength. The Champion endeavoured to hit the right eye of Molineaux, the left having been darkened, but the Moor warded off the blows with agility and neatness, although he went down from a trifling hit.

ROUND 27. Weakness on both sides, pulling and hauling, both fell.

ROUND 28. Cribb received a leveller, his distance being incorrect.

ROUND 29. Molineaux endeavoured to get Cribb's head under his arm, but failed. Cribb planted a hit on his right eye, knocking him down, his *peeper* materially damaged.

ROUND 30. The skill and bottom of Cribb was never more manifested. Molineaux, with a courage and ferocity unequalled, rising superior to exhaustion, rallied with as much resolution as at the commencement of the fight, his nob defying all the milling it had received, and contending nobly with Cribb right and left, knocking him away, and gallantly concluded the round by throwing the Champion.

ROUND 31. Molineaux threw Cribb, but fell over him and pitched upon his head, which so affected him that he could hardly stand. Richmond prompted him to go on, in hopes of Cribb being exhausted . . .

WILLIAM CROCKFORD,
fishmonger and gambler,
founder of Crockford's gaming club

Lord above, the same old question still – what befell in the thirty-first round, or whichever it was? Why do folk harp on that, as though 'twere in doubt? The facts ain't in dispute. Thousands saw what happened, your humble obedient among 'em – why, the whole world saw, bar Cribb and Molineaux themselves, who couldn't see at all, or hear, or tell what county they were in, even, beat senseless as they were, the Black on his feet and Cribb on his knees. As for Jackson, he was at the eye o' the storm, so to speak, which ain't always the best point of observation. I reckon it was too quick for him to follow. Oh, he was straight, and did what he thought right at the time – but he was wrong. Wrong as could be.

Here's what I saw, and know. The mill had gone both ways the best part of an hour, and how those two were still upon their pins, God alone could tell you. I never saw two men so dead and yet alive, disfigured so bloody you could only tell 'em apart by their skins, and not a hair's breadth to choose between 'em. They were that well matched I could not see a winner, but supposed they might both collapse simultaneous, and neither come to scratch again. The odds had shifted like the wind, mostly favouring Cribb, but that was sentiment only, and by the time I speak of there was no money in sight.

The Black was near blind, and Cribb little better, and if as some think Molineaux was the stronger, he had not strength enough to put his man to sleep, and nothing less would serve, for Cribb would continue while he had breath. They were mauling each other like sleep-walkers, floundering in the mud wi' the rain washing the blood and mire off o' them, and when they closed Molineaux shoved Cribb down and toppled over. The Black was first up, labouring like a

174

drunkard, and Pad Jones had to steer him to his corner. Molineaux was all in, swaying like a tree, but Cribb lay near senseless, wi' one hand pawing at the ropes trying to rise, when Gully and Joe Ward dragged him up on Gully's knee. I was closest to Cribb's corner, and he was gaping like a fish on a slab, with one eye open, but looked not to rise again by my reckoning. Molineaux, I'm told, was weeping as he lay on Jones's knee, and I heard Richmond cry: "No, no, Tom, he's beat! He's beat altogether!" He was pouring the bottle over Molineaux's head with one hand and pointing to Cribb with t'other, while Jones was kneading the Black's calves and pattering in his ear, though I doubt if he heard him.

This, then, was the order of events that followed, and you may take careful note of 'em:

Sir Thomas Apreece called "Time!", signifying the thirty seconds was by, and the men must come to the mark.

Captain Buckley Flashman, whose curricle was one of those forming the outer ring, had stepped down, and I saw him pass close behind the Champion's corner and stoop to say a word in the ear of Joe Ward, who was Cribb's bottle-holder. What it was, I know not, but Joe started up, looking wild.

Bill Richmond dragged the Black from Jones's knee and urged him, stumbling like a cripple, to the mark, crying: "He's beat! Oh, Tom, Tom, stand your ground!"

Cribb heaved up from Gully's knee, and fell full length. He dragged up to his knees, *crawling* towards the mark, with Gully beseeching him to rise.

Joe Ward tumbled through the ropes and ran to the umpires by the mark, where Molineaux stood. He was shouting (tho' I didn't distinguish the words just then) that Molineaux had bullets in his hands. In a moment all was babble, with Richmond calling Ward a liar, Pad Jones capering into the ring with his arms raised, laughing and crying like a mad thing that the Black had won, Jackson was standing a-gape at Ward, then turning to snatch the Black's hands open, which were empty, Apreece was crying: "Time! Time, Jackson!", Jackson gave a shout of fury and thrust Ward away, with Richmond howling abuse – and when Jackson turned back to the mark, Cribb was there, on his feet. Jackson cried: "Set to!" – and so they did.

Richmond was raging like a madman, screaming at the umpires, and at Gully, and at Ward, and two of the vinegars had to pull him from the ring. Jones was at Apreece's ear, shouting and swearing, with Sir Thomas shaking his head like a man helpless.

There you are, then. Those are the facts of the matter, and I never met a witness but agreed with 'em. Here's the marrow of it:

Molineaux came to the mark on the call of "Time!" Cribb did not – until after Joe Ward had bought him precious seconds with his (or Buck Flashman's?) lying tale of slugs in the Black's fists. Jackson was distracted long enough, examining Molineaux's fambles (as he was bound to do) for Cribb to clamber up to scratch. Apreece was crying "Time!" over and over, but what was Jackson to do, with both men at the mark, but bid them set to again and box away?

Nowadays, under the new rules, men have eight seconds to come to scratch after "Time!" is called. Molineaux was there with time in hand, but Cribb wasn't. 'Twas no fault of his, but the plain truth is that Molineaux won that mill in the thirty-first round.

MILES and EGAN, resumed

ROUND 32. Strength was fast leaving both the combatants – they staggered against each other like inebriated men, and fell without exchanging a blow.

ROUND 33. To the astonishment of every spectator, Molineaux rallied with strength enough to bore his man down, but both their hits were of more shew than effect.

ROUND 34. Molineaux had the worst of it. Cribb evidently appeared the best man, and at its conclusion the Moor for the first time complained that "he could fight no more", but his seconds persuaded him to try another round, to which request he acquiesced, when he fell from weakness. Cribb was greatly elated, but was too weak to throw his usual somersault. The contest lasted fifty-five minutes.

Remarks on the fight
by H. D. MILES alone

Molineaux in this contest proved himself as courageous a man as ever an adversary contended with, and Cribb's merits as a pugilist cannot but be enhanced by a victory over so tremendous an opponent. The Black astonished everyone, not only by his extraordinary power of hitting and his gigantic strength, but also by his acquaintance with the science. In the 28th [*sic*] round, after the men were carried to their corners, Cribb was so much exhausted that he could hardly rise from his second's knee at the call of time. Joe Ward, his second, by a little manoeuvering, occupied the attentions of the Black's seconds, and so managed to prolong this period sufficiently to enable the Champion to recover a little, and thus assisted him to pull through.*

---

* It is now impossible to say with certainty in which round this famous early instance of a "long count" took place. Miles in his Remarks says the 28th, but does not even mention rounds 24 to 28 in his running commentary. Egan (a Cribb enthusiast), although he details every round, makes no mention of the incident at all. Another theory is that it happened as early as the 24th, but from the descriptions which both Miles and Egan give of the progressive exhaustion of the fighters, it seems probable that it did not take place before the 30th round at least. That it did happen is not disputed, and while no blame attaches to Cribb or Jackson, it seems clear that Molineaux was robbed, and this was a widely-held opinion at the time.

177

His Royal Highness
GEORGE AUGUSTUS FREDERICK,
Prince of Wales,
later KING GEORGE IV

Molineaux, I maintain, *beat* Cribb! Curse me if he did not!

PADDINGTON JONES, *resumed*

His Royal Highness said that, sir? Then God bless him for an honest man and a true sportsman – aye, and a proper Englishman! Would to God he had been at the ringside, so we might ha' had fair play. I choke to this day when I think on it, and feel the red rage I felt then.

"You, you lousy thieving son of a bitch!" I told Joe Ward. "By God, the difference 'tween you and Dick Turpin is that he wore a mask! You're a damned chousing cheat, and to hell wi' you!"

"On my oath, Pad, Buck Flashman swore he saw you slip the bullets!" cries he.

"You lie, you bastard!" says I, tho' on reflection I'm not sure as he did. "Damn you all to hell, you and Gully and Cribb, for you're the first that ever stole the Championship of England!"

And that was the God's truth, of Ward, anyway, and no doubt Buckley Flashman. They were the cheats, and Cribb had the benefit. Tom Molineaux, my Tom, won the title that day, and all the world saw it, and more than one thought shame for the honour of the game, aye, and more than the game. "A black day for England, this," I heard one say, and another cried: "Bad work, bad work! The black deserved better." There were more'n a few frowns and shaken heads among the Fancy, and voices to echo what you tell me the Prince maintained. Aye, Molineaux *beat* Cribb indeed, damme if he did not.

Some held otherwise, course they did, and you may think, sir, that there was summat in what they said. One Corinthian, I mind, swore that a mill was ended only when one o' the fighters owned himself beat. "The nigger it was who cried enough, not Cribb," says he. "And what o' the rules, sir?" cries another. "Cribb did not answer – nay, *could* not answer – when time was called, and so forfeited the match!" "Come, sir, he answered in the end!" says the first buck. "Would ye strip the man of his laurels for a matter of a few seconds?" "Aye, if he broke the rule!" retorts the other. "Damnation, sir, what are rules for?" A third opined that by the *letter* o' the law it might be said that

179

Molineaux had won, ''but by its *spirit* Cribb was the better man, and I for one am proud of him, begad!''

I reckon that was the general opinion, among the public, who were behind Cribb to a man and not inclined to question the outcome. The professional millers said naught to me, and I didn't ask 'em, but I reckon Big Bob Gregson spoke for more'n a few by what he *did*. He'd wagered a cool thousand guineas on Cribb, but asked only for his stake to be returned: the winnings, sir, he would not touch, and what d'ye make o' that?

At all events, 'twas over and done, and no sense repining, or blaming Jackson, or Apreece, or anyone except those two dirty villains aforementioned. I could ha' swung for the pair of 'em, but, d'ye know, sir, when my first wrath had passed I could find consolation, too. In a few months I'd trained a raw black clown to hold his own – and better! – with the best Champion the game had ever seen. Fair's fair, mind. Cribb was not in primest twig. He'd counted Tom too cheap, wasn't better'n three-quarters trained, and should ha' milled on the retreat earlier than he did. It was the wind and rain that saved him. If Tom had had the sun on his body, Cribb would not have lasted to the half-hour. That boded well for the future; next time, thinks I, we'll meet Master Cribb in summer.

My one fear was that Tom might have been sickened. He'd had the damnedest melting – Egan reckoned it was the bloodiest, cruellest mill that ever was – and I've seen good men spoiled for keeps by less punishment than he'd taken that day. Both his ogles was swollen closed, his nose split in two places, a gash from his lower lip nigh to his chin, one ear part torn away, and the rest of his nob cut and rasped and bloody as raw liver. God, that right hand of Cribb's was a terrible thing! Tom's body was one mighty bruise, but at least no ribs was broke.

'Twas small comfort that Cribb, by what I'd seen, was in no better case. But he had suffered it all afore, and come again; the only way to sicken the Cribbs o' this world is to kill 'em. But Tom I was not sure of, and when we'd cleaned and stitched and tended him and put some soft peck and spirits into him, and settled him on cushions at the inn, and he was in his right mind again, I was all eyes to see how he might be. If he had gone into the blues, and moped silent, as I'd seen so many do, I'd ha' known that here was another promising chicken gone, but God be thanked that was not his sort at all.

Sir, he was like a wild beast! He raved, and whined, and swore, and damned if he didn't pipe his eye, and when he heard the Bristol boys downstairs hurrahing and cheering Cribb, it was all I could do to prevent him having at 'em. "They cheated me! They done robbed me!" bawls he, over and over, and beat his fists that were red raw in their swaddling, and flung himself about so far as he was able, what with his pain. "Ah beat him! Ah beat him! Yuh-all *knows* Ah beat him!" He plumps down in a chair, wi' the tears running down his swollen black face. "Oh, Pad! How c'd they cheat me thataway? Oh, Bill, Ah beat him!"

Richmond hadn't said above six words since the fight, he'd been that heart-sick, but now he was just fagged out and quiet, setting at the table with his hands clasped on the board.

"No, Tom," says he. "You didn't beat him. 'Member I told you, th'only way to do that was to put him cold to sleep."

"He din't come to scratch!" wails Tom. "That sunnabitch Joe Ward bought him time! Ain't that so?"

"'Tis so," says Bill.

"An' Ah had him down more'n a half-minnit! That's the rule, an' he din't make it to time!"

"Maybe not," says Bill, "but then he got up, an' started to fight, like I said he would. He didn't quit." I knew what he was thinking, sir: Tom was the one who'd said he could fight no more.

I guess perhaps Tom knew it, too, for he changed his tack. "'Twarn't *fair*! Ah had cramps wi' the cold, ma laigs wudn't answer! An' they cheated me! Lissen 'em singin' an' rejoicin', the lyin', gammonin', cheatin' bastards! Ah jes' hope they satisfied the way they won – cheatin' me!"

"Guess they are," nods Bill, studying his hands. "But I know one man who ain't . . . an' that's Tom Cribb."

Tom left off sniffing. "Whut you mean?"

Richmond gave him a thoughtful look. "I mean he wants your hide, boy." He let it sink into Tom's mind, and leaned forward across the table. "'Fore today, he didn't reckon you worth a peck o' coon-shit. Well, now he knows better . . . an', boy, he wants you real bad!"

181

You never saw a man's mood change so fast; I could have laughed to see the shades run o'er Tom's phiz – misery, astonishment, and then a great blaze of hope, sir, as if he'd seen a wonder. He almost threw himself at Richmond.

"You mean . . . Ah kin git a re-turn? He fight me agin?" He stared from Bill to me, the joy fair bursting out of him.

"He can't do other," says Bill. "Ain't that so, Pad?"

"The country won't let him," says I. "And he's a proud man, is Tom Çribb. Aye, you lost, Tom, but you gave him such a pasting as he never had before – and he don't like what happened in the thirty-first round any more'n we do. He'll give you a return – and then, watch out!"

Tom gave a great whoop and fell back in his chair, limbs all a-sprawl. He shook his fists, beaming.

"Hallelujah!" roars he. "Oh, great day! When, Bill, when? Oh, Bill, Pad, Ah swear Ah lick him nex' time! Ah *knows* Ah kin, honnist to Jesus! I *knew* it today, when him an' me was out theah! Ah got his measure! Oh, Ah knows how good he is – man, Ah din't think they was such a millin' cove in creation . . . but Ah's bettah! *Ah kin lick him!*"

That was when I knew for certain that we had a real miller on our hands, sir – a match for the Cribb he'd fought that day, and even for the Cribb who would come at him the second time. He'd forgot his hurts, his disappointment, and his rage all in a trice, so full of joy was he – at the prospect of doing it all over again! But, bless you, every good pug is dicked in the nob, or he'd not be a pug in the first place.

Even Bill had it in him to smile at so much eagerness. "Yes, you can lick him. You did . . . for a while. An' maybe Tom Cribb taught you sump'n today . . . what makes a champion, more'n any skill or strength or speed. Yes, sir – how to get up again. That's what you got to do now, the sooner the better. Moment we're back in Town, you'll write a challenge in the press."

Tom's face fell again. "You know Ah cain't write!"

"I can," says Bill, "and Pierce Egan'll do the flowery bits. You can make your mark . . . and then, Tom, my boy, you can learn to be a slave again, with Paddington Jones as your task-master!"

TOM MOLINEAUX, *pugilist*

To Mr Thomas Cribb, St Martin's Street, Leicester Square,
December 21, 1810

Sir,

My friends think that had the weather on last Tuesday, the
day on which I contended with you, not been so unfavour-
able, I should have won the battle; I therefore challenge
you to a second meeting, at any time within two months,
for such sum as those gentlemen who place confidence in
me may be pleased to arrange.

As it is possible this letter may meet the public eye, I
cannot omit the opportunity of expressing a confident hope,
that the circumstance of my being of a different colour to
that of a people amongst whom I have sought protection,
will not in any way operate to my prejudice.

I am, sir,
Your most obedient humble servant,

T. MOLINEAUX

BOB GREGSON,

championship contender, publican,
poet, and match-maker

Ha-ha! Aye, Cribb showed us the black's letter, asked us what it might mean. "It means tha'd best get thasel' fit, man!" I told him. "Did I not warn thee what'd coom on't if ye met the nigger half-trained? Man, ye were fatter'n a pregnant pig, and think thasel' lucky he did not flatten thee! He's a canny miller, the same feller, an' if tha's not doon to thirteen stone when ye coom to scratch wi' him again, God help thee. I lost a good thoosand guineas as I'd ha' won but for thy guzzlin', ye big-bellied booger! Fat, man - I say ye were fat!"

"I hear ye!" snaps he, short as ever. "But what's his 'different colour' to do wi' me?"

"Nowt," says I. "That's to the Fancy's address, man, not thine. He's tellin' 'em, polite-like, that he doesna want 'em cryin' 'Away, ye black bastard!' when he gits in't ring. But what noo, Tom? Wilt put thasel' in trim, an' meet him again?"

"I will, tho' I'd as soon not," says he, scratchin' at the stitches on his clock – man, ye'd ha' thowt he'd been shaved by a barber's drunk 'prentice. "That black's a fibber," says he. "It were a dear-bought three hundred quid. Nay, I grow old, Bob. Win or lose, 'twill be my last mill."

"Git oot, man, is that the way to talk? 'Me last mill', as tho' ye were sixty! Ye're but a lad yet," says I, "an' look ye here, Tom Cribb – git thasel' in fettle, an' the black'll not stand twenty minutes wi' thee, good miller an' all as he is! What? Git tha head up, man! We're coontin' on thee!"

"I'll never quit to him, at all events," says he, and that was a' I could get from him. Mind you, he was ever a quiet 'un, was Tom, but ye'd ha' looked for more spirit in him, would ye not, an' a sharp answer to the nigger's challenge? Nay, but he hung back on that,

184

turned a stopped lug to a' inquiries, and put it aboot that he'd no inclination to fight! I wondered at the man – aye, and if the larrupin' at Copthorn had given him his fill. God knows he'd got no profit from it, while the black had larned wi' every blow. And tho' he'd been beat, Molineaux was the cocksurest dandyprat still.

'Twas aboot six weeks after Copthorn that the patrons gi'ed Cribb a benefit at Fives Court. The whole Fancy was theer, three thoosand on 'em, young Queensberry, Sefton and Craven and them, a' the top millers, Cribb his sel', and Power and Richmond and Tom Belcher (but not Jem, who had fell oot wi' Cribb) and Jones and Ben Burn and Cropley and Mendoza and O'Donnell . . . oh, aye, and Molineaux, a' sauce and swagger. He was figged oot like a May Day cuddy, wi' a collar that high his chin was wheer his neb should ha' been, silk coat, roofles, a lace hanky in's cuff, and mair rings than a Haymarket hoor. Aye, and scented, an a'.

But this was the thing – ye'd ha' thought from his gait that Copthorn had never happened, or, if it had, that he'd won it! It was: "Ah! How-de-do, Mistah Cribb!", wi' a lordly smile and compliments on his benefit, and a few pleasantries aboot their mill – but not a word o' Joe Ward's antics, no 'plaints, and never a mention o' his challenge that still waited an answer. Talk aboot genteel; ye'd ha' thought he was the Duke o' Clarence.

Cribb spoke him civil and steady as ever, but 'twas the black that had the ease and settled way wi' him. I tell thee, viewin' the pair o' them, ye'd ha' said from his airs 'twas Molineaux was the Champion.

He acted it on't stage, and a', when he had the mufflers on wi' young Tom Belcher, laughin' and sparrin' at half-pace – and, man, even at that he fair danced him dizzy. Tom Belcher, ye know, took ower my chophouse afore I went to Ireland, and was used to say that in twenty year o' prize-fightin', he'd never been so foundered as in that brief breather wi' the black, "for I swear, Bob, I did not touch him above twice, and his left played rat-a-tat-tat on my nob like a woodpecker, as he chose."

Now, it happened that day I'd brought forrard a young feller, Rimmer, that I had an interest in, him being Northcoontry like mesel'. He made a good figure at the benefit, sparrin' wi' Cropley, and the

Fancy swore he were a prime chicken. Well, by and by up to me comes Bill Richmond, and after a bit crack he asked, had I a match in mind for the boy? Hollo, thinks I, what's i' the wind here? I said, maybe aye, maybe no, and what was't to him?

"Would ye have him go 'gainst Molineaux, mebbe?" says Bill.

"What the hell are ye talkin' aboot, man?" says I. "Thy lad's lookin' for a return wi' Cribb!"

"I'm weary waitin' on Cribb," says he. "He don't answer, and my Tom's gettin' stale. I want to keep him sharp, and seems to me Rimmer'd be a match, while Cribb's makin' up his mind."

"Coom up, Bill," says I, "that's a reet Banbury tale!" For who that had a challenge laid wi' the Champion would bother wi' a novice? "Are ye scorched, or what?" Ye see, I'd heerd word that Richmond had plunged at Copthorn, and his pockets was to let.

"Never mind that," says he. "Well, truth is we're bound to meet Cribb wi'in two months of acceptance, and blow me if I want to see Tom fight him in the month o' March—'twill be bitter cold as December, likely! But if you'll make us a match wi' Rimmer *afore* Cribb answers, why, when he does we can postpone legitimate and Tom can fight Cribb in summer. What say, Bob?"

He was a reet fly 'un, was he not? Well, 'twas good sense for him – and good business for me. Match-makin' was ever my game, and 'twould be a grand advance for young Rimmer to fight Molineaux, whose name was on every lip. Mind you, the black would mill him fra Hell to Huddersfield, but what o' that? The lad had his name to make, and he'd go broody on me if I denied him a tilt at the man who'd gone thurty roonds wi' the Champion. Aye, and the green fairy circle's a chancy place: many a novice has upset the odds, and young Rimmer might be one o' the lucky 'uns.

"What does Pad Jones think?" says I.

"When I want to know, I'll ask him," says Richmond, mighty short – and I wondered at that, and a'.

'Canst stand good for a hoondred guineas a side?" I asked him, and he swore he'd raise the wind, so we shook hands on't then and theer, and when I told Rimmer he danced on his hat for joy.

I wondered how Cribb might take it, but it made no matter to him. He cared not tuppence when he fought the black, or if he ne'er fought

him at a'; he was content to let the challenge lie until after Molineaux
had met Rimmer. Aye, and Richmond was in no haste now that he'd
put Cribb off 'til summer; May, says he, would be soon enough for
the mill wi' my lad – as I'd suspicioned, he *was* short o' brass, and
worse, he was in debt to the Land o' Judah, and vexed how to clear
himsel'. 'Twas rumoured that even the Prad and Swimmer was poult-
iced, but I know nowt o' that.

So what does he do but take the black to tour the country, wi'
exhibitions o' the Manly Art, and sparrin' matches, and showin' his
man off to the gapeseeds at markets and holidays for a tanner a time.
Molineaux was a canny wrestler as well as a miller, and there was no
lack o' farm loons and sojers and daft hicks eager to try a fall or put on't
mufflers wi' the famous blackamoor. 'Twas easy fare for Molineaux to
topple 'em, tho' for the most part I reckon they was satisfied to see
him strike a pose, bare to the brisket, for the half o' them had never
seen a nigger afore.

Now, this way o' goin' on was weel enough to get them a livin' and
steer Richmond clear o' Point Nonplus, wi' a dollop put by for the
Rimmer stake and expenses – but 'twas no life for a fighter, I can tell
thee. He needs to be settled, man, and reg'lar, and kept hard at the bit in
trainin'. They say Molineaux had been bad enough to manage afore, but
from a' I heerd he was ten times worse on that tour, traipsin' fra toon to
toon, wi' the folk gawkin' at him, and him up to a' larks at a' hours,
seldom sober, beddin' every mollisher that offered, and splashin' his
rhino on fancy toggery and toys and whatever trash took his fancy.

To make bad worse, Pad Jones parted fra him in disgoost at the
way he was kickin' up and wastin' his self, and Richmond not able
to rein him in. By what Pad told me later, Richmond had vowed that
Molineaux would be kept to the collar and no liberties, but when it
came to it, he let the black have his wilful way for fear he'd lose him;
there was high words among the three o' them, and Pad packed his
ditty and bade them fareweel. In his stead, Richmond brought in two
reet flash gills, Abner Gray and Joe Ward – aye, that verra same Joe
Ward that had humbugged Jackson aboot the bullets at Copthorn!
Never ask me how Richmond came to make his peace wi' that 'un,
or coaxed Molineaux into usin' him to spar wi', but so it was. Worse
yoke-fellers for a fighter ye could not find, but they came cheap likely,

and Bill would be coontin' his coppers. I wouldna gi' the reek off my dottle for the pair o' them!

When I heerd o' the way Molineaux was carryin' on wi' the bub and the burricks, and that Pad Jones had washed his hands of him, I says to mesel', Bob, I says, if ye miss this chance ye're a cloot-bobby. Straight I went to Pad and offered him the trainin' o' Rimmer. First off he shook his head, sayin' he didna like.

"What's likin' to do wi' it? Ye trained the black for Richmond, what hinders thee to train Rimmer for me?"

" 'Twould go 'gainst the grain, Bob," says he, doubtful. "If 'twere against any other fighter, I'd say aye and gladly, but not against Tom Molineaux."

"What the hell, man! Are ye feared Molineaux'll leather my chap, is that what ails thee?"

"If he does, and 'tis Lombard Street to a China orange he will," says Pad, " 'twill be because Tom's the fighter *I* made him – and made Champion o' England, if he had his rights. Nay, Bob, how could I train another milling-gloak 'gainst him?"

"Weel, Pad, I thought ye were a professional man," says I. "But since ye've gone soft on the nigger, seemin'ly, we'll say nae mair."

He swore he was not soft, but no turncoat, either – which was a daft start, for in those days milling men were wont to hold the bottle and give the knee against their best friends even, in the way o' business, and no hard feelings. It was the professional way, man, and none knew it better than Pad. I let it lie, while he pulled his lip, considerin', and he hemmed and hawed and then laughed and said, well enough, he'd take charge o' Rimmer. I asked why he laughed, and he said the fact was he couldna abide to be awa' fra the ringside when the black was fightin'. Did ye ever hear the like, eh? "But I'll do my best for your lad, Bob, never doubt it," says he, and gave me his hand. I knew he was straight, and my hopes went cockahoop high, for Rimmer would have the best knee in the game, and one that knew Molineaux like a book.

"Reet, my lad," I told Rimmer, "ye'll be on't road every day by six, get half a stone o' rump inside thee at noon, skip and lift and thresh that bag 'til tha's baked, Pad'll coach and breathe thee reg'lar, and by God we'll startle the nigger yet!" The lad went to work like a navvy, wi' Jack Power the Irish plumber as partner, and wi' Pad's guidance he shaped better'n ever I could ha' hoped. He had a miller's head on him, and was big and strong and speedy, and larned quick. Pad put him up to a' the dodges the black favoured – how he played at the head, so his left must be weel stopped, and that he favoured Mendoza's guard, but lost patience if his man milled on the retreat, and might be weel punished wi' a one-two stomacher, and all o' that.

Aye, Rimmer shaped reet handy, and a few there were who said he had the makin's o' another Jem Belcher. Cribb himsel' came to see him spar, and put the mitts on wi' him, and was weel pleased. Aha, Tom, thinks I, d'ye hope to see Rimmer do thy work for thee? Others wondered, too, and the buzz was that 'twould be grand if Rimmer should be next to bid for the Championship, as must surely follow if he beat Molineaux.

For the black was become badly liked since Copthorn. He was that cocksure and impident, and cut such a figure in his flash duds, and gave offence by his goings on, what wi' the sprees on his coontry jaunt, and he was foreign, and black – and ower a' that, he'd put the fear o' God into the Fancy by his showin' 'gainst Cribb. They dearly hoped that Rimmer might cut his comb for him, and never did a novice get such a cheer as went up fra the ten thoosand at Moulsey Hurst when my lad threw his shap over the ropes on the day.

Molineaux, for a' the lush and trollops he'd been trainin' on, looked better than I liked, bar a bit o' belly on him, and the odds were three to one for him when they went to the scales. Richmond and Bill Gibbons 'tended him, and didna Richmond glower when Pad Jones stepped up as leadin' counsel for Rimmer? Not the black, though; he laughed and clapped Pad on the back, and bade him tell Rimmer to watch oot for his left hand.

Aye, weel, we live and larn. For a' the good Pad's trainin' and advice was, Rimmer might as well ha' had Boney's mother in his corner. I saw my hoondred guineas fly awa' in the furst roond, when Molineaux saunters oot on his heels, smilin' and sparrin' easy, 'ticed my lad to let go wi' both hands, and flattened him wi' that same left. Four to one, and they'd barely set to when Molineaux put in left and right, and doon goes Rimmer a second time. And then a thurd, and a fourth, and damn my skin, the same tale for eight roonds. The boy made play game enough, but knew no more o' distance than a blin' beggar, while Molineaux stood off laughin' at him, made his stops as though he were pattin' flies awa', grinned a' ower his ugly black dial as he picked his marks, and when he struck, Rimmer went doon like a man shot.

By God, it galled the crowd, the way yon nigger strutted and smiled and tret the lad like a clodpole. There wasna a sound bar a groan whenever Rimmer went to grass, and wi' a bare ten minutes run he was a woeful sight, spoutin' claret like a cloudburst and fair dozzened by the hammerin'. I doot if any but Jones could ha' kept him on his gams, but after the eighth he shook his head at me. "The boy's foundered," says he. "I can do naught for him."

I asked Rimmer would he give up, and damme if he didna rally and rattle the nigger's nob, and milled him back, but Blackee weathered it, fibbed him doon yet again, and then set oot to pay him back. I never saw such savage millin', for noo Molineaux stretched himsel' and went after Rimmer like a tiger, fibbin' him a' roond the ring, feet and fists flyin' too fast to follow. Man, he was a grand miller, the black! Rimmer was game, but the crowd thought nowt o' him, but gave a' their voice in yells and curses and threats at Molineaux, shakin' their clubs and sticks, and I heered Cribb tell Baldwin, who had charge o' the vinegars, to look to the outer ring. The nigger never heeded the cat-calls, but floored Rimmer twice again, wi' the mob uglier by the minute, and when the lad, half-gone and oot o' his wits wi' pain, wrestled him Lancashire style below the waist and threw him foul, there was sic a hollerin' cheer that the umpires darsn't say bo! Again Molineaux floored him, again Rimmer threw him foul, and now I saw the black set himsel' to finish it for good and a' . . .

190

PIERCE EGAN, *interpolated*

... It was *all up* with Rimmer, who retreated to every part of the ring, closely followed by Molineaux, who put in a dreadful stomacher, which *floored* him. A scene now took place which beggared all description, during [which] Rimmer lay prostrate on the ground, the ring was broken, owing, it is said, from the antipathy felt against a *man of colour* proving the conqueror – if it was so, the illiberal were disappointed by this manoeuvre, as those who had taken the odds gained nothing by the event. Rimmer was completely exhausted, almost in a state of insensibility. It would have been a fine subject for the pencil of Hogarth to have delineated – here were *Corinthians* and *Coster-mongers* in rude contact; *Johnny-Raws* and first-rate *Swells* jostling each other; Pugilists and *Novices*, all jawing, threatening, but no hearing – the confusion was beyond every thing, sticks and whips at work in all directions, ten thousand people in one rude commotion, and those persons in the interior of this vast assemblage suffering from their attempts to extricate themselves from so perilous and unpleasant a situation. Twenty minutes elapsed in this *chaotic* manner, till the Champion of England, assisted by some brave fellows, once more formed something like a ring. Molineaux and Rimmer again *set to*, but it proved a short-lived advantage to the latter, notwithstanding extraordinary exertions were made to renovate Rimmer, to make him stand upon his legs. It was all in vain, during six more rounds Rimmer was so severely *punished* as to be unable to stand up, when he acknowledged he had received *enough*!

BOB GREGSON, *resumed*

So that was that, and that was a' – and enough, I'll tell thee! It was a lesson to me. I should never ha' made the match, for it broke the boy, and he ne'er fought again that I heerd on. But man, how was I to knaw that I was pittin' him 'gainst a miller that the best on God's earth couldna ha' stood up to, let alone a green lad? I tell thee straight, if Molineaux had fought like yon at Copthorn, we'd ha' had a black champion of England. Now, then! I said as much to Cribb, and a', and he gi'ed us his nod, solemn like, and says: "Aye, like enough . . . if I'd let him."

I'll tell thee summat else. Cribb saved the nigger's life that day at Moulsey, when they broke the ring. Man, they'd ha' killed him, for they were run mad wi' rage, hollerin' to be at him wi' sticks and clubs and owt they could lay hand on, and umpires and seconds and a' swept aside, and the poor bloody darkie kicked and trampled nigh to bits 'til Cribb and the vinegars threw back the press and dragged him clear! Pad Jones reckoned Cribb levelled more fellers that day than in a' his mills put together.

Aye, weel, we live and larn. Two hoondred quid that mill cost us, 'tween the stake and the blunt I was daft enough to wager on Rimmer. A' the benefit I had was the privilege o' watching Molineaux at work; he was a canny fibber. Mind you, if I'd been Cribb I'd ha' let 'em stamp the black booger six feet oonder.

Captain ROBERT BARCLAY ALLARDICE,
late 23rd Foot,
pedestrian, landowner, and agriculturalist

Sir,

I had not intended to reply to yours of the 15th, which on immediate perusal I was inclined to dismiss as an unwarranted impertinence unworthy of notice. On reflection, however, it seems possible that you may have addressed me without intent to offend, since the aspersions on my character which your letter contains are not your own, but those of others, and that your repetition of their slanders, however insolent in itself, may have had the not unworthy object of inviting me to refute them. The question remains open in my mind, but I give you the benefit of the doubt for the time being, and I shall avail myself of the opportunity to rebut calumny and at the same time satisfy your other inquiries which by their nature suggest that you may be an earnest if importunate seeker after truth rather than a mere echo of scandalous gossip.

I must warn you, however, that any publication outwith this present correspondence of the defamatory matter to which you have referred, will meet with a prompt response. I allude not to redress at law, in which personal experience leads me to repose no confidence, but to certain facts anent myself to which you have made adversion in your letter – viz., that in my youth I was accounted the foremost amateur practitioner of the pugilistic art, that I was known to perform the feat of lifting with one hand an eighteen-stone man from the floor to a table, and that I pursued a course of exercise and diet designed to promote a health and vigour which, I am happy to say, I retain even in my advancing years. Sir, you have been warned.

I proceed now to the statements which you attribute to Mr Charles Wheeler and an unnamed other party, touching my spar with Molineaux the prize-fighter at Jackson's Rooms in the summer of the year 1810. They say: "Barclay never forgave the nigger for beating him, and this, Mr Charles Wheeler, who knows Barclay well, assures me was the reason why the Captain took such an interest in Cribb's second match with the black and offered to train Cribb at his own expense."

That, sir, is a disgraceful falsehood. I bore no grudge to Molineaux, indeed, I held him in esteem *as a pugilist* whose ability marked him as worthy of the highest honours of his profession, and my motives in training and sponsoring Cribb were in no way whatever influenced by any emotion of rancour towards his opponent. My interest in Cribb had been kindled years before Molineaux's arrival in England, and in training him for the bout referred to I was but continuing the policy begun when he was first brought to my notice by Mr Jackson, when I sponsored, trained, and backed him for 200 guineas in his victorious match against Jem Belcher. It will not, I think, appear strange that having trained and sponsored a fighter to the Championship of England, I should be moved by interest and friendship to assist him again when his laurels were in danger from an adversary whose formidable powers all acknowledged, but the suggestion that I did so from feelings of spite and ill-will towards that adversary is beneath contempt and merely dishonours him who makes it.

One word more, and I have done with this distasteful topic. It has been supposed by the ignorant mass who imagine their own prejudices to be universal, that the determination with which my principal and I laboured to resist Molineaux's challenge sprang in part from an aversion to his colour. That, too, is utterly false. It has been truly said of Thomas Cribb that an opponent's colour or country made no difference to him. I may say of myself that had Molineaux been an Esquimaux or a Tartar, a Prussian or even a Frenchman, my feeling towards him would not have been altered by one iota from what it was. That I was concerned to keep the Championship out of a *foreign* grasp I am proud to acknowledge; that I was concerned to keep it out of a *black* grasp I most emphatically deny. That many of the public did not partake of my sentiments is true, alas, and a blot on our national escutcheon. That they *were* shared by the race of pugilists, who welcomed the Black American among them, and thought of him as one of themselves, is manifest, and found expression in one of many patriotic chaunts sung at Bob's Chophouse and those other houses of good fellowship where the milling professionals were wont to foregather. I quote it with apologies for its poetic shortcomings, but pride in its sentiments:

> Since boxing is a manly game
> And Britons' recreation,
> By boxing we will raise our fame
> 'Bove any other nation.

> If Boney doubt it, let him come
> And try with Cribb a round;
> And Cribb shall beat him like a drum,
> And make his carcase sound.

> Mendoza, Gully, MOLINEAUX,
> Each nature's weapon wield,
> Who each at Boney would stand true,
> And never to him yield.

I believe, sir, that his fellow pugilists' regard for Thomas Molineaux needs no other endorsement, and the association of his name with three of the worthiest Champions is ample testimony to his stature in the annals of the Prize Ring.

Now, sir, the particulars which you seek of my preparation of Cribb for his second bout with Molineaux might have been obtained without inconvenience from the work on Pedestrianism and Training by my friend and neighbour, Mr Thom, of Aberdeen, in which I assisted. However, to avoid any possibility of error leading to misinterpretation on your part, I summarise them herewith, commencing with an observation on the character of the Champion.

Cribb, on my first acquaintance with him in the year 1806, was in his twenty-sixth year, and endowed with such natural ability as to arouse peculiar interest in me. He possessed every attribute of the expert pugilist, save one. Being of a genial, quiet, and indolent nature, he had a deep aversion to that strenuous exercise essential to any person who aspires to success in the prize ring. In short, *he would not train*, being content to rely on his great scientific powers alone, and frequently pitted himself against the foremost and thoroughly trained opponents while himself in an ill-prepared condition, overweight, and in poor temper both mental and physical. On the occasion of his only defeat, by Nicholls, it is stated on good authority that Cribb came to the contest in a state of inebriation, which may well be true, for his easy-going and generous nature led him into companionable indulgence, and this failing, so fatal to any sportsman, but to a pugilist above all, was one which I was at pains to correct. Even then, his habitual resistance to a proper course of exercise, diet, and practice came near to being his downfall, as in his matches against Pigg and Gregson, in both of which he was entirely exhausted, and triumphed only through that indomitable refusal to surrender which endeared him to the public at large even more than did that pugilistic genius which (I believe) was born in him to a greater degree than in any professional fighter before or since.

His condition in his first encounter with Molineaux, for which I was not responsible (being occupied by military duties as aide to Lord Huntly) was far from satisfactory. He was too heavy and sluggish against a most dangerous opponent whom he had manifestly undervalued, whose one shortcoming was want of experience, and whose strength and skill on the occasion were hardly, if at all, inferior to his own. It was evident that only by subjecting himself to the most rigorous preparation could the Champion hope to withstand his redoubtable challenger when their struggle was resumed in circumstances which must necessarily be more favourable to the American by virtue of his youth, anticipated improvement in skill, a less inhospitable climate, and, perhaps more than all the rest, the confidence accruing from his admirable showing on their first encounter.

I therefore began by removing Cribb from London, where the crowded confinement of the city and its unwholesome air had combined with his slothful and irregular mode of living and the influence of boon companions, to render him corpulent, big-bellied, full of gross humours, and short-breathed. When he arrived at my seat near Stonehaven, Kincardineshire, he weighed full sixteen stone and could walk ten miles only with difficulty. I prescribed a diet of beef, mutton, strong beer, stale bread, and Glauber salts, with a strict prohibition of butter, cheese, eggs, and fish, and subjected him to a course of physic, consisting of three doses, but did not yet commence his sweats. For recreation he walked about as he pleased, and spent many hours strolling the woods and plantations with a fowling piece; the reports of his gun resounded every where through the groves and hollows of that delightful place, to the great terror of the magpies and wood pigeons.

After amusing himself in this way for about a fortnight, in which he became accustomed to his diet, the absence of domestic comforts, and the discipline of regular hours, he commenced his regular walking exercise, which at first was about ten or twelve miles a day, increasing to eighteen or twenty. At first he was strongly disinclined to march such distances, so I took to filling my pockets with pebbles, and when he proved laggard I would pelt his shins severely, which stimulated him to pursue me, vowing revenge, but never able to overtake me. Twice a day, morning and evening, he ran quarter of a mile at the top of his speed,

197

and in consequence of these exercises and the physic his weight was reduced, after five weeks, to fourteen stone and nine pounds. This being still too heavy by a stone and more, I commenced his sweats, walking him under heavy loads of clothing and putting him to lie between feather mattresses. In this way, and with such purges and emetics as were necessary, he was further reduced, over four weeks, to thirteen stone and five pounds, which I determined to be his pitch of condition, beyond which he could not go without weakening.

He was under my care eleven weeks at Ury, from early July until a few days before his second bout with Molineaux in September, with two intervals of a week apiece in which I took him on a course of strong exercise in the Highlands. We walked sixty miles to Mar Lodge, in two days, and I was satisfied that he could have walked as far again without distress. He continued his regular exercises with zest in the splendid surroundings, and I believe his strength and wind were more improved by these Highland journeys than by any other part of his training.

Besides his regular exercise at Ury he was frequently engaged in other rural pursuits, ploughing, pulling carts, and felling trees, which he greatly enjoyed. Of pugilistic practice he had as much as seemed necessary, which was little enough, for once in condition his speed and science were beyond improvement. His hands were truly remarkable, the knuckles having hardened by long use into a sort of carapace with which he could strike the knotted bark from a mature ash tree, which he did once negligently during one of our walks. I forbade any repetition of this extraordinary feat in case of injury. We sparred with the gloves occasionally, and on visits to Stonehaven he gave lessons to the local youths, with whom he became a firm favourite.

On this head I feel bound to own that during our near three months together I conceived an increasing affection for him. He bore my tyranny with great good humour, pebbles and all, and his conduct and demeanour were proof

198

that, contrary to mistaken opinion, professional pugilists are, with a few exceptions, among the most gentle, modest, and good-natured of men. It may be that this becoming tolerance springs from the knowledge of their prowess, or, as I have heard it ventured, that vice and ill feeling have been beaten out of them and remain on the ground with their blood. It is a matter for conjecture, but whatever the cause I can assert that in my experience, "the better the miller, the better the man," and point to Gully, Gregson, Jackson, Mendoza, Jones, Pearce, and many others to establish my case.

Cribb conducted himself with much propriety in Scotland, and showed his humane and charitable disposition on various occasions. I remember, when walking on Union Street in Aberdeen, he was accosted by an old woman in great distress. Her story affected him, and the emotions of his heart became evident in the muscles of his face. He gave her all the silver he had in his pocket, and was rewarded with: "God bless your honour, y'are surely not an orn'ary mon!" She spoke truer than she knew.

Sir, I have allowed myself to be carried beyond the scope of your inquiries. It remains for me to say only that when the period of his training was complete, Cribb was, by his own admission, in the best condition of his life, enjoying good spirits, and confident of success. He weighed thirteen stone and six pounds.

I remain, sir,
Your obedient servant,
Allardice of Ury

PADDINGTON JONES, *resumed*

I'd ha' given the world and every single thing in it, to be by his side when he met Cribb again. That's the lasting sorrow o' my life, sir, and I know it's a selfish one, but what I told Bob Gregson was gospel true: I'd made Tom Molineaux, so far as a trainer ever can make a fighter (for the man must have it within him), and I wanted to share in his glory. That's only human vanity, course it is – but not vanity alone. Truth was I'd put such heart and soul into training him for Copthorn, so much hard graft and hope, so much of my own self, if you follow me, that 'twas almost as if we'd become one, Tom and I. And I knew, when we was choused out o' the fight by those dastard villains, that we'd come again a second time and take what was rightly ours – and 'twould ha' been *my* knee he rested on, and *my* hands to rub his flanks and ease his limbs, and *my* fingers to staunch and close the cuts and anoint the grazes, and *my* words in his ear when he'd fibbed the Champion of England into a blind bloody hulk in the third round . . . but, lo! I was not there, sir, not in his corner, nor within the outer ring, even, but perched on a farm cart where I'd paid a bob for a view, among all the chawbacons who'd never heard o' Pad Jones. That's sinful pride, ain't it, though? But you understand my feelings, I know.

I'd no one to blame but myself, mind. 'Twas I threw in my hand and left him, at Bedford, I think it was. Bob Gregson has told you how and why. Bill Richmond had sworn that there would be an end to Tom's slack ways, that he would buckle to training and leave off the daffy and doxies and stuffing and riotous living that had so spoiled his condition afore Copthorn – but he did not keep his word, sir. I would have had Tom back at the Nag and Blower, under my eye, training hard, but Bill it was who said we must take to the road with him. I was dead against it, sir, but Bill needed the dibs, and was sure the country air must benefit Tom, and what should hinder my keeping him in trim on tour as easy as in Town?

Fine talk, sir, and all gammon. We had not been on the road a week when the great black simpleton was at his tricks again, lushy drunk and skirt-smit, gorging as he pleased, and a stone heavier. I'll not weary you wi' the tale of it, save to say that it got worse wi' each town we visited: Tom the idol o' the mob, grinning like an actor, swallowing flattery and liquor by the gallon, ogling the drabs, and abed until noon. I reasoned with him, sir, I begged him, but 'twas no go. His reply was ever the same:

"Ah whupped Cribb once, Ah whup him agin. By'n' by, Ah train down good, like Ah did befo'. Git my weight below fo'teen – but, Pad, ain't no sense to doin' it *now*. You want me trained *off* an' weak?"

"I want ye fit to fight Rimmer," says I, for that match had been made, "and that you'll not be, the way you go on!"

"Oh, pore ole Pad!" cries he, grinning and cuffing at me in play. "All a-worried 'cos Ah's 'joyin' maself! Why, Rimmer ain't but a Johnny Raw! Ah trim him up wi' one hand – an' *then* we get ready for Massa Cribb, ho-ho, fee-fie-fo-fum! An' if Ah has me a li'l fun wi' the gals, whut's to matter? Had me plenny 'fore Copthorn, din't Ah – an' Ah was in's goodish trim as Cribb, weren't Ah?"

"Aye – and lost, blast your black ignorance!" cries I. "If ye'd ha' heeded me ye'd ha' been a stone lighter and a foot faster, and had him beat in twenty minutes! And been Champion this moment – wi' *Cribb* beggin' for the return!" But 'twas like arguing wi' a kid, sir, a great heedless babby.

Only once I thought to win him to a better course, and that was after Jem Belcher's funeral. Poor Jem had been as good as the best, but the loss of his peeper put paid to that, and he'd been only the ghost of his self since Cribb beat him the second time. They reckon his health was broke by the month he spent in limbo at Horsemonger Lane after that mill, which the beaks held to be a breach o' the peace, and clapped him up. Consequently he grew morose, and business at his crib in Frith Street fell away, folk being disinclined to take their wets from a blue-devilled landlord. They say he died of an ulcer on the liver, but I reckon 'twas an ulcer o' the heart. He was only thirty years old.

We were bound to leave off our tour and come to Town to see him laid away, for all the Fancy turned out, pugs and amateurs. We three rode with Gregson and Ikey Bittoon in the second coach – four coaches there were, one of 'em glass, a mute wi' a plume o' black feathers before the hearse, and such a crush at Mary-le-Bone we could not have come to the grave if Big Bob and Bittoon had not cleared a path, Ikey heaving the files aside crying "Make vay, you heathens!" and blubbing like a skirt. He was not alone, sir; many a pug piped his eye to see such a Champion as Jem filled in at last. He was Jack Slack's grandson, sir, did you know?*

Tom was quite knocked over, and wept floods, not that he'd known Jem long, but the occasion was such as he was not accustomed to, and it being so solemn put him in awe. "Po' feller, po' ole feller!" he kept saying, and asked me how Jem had come to hop the twig so young. I told him it came of not keeping himself in trim, what with daffy and late hours and not minding exercise and diet, and Tom's eyes fair started from his head.

"Pad," says he, " 'tis a warnin'," and vowed to live clean henceforth, which he did for the rest o' that Sunday, and went to evening service at St Martin's, too. We were to go down to the country again on the Tuesday, and on the Monday night what does he do but get raging lushy and picked a fight wi' Jack Power for calling him a chimbley-sweep, and they hammered each other half round Leicester Square before Jack cried enough, and then my bold Tom goes off to the theatre wi' *four* bits o' Haymarket ware on his arms, that damned Janey Perkins foremost, and came home in a hurdle half-naked, laughing and bragging how he'd pestered all four, and Janey twice.

I as near threw in my hand then and there, but was prevailed on by Richmond to stay wi' him, and so we set off on our travels again, with Tom promising reformation, and swearing I was the only trainer for him. And I'd ha' stood by him, sir, if only Richmond had backed me, but I soon saw his interest was in the takings from Tom's sparring

---

* Jack Slack, a Norwich butcher, became Champion of England in 1750 when he beat the famous Jack Broughton, codifier of boxing's first laws, inventor of the boxing-glove, and in later years a Yeoman of the Guard. Slack was the central link in a dynasty of great fighters; grandfather to Jem Belcher, he was himself grandson of the "Father of Boxing", James Figg, first Champion of England (1719–34) and the subject of one of Hogarth's finest portraits.

and wrestling shows, while his man went to the devil. "All in good time, Pad," he would say to my protests. "Once he's done Rimmer we'll have the gelt to tide us over, and ye can set to work in earnest. Let him be just now, can't ye? Naggin' can't but distemper him.'

What haunted Bill, you see, was the fear that if Tom was irked he might cast off and find another backer. So he indulged Tom, who became more wayward and insolent by the day. D'ye know, sir, I sometimes believed he was dicked in the nob, the way he went on, as though he were *trying* to ruin his self? And his moods, sir! Why, at Salisbury, where he was sparring wi' all comers for a shilling a time, a blacksmith who was the local terror challenged him to a reg'lar mill for a hundred guineas, which would ha' been the easiest of pickings – and what d'ye suppose Tom did? Locked his self in his room, sir, and would not come out, not for anything! And that against a man he could ha' eaten for supper!

But his drinking and dallying were too much, and at last I could brook no more of it. I had lost count o' the times I'd vowed to quit unless he came to heel, and each time he had played the simple darkie, ever so sorry and please to forgive him, and had wheedled and grinned me into staying, which God knows I wanted to do. But at Bedford, when he rolled in shot at dawn and spewing, wi' a hussy on his arm, and I pitched into him – well, sir, he was too sour and ugly to wheedle, but damned my eyes and told me I might stay or go to Hell as I pleased. Richmond said no word . . . so I went.

Gregson's told you how I thought twice about taking Rimmer in hand, but he ne'er guessed why I accepted. If the boy had had a pauper's chance against Tom, I'd not ha' touched him – what, go to work to smash what I'd been at such pains to build? Never at any price. But I figured I might bring him on sufficient to give Tom a run for his money (for he had the makings of a good heavy man, did young Rimmer) and scare him into sense, maybe. A foolish notion, you may say, but the truth was I wanted Tom to beat Cribb and take that title as I wanted salvation, whether I was in his corner or not. That was why I trained Rimmer.

Well, you know what came of it. Tom was fat, and Tom was sluggish wi' good living, and Tom fought at half-pace, and even so Tom made a damned promising chicken look like an old woman, damned if he didn't! In eight rounds he never broke sweat, until the lad stung him, and then tore the heart out of him with such speed and vicious science – and he terrified that assembly, sir, and for all I know he terrified Cribb, too.

I was blowed if I knew what to make of it. It crossed my mind (as it had crossed it before) that perhaps he knew his business best, and I knew mine not at all, and he could go his own way and half-ruin his self wi' loose-living – and still fight like a Champion. He believed it, and for all that good sense told me different, I could not deny it, not after Copthorn, nor Moulsey Hurst neither. One thing only I was sure of: that if he trained only so much as to give him the wind and legs for twenty rounds, then the Cribb that I knew could not stand against him.

Perhaps Bill Richmond concluded the same, for by all I heard that summer he took no great pains wi' Tom, but was content to have Joe Ward and Abner Gray spar wi' him when they was touring the country, and when they returned to Town 'twas Tom Belcher and Bill Gibbons who saw to his training, such as it was. Cribb was in Barclay's hands in Scotland by then, and you may be sure the rumours flew thick and fast, but 'twas all gas and speculation; never was a mill so talked of, with so little news of the millers. More than once I thought to tool down to the Nag and Blower and offer my service again, but word reached me that I'd have no welcome home from Bill Richmond, so I let it be. But I was sorry, sir, aye, heart-sick sorry, and much regretted my leaving Tom at Bedford, yet consoled myself that I done my duty by him in his beginnings. I could not flatter myself that I had more to teach him, or that my knee would support him better than another when the time came.

PIERCE EGAN, *resumed*

I can't think why you should want to examine me *viva voce*. There's enough spice and colour in my written accounts, surely – you've read my *Boxiana*? Well, then! Points I may have overlooked? Well, I dare say; one can't set down every little thing. Points, eh? Let's see . . . oh, Dick Christian's bit of fun about Marriott and the farmer who wouldn't take a cheque – aye, that was a lark . . . no, I don't believe I ever recorded it. Very good, we'll come to it in due course . . . I'm your man, sir, fire away.

Cribb and Molineaux . . . Molineaux and Cribb . . . the Black Diamond versus the Black Ajax, for the second time. Gad, that was a mill that set the Fancy back on their heels . . . oh, better than the first fight, by far – and *that* had been a historic set-to, if you like. But the second match took our breath away, so sudden, so unexpected, not at all what we had imagined it would be. After the first encounter, no one supposed we should have such a drama again; well, we were out there.

Even as interest in the first bout surpassed anything that had gone before, so with the second it was agreed that there had never been such excitement in the memory of man. Ossa was heaped on Pelion; the country was sated with boxing-mania, and it was *the* event of that year o' grace 1811! Aye, the year the Regency began – and who cared for that when the Championship of England was at stake, with black hands clutching at Britannia's crown? That was the summer when Wellington thrashed the French at Fuentes d'Onoro, and Soult was given his medicine at Albuhera, but neither action could compare with the Battle of Thistleton Gap! The massacre of the Mamelukes was small beer to Barclay's mysterious doings in the Highlands, and Cribb's correspondence with the *Edinburgh Evening Star* over the latter's protest at the sums being wagered on the fight ("Blush, oh Britain!") quite knocked Bolivar and his Dagoes into the shade. The conquest of Java wasn't in it with a squib on the Moor's improving science, I can tell you.

205

I'm sure the wagers far exceeded the betting on Copthorn, and there were some dooced queer ones, like the London baker who backed Cribb with every blessed thing he owned - blunt, personal property, even the lease of his house, seventeen hundred quid's worth — or the two Corinthians whose stake was a new suit of duds, with linen, gloves, walking-stick, and a guinea in the pocket, for the winner.

Well, you may judge the frenzy from the to-do there was over the scene of the bout. You know how down the beaks were on mills, with bailiffs hounding 'em from one county to the next, fighters arrested, and all that rot — not for the Cribb—Molineaux return, though. Why, the corporations of our northern towns were fairly *bidding* for the bout to take place within their bounds, and half the sporting gentry in the shires were offering their private land! The patrons were leery, though, and fixed on Crown Point in Leicestershire, with the ring itself close by at Thistleton Gap, where three counties meet, Leicestershire, Rutland, and Lincolnshire, just to be safe. They needn't have fretted — every magistrate in Rutland was at the ringside, and such a turn-out of the Quality as never was seen: Young Q, Yarmouth, Pomfret, Baynton, Craven, Mellish, God knows who else, and every leading professional in the game, all come, horse, foot, and carriage for the battle of the century, a hundred miles from Town, and no railways in those days!

There wasn't a bed to be had in the three counties the night before; every one had been bespoke days ahead, and the hostelers of Leicester and Oakham and Stamford and Grantham rejoiced. The roads were black with people, thousands on thousands, and every kind of conveyance, on the morning of the fight, and in the press to get to the field no end of trees were broken down and hedges uprooted. It was stiffish country, much of it plough, but the weather was fine and warm which raised the hopes of those with their money on the Moor, who became an object of even greater fear and jealousy to the friends of the Champion.

Dick Christian and I were early on hand, Dick giving me a lift on his mare, and arrived in time for the altercation about where the ring should be. Molineaux's last two fights, with Cribb and Rimmer, had both been interrupted by the crowd breaking the outer ring, so this time there was to be a stage, twenty-five foot, which should serve to keep the mob at bay and give them a better view. They'd picked on a fine piece of stubble, but the farmer wanted fifty quid for it, and wasn't about to accept a cheque. "Oi doan't know 'bout they fancy papers," says he. "Fifty in me 'and, or foight summers else."

"'Pon my word!" cries the commissary-general. "Ain't my sign manual good enough?"

"Good enough for 'ee, milord," says Turvey, "but not for me. Oi doan't know 'ee, do Oi?"

They swore the cash wasn't to be had, in flimsies, it must be a signature to pay.

"Awright," says the stout yeoman, "show me a name as Oi knows," and old George Marriott was found, who knew him, and that was fine.

"Set to, and may the best man win!" cries Turvey, flourishing the cheque. "An' here's my paper as says the nigger'll draw first blood!"

So they set up the stage, with an inner ring to enclose the handlers and Swells (and your humble obedient of the Press) with another beyond for the vinegars. The assembly was now thousands strong, so the first ranks lay down, the next knelt, and the rest stood. Beyond them again were the vehicles of every description, and the horsemen, some astride and others, like Dick Christian, standing on their saddles like so many circus acrobats. I never saw a finer turn-out of the Fancy, from the peer of the realm on the box of his four-in-hand to the rustic in his clouted shoes, the Corinthian with his caped coat and eye-glass and the peasant chewing on his straw, the dandy cavalry officer on his bang-up bit of blood and Old Crocky smiling and nodding among the legs as they bawled their prices – that was sporting England, then, and where has it gone today?

A few minutes after noon there was such a roar went up: "Cribb! Cribb! God bless you, Tom! Huzza for Bristol!" and hats were flying and the whole vast arena rose like a wave as the Champion hove in view and jumped to the stage. He bowed to the spectators and bound his blue ribbons round the palings of the ring, and as Dick says "He was in beautiful condition, fine as a star, just like snow aside a black man." On his heels came Molineaux, vaulting the rails with great spirit, waving and smiling, and getting not a bad greeting, though not so loud as Cribb's. They had weighed before, Cribb at thirteen six, the black at thirteen two, and you should have heard the gasps when the announcement was made, for each was lighter by a stone than in their previous mill.

I was hard beneath the stage, and had the best opportunity for viewing the men and their attendants: big John Gully shedding his coat and talking to Cribb, Joe Ward arranging his bottles – he had been on Molineaux's tour in the spring, but was now returned to his true allegiance; Bill Richmond, frowning and snapping at Gibbons, who bore the bottle for the Moor. "Ah, Pad Jones, where art thou, trainer *par excellence* and second without peer? Africa has disdained thine aid, or so 'tis said by the Knowing Ones at the Fives Court and the sibyls of Randall's Hole-in-the-Wall and Bob's Chophouse."

That tidbit is taken from my notes made by the ringside; fine prose, don't ye know, for those fair readers who are wont to hide loose sheets from *Life in London* inside Paley's Lectures. Where's my old note-book? Ah, here it is, my little reader with impressions from that memorable day. Let's see . . . "Cribb in prime shape . . . trim as a lightweight . . . Barclay withdrawn, thoughtful . . . has reduction in weight impaired Cribb's stamina? . . . Molineaux peels well . . . lighter than expected . . . rather good-looking for a man of colour . . . body of a black Hercules . . . Cribb composed, but M. appears disturbed, walks stage with hasty steps . . . anxiety of multitude beyond description . . . Barclay calls up to the stage, Cribb nods . . . M. shuffles in a little dance, limbering his arms . . . Richmond and Gully bring their men to the mark . . . the umpires confer . . . the white hand and the black clasp in respectful salute . . . silence, forty thousand eyes gaze on the mighty twain . . . they see only each other . . ."

HENRY DOWNES MILES *and* PIERCE EGAN,
resumed

At eighteen minutes after twelve they set to; betting three to one on Cribb, and six to four in his favour for the first knock-down blow.

ROUND 1. Sparring for about a minute, both men wary, when Cribb made play right and left. The right told slightly on the body of Molineaux, who returned lightly on the head. A rally now ensued, but they exchanged their blows at a distance not to do very great execution. Molineaux received a dexterous blow in the throat, which sent him down, but not considered clean.

ROUND 2. The *claret* was perceived to issue first from the mouth of Cribb, Molineaux planting a flush left on setting to. A most terrible rally now ensued by mutual consent, the Champion planted a severe body hit with his right, which Molineaux returned on the head with his left flush. They both fought at half-arm's length, and about six good hits were exchanged with great force, Cribb fibbing at the body, Molineaux punishing his opponent's nob. They closed, and after a severe trial of strength Molineaux threw the Champion heavily. Odds five to two, then six to four on Cribb.

ROUND 3. On setting to it was seen that in the last rally Cribb's right eye was nearly closed, and now another equally sanguinary and ferocious followed, after sparring for wind, in which essential Molineaux was evidently deficient. Cribb put in a dreadful "doubler" on the body of his opponent who, although hit away, kept his legs and renewed the attack with such ferocity that the backers of the odds looked blue. The science of both men was extraordinary, that of Molineaux being quite equal to that of the Champion; the speed with which they moved and struck was astonishing, the blows and stops almost too rapid for the eye to follow. There was a marked difference in their method of fighting: Cribb hit right and left at the body, while the Moor aimed at the nob alone, and with much judgment planted several dexterous flush hits, that impaired the eyesight of Cribb, and

209

his mouth bled considerably. This rally lasted a minute and a half, milling beyond anything seen in memory, until they closed again, when Molineaux again threw Cribb with astonishing force. The superiority of the Moor's strength was evinced by his grasping the body of Cribb with one hand, and supporting himself by the other resting on the stage, and in this situation threw Cribb completely over upon the stage, by the force of a cross-buttock. To those not *flash*, the mere appearance of things was in favour of the Moor, odds fell again, but Cribb's tried game still kept him the favourite. Captain Barclay, who had left his carriage after the second round to advise Cribb, now spoke to him again.

ROUND 4. Molineaux's wind could not be depended upon, but the head of Cribb was terrific. Although he was bleeding from every wound, he smiled with confidence, and rallied in the first style of manliness, hitting right and left at the body and head, but Molineaux fought at the head only. He was so successful with the left hand that he planted many flush hits. By this means, both Cribb's eyes were now damaged, the right completely closed and the left nearly so. His face was dreadfully disfigured, and he bled profusely, but Molineaux evidently was in great distress, his chest and sides heaving fearfully. Cribb smiled again at such a favourable omen, and renewed the rally with a heroism perhaps never excelled, and in point of judgment most adroitly timed. Hits in abundance were exchanged with great force and speed, Cribb still fighting at the "mark" and Molineaux at the head. At length Cribb fell, evincing great exhaustion, both eyes now being darkened, which moved his seconds to a terrible expedient. Gully, with a lancet, cut open the great swellings beneath his eyes, the blood issuing forth in floods as a consequence, but with the swellings thus diminished his sight was cleared. *Odds seven to four on Cribb.*

ROUND 5. Molineaux commenced a spirited rally, and the execution on both sides was truly dreadful. Molineaux had the best of these terrific exchanges, and Cribb fell from a blow, and in falling received another. This excited some murmurs and applause from the partisans of the contending heroes, but on reference to the umpires was declared "fair", Cribb's hands being at liberty and not having yet touched the floor. Odds of all kinds offered, Cribb showing signs of weakness, but Molineaux sadly distressed for wind.

210

ROUND 6. Flash side, amateurs, professionals, and Knowing Ones agreed that this round must settle the contest, the pace and punishment of the previous exchanges being beyond the powers of both men to continue; one or other must gain the advantage. Molineaux, from want of wind, lunged right and left but gained little from it. Cribb avoided his hits neatly, and put in a right of great force and swiftness, but Molineaux stopped it exceedingly well. The science of both men was wonderful in their exhausted state, but now came the blow which it seemed must decide the fight, Cribb feinting and delivering so destructive a hit at the "mark" that it appeared not only to roll the Moor up, but seemed as if it had knocked the wind completely out of him. He, however, returned to begin a rally, seemingly anxious to go in, but still sensible of the ugly consequences. He seemed bewildered as to what manner he should conduct himself, appeared almost frantic, and capered about in an extravagant manner; he hit short and was quite abroad. Cribb followed him round the ring, and after some astonishing execution, floored him by a tremendous hit at full arm's length. Five to one Cribb.

ROUND 7. Molineaux seemed lost in rage. He ran in, and undoubtedly did some execution, but Cribb stood firm and changing his style, put in several straight hits at the head and throat. Molineaux bored in till he fell.

ROUND 8. Molineaux, still desperate, rallied, but his distance was ill-judged. Cribb nobbed him in fine style, got his head under his arm, and fibbed him till he fell.

ROUND 9. The Moor, running in, had his jaw broke from a tremendous left of the Champion, and fell as if dead. He did not come to time by full half a minute, but Cribb, wishing to show his superiority, gave away his chance, dancing a hornpipe about the stage.

ROUND 10. With great difficulty Molineaux got off his second's knee, only for fresh punishment. The Moor, still game, made a desperate though unsuccessful effort, and fell.

ROUND 11. Here ended the combat. Cribb gave away another chance in time, but Molineaux's senses were absolutely hit out of him; he was perfectly unable to stand, and a Scotch reel by Gully and Cribb announced the victory, while the very welkin echoed with applause. Molineaux was taken out of the ring senseless and could not articulate;

his jaw-bone and two ribs were fractured, while Cribb scarcely received a body blow, though his head was terribly out of shape.

Remarks on the Fight
by H. D. MILES alone

This battle, which lasted only nineteen minutes ten seconds, left no doubt as to the superiority of Cribb. The science of Molineaux was quite equal to that of the Champion, but the condition of Cribb was far better, his temper more under restraint, and although there was no question of Molineaux's courage, which almost amounted to ferocity, Cribb was his superior in steadiness and self-possession.

During the battle the spectators gave applause to both combatants, and many were surprised that Molineaux should have found himself necessitated to relinquish the palm in so short a time, when he so obstinately contested with the same opponent thrice the duration so very recently. It is to be considered, that in the first combat Cribb was full of flesh, and by no means in prime condition; and again, that in this [second] battle, although Molineaux had acquired an increased degree of science, he had by his own conduct impaired his stamina.

Although it has been acknowledged that applause was mutually given, and that Molineaux in every point had fair play shown him, it cannot but be granted that the exulting clamour of congratulation, proceeding from the Champion's friends, when even the slightest advantage seemed to favour him, must have tended to hurt the feelings of the man of colour, and very probably to have cowed him. It should have been considered that Molineaux was a stranger, that he stood indisputably a man of courage; that he came to the contest unprotected and unsupported by friends of note; while his opponent commanded the patronage of the leading men as well as the natural partiality of his countrymen in his favour.

Much has been said of Molineaux's savage denunciations against Cribb; of his vapouring professions of what he should like to do to him; and these were thought sufficiently disgusting to have excited animosity against him. But granting that Molineaux was brutish enough to make use of many of the barbarous expressions imputed to him, we certainly ought to take into consideration the circumstances under which they were uttered. The black could not but be sensible that Cribb was better supported by his many surrounding friends than himself. He knew and felt that Cribb was under the care of the first trainer of the country, while he was left to the government of Tom Belcher and Richmond, who made him an instrument of getting money, by carrying him round the country to exhibit sparring, and, to keep him in good temper and pliable to their wishes, allowing him to drink stout and ale by gallons. It is said that on the morning of the fight he bolted a boiled fowl, an apple pie, and a tankard of porter for his breakfast.

When all these circumstances are considered, by an unprejudiced mind, it cannot be denied, that whatever national pride we may justly feel in our Champion's triumph, and admiration of his pluck and manly prowess, we cannot but admit that the man of colour was a formidable antagonist, and one who, but for his own imprudence, might have won fame and fortune in the pugilistic arena.

PADDINGTON JONES, *concluded*

I know the question in your mind, sir: if I'd stayed wi' Tom at Bedford, and done my best by him, 'spite of his boozing and whoring, and seconded him at Thistleton – would he ha' won? No, he would not. Cribb was the better man, in the end, if not in the beginning, for Tom fought like a god them first three rounds, left hand, left hand, hammering his nob and closing both his peepers; I never seen cleverer milling, and if Gully hadn't lanced his face, Cribb was done for. But he came again, sir, as Cribb always did, and Tom was bellows to mend, and Cribb punished his midriff 'til he caved – and *that* was clever milling, too, and won the fight.

If Tom had been in condition – ah, *if*! Sir, you might as well say "If he'd been white" or "If pigs could fly"! No one could put him in condition – as you know from all I've told you. I've blamed Bill Richmond for being soft wi' him, but the God's truth is Bill could not manage him, either; no one could. Not even Barclay. And d'ye know, sir, if Barclay had had charge of him, and forced him wi' a gun at his black poll to train as Cribb did – aye, if Barclay had trained the pair of 'em in harness, and they'd been set to both in prime twig . . . well, 'twould ha' been the greatest mill of all – and Cribb would ha' won it. He'd ha' fought no better than my Tom, but he'd ha' fought that moment longer. He had that within him that makes a Champion, you see.

So there it was, and I came away from Thistleton blue-devilled beyond telling. I was so sad, sir, that I went on the mop in Stamford and slept blind bottled in a haystack. Next morning the whole town was agog and cheering, and on a Sunday, too. Boney's gone to roost, thinks I, but what should it be but Cribb and his party driving through in a barouche and four with ribbons flying, barely able to move for the clamour, every window crowded with folk waving, and blow me if the church bells did not ring on past the hour, and the people came out from the services to gaze on the Champion and huzza him with

214

three times three! They toured the villages about, I believe, cheered wherever they went; never was such rejoicing since the Peace.

I knew one place where there'd be precious little celebration, for I'd learned that Tom was lodged in a ken at Grantham. Pad, I thought, you should go to see him; bygones is bygones, and I was curious, too, to see how he did. Grantham was a tidy step for a man with a head like a hive, but I had a lift on a wagon part of the way, with a party of 'prentices who drank Cribb's health at every milestone, and came to the town towards evening. Here again the streets were thronged with merry-makers, and the boozer where Tom lay likewise. I knew where I was the instant I set foot in the tap and heard a cry of "Burn my britches!", for sure enough there was stout old Bill Gibbons, who'd held Tom's bottle, repelling boarders at the stair foot, with his bulldogs growling assistance. He was a famous fancier of tykes, and those bulldogs grew more like him by the day, being fat and wheezy and leery-eyed, down to all the tricks.

"Vhy can't ye let the man be?" Bill was saying, and I saw he was holding the press-gang at bay. " 'E don't vant to see ye, nor does Richmond, nor do I! Write votever comes to mind — ye alvays do."

"Will he challenge Cribb a third time?" asks one.

"I'll challenge *you*, Smart-boots, if ye don't pike!" cries Bill, flourishing. "Vill you brush, or must I draw your corks?" He would not let them by, but I caught his eye, and asked him what news of Tom and Richmond.

"Come avay from these earvigs," says Bill, and drew me a little up the stairs. "An' if any loose fish wentures to follow," he told the scribblers, "Nero an' Nelson 'ere vill see 'im put to bed vith a shovel." The bulldogs sat like Gog and Magog on the bottom step, ugly as sin, and the press-gang shied off.

"I'd keep clear, Pad, if I vas you," says Bill, looking glum. "There's naught to be done vith either of 'em. The black's bad in body an' wuss in sperrit. The sawbones 'as 'ocussed 'im, an' I dare say done 'im more 'arm than vot Cribb done, but 'e's been flappin' 'is trap like a fish-vife, an' Bill's been answerin' back, not as you'd vish to 'ear 'em."

He told me that Tom and Richmond had fallen out bitterly, and spent half the night blackguarding each other. "Molineaux begun it,

vunce they'd set 'is jaw-bone, cryin' as Bill 'adn't paid proper 'eed
to 'is trainin', an' should 'ave kep' 'im up to the collar, like vot Barclay
done vith Cribb. 'If I'd 'ad a breather like Barclay, I'd 'ave fibbed
Cribb foolish,' sez 'e. Vell, Bill 'ad been patient, but he vosn't 'avin'
that. 'Vhy, you could 'ave been Champion, you black blubberhead,
but you 'ad to bake yourself with sluts an' flip!' Vould you believe
it, Pad, Molineaux said Bill should 'ave *made* him train right! 'Ow
vos that for himpiddence, eh? An' Bill yelled, couldn't 'e do *nothin'*
for 'is self, no, 'cos 'e vos still a bloody *slave*, an' 'e'd done vith 'im,
an' 'e could go to 'ell in a 'ansom!

"Arter that, Molineaux said Bill could give 'im 'is money an' go
to 'ell 'is self. 'Vot money?' cries Richmond. 'You lost your stake, I
lost every meg I 'ad, ve ain't got nuthin' but browns an' vhistlers, an'
ve owes Tom Belcher a 'undred quid trainin' expenses – an' you can
pay your whack o' that, an' all, you baked-up barstid!' Then Richmond
flung off, an' drunk 'is self castaway, an' ain't stirred out 'is bed since,
and Molineaux's mopin' abovestairs, suckin' gruel through a straw.
An' I'm a-keepin' the pen-vipers away, more fool me," says Gibbons.

I asked, were they scorched altogether, and Gibbons said, all but
fifty pounds that Gentleman Jackson had taken up as a subscription
for Tom. "But vot vith the sawbones, an' vot Richmond's drinkin',
an' the score for their room, an' settlin' of their side-bets, they von't
'ave as much change as'd buy a workus supper in Lent," says Bill,
shaking his wattles. "They owes *me* vages, four pound ten, but I
reckon I shall 'ave to look elsewhere for my inwestment in the Funds."
He was a cheery cove, Gibbons, and a good 'un to stand by Tom and
guard his door from the press-gang, who'd have pestered him to death
with their questions.

Another he turned away was a foreign chap, a French refugee, I
think, who told us he was a painter, and wished to take a study of
Tom's head for a picture he was making of the fight. Jericho, his name
was, very polite and graceful, but Gibbons put him off quite humorous.

"Mister Molineaux ain't in 'is best looks today," says he. Jericho
showed us a sketch he'd made of the mill, with Tom and Cribb squaring
up, nothing like the thing, course it wasn't, and to crown all, he'd put
trousers on 'em. He had to, he said, 'cos when the painting was shown
it would never do for ladies to see 'em in tights. We told him 'twas

a bang-up piece of work, and that he'd hit the likenesses to admiration, and he went off well pleased.*

Hearing how he'd fallen out with Richmond, I wondered if I might not do some good by looking in to see Tom. Gibbons was doubtful, but took me up, and as we came to the door we heard a mighty cheer from the street, and shouting and confusion in the tap below. We thought nothing of it, but went in, and there was Tom, lying in an armchair with his ribs strapped and his jaw in a sling and his clock that swole it looked like a dumpling in a clout. The curtains were drawn, and only a solitary glim on the board. "Who dat?" he croaks, and 'twas as if he spoke through a blanket.

"Vot cheer, Tommy!" cries Gibbons. "'Ere's a old pal come to wisit on you, Pad Jones as ever vos!" He lit another brace of glims, rubbing his fat paws. "All's bowmon, eh, boys?"

Tom blinked, and glowered at me. "Wha's he want? Din' ask for no vis'tors. Ah's sick! Lemme be!"

I said I'd come to see how he did, and he gave me his surliest scowl. "How Ah does? How you *think* Ah does? Ah got a bust jaw an' busted ribs – that's how Ah does! That whut you come to see?" He gagged with the pain of his jaw, and groaned. "Come to see me now Ah's beat – that why you come?"

"Vhy, Tommy, that ain't civil!" says Gibbons. "Vot, when Pad's come to inkvire arter you, friendly-like!"

"Oh, sho', Pad come *now*! Din't come befo', when Ah need him! Lef' me to that scut Richm'nd, as blames me 'cos Ah gits beat!" All in a moment, sir, he began to snuffle and sob like a kid. "Ah cudn't help it, damn him! Done best Ah cud – best Ah knowed how! An' wha' did *he*

---

* The temptation to identify "Jericho" with Theodore Gericault (1791–1824) is at first overwhelming. The great French painter did indeed make an etching, *Boxeurs*, in which the fighters are undoubtedly Cribb and Molineaux, and while it is somewhat romantic, and depicts the combatants in trousers, it is plainly the work of an artist who has studied prize-fighting at close quarters, and the head of Cribb appears to have been drawn from life. On the other hand, there is no evidence that Gericault visited England before 1820, when the controversy over his famous painting, *The Raft of the Medusa*, drove him across the Channel. In 1811 he was a young artist studying in France under Guerin, and with the countries at war a clandestine journey to a boxing bout in Leicestershire, while not impossible, would have been a hazardous matter, even for one who was a sports enthusiast. The mystery of "Jericho" remains.

do, bastud Richm'nd wi' his trade'n his eddication, dam' white nigguh! Wha' did Pad do? They was goin' make me champeen—me, the iggerant *black* nigguh! Why'nt they do it *right*, they so smart!''

Sir, what could I say? How could I reproach him with all the times I'd pled and warned him, or tell him 'twas only his self to blame, and him a-laying there broke and crying? I stood mum, while Gibbons tried to soothe him.

''Now, don't take on so, Tommy boy! Ye'll on'y pain y'rself an' do your peck-box a mischief! Vot's the use o' that, eh? You rest easy, an' if you ain't inclined for conwersation, vhy, Pad von't mind, vill ye, Pad?''

Tom sniffed, wiping the blubbers from his cheeks, and let out a wail. ''Oh, Ah's po'ly sick! Oh, Pad, why'd ye leave me? Nevah did befo'! Why'd ye be-tray me thataway?'' He was a hellish sight, sir, ever so miserable, mumbling at me. ''Ah cud ha' beat Cribb! You know dat, Pad! Beat him fu'st time, at Copthorn, cud ha' beat him yes'day, if on'y . . .'' From whimpering he fell a-raging again. ''An' Ah will! Ah fight him when Ah's rested an' better! Lick him good, an' Ah do it ma own self, 'thout Richm'nd or nobody!''

It would ha' sickened you to hear him, sir, blaming all but himself, bragging what he knew was a lie, mortified to bits at the truth he could not stomach – that he might ha' been Champion but for his own folly. He lay back in the chair with his eyes closed, breathing heavy but quiet now, and I was uncertain whether to go or bide when I heard a heavy step on the stairs and then on the threshold, and when I turned I saw what all the shouts and cheers had been for belowstairs a moment since, for the man in the doorway was Tom Cribb.

He gave a nod to Gibbons and me and stepped into the light, and lord! he was a prize study! His phiz was like a ploughed field, all swole and rainbow colours about his eyes, stitches in the great gashes where Gully had lanced his cheeks, his nether lip split in two places, the whole right side of his head flayed red, and the ear twice its size. He was a proper handsome cove as a rule, but that day he was fit to scare crows.

He came into the room, and Tom gave a croak, staring as at a ghost, and neither said a word. Tom was that startled he made as though to rise, but Cribb stayed him and held out his hand.

"How are ye?" says he, short as ever, and Tom blinked open-mouthed, and took his hand. He was taken flat aback, but after a moment he braced up in his chair, wincing, but his own man again.

"Tol'able well, thank'ee," says he, mighty proper. "Kin'ly to set down?"

Cribb drew up a chair and sat by him, and they took stock of each other in silence. Their figureheads were so put out o' shape 'twas hard to guess what they thought, but Tom had thrown off his vapours altogether, putting on his best airs for the Champion, while Cribb looked damned grim, but unsettled, as though doubtful how to go on, now that he was here. At last he spoke, still short:

"Well, ye could look wuss, I rackon!"

Tom sat a spell, considering how to reply. "Them's turr'ble welts 'neath yo' ogles," says he.

"Slept wi' four pun' o' prime rump on 'em," says Cribb. "Us cuts up easier'n you black chaps do, seemin'ly. How's the jaw, then?"

"Oh, doctor say it be fine . . . thank'ee."

"Do 'e, now? Ha! Half they country sawbones should be mendin' roads! Best let Doctor Craig o' Mount Street see to it, when ye're back in Town. He'll set ye to rights."

" 'Bliged to ye," says Tom, and there was silence until Cribb spoke again, sharp as a sojer at drill:

"Ye won't be relishin' your vittles for a while, I'll lay. Bread an' milk, mostly?"

"Ah ain't hungry."

"Likely not. A bellyful o' my own blood han't given me much appetite, neither. Damme if I ever felt less gut-foundered!"

They fell silent again, and Gibbons and I looked at each other thinking that this was uncommon talkative for Cribb, when he was sober, leastways, but he was making heavy work of it. Having come to ask after Tom, paying his respects like, he was at a loss what to say for the best, and Tom being on his dignity again, blowed if they didn't 'mind me of two old dowagers gabbing genteel across the tea-cups. Cribb frowned and shifted his stampers, and at last Tom asked if he'd take a dram, but Cribb said, no, he was kindly obliged but his mouth was too raw for spirits. He asked where Richmond was, and at this Tom grunted and glared like a 'vangelist.

"Don' ask me 'bout Richmond! He ain't mindin' me no mo'! Sunna-bitch done lef' me, on 'count o' . . . o' yes'day!' "

"Jimminy!" cries Cribb. "Ye don't say! Well, damme if that ain't like a nigger! Turn your back an' he's off, an' granfer's watch wi' him . . ." He stopped short, confused, and made haste to ask Tom what he would do now.

"Don't know, yet. See when Ah's mended."

"That won't be tomorrow!" snaps Cribb. "No, nor next month, wi' they ribs an' jaw." He was looking vexed. "An' Richmond's hopped the wag." I could read his thoughts, sir, plain as print, and twice he made to speak, and twice thought better on't. He glanced at Gibbons and me, and then asked Tom, mighty offhand, if he had lost much on the fight. Tom said pretty cool that there was no trouble thataway. "Gen'man Jackson took up a 'scription fo' me."

"Fifty guineas won't go far!" says Cribb, not thinking – and I wondered, sir, how many o' those guineas had been Cribb's. Tom shot him a look, and then asked, with great composure, I thought, if Cribb had backed himself, and how much had he won?

"Four hundred quid. Cap'n Barclay cleared ten thou'."

Tom smiled for the first time. "Guess we in the wrong business. Ought to git ou'sel's a couple o' prime chickens."

"Aye, p'raps," says Cribb, and I saw he had something on the tip of his tongue, and was studying how to put it, but after a moment he rose with it unsaid.

"Best be away, I rackon," says he. "Glad to see ye ain't took too much harm."

"You likewise." Tom held out his hand. "Mighty 'bliged to ye fo' stoppin' by."

They shook hands, and Cribb hesitated a second, frowning, before he went to the door. He stopped there, chin on chest, and then turned again.

"When ye're well again, an' so be ye're inclined, give us a look in at my parlour, the Union Arms in Panton Street." He clapped on his hat, head high, and touched the brim to Tom. "There'll always be a pint an' a chair by the fire for the best bloody miller I ever did see!"

He gave a quick nod to Gibbons and me and went off downstairs, and we heard them huzzaing him into the street.

PIERCE EGAN, *concluded*

Why was there never a third mill? Bless you, because neither of 'em had the stomach for it, that's why! Cribb, remember, had been retired in all but name for two years, taking his ease in comfort until fellows like me and the sporting public bullyragged him back to the ring to thwart the Black Peril; he reckoned he'd done his duty, and saw no sense to being knocked about to prove again what he'd proved twice already. Besides, oxen and wainropes wouldn't have got him back 'neath Barclay's wing a second time; why, he told me he'd sooner fight Molineaux any day than go through another training from our energetic captain. No, London had turned out by tens of thousands to cheer him home from Leicester, given him a dinner to live in song and story, presented him with a silver cup and oceans of eulogy, and honest Tom Cribb was well content to call it a day.

As for Molineaux, it's my belief he met his fate at Thistleton Gap. Having swaggered into two mills puffed up with conceit, he'd come face to face with the awful truth that he never could beat Cribb. He knew he was as good, as clever and quick and strong and brave, but that Cribb was still too much for him – if only because Cribb would train and he would not. Oh, he put out challenges enough, and pretended the Champion never answered; Cribb, for his part, swore that he had, but had heard no more from the Moor – you've read all about it in the *Leicester Mercury*, I dare say, and felt none the wiser. The truth was that Molineaux was glad to strut and pose and bask in his glory, but for all his big talk and challenges he was no more eager than Cribb to endure another such hiding as they'd given each other at Copthorn and Thistleton.

Nor was anyone else. Not a soul, out of all the good millers of the day, was willing to challenge either of 'em! Those two titanic battles had set 'em aloft and apart; it was a case of Cribb first, Molineaux second, and the rest nowhere. That suited White Tom, with his championship laurels safe upon him, and it suited Black Tom, too, for even in defeat his name and fame were a passport to easy pickings, and he could jaunt about the provinces again, raking in the rhino from rustics who were all agog to see the fabled nigger who'd fought the Champion twice. That was nuts in paradise to Molineaux; he could preen and brag to heart's content, indulge his taste in high living and coats of many colours, spar a little here, wrestle a little there, and riot to excess among the fleshpots, vinous and Venus, ha-ha! with no Paddington Jones to hound him – and, better still, no Richmond to share the booty.

You've heard about the great African Civil War – Richmond v. Molineaux? No? Well, you know they fell out after Thistleton, exchanging dog's abuse and going their separate ways, but that was only the beginning. A few months later, what did Richmond do but have Tom *arrested* on a ca. sa. – *capias ad satisfaciendum*, which means, my chums of the wig and gown inform me, a writ whereby a plaintiff has a defendant jugged until he coughs up. It's gone out now, I believe, but in those days it meant that poor Tom found himself admiring the inside of a spunging-house with the prospect of debtor's prison to follow. Heaven knows what the debt was – money owed to Tom Belcher, or some such thing, which Richmond had paid and was dunning Tom for his share – or who settled on the Moor's behalf. Some said Sefton or Alvanley, and others Old Cripplegate (which I can't credit, for that 'un wouldn't have bailed his own mother), but one way or t'other Tom breathed the free air of England again – and wasn't he full of charity, just, towards his old pal Richmond? He soon found that he had other cause for grievance.

Before the ca. sa. business, Tom had spent some months on his rural exhibitions, but fighting no regular mills, as I said, until a challenge came from one Jack Carter, a promising chicken who, being a Lancastrian, was a protégé of Big Bob Gregson's. My guess is that Bob, being fly as they make 'em, and knowing that months of boozing and frolic had played the dooce with Molineaux's condition (such as it ever was), believed that his young giant might make a name for himself by trouncing him – 'twas the Rimmer business over again, if you like. However, the match had been put off when Tom went to clink; now that he was out, it could go forward – and who d'you think emerged as the match-maker, eh, and Carter's principal second? Why, none other than Tom's erstwhile guide, philosopher, and friend, and now sworn enemy: Bill Richmond! And when the battle is joined, who seconds Molineaux? Who but the cove who cheated him out of victory against Cribb at Copthorn – honest Joe Ward!

Do you begin to have an inkling, my dear sir, that the allegiances and alliances of the prize ring are somewhat more confused than the intricacies of the Spanish Succession, and that its rivalries and vendettas cast the petty intrigues of the Borgias quite into the shade? Observe how A sponsors B against C, to whom A was lately grappled by hoops of steel, while C is supported by D, who previously engineered C's downfall. Incredible, you say? By no means, say I, nothing out o' the way, as the old lady said when she stepped unexpected into the ditch.

Well, the mill took place near Banbury, at a spot convenient to four counties in case the beaks intruded. A distinguished company of noblemen, amateurs, and pugs assembled, in expectation of a famous set-to, for 'twas Molineaux's first combat since his defeat by Cribb, and the Fancy was a-buzz with the news that Richmond was backing Carter out of spite against his old pupil, and that Tom had vowed to pay him out by licking Carter to nothing.

Alas, for our hopes! That mill, my friend, became a byword as the worst in living memory, a ludicrous pantomime unworthy of the word "fight", and beneath anything since Falstaff took the field at Shrewsbury. Why, 'twas so disgraceful that some were sure it must be a cross, but Captain Barclay swore it couldn't be, because Gregson would never be party to anything smoky, and besides, if Carter had wanted to sell the fight he'd have found a less foolish and obvious way to do it, and his behaviour was not a whit worse than Molineaux's anyway. Thus Barclay, and I *incline* to agree with him, but I ain't sure. However, you must judge for yourself. I'll tell you what happened, and if you think I'm pitching a *Banbury* story – well, ask Barclay or Ward and they'll vouch for it.

It was a rum go from the first, for when the umpire announced that the winner should have a hundred guineas, Carter demanded to know what the *loser* was to have! Richmond gnashed his teeth and rolled up his eyes in despair at such folly, but Gregson was fairly stunned, and cried out: "Nay, Jack, never talk o' losing, boy! Tha moost win, the chance is a' in thy favour!'' Molineaux, sitting on Ward's knee fat as Beelzebub, left off scowling at Richmond to shout with laughter.

Then they set to, if that's the word, for I'll swear there have been bloodier quadrilles at Almack's than that first round. For two minutes they pranced round each other without touching, and then Carter, nervous as a kitten, gently stroked Molineaux on the chin, and the Moor tapped him back with the utmost gentility. This exchange rendered both men cautious, not wishing to undergo such punishment, but presently they closed, and Molineaux fell down, showing signs of distress and alarm.

Coming to scratch again, they began to whale into each other delicately, but Tom accidentally stinging the other, Carter became excited and thrashed away in earnest. Tom, grunting like a Berkshire hog, and debilitated no doubt by his months of guzzling and amorous exertions, retreated ponderously, but what dumfounded the Fancy was that he seemed to be in an extremity of terror, shying off whenever Carter bore in, capering wildly, hitting without regard to distance, and bellowing whenever Carter got home. Every round, almost, ended with his going down, often for no apparent reason, and once he fairly bolted from Ward's knee and scrambled out of the ring, crying "Help! Help!" Barclay it was who persuaded him back, and the farce continued. We couldn't credit the evidence of our eyes.

You think I'm bamming? As God's my witness, it got worse, for as Carter, seeing his man so abject, grew in confidence, so Tom descended to the depths of poltroonery. Once he dropped to one knee, seized the ropes in both hands, and bawled: "Foul! Oh, he done hit me when Ah's down!" when Carter fibbed him. They explained (what he knew perfectly well) that you can't be down until both knees and one hand are on the ground; he stood rolling his eyes and whimpering, and two minutes later he was racing round the ring howling that Carter had bit him in the neck! Ward looked, and swore there were no teeth-marks, and in the next round Tom began howling that Carter had bit him again! He fairly ran from the man, crying "Murder! Murder!" and cowered in a corner of the ring, wailing "Oh dear, oh dear, 'tis cruel, cruel!"

There was amazement and disgust all round. "This is the man who stood an hour against Cribb?" says Barclay to me. "I'll not believe it!"

224

No more could I; Joe Ward had to hold him in the ring by main force between rounds, coaxing and pleading and threatening and even pouring rum into him, but all to no avail. Courage aside, Tom was dead beat by now, labouring like a whale and not an ounce of wind left in him; for twenty-five rounds of milling (if you can call it milling when a man flops down and lies there cringing) he'd been a pitiful parody of a fighter, and when Ward pushed him to scratch for the twenty-sixth it was odds on he'd collapse whether Carter hit him or not.

And at that moment, so help me, Carter *fainted*! He did, sir, 'tis no word of a lie, swooning on Richmond's knee like a bride with the vapours! It seemed impossible, for he was a big, tough, active heavy-weight, and such punishment as he'd taken from Trembling Tom wouldn't have hurt an infant. Richmond was in a fine frenzy, working at him while Gibbons plied the bottle, and Gregson, seeing victory snatched from his grasp, was near to tears, crying: "Jack, Jack, what's thee aboot, man? Git oop, git oop, lad! By God, if tha willna git oop for me, git oop for Lancashire!" He might as well have sung psalms to a dead horse. Carter lay like Ophelia through the call of "Time!", and Tom, altogether played out and wheezing "Oh dear, oh dear!" was declared the winner.

What an uproar there was! "Universal dissatisfaction", my colleague of *The Times* called it, and you may say he was right. They were waving hats and canes, shouting "Cross!" and "Sold!" and pelting the recumbent gladiator with coppers, while Gregson pleaded for the mill to continue, for Carter had opened his eyes and whispered "Stop a bit, stop a bit!" which gave hopes of revival. These were dashed when a little chap with a doctor's case scuttled through the ropes, whipped out a lancet and cup, and in a twinkling of an eye had bled Carter as neat as you please. That settled it, there was no continuing with the man's vein opened, the shouts of execration and disappointment redoubled, and the sporting peer who'd let Carter change in his chariot, flung out his clobber in disgust, crying: "Carter, you louse, take your miserable weeds and be damned to you!" They never discovered who the medicine-monger was; Gregson swore he was none of his.

Tom was paid his prize to an accompaniment of hissing and shouts of "Shame!" Ward bustled him away to a chaise, and that was the last view I ever had of the Milling Moor who had shone so briefly like a comet in the sporting sky, slumped with his ugly black face bowed and the fat heavy on his arms and body. Barclay nudged me and says: "Barely a mark on him, for all Carter's heroics, do you see?" It was so; even in his poor condition, terrified and shirking, he had gone twenty-five rounds with a mighty handy heavy man and still contrived to slip and stop most of the blows rained on him – and hardly struck back at all.

Well, as a fight it had been a disgrace, but it was also a mystery, and the Fancy couldn't fathom it. What the devil had been the matter with Molineaux? That was the great question – not whether Carter had sold the fight or not. It was past belief, and no accounting for it. How, it was asked, could the once brave and splendid competitor of the Champion have so degenerated? How, I was asked, "did the Hero become a *cur*"? What could have wrought the change in the Black Ajax, the all-but-conqueror of Cribb whose "dauntless courage had matched his wondrous skill"?

The popular view was that dissipation had so destroyed his powers that he knew he was no match for Carter, and was terrified in consequence. "Niggers have no bottom", "Scratch a black and you'll find a coward", that sort of talk. Joe Ward had the answer to that, though: "Tom were no coward. Cowards don't take what he took from Cribb. 'Sides, rum an' rogerin' may ruin a man's constitootion, but they never hurt his game that I heard on. No match for Carter? Bli'me, baked and boozed and breathless as he was, he could ha' done Carter wi' one hand, if so minded!" Then why, Joe, was he not so minded? Joe don't know; it beat him.

Barclay, who knew more of fighters and their condition than anyone, wouldn't credit that any amount of debauch could have turned a brave man into a poltroon, but there were those who wondered if Tom hadn't been *mad* all along, and been suffering from a fit. Others wagged their fat heads over the Unpredictability of Savage Natures, the Primitive Emotions of the Negro Race, and so forth. One chap said you never knew with niggers, look at cannibals, what?, but another reminded him, solemn as you like, that 'twas Carter who was supposed to have bit Molineaux, not t'other way round.

What do I think? Only this, that if he *was* queer in the attic, or a

226

coward at bottom, it was uncommon odd that a year after the Carter mill Tom Molineaux should have fought one of the bravest battles of his life. His junketing had taken him by then to Scotland, you see, and there he met and beat Fuller, the Norfolk printer (another pupil of Richmond's, *nota bene*!). No, I wasn't there, but Joe Ward, who was, told me he'd never seen the like, for Tom, untrained, overblown, and in the poorest trim, had shown masterly science and style, and was game as a terrier, the very image of what he'd been against Cribb.

How, then, do I explain his shocking display against Carter? An "off day"? No, that won't do. Oh, we know that every fighter has 'em, but they don't run blubbing round the ring squealing "Help, murder!", do they? Well, I can't account for it – but I'll tell you Pad Jones's opinion, when I put the matter to him. He didn't see the fight, but he knew Tom better, perhaps, than any man in England, and it was his belief that Tom was *playing the fool*!

"And letting folk think he was the poorest kind of craven?" says I. "Come, Pad, what man in his right mind would do such a thing?"

"Tom would," says Pad.

"Never! What, for twenty-six rounds, while the whole Fancy shouted its disgust and contempt of him? Why in God's name should he do such a thing?"

"Mebbe to show *his* disgust and contempt o' *them*," says Pad.

"Oh, come, that's doing it too rich altogether! What cause had he to harbour any such feelings? No, no, Pad, that won't do!"

You've met Jones – well, you know his trick of talking sideways, with that little smile, and all of a sudden he'll level those grey eyes at you, straight and steady? So he did now.

"He did not like us, Mr Egan. He did not believe we treated him fair. Nor did we, sir. We robbed him o' the Championship of England, and we abused and insulted and made mock of him when he was doing his best and showing us milling as good as any. Oh, I know – none better! – what an ugly customer he could be, with his bragging and bounce and nigger airs, and the offence he gave with his insolence and carrying on and all o' that. He was a great ignorant babby, and a brute, if you like, and the Lord knows I had my bellyful of him and don't excuse his faults – but he was a stranger in a strange land, and the Fancy at his fights was never what you'd call even-handed, were they? Natural enough . . . but we could ha' been kinder.''

Well, some of this I'd thought myself, as you'll know from my *Boxiana*, where I opine that Tom had to contend with a prejudiced multitude, whose hostility was as great a hazard to him as his opponent's prowess, that he knew his unpopularity, and that it could not help but depress him. "Still," I told Pad, "if he felt himself badly used, I can't for the life of me see what good it did him to play the frightened lunatic in the mill against Carter! You say he was showing his contempt of the onlookers? Well, then, he failed, for they didn't know it!''

"Tom did, though," says Pad.

"And much good it can have done him! Why, all he did was make a fool of himself – aye, and of the fight game!''

Pad gave his little smile, looking sideways. "Ain't that just what I've been saying, Mr Egan?" says he.

So there you have the philosophy of Paddington Jones, my dear sir, and you must make of it what you will. I've told you all I can of Molineaux, for as I said, I never saw him again after Banbury, and heard only snatches from time to time, few of them pleasant. Exhibitions, sparring matches in the provinces, a mill in some godforsaken spot now and then, a brawl or two, but always, alas, a downward course. My stars, what a waste that was! What folly! There never was a pugilist with greater gifts, or one who squandered them so foolishly. He could have risen to the heights . . . why, for a moment he did. But there were two fighters he never could beat. One was Tom Cribb, and t'other was Tom Molineaux.

BILL RICHMOND, *concluded*

I ain't proud o' what I did to Tom after the fight at Thistleton Gap. I mean leaving him, and the ca. sa., and having him spunged up, and making the Carter match, and all o' that. But I ain't wearing mourning for it, neither, and I guess I'd do it again, given the time over. I was crazy mad, and hated him something vicious for what he'd done. Not for the money we owed Tom Belcher, that was nothing, just an excuse to do him spite. No, I hated him for the pain and disappointment, for all the hopes he'd spoiled, for the way he'd had the prize in his grasp and threw it away. He could ha' been the Champion, the *black* Champion of England! He threw it clear away.

I used to dream 'bout that Championship, long ago, when I was a young miller, and thought myself a prime chicken. But I soon saw 'twould never be, for me, and time passed – and then came Tom, and when Buck Flashman and Pad Jones showed me what was in him, oh, ten times what there ever was in me, or any other fighter I ever saw, black or white . . . then I dreamed again, and knew such a burning ambition as I'd never felt for myself – to see him cock o' the Fancy, Champion of England, and pay back all those years and sneers and see their pride humbled and their insults thrown back in their teeth, and a black man, not a *half-human* like me, but a *real* black man take their precious jewel away from them! Their Championship, their game that they set such store by! Mister, I could ha' died happy then, knowing they'd had to eat the crow I'd etten all my life, and bowed and smiled and looked real civil while I et it, damn them all!

Guess you think the Championship of England ain't worth that much hate? Mister, you don't know the English. Guess you think I must be dicked in the nob to feel the bitterness I feel? Mister, you ain't a nigger . . . and you never been a slave.

Tom could ha' done it. If he'd had half my will, half o' the fire that was in my guts, sure, he could ha' done it! But he did not. Well, you

229

know why, by now, and what's the use to talk o' that? Maybe you think I was wrong to feel such spite at him. See here, mister, if he'd done his best, if he'd worked, if he'd trained, if he'd tried a lick, godammit! — d'ye think I'd ha' *blamed* him for getting beat by that son-of-a-bitch Cribb? No, sir! I'd ha' given him the shirt off o' my back! I'd ha' stood by him, and loved him like a son! But when he got beat as should never ha' got beat, but for his own jackass cussedness — and then turns and blames *me* ... well, then, I'd ha' seen Tom Molineaux in Hell! I get the shakes and the fury just to think on it, even now.

I made the Carter match to pay him out, sure. I hoped Carter'd whip him, maybe learn him sense — maybe even hoped Tom might still come again 'gainst Cribb, I don't know. Well, I was paid out myself for my spite, worse'n I could have 'magined. I hoped to see him beat, but I took no pleasure to see him *shamed* — to see a black man shamed. That was the awfullest thing, to see him blubber and whine and run white-livered from a man that wasn't fit to tie his laces. Pad Jones figures he did it a-purpose. I don't see that, but I don't know, and I don't dam' well care. I was sickened, and cursed the day I ever saw him, wanted to forget all 'bout him.

But 'twas not to be. I was down in Scotland next year; there was some good mills there in '14, and there was a boy, Fred Fuller, had been a pupil of mine, I'd brought him forward at the Fives Court, taken him on tour to Yorkshire, good heavy man — well, he was in Scotland then, and when I heard he had a match, I thought to go to see it. Mister, when I learned his adversary was Tom, I dropped the notion. I had no wish to see *him* — and yet, all that day of the mill, which was at Paisley, no distance from Glasgow, where I was, I found my thoughts turning to it, I knew not why. The talk was of nothing else; every amateur in Scotland had gone, the Paisley road was a-throng with folk at first light, and they say there was a hundred carriages about the ring. "No, I'll not go!" I said. "Likely 'twill be another such disgrace as his fight with Carter." So I stayed in the town, and thought: "Damnation, I wish I was there!"

That night I heard the sheriff had stopped the mill in the fourth round. Hoping to learn more, I hung on a group of swells in a sporting ken on the High Street, and their talk was all of the science on both sides, and how Tom had fibbed well at the head with his left, until Fuller had planted him a desperate ribber, at which Joe Ward, who was seconding Fuller, had called out in fun that if he hit so•hard the fight would be over too soon. "Then the damned sheriff and his damned constables broke the ring!" says the swell. "So the mill was o'er sooner than Ward thought, and a damned shame!"

"How did Molineaux shape?" asks one.

"Oh, quite famously, but too stout by stones, and short o' puff!"

"But not of conceit!" cries another. "Why, the black villain swaggers up to the sheriff, bold as brass, and told him if he had known they were to be interrupted, he'd have finished off Fuller in quick time! Well, the mill's to go forward on Tuesday, so we shall see if he makes good his boast!"

Mister, I could ha' laughed aloud. There was no good reason why I should 'bate my enmity to Tom one bit – but when I heard that, I could just see him, full o' bounce and sass, fronting that sheriff, and crying something like: "Why, m'lawd, ifn yo' lawdship had jes' *told* me you was a-comin', Ah'd ha' had this white pug laid out all cold! Say, m'lawd, cain't we have jes' one mo' round? Ah's five to four fav'rite – you cud git yo'self some o' that Molineaux money, why don't ye?" Aye, something like that. I'd heard it before.

I was there on Tuesday, and I'm right glad I was. Oh, Tom was in worse shape, even, than against Carter, and Fuller was no milling fool. I thought to speak to him 'forehand, but kept back after all, for when I saw Tom I still had no mind to be noticed by *him*, as would have happened if I'd spoke to Fuller.

So I just watched, and wished Pad Jones could ha' been at my side. Tom was full o' flesh and gasping to be heard in London, he was ever so slow on his pins, and when he struck I knew his power was gone, his guard was clumsy and he took hits that he'd ha' stopped or slipped with his eyes shut three years back. But, mister, one thing had not gone, and that was his spirit. Anyone thought Tom Molineaux lacked game and bottom was proved wrong that day; he was too weak to put Fuller down, and Fuller, hard and fast and clever as he was, with a grave-digger right, could not knock Tom off his legs. There never was a set-to like it, for it lasted above an hour *with but one half-minute's rest in all that time*! It's the truth – they fought but *two rounds*, the first of twenty-eight minutes, the second of *forty*, such a thing as was never known in a prize-fight, and the two men hammer and tongs all through.

It was a cruel, bloody affair, for Fuller had a gift for the heavy nobbing return, and Tom played at the head as always. Oh, if Pad had only been there! For just now and then, and only for a moment, that big black hulk with his belly flopping o'er his britches, bleeding like a slaughtered ox and winded fit to die — just now and then, he'd lift on to his toes, and that left hand would go like a bolt o' lightning, smack-smack-smack and Fuller's head rocking on his shoulders! He was a game chicken, too, with his nose busted and one eye closed, and back he'd come for more. They rallied, retreated, closed, fought at half-arm and distance, and every second I thought Tom must go down dead beat, but still he milled away, until Fuller levelled him with a right upper-cut that should ha' killed him, but there he was again, at the call o' "Time!", laughing out of a phiz that was dripping claret, telling Fuller his time was come.

That was the first round, and in the second — forty minutes, mind! — Fuller was bellows to mend and failing. Tom was done, but the slower pace was nuts to him, and the science that was still in him began to show as he shifted his body but not his weary feet, ducking and slipping like Jackson on the handkerchief, until Fuller was at a standstill.

Then Tom went for him. God knows, mister, where he found the strength, but he milled that man to death, left hand going like a repeater, hitting him away every time, 'til he had him cornered and ripe for the down-cut that would ha' finished him — and damme if that snake Joe Ward, stooped by the post, didn't clip Fuller's ankle and down he went. It saved Fuller, no error 'bout that, and Tom's second, an Irish galoot, yells "Foul!" I reckon Ward, who was up to every dodge, figured the Scotch people wouldn't know that one, when a second pulls down his man to save him from being laid away for keeps. But the umpire did, and gave the fight to Tom on a foul.

I didn't go to him. After all there was between us, I thought best not. I heard one man say it was a real "Molineaux mill", on account of ending in dispute and ill-will, but another said that for his money the Scotch people had been lucky to see such a prime specimen of

English prize-fighting. He was right there, and I left the ground with a heavy heart, to think o' that mighty miller that I'd helped to make, me and Pad, that should ha' been Champion, but gone to ruin now.

For he had fallen in with Abner Gray, that Tom Belcher and I had employed to spar wi' Tom years before, after Pad quit us. He was a no-account person, but convenient at that time, and lately had been around the provinces with exhibitions and piddly little matches at fairs, third-run things where they put in old beat pugs wi' a bellyful o' beer to get hammered by the local chawbacons. Abner was a scut and a leech, and Tom must ha' been a godsend to him, with his name and fame still sticking to him along wi' three extra stones o' fat, but I was sick to think o' him in such company. I heard of him now and then, in Scotland and the north country, but nothing of consequence, and I guessed he had given up the game.

About a year after the Fuller mill I was down to Scotland again, on behalf of George Cooper, who conducted a boxing school in Edinburgh. You mayn't know of him, but he was a pupil of Pad Jones's, and I'd had a hand in bringing him on a couple of years before when he'd been a novice. It was after I'd taken leave of Tom, and you might say 'twas "off wi' the old love, on wi' the new", but that's the way o' the Fancy: one chicken goes to roost, so you find another. From the first Cooper had been as pretty a natural miller as ever you saw, another Mendoza for footwork, five foot ten, twelve stone, clever as a monkey, and fibbed hard two-handed; only one thing lacked, and that was strength o' body. He had no constitution. 'Twas the damnedest shame, but no amount o' work could better it; as Barclay used to say, he was one o' those who "trained off" 'stead of "on". But he was *so* quick and full o' style that we must give him a run, for as Pad said: "He hits like a hammer, and is too fast to be hit his self." So it proved in mills with Harry Lancaster and Bill Jay, but George went down to Tom Oliver, boxing him blind for six rounds and growing careless, when Tom nailed him. Now George was in Edinburgh, as I said, and when he wrote asking me to hold the ring in a match his gentry pupils were making for him, off I went north, for old times' sake. It was older times than I'd bargained for; his opponent was Tom Molineaux.

There was no backing down, even had I wished — and tell you the truth, mister, I did not know whether I wished or not. I'd thought nothing but ill o' Tom until his fight wi' Fuller, but that day, when he'd showed so game, and just now and then like his old self, I'd felt my feelings change somehow. I could never put from my mind all the misery and pain he'd caused me, but it was not in me to bear grudge, neither, not now, when 'twas all by and done with. I can't put words to it, 'xactly, but I guess if you've been concerned in some one, and tried to make him into something, then even if evil comes 'twixt you ... well, hang it, you don't forget the good times, and could wish the bad had never been, and even if you can't forgive in your heart, why, the grudges don't seem worth having. Not to show, leastways.

The mill was at some little place in Lanarkshire, March 10, 1815 – I recall the date 'cos it was the day we heard Bonaparte had 'scaped from Elba and was back in France, you know, 'fore Waterloo. There wasn't a drag or a prad to be had in Edinburgh at breakfast, and thousands had been on the road to the fight 'fore daybreak – say, and other thousands had gotten the wrong office and arrived some place else! But it might ha' been Moulsey or Tothill Fields, so great was the crowd and the carriages, and as I made the ring, I thought, yes sir, they still come to see the Black Ajax.

It took me flat aback, tho', when I laid eyes on Tom, coming to the field wi' Joe Ward at his elbow. He was twice the size of a year ago, the fat hanging on him in dewlaps, his phiz all broke and scarred, and white sprinkled in his hair like powder. I was talking to George Cooper by the ring when the roar went up, and I looked round, and thought hardly to recognise Tom, he was so beat up, and old somehow.

He looked across the ring and saw me, and said something to Ward, and then sat himself down wi' his back to the post as though to rest. Back of Ward there was a couple o' flash coves who'd come wi' them, and two or three mollishers all decked and painted, laughing and preening, and I thought, brother, you sure been training the way you know best. Abner Gray was there, and handed down Tom a bottle looked like stout, and Tom drained it right off. He must ha' seen me watching, for he looked 'round at the doxies and then at the bottle, and then grinned at me with a little nod. 'Twas so unlooked for I didn't know what to think. Oh, confound it all, said I, and went over to him.

"Hollo, Bill," says he, squinting up.

"Hollo, Tom," says I, and he reached up a hand and I took it.

"Din't know you was a commissary-gen'ral," says he, and I told him George Cooper had asked me to hold the ring. "You ain't in his corner, then?" says Tom, and I said no. I told him I'd seen him fight Fuller last year, and that he showed pretty well.

"Well 'nuff to win, no thanks to this sunnabitch," says he, pointing to Ward. "Say, Joe, if Cooper ribs me good, mebbe you'll pull *me* down, hey? Ye saw that, Bill, the trick he served me? Weren't that the damnedest thing?"

"I was Fuller's man that day," says Joe, sour as usual. "I'll do as much for you, aye, or for any man as is on my knee."

'Speshly if he's Tom Cribb," says Tom, winking at me. "Say, Bill, you're commissary – you mebbe take a good look at Cooper's hands, see he hasn't got no *bullets* in 'em!"

"Why, ye sooty villain!" cries Ward. "Have I not told thee once, an' a thousand times, 'twas Buck Flashman's ploy, not mine!"

"Sho' 'nuff, Joe," says Tom, "sho' 'nuff." He was not smiling, mister, nor angry neither, but sighed weary-like and shook his head. I asked him what he'd done this year past, and had he settled in Scotland.

"Guess not. Me'n Abner's goin' over to Ireland pretty soon, do a little sparrin' an' ex'bitions," says he. "Give lessons, mebbe, teach 'em a bitty Cum'erland style rasslin' an' that."

"What d'you know 'bout Cumberland rasslin'?"

"More'n the Paddies, Ah guess. Easier'n millin', that's fo' sho'." He gave another sigh and put up a hand 'gainst the sun. "Tirin' work, Bill, tirin' work. Don' know why I made this match, even. They say Cooper's a prime chicken, fibs real hard."

"Hundred quid a side, that's why ye made it!" says Joe. "Here's the scales, so shift your black arse!"

They weighed, Cooper at twelve four and Tom at seventeen, which I reckon would ha' been more, but the umpire slid the gauge along the bar when no one was looking, for decency's sake. Seventeen stone, mister, and him but five foot nine erect!

The umpire read the articles, Cooper skipping a little, Tom standing slumped wi' his belly glistening like a whale's back, and every now and then he would give me a shot of his eye sidelong, as though reflecting on something. He muttered once to Ward, who nodded, and when the reading was done he says to me:

"Say, Bill – care to gi' me yo' knee?"

I couldn't see what he meant. "Joe Ward's your second."

"Joe don' mind holdin' the bottle. Ah'd take it kin'ly if you'd pick me up, be ma senior counsel."

"But I'm commissary!"

"You done that, staked it out an' all. Anybody can mind the ring." He gave me a wink and that great darkie grin. "You don' mind? Kind o' like to have you in ma corner, bein' ma las' mill, likely."

"Your last mill? Why, how you talk!" Truth to tell, mister, 'twas so unexpected, after all of everything, I knew not what to say. Not a word 'bout our differences, or ca. sa., and he was asking me to pick him up. "What d'ye mean, your last mill – why, you'll have mills a–plenty in Ireland!"

"Not reg'lar mills, not thisaway," says he, nodding 'round at the great throng beyond the ropes, thousands on 'em lying and kneeling and standing. "This Cooper's a top-notcher, ain't he, an' Ah don't reckon to find many such in Ireland – 'sides, Abner's no hand at all at match-makin'." He laughed, that big melon-splitter of a laugh. "An' Ah ain't all that in-clined to matches wi' bustlin' young chickens these days." He tapped me on the shoulder, that old coaxing way. "What say, Bill? Gimme a knee?"

Mister, I felt ... I don't know what I felt. "Damn you, Tom Molineaux! Damn you to Hell!" says I, and he stood there grinning all over that ugly scarred phiz. "Damn you! I'll give you my knee!"

"You ain't so green, Bill Richmond!" cries he. "'Bout time you's on the winnin' side! Ain't had that many chickens to run, lately, hey? Git back to Town, presn'ly, git roun' the Fives Court, hear the boys askin' 'Where you been, Bill?' 'Why, Ah's been up nawth, pickin' up Tom Molineaux!' 'Lan' sakes!' says the boys, 'you in the swim again, Bill, jes' when we's reckonin' you done up an' gone to roost.'" He was laughing at me, damn him, drawing me to his corner. "Like ole times, hey, Billy boy?"

I dare not answer him, mister, but went to Cooper and the umpires, who gave their consent soon enough, but puzzled I could see. Tom was at his bottle again, wi' the mollishers tittering 'round him. I hustled 'em away and gave him my knee in the corner; 'twas like holding up an elephant.

"Cooper's got no body, they sayin'," says he, resting back on me. "Cain't take middlin'. Ah guess Ah give him the one-two an' away, likely. Hey, Bill? Git him on the mark, fold him up, hey?"

"Never you mind his goddam middle! You're too dam' fat for one-two and away! Who the hell you think you are — Mendoza? You play at his head wi' your left, nob him senseless!" I knew Cooper was too fast by yards, and Tom must fight at distance or be dead of exhaustion. "Let him come to you, give him the left! Go for his brows, mind! Don't chase him, he's too nimble!"

"Oh, Bill, he ain't but a novice! Ah licked Fuller, din' Ah, an' you cain't tell me this Cooper'd be any bait fo' *him*!"

"Forget 'bout Fuller — this fellow's fast and he's clever and he ain't no novice! How d'ye feel, Tom? Legs easy? Then don't tire 'em — stay back, let him come in, then left-left-left!"

"Sho' 'nuff, Mass' Richmond! Like you say, mass'! Ah trim him up jes' how you tell me!" I could feel him laughing. "Say, an' when Ah comes back f'm the Wild Goose Nation, how 'bout we challenge Tom Cribb again? Lissen, Ah cud lick him right here an' now! Think Ah cudn't?"

"Tom, I'm giving you my knee," says I, "but don't dare talk to me 'bout Cribb, not now, not never!"

"Tell ye why Ah cud lick him — 'cos he'll be fatter'n Ah am this minute, beatin' his belly in Panton Street, wi' ale by the gallon!" He gave another great sigh. "Say, this is real comf'table, ain't it, tho'? You got a fatter knee'n Pad Jones, ye know that?" He was silent a moment, watching the umpires making the scratch, and the timekeepers setting their repeaters. "Wisht ole Pad was here, too," he said.

"Come to the mark!" was the cry, and he heaved up off my knee, putting a hand down to clap my shoulder.

"Go on, Tom," says I. "Left hand, mind."

HENRY DOWNES MILES, *concluded*

ROUND 1. Silence prevailed, and the Caledonians appeared anxiously interested to witness the opening attack. Considerable sparring took place, both being aware of the milling talents possessed by the other. Molineaux commenced offensive operations right and left, and Cooper, in return, put in a sharp bodier, but received a hit which sent him under the ropes. Six to four Molineaux.

ROUND 2. Milling without ceremony, and both the combatants on their mettle. Molineaux planted a sharp nobbler, but received two tremendous rib-roasters that made him wince and gasp for breath. Some blows were exchanged; in closing, both went down.

ROUND 3. Molineaux, with the most determined spirit, kept fighting at his opponent's head, while Cooper directed most of his blows at the body. Some heavy hits, and in a desperate rally against the ropes the claret was first observed on Cooper. However, the round ended to his advantage, for he hit the man of colour through the ropes. Seven to four Cooper.

ROUND 4. Molineaux appeared at the scratch rather distressed. Cooper, full of gaiety, took the lead and floored Molineaux in grand style. Two to one Cooper.

ROUND 5. The superiority of Cooper was conspicuous. He stopped the fury of the Black with skill, nobbed him at will, and again hit the man of colour down. Any odds Cooper.

ROUND 6. Molineaux was growing weak. Cooper, having the best of him, eventually put in a tremendous facer, which floored the Black like a shot.

ROUNDS 7 to 9. In all these rounds the best of the fighting was decidedly on the part of Cooper. Molineaux was hit down every round.

ROUND 10. The Black, still determined, rallied Cooper against the ropes, and some hard fighting followed, but Cooper planted so desperate a blow on his opponent's body that he went down quite rolled up, his head falling against the post.

ROUND 11. Molineaux, despite his defects and falling off, astonished the ring from the gallant manner he fought this round. Some terrible exchanges of blows were witnessed, when the Black again rallied Cooper to the ropes. In closing, Molineaux was severely fibbed, but broke cleverly, and felled Cooper by a heavy blow upon his face. From great exertion, however, Molineaux fell exhausted. This rather reduced the odds.

ROUND 12. Cooper appeared at the scratch eager to finish the Black, whom he nobbed repeatedly, and completely hit off his legs. The man of colour was sick, and brandy was given him to recruit his declining spirits. Any odds, but no takers.

ROUND 13. Molineaux was sent down as soon as he toed the scratch.

ROUND 14. The Black could scarcely leave the knee of his second, and upon meeting his man he was again floored. The battle was thus at an end, twenty minutes only having elapsed.

From the superior style of Cooper, he rose high in the opinion of the Scotch fancy, and entered the ring in good condition. Molineaux trusted principally to his weight and length, neglecting any preparatory care of his health, so that the right-handed blows of Cooper proved irresistible. The tourney was well conducted, and afforded a high treat to the northern admirers of boxing.

From Scotland Molineaux went on a sparring tour into Ireland, travelling over the northern parts of the country, teaching the stick-fighting natives the use of their fists; an accomplishment which might save many a jury the trouble of a trial ending in a verdict of manslaughter or even of murder. But the sun of his prosperity was set. Intemperance, and its sure follower, disease, brought down the once-formidable gladiator to a mere anatomy. Molineaux was illiterate and ostentatious, but good-tempered, liberal, and generous to a fault. Fond of gay life, fine clothes, and amorous in the extreme, he deluded himself that his strength of constitution was proof against excesses. Alas, poor Molineaux! Peace be to his manes! He was a brave but reckless and inconsiderate man, on whose integrity and straightforwardness none who knew him ever cast a slur; nevertheless he was the worst of fools, inasmuch as he sacrificed fame, fortune, and life . . .

EPILOGUE

Tom Molineaux died on August 4, 1818, aged probably thirty-four, in the bandroom of the 77th (East Middlesex) Regiment, at Galway, where he had been befriended by two black soldiers. His claims to fame are his two fights with Cribb, the most celebrated bouts in the early history of the ring, and the fact that he was the first and, for all we know, the best in a long succession of great black heavyweights. Sporting comparisons are more odious than most, for every generation loves to believe that its champions are superior to all who have gone before; in sports where achievement is measurable, the records of times and distances appear to justify them, although one can never tell how athletes of old would have performed given modern equipment and modern marks to aim at. Boxing has no times or distances on which to base comparison, and its rules and conditions have changed greatly, but anyone who studies the history of the prize ring over its two and a half centuries must surely doubt whether any modern champion, unskilled in wrestling, used to three-minute rounds, unaccustomed to being hit repeatedly by bare fists calloused to a degree unknown today, and, most vital of all, depending on heavily-padded gloves to protect his hands, could endure for long the savage exchanges of the golden age of bareknuckle fighting. But talk of "the greatest" is always futile. Molineaux has his place in social as well as in sporting history, and he did his profession and his people good service.

Bill Richmond moved from the Horse and Dolphin to rooms in Whitcomb Street, Haymarket, which were "highly patronised by the nobility", including his friend Byron. A popular and respected figure, noted for his pleasant manners and excellent conversation, he remained a sought-after instructor, second, and master of ceremonies, was a first-class cricketer, and still a formidable boxer well into his later years; at the age of fifty-three he beat Jack Carter, Molineaux's old antagonist, in three rounds. In 1821 Richmond was one of Gentleman

Jackson's security "heavies" at the Coronation of George IV; they also included Cribb, Carter, and the then Champion, Tom Spring, all dressed as royal pages. Richmond died on December 28, 1829. He was sixty-five.

Paddington Jones's long and active career began in 1786 when, at the age of twenty, he beat one Jack Holmes for a stake of half a crown. He became champion at what would now be called welter-weight, but frequently fought the heaviest men of the day. Jones, who was credited with having fought more bouts and seconded more boxers than anyone before him, died at his birthplace in Paddington in 1833, aged sixty-seven.

Tom Cribb, the most famous of bare-knuckle boxers, never fought again after his contests with Molineaux, although he continued to be recognised as Champion until his formal retirement in 1822 in favour of Spring; he had held the title for fourteen years. By all accounts a superb boxer and a genial and kindly if uncommunicative man, it was Cribb's extraordinary courage and refusal to admit defeat that endeared him not only to the Fancy but to a far wider public; he may fairly be called the first superstar in the history of sport. In 1814 he was the main attraction at an exhibition given before crowned heads, including the Tsar of Russia, and other allied leaders visiting London to celebrate the peace, "and the veteran Blücher eyed him with more than common attention". His later life was marred by business setbacks and domestic troubles, and he died after a long illness at the home of his son in Woolwich, on May 11, 1848, at the age of sixty-seven. An imposing monument in the form of a stone lion was erected over his grave in Woolwich Churchyard.

GLOSSARY

above par	tolerably drunk
ale-draper	publican
all's bowmon	all's well
angelic	single young woman
apartments to let	empty-headed
area-sneak	burglar through a house's area
baked	exhausted
ball of fire	glass of brandy
ballum-rankum	dance by naked prostitutes
bamming	being funny, humbugging
Banbury tale	silly, roundabout story; hence, a lie
bang-up	most stylish, à la mode
barker	pistol
bartholomew baby	a doll, gaudy person; hence, a clown
beak	magistrate
belch	beer, porter, etc.
Black Beetles	lower orders
blackleg	sporting gambler or sharper
blate	frightened
blue tape	gin
blunt	money
bottom	pluck, grit
boxing a charlie	trapping a watchman in his box
breathing	exercising
breech	backside
bridle cull	highwayman
browns and whistlers	counterfeit coppers
brush	go away quickly
bub	beer
burned to the socket	dying, done for; hence, penniless

243

burrick	prostitute
bushed	poor, without resources
buz-gloak	pickpocket
buzz	talk, rumour
case	suit of clothes
castaway	drunk
casualty	a nonentity
cattle	horses
charlies	watchmen
cheese it	stop it, desist
chipper	lively girl
chived	lit. cut, hence gone away
chouse	cheat
circumvendibus	roundabout way
claret	blood
clock	face
clunch	a lout, a lumpish fellow
conk	nose
cool Nantz	brandy
crack the whid	to talk sociably, to joke
crapped	hanged
crib	a house
cross	a "fixed" fight
cry rope	to warn, hence inform
cut	drunk
cut his pigtail	resign commission
Cyprian	a harlot
daddle	hand
daffy	gin
darbies	fetters
delope	to fire wide deliberately
dial	face
Diamond Squad	fashionable society
dibs	money
dice	teeth
dicky	paltry, inferior
dicked in the nob	mad, silly

dive	to go slumming, hence a low establishment
dorse (doss)	to sleep
doxy	loose woman
dozzened	stupefied
dub your mummer	shut your mouth
duds	clothes
dummy-hunters	pickpockets (of wallets)
earwig	eavesdropper, hence to listen
edge	encourage (cf egg on)
eye-water	gin
facer	a blow in the face
fadge	be suitable (Won't fadge = won't do)
famble (fam)	hand
family	underworld
Fancy	boxing, sporting fraternity
fib	to box, to punch
file	a person
fives	fists
flash	loosely, relating to the underworld, but also disreputable, showy; thieves' language
flash the hash	to vomit
flimsy	a bank-note, money
fly	cunning, aware
fly-flapped	whipped at the cart-tail
foxed	drunk
fussock	lazy fat woman
futter	to copulate
galoot	a soldier
gams	legs
gelt	money
gig	fun
gill	a fellow
gloak	synonymous with *gill*
go-alonger	simpleton
gone to roost	dead, done for
Grand Strut	Rotten Row, Hyde Park
gun	to examine (took a gun = took a look)

gut-foundered	hungry
Haymarket ware	a prostitute
heavy wet	porter (drink)
high ropes	angry, excited
hocus	to drug, hence to deceive
Holy Land	back slums of St Giles'
hop the twig	to die, to go away
hop the wag	to play truant
hopper-dockers	shoes
hot house	brothel
ivories	teeth
jigger	door
jobbernowl	a fool
juggs	breasts
ken	a house, place of resort
knee	a second (boxing)
lawful blanket	wife
leery	wary, cunning
leg-men (legs)	bookmakers' touts
lickerish	lecherous
lillywhite	a Negro
limbo	prison
lush	strong drink
lushy	drunk
mag (meg)	a ha'penny
mauleys	boxing-gloves
mellow drain	sociable drinking
mill	(n. and v.) fight, to box
mint sauce	money
mollisher (moll)	a prostitute
monkey	£500
mop, on the	on a drinking spree
mot	a low woman
mufflers	boxing-gloves
muslin	girl
mutton-monger	a ladies' man, a rake
muzzler	upper-cut (boxing)

nap (nab)	catch, arrest
nix	nothing, hence an emphatic negative
not a feather to fly with	penniless
nuller	a boxer
nun	a harlot
nuts (nutty)	something delightful, sweet
nymph of the pavey	a prostitute
office	private information of prize-fight venue
ogles	eyes
Oliver	the moon (depending on whether the moon is shining or set, Oliver is said to be in, or out of, town)
out-and-outer	splendid fellow
Paddington frisk	a hanging
pads	street robbers
pattering the flash	speaking thieves' cant
panny	small house (*family panny*, underworld resort)
peck	food (*peck alley*, throat, *peck-box*, mouth)
peepers	eyes
pewter	money
phiz (phizzog)	face
pick up	to act as second (boxing)
pike	run away
pilot	a watchman
pimple	the head
pippen	a good fellow
Point Nonplus, off	without money or credit
poulticed	mortgaged
prad	horse (*pradster*, horseman)
prig	to steal, a thief. Also *prigger*
put to bed with a shovel	buried
racket	a fraudulent or criminal operation
rapper	false witness
rattler	coach
reader	notebook
red tape	brandy, spirits (cf. *blue tape*)

rhino	money
roll of soft	sheaf of bank-notes
ruby	blood
rum	queer, but also excellent
sarsy (*sassy, saucy*)	impudent
scorched	short of money
screwed	burgled
shap	hat
sharp	a sword
shiner	black eye
shiver	to shake the fist
shoot the cat	vomit
shot in the neck	drunk
shove in the mouth	glass of gin
skirt	female
slum	nonsense, foolish talk
smoky	suspicious, underhand
snitch	betray
snyder	a tailor
sow's baby	sixpence
spangle	a seven-shilling coin
Spike Hotel	prison
spunging house	preliminary prison for debtors
stampers	feet
stash it	desist (''stow it'')
Steel, the	Coldbaths Field Prison (''the Bastille'')
strap	to copulate
Tick River (*up* or *in*)	deep in debt
tiger	groom
titter	young woman
toco	punishment
togs (*toggery*)	clothing
town tabby	Society matron, dowager
trap	mouth
tulip	a showy person, would-be ''Swell''
vis-à-vis	carriage with facing seats
vinegar	guard at a prize-fight (also *whip*)

wet	drink
Wild Goose Nation	Ireland
winder	a body blow
winker	bright-eyed girl
wistycastor	a powerful blow at boxing
whiz	talk (n.)

Some of these expressions have other meanings also. The definitions listed here are those applying to the text.